T0367593

THE UNWANTED BABY THE SEQUEL

A Father with Custody

LONE WOLF

WESTBOW
PRESS®
A DIVISION OF THOMAS NELSON
& ZONDERVAN

Scripture taken from the King James Version of the Bible.

WestBow Press books may be ordered through booksellers or by contacting:

WestBow Press
A Division of Thomas Nelson & Zondervan
1663 Liberty Drive
Bloomington, IN 47403
www.westbowpress.com
1 (866) 928-1240

ISBN: 978-1-9736-3669-4 (sc)
ISBN: 978-1-9736-3668-7 (e)

Print information available on the last page.

WestBow Press rev. date: 08/16/2018

Contents

1

At the eight week of development inside my mother's womb, I had lungs, ears, and eyes' I also, had a brain. My nerve cells were branching out connecting to one another. My brain was operating and recording everything which was happening from this moment in development. My brain would remember everything, and put it in one of my special storage cells from now through out my mom's pregnancy with me. This, story begins inside the womb of my Mother. I will tell you the story as I recall. I remember the first disagreement my parents had. I am inside the womb I am defensive less for myself. I recall mom saying to my dad. "I told you, you time after time, I did not want to get pregnant." "You give your word this would not happen to me." Then, dad said, "I'm sorry, I only wanted a child." Mom responded back and said, "You won't be the one carrying this thing around inside of you for the next nine months, will you?" This would only be the first of many arguments I would recall to memory of the two having. Their arguing was almost always over my being born into the world. Dads' work was always in some place other besides the state which we lived, and he was almost not ever home, I imagine for some reason that him and my mom never got along so well when they was together. Well, after this argument today, was finished and both stopped cussing each other for what seemed to have went on for hours, at last everything seem to have settle. I remember dad and mom had been drinking large amounts of, alcoholic this day, or I should say the three of us where drinking this

1

day. Because, everything that mom drinks I drink as well, when mom smokes I smoke as well. It was not long afterwards all three of us where intoxicated. The alcohol that mom drank had now put me too sleep. Dad was only staying for a couple of days, and this was as long as he ever stayed at any time he came to visit with us.

2

I Wish Dad Would Not Leave

I did not want dad to leave today, after all the bad things mom had been saying about me, growing inside of her belly. I wish, I had a voice today to speak with and say dad please don't leave! I wanted to tell dad I was petrified that mom might try to do something like maybe try to kill me so I would never get the change too be born. However, keep in mind I have no voice at this stage; we don't seem to have any right? After dad was gone and returned to his home in, Missouri, I would hear other pregnant woman saying to mom how precious their babies were inside their womb. I wonder what I look like, I wondered if I was a beautiful baby I wondered if people would say too mom that I was a beautiful baby. I would hear someone ask the other woman who already had their babies; oh can I hold your baby? I would hear women talking to their unborn babies inside their womb; I wished mom would talk to me nicely and stop saying I was a little thing that she wish she could get rid of. I could hear women saying how much they loved their baby, and how happy they would be when their baby arrived so that they could hold them for the first time. I remember one woman who used to sing a la-la-bah song to her unborn baby. The song was. Hush little baby please, don't cry Mommy's goanna buy you a mocking bird. I use to enjoy hearing this song so much. I wished Mom would sing this song to me. The only time I remembered mom saying anything directed to me while I was inside her womb was, I wish I could just get rid of you.

3

Mom Tells Her Baby She Want's Rid of It

I could hear mom say awful words about me, such as I wish I could just take something so you would disappear. She would say she, had been such a fool to have ever let such as this happen to her.

I could tell that my mom was even crying sometimes about this pregnancy. Now, as I was beginning to grow through the different stages inside of mom's belly I began to stay awake more, and kick more, this was something normal, and nature's way of doing things. Well, the more I stayed awake and the more I kicked the more mom would cuss me calling me more bad names. Once she said, "If you don't, stop kicking her, she was going to reach inside and knock me silly." One day I heard mom talking to a man an acquaintance of hers. She told him "She wished she could just go off some place and get blind drunk." The man said "Well, let's go then." So the two of them or the three of us went off to get drunk. Again, whatever mom does, her unborn baby does as well, because what goes through mom's blood goes into the baby's blood. There would be many times for me too saving alcohol in my blood, as well as some other harmful things to come. I would learn to hunger after, for cigarettes and marijuana. Now, after mom's man friend joined with her at this place that played loud music, it was not long after that I began to feel numb and sleepy. I am sure this is what mom wanted, for me to become, immobilized so that I would not kick her. This bad judgment of my mom to drink and use drugs would later in my life cause me to crave the use of alcohol all the time. I looked forward every day to having beer and whiskey, and marijuana instead of the nourishments of milk my mother was suppose to be furnish me with. {Please mothers, if your baby could talk while they were inside the womb they would say please, don't give me drugs, and drink alcoholic and smoke cigarettes and use marijuana. I don't want that slop poured down here where I have to live for the next nine months.}

4

Moms Car Wreck

Once mom and I had stayed an entire Saturday afternoon, at her favorite drinking place that played loud music, and everyone was talking loudly, and swearing with their words, the place was reeking with cigarettes and marijuana burning. Mom swallows down and large lung full of the cigarette she was smoking it brought a cloud of reeking smoke inside my home. The smoke burned through the tubes that were feeding my tender body. I was by now having nervous tremors, when I did not get the daily amount of alcohol and cigarettes, and the marijuana. However, today as we left this place, mom walked outside and fell to the ground. It did not hurt me, at least not as much as it had hurt mom. She was swearing saying who left this here for her to trip over her. The only thing she had tripped over were her large feet that she was too drunk and high on the marijuana to pick up.

I remember I was getting extremely sleepy from the drinking mom just finished. I remember we got into moms car, and, as we are driving along an old country road back home, she must have fallen asleep at the wheel. I recall the car ran off the road and over a big hill, and then the car began to flip over, and over. I guess the car must have rolled over at least four times when we landed upside down in the shallow of a creek at the bottom of the cliff. I judge we had been there for several hours before anyone had come along to take notice of our wreck. Mom had been in and out of consciousness, and I could hear her from time to time her calling out for someone to help her. I could also smell a strange odor that was not alcohol. I had never smelt this before. Then, I could hear voices outside moms womb, I could sense that someone knew she had wreak the car and people were pulling on mom trying to get her out of the smashed up car. One of the voices I heard was familiar; it was the voices of the man who had talked mom into coming to the bar to get her drunk in the first place. The man was telling all the other people who had now gathered they needed to hurry, because the gas tank was leaking, and the car might explode at any time?

I remember hearing sirens coming, then at last, the first responders, the police, and the fire trucks were here. I could tell that a very large group of people gathered around to see what had happen. The first responders arrived on the scene first. The team had sent a couple of men with ropes to the bottom of the cliff where we had rolled, too. After they had put mom onto this flat board then pulled it to the top of the cliff, the ambulance screamed off toward the hospital some sixty-miles away. Mom was still losing and regaining consciousness. After we had arrived at the hospital, I heard one of the emergency room doctors say she had some swelling on her brain, and that she could slip into a coma. I also, heard one of the doctors say your baby appears to be doing just fine. Finally, mom regains consciousness and was able to stay awake. It was then, I heard mom ask one of the doctor's, "Well, I am sure I must have lost the baby haven't I?" "No, the doctor answer, your baby is going to be just fine." However; the doctor did say, they would need to run more test. I knew when mom heard that I was going to be just fine, that she was not fine. I heard her say to the emergency room doctor, "Oh, so I am still pregnant?" Yes, you are still pregnant. I heard her, say in a low voice that no one else could hear, "that's just great, I still have this little thing to carry around." I believe there must have been angels there this day protecting me. I believe today there must have been angels assigned especially to me from the very first day I was a conception, or else I would not be able to tell any of this story today. Oh, but the time I was going to be in for after I was born into this world? No one could ever imagine what was going to take place in my life. You would never believe that one little human could have ever experienced such misfortunes as what I was about to go through and live. After our return home from the car wreck, I was hearing loud music through the night, every night. It was difficult to sleep at anytime; I was not getting the rest a baby growing inside their mother's womb needed, for the proper development. I was frightened to fall asleep, petrified mom was going try and do away with me, not that I could have stopped her anyway. Although, I knew if something should happen to me I would go to a phenomenal place where nothing could ever again hurt me. Heaven will be waiting on me if something should happen all babies go there. Still, though, as baby I wanted the opportunity of being able to see the world.

5

'A Story from the Bible'

Ecclesiastes: 3: 1{KING JAMES} there is a time for everything, and a season for every activity under the heaven: 2.A time to be born and a time to die, a time to plant and a time to up root. 3.A time to kill and a time to heal, a time to tear down and a time to build, 4.A time to weep and a time to laugh, a time to mourn and a time to dance, 5.A time to scatter stones and a time to gather them, a time to embrace, and a time to refrain. 6. A time to search and a time to give up, a time to keep and a time to throw away 7 A time to tear and a time to mend, a time to be silent and a time to speak, 8.A time to love and a time to hate, a time for war and a time for peace. I will never know why a man and a women wanted to have a common interest in each other, and being completely mindful of what the two of them were doing create an innocent life to come into this world, and often before the birth it would be hated so much. It would appear too me the conception of a birth would be the most wonderful thing that could ever happen in two seems people's lives. GOD told the first man and women. Go and populate the earth. GODS word did not say go conceive, and kill all of your un-born babies nor, did GOD say, go and conceive, and hate your un-born baby while it is developing, and then afterwards hate it and reject it. With all the anger, mom had about being pregnant with me I was indisputably, a frustration to her. I would be time after time reminded of this throughout my mom's pregnancy, of her frustration

I was living inside of her. After my birth and throughout my entire life the neglectfulness mom showed toward me and the favoritisms she showed towards a younger brother and a sister that would be born later was always something that hurt deep inside me. Now, as we we're still waiting in the doctor's office for my arrival I'm still collecting everything that's being said, as if I'm a computer keeping everything stored in my memory. During the past nine months' I have had to absorb everything that mom has done, even though I did not want to, I had no choice; I had no choice because there are no laws that protect the un-born, even though I am a living breathing human being. They, say that I am not a human, even though I am, and I have been since conception.

6

My Birth

There are no laws that will protect the unborn, the law looks at us and says because we live inside our mom's womb, it is the woman's choice to do what she wishes to do to us, even murder us because we cannot talk to express our feelings that, we want to live. You see, I'm a human living inside my mom's womb, I did not ask to come to this world, the mother and the one who the father is decides on this so? We need someone to speak up for us and say we have a right to be born, a right to be taken care of while we are in our mom's womb until we are born? At last, it was time for me to come to meet the new world. Mom asks a neighbor drive her to the nearest town with a doctor, which was just over fifteen- miles away. I remember this day; mom was carrying on something outrageous. I heard her say to the doctor, "She can't stand this any longer." I would never know why my mother never loved me from the beginning of her pregnancy and throughout the years. After we arrived at the doctor's office, he told mom go into this room and wait, that it was not time. We were only in the small room for a short time when mom yelled for the old doctor and told him, he was going to have to hurry up and get this thing out of her just then, the old doctor came back into the room and told her to push. After about the third push, I came out to meet the world.

The doctor slaps me on my hind parts and I begin to cry. As I mentioned earlier in the story, I remembered everyone carrying on about how precious their babies were, and I was hoping that someone was going to say the same thing about me when I was born. Well, the old doctor's nurse took me and cleaned me off, then handed me to my mom for her to hold me for the first time. However, it was just as I had expected she never said anything to me. She had not pulled me up close to her and said I love you; it was like she was holding an old dish rag. Oh well, I thought maybe, this would come later? But, I remembered how she felt about my being inside her belly for the past nine months. There was not a day that had passed over the entire nine months that she had not curse and raved about me being inside her. She had said things such as, 'I wished there was something I could take so you would just go away." Dad could not be here for my arrival into the world. Dad was working at his out of state job as he always had. It seemed that in the 1950s a women needed looked after longer after giving birth, than what they do today. In those day's it was often weeks after giving birth that a women would need the care of someone to help them. I was going to get to meet my grandparents for the very first time. Mom always comes to granny to look after her until she could get back on her feet for anything. I guess granny was just as good of a mid wife as you could find. However, going to my grandparents for the first time I was wondering, if I they would love me or, would they reject me as mom had done? Then, as we pulled up in front of the old house granny lived in she come running out as if she was a twenty-year old woman. Then, the old woman with wrinkles from age and hard work took me from my mom's arms and carried me inside, sitting down in an old wooden rocking chair. This was the first time for me to feel loved.

I would never learn why I was only attached to my grandparents from my father's, father and mother. I would only meet my grandparents on my mother's side a short few times?

These grandparents lived in another state and only once a year they would ride a bus to our state for a week visit with us. I remember my first birthday present from these grandparents; it was a pair of girl's jeans. I recall my grandfather from my maternal grandparents was a very large man, he had long white hair and this grandfather was half Cherokee Indian. I remember he could speak in his native language. I have been throughout my life interested in the heritage of this blood line in my ancestry? However, each time I have inquired I was at a dead end? I was told that this was something which the family had kept a secret, mainly because my grandfather's father, my step grandfather was German and this embarrassed the family that he married an Indian woman.

However, I would only acquire little information about my Indian heritage. I did learn that my Cherokee step grandmother had been wearying the traditional Indians woman's dress one day when she apparently got too close to their camp fire and the dress caught fire and she burn to death.

I remember, granny had now pulled me up close to her chest and she began to sing me a song. The song, granny was singing, was a song I heard when I was still inside my mom's womb. The song that granny was singing to me was. "Hush little baby please do not cry, Granny's, going buy you a mocking bird." At last, I felt totally safe and loved in my granny's arms. However, all the love and comfort I was feeling would not last but for only for a short time. My mom was back, on her feet and was able to take care of herself, I had to leave granny's house to go live with my mom. I knew I was going to miss having granny hold me close to her chest, and singing songs that soothe me down to my soul. Somehow, I knew there would be no one to hold me or, pull me up close to them and sing to me after I left this house of love? Mom would put me in this dark closet and shut the door, often for hours at a time, to block out some of the noise from my crying. I remember crying myself to sleep so many times. I had the idea when it came time to feed me my bottle mom would hold me, because that was the way my granny did it when she fed me for the first time. Mom however had her own way to do things and it was much different than the way my granny did things for me. Mom would put a cold bottle of milk in my mouth, propped it up with a pillow, and walked out of the room.

7

Special Love

However, the good times would return. Mom always left me with granny when she needed to go out of the house, she would tell granny all I did was cry, and she could not take a squalling child with her. Mom would never call me these bad words in front of granny, but when we were along she would call me horrible things, she would say she wish this squalling brat would shut up. Sometimes, she would say she would like to knock me silly, and there had been a time or two that she had hit me when I would wet or dirtied my diaper. Then, if the hit left a burse, it would be a long time before we would go around anyone, especially to granny's house. I remember, I would cry myself to sleep from being hungry. However, each time we came to granny's house it would always make me happy, I was happy because I knew I granny loved me. Then, another dreadful day came. I had turned five months old. Mom told granny and pa that she was taking me and going to Missouri to live with my dad. I remember granny started to cry and she said "I guess we will never see our little boy again" granny and pa had started calling me their little boy.

8

Granny's Broken Heart

I have not spoken much about pa, mostly because pa always worked long hours six days a week, and it was granny I spent most of my time with. Pa was a man of few words but when he spoke, you had better listen, because pa was the type of man, who believed in saying what he, meant, and meaning what he said. However, pa spoke up and said, to my mom with a tear in his eye and pointing his finger toward mom said; "you had better bring our boy back to see his grandmother and me." Then, pa had something more to say. "If you don't bring the boy back to visit, and we have to get on a bus, to come to Missouri, It will not be big enough for you to hide in." After getting hugs and kisses from granny and pa, mom still carrying me as if I was a rag doll, we walked up the three steps to get on the big greyhound bus and were off to a big city in Missouri. The trip took a long time, and I had become restless and had begun to cry throughout the trip. Mom had stuck a cold bottle of milk in my mouth and this satisfied the restlessness for a while. The thing that would have work best would have been for mom to pick me up and held me, close to her. However, there are many babies just as the baby in this story who never experiences the love they need and deserve from their mom or dad. The long journey from our little town in, Arkansas, to the big city in Missouri ended at last.

Dad was waiting at the bus depot to pick the both of us up to take us to his place. Dad had lied to his landowner about having children.

Dads' landowner told him upon renting the apartment they did not rent to families with children so dad told the land owner, his family was in the graveyard. The landowner sympathizes with dad at what they believed he had lost his family and had died. Actually, dad did not lie to his landowner. He had dropped us off at the cemetery and later came back to pick us up. Then, when the landowner learned what a trick he had pulled they found it so funny that they decided to let us stay. Mom stayed home each day, and I stayed in the playpen everyday all day or, at least until I learned to crawl out of the playpen which would be a mistake.

In about the ninth month I had learned to get out of my playpen prison, and begun to get, into everything that was in my sight, and mom was not enjoying this at all. Mom told dad she was having a nervous breakdown over me, and that he would have to do something.

9

My First Birthday

Nothing had changed as for any attention to me which I needed from mom and dad. Dad worked all day, come home, bathed then got blind drunk, this was a daily practice for both him and mom. Mom now told dad that I was such a burden on her, she said, I was so not very bright, and that I did not know how to listen to anything she said to me. She also said, "I think there is something wrong with him." Dad said, "this was expected from a one year old and it was likely something I will grow out of." However, mom's reply was, "he sure better hurry up and grow out of it, because I can't take much more of him." One day after mom put me down in the playpen, and later found that I had learned to climb out and was playing in the dirty clothes room, she pulled me up by the arm and gave me the flogging of my life for getting out of the playpen. She took me down to a dark damp basement where she tied a rope around my ankle, then tied the other end of the rope to a cement support in the basement, this is where I would stay often from early morning, until just before dad was to come home from work that evening. The way things had been going I was wondering if I would ever live to see my second birthday? I was thinking you where suppose too have birthday presents and a party for your birthday with someone signing and a happy birthday song too you. Although I had never expected to see this day I was turning one year old. But, there were not one presents, no signing, and no cake dad said there were no presents because time were hard and money was hard to come by. It had now been almost a year since I had seen my grandparents, and I remembered mom had promised granny and pa she would bring me back to visit with them. One night as I was listening to mom, she told my dad she had no plan to take me back too Arkansas to see my grandparents. She said, "If they wanted to see me again, they would have to get on a bus and come to Kansas City too see me." This was alarming news for me. I did not know if I would ever get to see my grandparents again.

I was now beginning to cut teeth, the pain was unbearable, the discomfort of this caused me to cry out with pain most of the day and night. This caused mom to become even more upset than I had seen her in the past. She was calling me names that I could not say again. After having my first birthday mom told dad that she had to go to work, that staying in the house every day watching me she was not going to be able to stand it any longer. I was looked after by a friend of the family's to sit with me. Although, the sitter would at least feed me and change my diaper more often, than mom had she, still pretty much overlooked me as well talking on the phone for most of the day, the same as mom did. I went to the sitter five days a week, and sometimes I would be there for as many as five days straight before I would see my mom and dad. I guess it was just as well, because it was no different there with the sitter then it was at home. Then, at last another year had come and gone and I was turning two years old. I was having my second birthday and this one would be a little different from the first birthday, as my granny and pa had come on a greyhound bus from the little town in Arkansas to Missouri, too be here on my second birthday. Well, this birthday my granny and pa made sure I had a birthday cake with two candles on it. This year I had ice cream, and cake with presents that granny and pa brought from Arkansas, this was a great birthday. I would like to have told granny and pa that last year I never received anything for my birthday, not even a birthday cake. I would like to have said also, I would not have had anything again this year if they had not come to visit me. Well, my grandparents visit ended sooner than I wanted and now they had to get ready for their journey back to Arkansas. Granny was crying and even pa had a hidden tear in his eyes behind his rough exterior. Granny asks dad "please, let me come back to Arkansas to live with them?" I know this would have made my happy mom very happy, but dad said, 'no maybe later." I was here and it looked as if I would not ever get out, unless either a miracle or something terrible happens to me. I was growing and wanted to go outside too explore the things that were out there for a two-year-old boy. I was keep behind locked doors with much of the time spent in the dark damp basement as if I had some type of contagious disease. The baby sitter would take me as well to that dark damp basement and leave me for hours there alone. However, at the sitter's house she would let me have enough rope so that I could walk and crawl around, where mom would always tie the rope around my ankle not leaving enough for me to move around, most of time she tied the rope around my waist, so that I could not move at all. I stayed tied with the rope sometimes for an entire day, I ate there, and I slept there, and played there with a teddy bear given to me by my granny I went to the bathroom here. My life at times looked to have been at a standstill for me, as if it was not ever going to end. However, years passed slowly and I was now turning five years old. I guess I was becoming a major problem for my mom. The baby sitter stopped looking after me; mom was going to need pay someone else double the amount of money she had been paying her friend. This was an inconvenience, which caused her to become outraged she told my dad that all her pay check went to a baby sitter. While I was too young to know anything about the BIBLE GODS words says which I later would learn,

MARK 10:16 [KING JAMES] And HE took them up in HIS ARMS, put HIS HANDS on upon them, and blessed them. Well, if I had have known about the scripture then I would have asks GOD to bless me, by letting me go live with my Grandparents. Mom told dad he would have to do something with me and it never mattered to her what it was as long as it was something.

10

Going to Live With Granny and Pa'

I expect all good things are worth waiting for. I had now turned three years old granny was not able to make the long trip from Arkansas to, Missouri for my birthday this year, and it was as the years before there was no money for even a simple birthday present? Then, one day just out of the blue my dad made a call to granny and pa too ask if they still wanted me to come live with them, he told her it would most likely be a permanent stay. Granny did not hesitate she said, she would be on the next available Greyhound bus she could on. I spoke with my granny on the phone and she promised me she was coming to get me. Now, the anticipation was building up inside me, as I waited on granny to get here to take me away from all of this. My heart felt as if it were beating a hundred miles per hour. I told my baby sitter I was going to Arkansas to live with my granny and pa and I was never coming back. Up until now this was the most exciting day of my life. The next day granny arrived just as she had promised me she would. All my things were ready, mainly an old teddy bears that granny and pa gave me for my birthday. I was ready to leave as soon as granny and pa got here. I wanted to leave at once but granny said, "She needed to rest for the night and we would leave the next morning granny promised me we would leave at the first light, and I knew granny would never break her promise. Granny would always tell me things from Bible, and this was one of those sayings granny said, that was in the Ten

Commandments: EXODUS: 20:20, you shall not bear false witness against your neighbor. {KING JAMES}. Sleep was not easy tonight, as I lie there beside my granny thinking about living with her and Pa, an old woman and man who first showed me they really loved me.

I remembered, the very first song granny sang to me, and when we got back home to granny's I was going to ask her to sing this song to me again? Then, at last the long night was over and the sun had begun to come up on this Saturday morning. Dad was getting everything ready to take granny and me down town to the Greyhound bus depot. Dad seemed somewhat troubled about me having to leave, but he also knew if I did not go that, he would never have any kind of peace with my mom. Dad also, knew that his mom would take as good as care of me as anyone could. I had never seen my dad cry before; he always had a rough exterior the same as pa, dad had told me that men was not suppose to cry, that crying was for girls, but his real hidden emotions, where showing today, because today, I could see one of those hidden tears behind his rough exterior. Mom said she could not come to the bus station with us, because she had other things to do. Then, as granny and I went too go on board, the big Greyhound bus dad gave both granny and me a hug, said, "Good-bye, and takes care."

11

A Bag of Candy from a Stranger

Looking through the eyes of a three-year-old boy, the bus was the biggest thing I had ever seen. Every seat on the bus had someone seated in them. It looked like if everyone knew the other person and each one was having something to say with the person in the next seat to them. The smoke from almost everyone's cigarette was something of a well-known and unpleasant stench. I had been familiarized too this smoke from the time mom carried in her womb, and dad smoked as well. It was as if I had smoke cigarettes myself, and I just as well had, because the second hand smoke which I had no say so about, taking in a lungful of the nicotine into my lungs was as bad for me as it was if I had smoked the cigarettes myself. It surprised me however, when I watched as granny put one of those cigarettes in her mouth and had lit up

I had never seen my granny smoke before. Granny had much rather had a dip of her {Garrett snuff}. Granny said, dipping snuff out in public did not look lady like so, she would wait until it was dark on the bus too does this when no one would see her put the snuff in between her lips . After we had been on the bus for three hours, stopping in every little town along the road, and some of the towns you would not ever know was here, unless you where told by the bus driver. Then, at last we came to a town when the driver told everyone over the PA system that we would be stopping for a thirty minute break, so everyone that wanted to get off and eat they could? The driver said the bus will leave you behind if you are not back in thirty minutes. Granny had walked to a snack bar too buy her and me a sandwich, when somehow I got loose from granny in all the crowd of people. Then, a short powerful looking built man, with a long ugly scare which ran down the left side of his face, come up to me and asks, "hey little boy, are you lost?" I said, "Yes sir, I can't find my granny." Then, the man said, "Why, I can help you find you're granny." He said, just take my hand, and as soon as I go to the restroom, we will have some of my candy and I can take you to find your granny." Boy, that candy sure sounded really great, I had not had candy in a long time, and I was sure was getting hungry for some too. Then, just as the man reach down to take my hand in his hand and as we were walking towards the men's restroom granny showed up and jerk me away from this stranger. Granny of course had something to say to the strange man who was taking me away, now with all the chaos that was going on, the bus terminal detective came and granny give explanation to him what was happening and the detective took the man away.

We later learned this man was a bad man, and he would have hurt me if he had taken me out of sight. Granny told me, not to ever go away with a stranger again. After, the police had arrested the man; we learned he was wanted in two other states for child molestation. Well, it was about two A.M. When the long ride on, the big greyhound bus arrived to our little town of, Arkansas, and the driver stopped alongside the road to let granny and me off, pa was waiting alongside the road of the sleeping little town and it was only a short walk off the main road to granny and pa's little house.

EPHESIANS 6:4 {KING JAMES} And, ye fathers, provoke not your children to wrath: But bring them up in the nurture and admonition of the LORD {KING JAMES}.

The purpose of parental discipline is to help your children, grow, not to wind up, a discouragement or an embarrassment to your family. Parenting is not easy-it takes lots of patience to raise children in a loving, CHRIST-honoring manner. However, frustration and anger should not be cause for discipline. Instead, parents should in love, minister to their children as JESUS minister to the children HE loves. This is vital to children's development and to their understanding of what CHRIST is like. {Also KING JAMES} [COLOSSIANS 3:21}. I would have given anything to have GOD loving parents or, loving parents at all for that matter. However, GOD had bless me with grandparents who stepped up and filled that empty place, and I could not have had any more love than these two old people showed me. They tried to raise me in a GOD loving, GOD fearing home. Granny and pa prayed continually to GOD, and for things that I did not see anything to be thankful for. I had been with granny and pa, now for about two months when mom called. She said, she was expecting another child and it would be due sometime in January 1957, she told granny, she would need to come, and stay until she could get back on her feet. Of course, granny would not have turned anyone in need away, not even an old stray dog. It was not long after mom called that dad arrived with mom, and sure enough, she was going to have another baby. Why mom wanted another baby, I could not understand. She hated the pregnancy with me, and to me it seems she hated me since the first day I was born. But, I suppose I was too young to understand why? I seem to have made her so nervous she told dad I was going to cause her to have a nervous break. Dad brought mom to grannies and, dad was only going to stay for a few hours and he would be back on his way to, Missouri. Then, on January the 28 1957, mom gave birth to a baby girl. This birth however, was much different from when mom gave birth to me. All of the taking on mom did about her baby girl, oh how beautiful, you are so precious, you are just an angel. It made me want to be sick. Well, mom stayed with granny about three weeks after my sister was born, and I really thought that was too long. However, mom called dad to come back too Arkansas too pick her and my baby sister up. Mom told granny she would not be taking me back with her. Mom said, 'I was just too much trouble for her to care for, and that she could not afford to pay a baby-sitter for two kids. Mom told granny, 'if I become more than could handle they could do whatever they had to do with me.' What mom said, to granny would have hurt most kids of five years old, but it never troubled me because, I never wanted to go back with her anyway. Now, that mom and baby sister had left to return to, Missouri. I did feel that my sister would be taken care of and loved by this woman that was supposed to have loved me as well. However, here at granny's I knew I was loved and I felt safe with granny and pa, there could not have been a safer more loved place on this earth than with my granny and pa.

12

A Winter Wonderland

Winter here in the northeast part of Arkansas, was always cold, during this time of year. It was a time of year which most of the kids in our little community could take pleasure in, because the more snow we had, as a rule they would cancel school as the school buses could not run, and that meant school would be turned out until the snow melted from the roads. The first snow fell in February, this year, and I remember awakening to see the first snow at granny and pas,' it had covered everything outside. It looked as if this was something from a fairy tale picture book. I guess this sight was about the most beautiful thing I could remember looking at. The soft white snow hung from the trees unlike anything I could ever picture. Everything that surrounded me looked isolated, it was as if I had awakened, and was in a land beyond some place only the imagination could go to. The enthusiasm of just looking through the window and waiting on granny to get me dressed in warm clothing so I could dash out to run through the blanket of snow, the excitement of today day I will cherish always. Sometimes, I still have visions of that morning especially each time I see a snow, watching the little rabbits hopping across the snow covered ground trying to find their home buried someplace beneath all this white beauty. I can often see pa and me that morning building a wondrous snowman, with corncob pipe, button eyes, and a carrot nose and of course, granny made a hand knitted scarf to wrap around our big frozen snowman. Although, my granny and pa have now passed from this world to live in GODS world, sometimes these happy remembrances are as if I have fallen asleep and it all only happens yesterday.

13

Grannys' Spring Cleaning

March had arrived and old man winter seems to have gone away as quickly as it had begin.

Spring of the year was coming in this year like a lamb. Granny said, that if the spring came in like a lamb it would leave like a lion, as a child I never knew exactly what that meant other than I later learned it was some kind of old folk lore or an old wise legend that the older people believed in?

The big mystical snowman, which pa and I had rolled from a small snowball, had now begun to melt away a little each day until at last it had completely liquefied leaving no sign that it ever existed. There was something new now in the air, and it was the fragrance of the coming spring air, the fragrance from all the newly growing flowers and the smell of fresh cut grass made this a very special and exceptional time of year. Granny said, "Everyone raised their windows in the spring of the year, and opened all the doors in their houses to let the sweet smell of spring come inside to fill their houses." Granny said, "This was the time of year everyone should do their spring house cleaning." I believe it would not made any difference what time of year it was, grannies house was always clean enough you could have in actually eaten from granny's floor, and it would have been as clean as if you had used a plate. Granny believed that cleanness was next to GODLINESS. However, I never found this to be scriptural. Granny always did the same thing ever spring, she opened ever window in the old house, took down, and washed and ironed ever curtain in the house, she carried out the feather mattress, hung them over the clothesline, then she would take a broom stick and beat the mattress until, you would believe at any moment all the feather would come bursting out of the mattress. Granny moved everything she could outside and washed it with 'bleach, granny said, bleach would kill any germs." Everything from the floors up the walls, even the ceiling was sweep and washed.

14

Spring Storms

I remember lying awake late at nights, when the spring storms were always sure to come, I would lie in bed watching the lighting which would flicker through the thin curtains which hung so neatly and wrinkle free from the windows. Granny's' curtains were wrinkle free because after she had washed them she also starched and iron them, granny had a thing about wrinkles in everything I remember granny even ironed my under shorts and tee shirts. Then, as the flashes from the lightning caused things to a small boy of five years old to look like monsters were standing in the room. I remember many times I would pull the covers up over my head so I could not see these horrible monsters standing here in the room with me. Sometimes the bursting of the thunder would cause the old wood frame house to tremble and squeak, and this would cause me to spring from my bed over into pa and grannies bed which was in the same room. Then, as I lay cuddle there between the only two people in the world who had ever showed me any love. I felt completely safe through the raging night's storm. It was May 1957, four months after the birth of my baby sister, dad called to tell granny mom was pregnant once again, and would be having another baby in February of 1958, Even as a child, I thought why mom would want even more children, after the rejection she had showed towards me? Summer was approaching, and I would get to see my baby sister for the second time since she had been born,

I knew, because mom always come to granny when she was having a baby. However, I had my summer planned for now, and besides they would not be here until January. My childhood days were much different from those of a child today. Unlike today, there were no video games to keep a child pinned inside the house. Our days were full of being outside most of the time with a self made toy. There were no computers to surf the web with, and I could only watch television at certain times usually Saturday morning when the cartoons were on.

However, as the summer went hurriedly by and finished much too soon for me, it would soon be winter once again in the little town of, Arkansas. The snow would again cover the town and again, I was looking forward to going outside with Pa to build another snowman as we had the year before. The snow came in December that year, and again pa and I went out to put together another big frozen man. The temperatures however, got to cold before pa and I had finished, and granny said, 'I would have to come inside, pa stayed and finished what we liked having him complete'. Granny said, "People got frostbite when it was this cold." Well, frostbite was something I never knew anything about, but granny said, "It was when you got to cold and your fingers and toes would turn black, and then the doctor would have to cut them off." Well, I did not know if granny was just telling me this to scare me into coming inside or, not. I did know that granny had never told me a lie before, granny and pa, was awful strict about telling the truth. Therefore, I took her word, besides I never wanted any fingers or, toes too be cut off. So now, I sit looking out the window at the big frosty snowman that was sitting there in the middle of the enchanting scenery of all the snow that lay upon the ground. Then, as I was looking at the enchanted snowman, I asked granny, "would it be alright if we moved the snowman inside the house?"

Granny said, "why heavens no child, the snowman couldn't last more than fifteen minutes in here with the stove burning, it would melt away, leaving nothing but a big puddle of water". Well, I thought on this a while more, then I said, "granny could we let the fire burn out, and then bring the snowman inside?" Granny said, "Why then we would be as frozen as the snowman in no time if we let the fire go out." Granny finally said, "We could bundle up really good and go out long enough to build another, snowwomen to sit beside the other one." I named them pa and granny. Every day that I could not go outside I would sit in front of the window and look out at my two snowmen and snowwoman that sat so cold looking in the middle of the yard. Then, there would be days that the temperatures would warm up enough that granny would let me out of the house for a while. Of course, when the temperatures warmed up the snowmen would start to melt away a little each day, and soon there was nothing left but a big wet spot where they had once sit.

15

A Vivid Memory of the Old House

My memory of my granny and pa is they was just plain country people, underprivileged from most of the luxurious things in life, they were unsophisticated people who loved the LORD and worked hard to pay their bills and to put food on the table. Granny picked cotton when it was in season; cleaned houses did washing and ironing for those who had money when the cotton season was over.

I never knew exactly what my pa did at his work, I knew he worked at a rock crusher through the week, and on Saturday, he would go to the cotton patch with granny. There was never any kind of work done on Sunday's at granny and pa's house. My grandparents believed firmly this was GOD'S day, and you should do nothing on this day but rest and be thankful for what you had, regardless if it was nothing but a bowl of beans and cornbread. Pa said, GOD says in the book of GENESIS Chapter 1. In the beginning GOD created the heaven and the earth {KING JAMES}. . GENESIS: Chapter 2.verse 2 {KING JAMES}. And on the seventh day GOD ended HIS work which HE had made, and HE rested on the seventh day from all His work which HE had made. Then pa said, in the book of.1THESSALONIANS 5.16. {KING JAMES}. Rejoice evermore, 17. Pray without ceasing. 18. In everything give thanks: For this is the will of GOD in CHRIST JESUS concerning you. Paul was not teaching us that we should thank GOD for everything that happens to us, but in everything. Evil is not from GOD. However, when evil strikes, we can still be thankful for GOD'S presence and for the good that HE will accomplish through the distress. However, I would not understand these things until I had become an adult, because I could not see anything we had to be thankful for, we were poor and had very little, but still pa and granny would always thank the LORD no matter what.

I believe a house could have fallen in on pa and he would have said, 'thank you LORD'. The old house we lived in only had four rooms to it. There was no running water to take a bath, granny would hang a sheet up close to the old wood burning stove and put a pan of water on the stove and this was how I took my bath. Our toilet was a little outhouse behind the house, it had one hole that you sit on, and it always had a very bad stench and more so when the summer arrived it usually had spiders. Now, this little house was a place, which you surely wanted to visit before you went to bed, especially if it was during the winter. There was a number of places throughout the old wood frame house you could see the outside showing through the boards. The rooms were always cold during the winter, especially at night after the old wood burning stove burned the last stick of wood. I recall the old house so plainly even after all these years. I cannot recall the old house ever having a coat of paint put on it or, at least on the outside, the floors were made of plank board, except in the kitchen and this was linoleum, and granny was particular about her kitchen, not a speck of dirt would be seen any place in the kitchen. The rooms had wallpaper on them except where it had worn off, and you could see the outside. The roof was tin, and I remember I use to love falling asleep listening to the rain hit the tin roof. I remember many rainstorms that granny would have to go through the house putting pots, pans, and buckets to catch the water, from the leaky roof. Although times were troublesome in those days, I suppose granny and pa's prayers were answered; after all because I do not ever remember a day that we did not have something on our table to eat even though it might be no more than a bowl of red beans and a pan of grannies homemade Cornbread.

Pa and granny believed in giving the LORD thanks for even this? I recall one meal PA asks me to offer the blessing for our food. I said, good bread, good meat good LORD let's eat. Oh, no but that was not the blessing pa had expected to hear from me? Pa's face turned the color of the beets that were on the table. Pa immediately said, boy I will have no such blasphemy in this house, he ordered me to leave the table at once and to go to the back of the house. But, pa I said I haven't ate yet? Pa said, and you want eat at this table until you have learned to respect the LORD and my house? You pray that the LORD forgive you for such blasphemy and remember how you were taught to pray for your food. Then, tomorrow night when you are ask to offer the blessing you will have remembered.

Well, not only was my mouth watering for those pork chops and mashed potatoes and gravy, my stomach thought my throat had been cut before I was allowed to eat again? Well, guess what it was at last supper time again and after we had all sit down pa said, son. I believe it's your turn tonight to say the blessing? Yes sir pa I said.

This time I started with. Dear, LORD we are blessed tonight for this bountiful meal before us to fill our mortal bodies with, we thank you LORD, thank you LORD for pa and my granny for providing it for us, and pa and granny said amen. Pa said that's much better son.

I still have remembrance of the summers of looking down the road on a Friday afternoon at granny and pas' house and watching pa as he walked toward the house with a big ripe watermelon under his arm.

16

More Indian Family and a New Brother

It was time now that I would be introduced to another family member who would later become, very close to me. This woman would be my forever best friend and aunt; I would come to love her very much. This family member was a half sister to my granny and everyone just called her Aunt Annie, even though she might not be been their Aunt they called her this anyway. I would never learn my ant Annie's real name. All I knew was she was half Indian, and this was easy enough to see as she had very high cheekbones, her eyes were dark and set close to each other, her skin was a dark-red color, and she had beautiful long black hair and was a very tall women. I remember a few times my aunt Annie spoke to me in her Indian language. Although this side of my Indian heritage was on my parental side of the family, and it was a half sister to my parental grandmother I as well never learn the background of this native heritage, this too was somewhat of a secret for some reason that I would never know?

My aunt was someone else who loved me very much and would have wrestle with a grizzle bear for me; I believe she would have won the battle too. I believe she was maybe the first person who let me smoke my first cigarette. She was the most good-hearted old person I would ever be acquainted with. Why, my Aunt Annie would have given even a stranger the very last nickel to her name. Anytime, I wanted anything, such as a soda pop, candy or, even cigarette's aunt

Annie had a charge account at one of the country stores, and she told the owner that anytime I came in for anything I wanted, to let me have it, and charge it to her account. It was now February, 22nd, 1958; mom gave birth to a baby boy, her third baby this one on Once again, and granny took care of mom until she was back on her feet. Then, the second week of March, mom called dad to come pick her and my sister and brother up. Dad drove down from Missouri that day and all four of them went back to Missouri. I had to wonder how it was that Mom could afford to pay a baby sitter for two kids now, and she said when I was the only child that she could not even pay for one. I really knew why, she had for some reason, since the day she found out that she was pregnant with me decided she did not then nor was she ever going to love me.

17

No Love Changes Lives

A choice to start a family is a serious life changing event for both a young mom and a young dad and more so for the baby to be. I am the perfect example of a baby that my life was changed, because I never felt or knew the love from my mom or dad. I have gone through a complete life with this feeling of being unloved and unwanted. I hunted for this attention through my infant years for my mom to pick me up, to hold me close to her, and tell me she loved me. I waited through my toddler years for mom to tell me she loved me, it never happened, I waited through my adolescent years for mom to tell me she loved me, it never happened, I waited through my teenage years, I waited through my young adult years and one day after sixty-two years later just before the death of my baby girl I heard mom say; I love you was it an accidental, or was it a miracle? Today, at sixty-five years old my dad has since passed away. However, my mom is still living at the age of eighty-four and our living five thousand miles apart we now from time to time have phone conversation with each other. Now mom has started to tell me she loves me, it feels a little peculiar but, she does at least say it, I try hard to accept that she may have changed and that she means this and I hope it comes from my heart when I say to her that I love her as well.

Of course it would not have been completely possible for me to have remembered every word said, about me from the eight week of pregnancy. But, I learned through researching medical journals that I had a brain which had developed at the eight week of pregnancy. A baby has its eyes, nose, ears, mouth, and all its vital organs. In addition, I went back to the places and talked with elder people who knew my family during this period and was gave me information that confirms most of my story. Since, I did have my brain at the eight-week I knew my mom rejected me through my life.

This is why my book began here. In addition, somewhere deep inside my subconscious mind I believe all these things actually happened as I write them from the eight week of mom's pregnancy.

However, at this point I plead with the young mom and dad to be a woman and man enough to take the responsibility of the life that the two of you have produced. Love this life through the term of pregnancy, talk to your un-born baby, let your baby hear you voice, let your baby feel your love towards him or, her. The life inside of you can feel whether or, not you want and love him or, her. Imagine now at the eight week, just a mere two months after conception you have a living human life growing and living inside of you. It now has a brain, nose, eyes, ears mouth and a face that looks like you or, dad. All of the baby's vital organs are working and functioning just as yours is, and now you choose to take this innocent living life away. So, even if you cannot love the little miracle inside of you. At least give it a chance to live with someone else who will love this baby.

18

They Would Not Let Me
Start to School

September 1958, School was starting. However, I would not be allowed to start school this year. I would not turn six until October 22, of this year and since school was beginning in September, I could not start until, the following year of 1959, when I would be seven. In 1952, we did not have a preschool or even a kindergarten. I was all but one month of being old enough to start to school this year.

Well, having to wait another year to start to school was ok by me. This would give me one more year to be free. This year however, went by much too quickly than I wanted, and at last the year had come and gone and it was the dreadful day for me to go to school for the first time. I think just about every kid remembers the frightful first day of school. I know I will always remember my first day, as I went kicking and screaming, in disapproval against this.

However, with the objection I put up I was still sitting in the first grade at the start of the school year. Before the day was over I had fallen in love with my teacher. She was not at all; as I had been told, she was going to be. Everyone told me the year before the teacher would have a long crocked nose with a big wart on the end of it, and if I said anything without her asking me she would make my nose look exactly as hers.' My teacher was just the opposite of everything I had been told

40

that she would look like. She was a lovely woman with a big smile and a soft voice. She told me that everything was going to be all right and she would not let anyone hurt me. I think I must have instantly trusted her from that moment. But now, an unexpected thing was about to happen in my life, and something I was certainly not going to enjoy. It was around the middle of the school year when dad called granny and said, 'he was coming after me to take me back to Missouri to live with him and mom.' I would very soon understand why I was wanted back in the family, and it was not because mom, had a change of heart and suddenly started loving me, but I was now seven years old, and this was an important age in this day and time. Granny talked to dad until I thought her face would turn blue, granny said, "why, if you take him out of school in the middle of the school year he will fail his first grade. But, my dad was my dad, and he was not listening to anything my granny had to say. He said, 'have the boy ready I am coming to get him." Dad arrived on the weekend and when granny had to say good-bye to me, I will always remember how the tears were rushing down her old wrinkled face. I thought something was going to happen to granny's heart, as she looked as white as the first snow I remembered seeing at granny and pa's house. Pa, being a man was trying not to let his tears show as much as grannies were, but no matter how much he tried the marks from the tears was on his wrinkled old face as well. My Grandparents treated me as if I was their own son, and I did not really know the difference, because I thought of them as if they were my parents.

Granny and pa were now getting old or at least to a small boy it seem that way, and some day I was going to have to give them up to go live with the LORD. I could not picture how my life was going to be without the two old people who had given me so much, love and a home to live in. Now, that I had been pulled out of school and being settled down with a loving home environment, life for me was once again about to change for the worse.

I was about to learn not long after I was back in dads and moms house the reason for my coming here, it was not because there had been a change of heart, and they had started loving me?. I was now seven and a half years old; this was old enough to watch my younger sister and brother. Seven and a half years old was old enough to change diapers, and feed a bottle to my younger sister and brother and to give them a bath. I would be accountable to do these things as soon as I arrived here.

The schools here were much different from the school back in Arkansas. There were twice as many kids in one room. The teacher did not have time to spend with one student, and when you did not understand something, it upset the teacher, they would tell me to pay attention, and I would not have to ask the second time. This was indeed an unhappy time for me; I was failing in every subject. I believed part of this was because I missed my grandparents. Back home in Arkansas after school in the evening granny would sit down with me and help me with my school homework truth be told sometimes granny actually did my homework for me.

Here, when dad and mom come in from work their first order of business was to start drinking and getting drunk, if they come home at all. When they never come home after work that meant they had stopped at the neighbored bar for a few beers and mixed drinks, and would be home when they got home. I knew when the two of them come through the door that everything had better be in order because the two of them were going to be drunk. Sister and brother had better be bathed, cleaned, and feed and in bed asleep. This went on for the rest of my school year. I believe it was here that I first began to believe in miracles' because one was about to happen. This, miracle was going to be the first of many yet to come as I looked back at my life at the times when there would have been no way that I would have made it through without a guardian angel. Granny called one day and told dad once more that if he would let me come back to stay with her and pa they would take care of all my expenses to raise me. Dad talked this over with mom for a short while, and called granny back and said, yes but it would have to be permanent. I was not to come back and he was not going to help with anything, this was going to be a sealed deal. Of course, granny agreed, "it was a deal." I felt like I had just been sold, but I knew my new owners would care for and love me with all their heart. This was one of those miracles GOD preformed in my life. Granny said, 'there was nothing impossible for GOD to do,' and I believed it. Granny said, 'once JESUS raised HIS friend from the dead.' Lazarus.

When, granny would tell me something from the Bible she would always read it to me, and this was in the book of JOHN: 11:39 {KING JAMES} JESUS, once more deeply moved, came to the tomb. It was a cave with a stone laid across the entrance. 39. JESUS said, take away the stone. Martha, the sister of him that was dead, saith unto HIM, LORD, by this time he stinketh, for he has been dead four days. 40. JESUS saith, unto her, said I not unto thee, that, if thou wouldest believe, thou shouldest see the glory of GOD? 41. Then they took away the stone from the place where the dead were laid. And JESUS lifted up HIS eyes, and said, FATHER, I thank thee that thou hast heard me.

42. And I knew that thou hardest me always: But because of the people which standby I said it, that they may believe that thou have sent me. 43. And when HE thus had spoken, HE cried out with a loud voice, Lazarus, come forth. 44. And he that which was dead came forth, bound hand and foot with graveclothes: and his face was bound with a napkin, JESUS saith unto them, loose him, and let him go. That weekend I felt as if JESUS had given me my miracle as dad and I were on our way to take me to Arkansas. Some place about half way between our trip I had fallen asleep, and when I woke up there was a police officer shinning a flashlight in the back seat where I had been sleeping I said. 'Hey mister, "I'm going to Arkansas, to live with my granny." The police officer replied and said, "Son if your daddy don't slow down you're not going to make it to Arkansas." Dad had been driving around a hundred miles per hour when the police office got him stopped. Dad always drove an old car just as fast as the speedometer registered, if it registered 150 M.P.H. That was

how fast dad drove the old car. The rest of our trip only took a few more hours and at last, I was at granny and pa's house. The following Monday after I had come back to live with granny, she enrolled me back into school. There were only two month left in the school year, but granny explained, there was a law that said, I had to be in school regardless? Now, since I had been in and out of school, so much my grades were below passing, and I was going to have to take the first grade over. However, this was all right with me just as long as I was with my granny and pa I could stay in the first grade until I was an old man. It was now May 1960, Summer here in the sleepy ruel little town of; Arkansas hardly no one got in a hurry to go anyplace, everyone walked about leisurely to wherever they wanted to go. Everyone drove their vehicle in the same manner as each one walked, unless of course dad was in town. Every day, here in the sleepy little town seemed as if it were a Saturday, which was all right for a kid. The women all stayed home to clean their homes, and each woman had her own washday which they washed clothes and hung the clothes out on a clothesline to let the gentle breeze dry them. You could always smell the aroma of some women cooking fresh baked bread or, homemade pies and cakes. I always loved the summer fragrances that filled the air in our little community. It would be difficult decision for me to make if I could go back in time to one of my childhood days, and enjoy reliving just one day. There were so many days at granny's house that was good memories that I could not choose the one I most favored.

I recall a time my little playmate a girl the same age as from next door to granny's and pas' house who was also my childhood sweetheart. We would pretend we were married; I would make believe I would go to work then come home to a wonderful meal prepared after my hard day's work. The meals were of mud pies she had put together, and I actually ate these mud pies. I would always shove a mouthful of her mud pie into my mouth gulping it down and telling her how delicious her pies were and that no one could make a pie as good as she did Then, as night fell on our lazy little town the two of us would sit under a corner street light near our houses, we would talk about the things we wanted to be and do when we grew up. We talked about really being married to each other someday. We talked about our profession, mine was to become a writer, and she wanted to be doctor so that she could cure all the sick people in the world. If I could choose a time in life to return to, when I was a child, I might choose the time. I recall the day I had skipped school and had slipped off to a nearby creek too just lie around in the sweet smelling grass. I would lay there sneaking a smoke from a corncob pipe, which I had found. Then there was a time which I would not wish to ever experience again. I had watched granny many times put a pinch of her Garrett snuff into her lips. I had took some of this snuff one day and I slipped off to my favorite place at the creek and after trying to us the exact same method granny had done I started to put the snuff into my lips, but the powder went up my nose. This had to be the most awful thing I had ever experienced in my life. My nose was burning, my eyes were watering, and everything around me went to spinning so fast it felt as if I was going to spin off the face of the earth. I could not imagine how granny used this awful stuff. I often look back now some sixty five-years past and it is as if as if it all took place just yesterday.

19

The Mumps

It was now the winter of nineteen- sixty this was in an era which medicine had not yet fully advanced as it has today, there was not so many vaccines in this day and time? So, when you caught something contagious you usually just suffered it out with homemade medicine and, of course I always had some of granny's homemade chicken noodle soup this was good for just about any contagious thing you could catch. I recall a contagious childhood illness that I remember all too well.

It was the winter of 1960, October the 22, and on my eight birthday, I had caught something called the mumps. This was something which effected your jaws and if you caught them you wanted to have them in both jaws at the same time and have it over with because if you only caught them in one jaw, it would be sure the other was sure to come later in the other jaw and it would be the same thing all over again. Luckily, I had them in both jaws at the same time. These mumps caused you jaws to swell along with your throat with a pain that you would never forget. There was not much that you could do for these mumps; there was no medicine that you could have that would make them go away. I think maybe, if you could look on a positive side of having these mumps it would be you for sure were excused from going to school for the period of time it took for the swelling and fever to leave. This commonly lasted around two-weeks so I suppose maybe, there was something after all that was good about this, as you could not go school while you had these, and you got a lot of attention and ice cream.

20

The Measles and Blindness

After having been ill with having the mumps, my wish was, I was through catching anything contagious again at least for a while I think maybe, even having to go to school would have been much better than being sick with all these horrible illness?. February 1961, I had caught the German measles. These were the most dangerous type of measles you could fall victim to. Granny put me in a dark room which she covered all the windows with aluminum foil so that no sunlight could come through. The only light in the room was from a dimly burning light from a kerosene lamp sit in the farthest Conner. Granny would take my temperature about every hour and give me Bayer aspirin for my fever, 7up to drink and of course the healer of everything granny's homemade chicken noodle soup.

Granny would put sunglasses on me to protect my eyes from the ceiling light when she came in to check on me. I never understood why I had to stay in the dark room while I had these measles, but granny said; that the light would damage my eyes and she wanted to take every safety precaution she could to safeguard me, this at least was granny diagnosis. However, regardless of all the precautionary measures, which granny took, I remember the day I was lying in the dark room with only the dim light of the kerosene lamp and a faint light that shown beneath the door from the next room, when everything went completely dark.

After all the safety measures and superior care, granny had given me I had now lost my eyesight completely. I was as blind as a bat. I scream in terror at the top of my weak lungs for granny to come at once. I could hear granny as she came running through the house rattling and knocking things onto the floor as she came to my frightful cry for help. The door to my room made a squeak when granny opened it to see what I was screaming for? By the time granny reached the bedroom I was in the floor crawling towards the door. Granny I cried I am blind, I can't see.

The room was no longer dark from granny having it this way to protect my eyes; it was dark because I had now lost my eyesight. I could fell warmth on my face from the kerosene lamp granny was holding next to my face. I will always remember how freighting this day was for me. I was just a child and now I was going to be blind for the rest of my life. I had so much planned to do, so much to see, so many places I wanted to visit, but now I was going to have to accept that I was blind and would need someone to care for me all the days of my life.

I listen as granny was praying and saying, "Oh, please LORD, does not take my boys eyesight away." Granny had taken hold of me, pulled me up close to her, and started to pray some more, as I had never heard anyone pray. After about an hour of praying granny said, "She was going next door to call the old doctor to see if he could help." Granny was not gone for more than about fifteen minutes when she returned to tell me the doctor would come by to look at my eyes after he had closed the office. Next granny walked to the neighbors to ask the woman of the house if she would come and sit with me until she could walk to the drug store for some eye drops to put in my eyes. The old neighbor women must have been at least one hundred years old, but she could walk faster and get around better than any twenty years old I had ever seen. I would have wage she could have sprint a hundred yard dash without breathing hard. When the old women came through the door to the dark room where I was at she was praying just as I had heard granny pray. Except her prayers were in a language I did not understand, nor had I ever listen to anyone pray in such a matter. The old women would beat her fist into the other hand, and when she did she would say things I never understood. She would talk directly to the devil, and say in the name of the LORD you dirty devil you, and you take your hands off this child. I later learned after growing up that the old woman was a Pentecostal and she was praying in tongues. Well, I was thankful when granny came through the door and began putting drops in my eyes at once, then about every hour she would put more in, by now she had moved into the room with me permanently just sitting beside my bed in her old wooden rocking chair praying and rocking.

That afternoon the old doctor came by as he had promised. I could hear him as he walked up to my bed that I was lying in. He then said, he was going to shine a light in my eyes and for me to say whether or, not I could see the light. Well, I never knew if he had turned on the light, because I never did see any light. This is a mystery, he said to my granny, but something from the measles has caused the boy to be blind. He told Granny to, just keep doing what she had been doing with the ointment, and he said this ointment is something new and it surly could not hurt to keep using it. The doctor said he would check by in a couple of days to see how things were going. After the first three days there was still no difference, I still could not see my hand in front of my face. I could hear granny sitting in the chair next to my bed praying and crying just about all the time often the crying that was just awful to listen too. Then, I could hear pa when he would come in from work and he would tell granny, now mother that crying is not going to help the boy. He would say it is no fault of anyone's it is just something that happened, and they had to stand on their faith that GOD would hear their prayers and that HE would restore my sight.

21

Granny Praised the Lord

It was about the seventh day, Granny had been doctoring my eyes, and the doctor had returned to check on me. He told granny this was puzzling to him, that he recommends a specialist check my eyes. The eight day now of my being blind, I told granny I thought I was able to see streams of light, and I could see a figure of her sitting next to me. Well, granny jumped up from her old wooden rocking chair and started to dance around the floor and we were Baptist, so I had never seen my granny dance before, this was just something which the Baptist did not do. However, from what I could make out of the dim figure of her dance she was performing, it was a remarkable sight to see.

Granny was giving praises to the LORD and shouting boy, "The LORD has given you your sight back; the LORD has given you your sight back, praise the LORD!" Well, after she had finished her victory dance, and the excitement had calmed down granny said, 'quick boy put these sunglasses on to protect your eyes'. Well, I still had to stay in the dark room for another three days. Granny said, 'she wanted to be sure that all the measles spots were gone but I was seeing as well as I had before.'

Granny said, "This was a miracle from the LORD was what this was, and that we should be thankful for HIS miracle". Well, at last, granny let me returned outside to play again, something that for a while I was afraid I would never get to do.

22

Adventure of Two Ho Bos'

Summer was now in full swing and I was going to be a nine-year-old boy in October now being the inquisitive kid I was I was continually being a nine year old exploratory kid. I was getting into everything I could get into, and believe me I was going to explore some things this summer that I would later wish I had left unexplored. Why, I don't believe old Huckleberry Finn himself, could have gotten into more of a disorder than, I was about to get into this summer. About a half of a mile from granny and pas' old house was two railroad tracks where a freight train ran through once in the morning and again in the afternoon. The train usually never stopped, unless it had to drop of a boxcar with merchandise, when one of the local merchants had occasionally ordered feed or other supplies from somewhere afar off. Most of the time there was always two or three old empty boxcars sitting on the sidetrack. Well, Saturdays as a kid growing up the little town of around four hundred people here, there was not much fun stuff to do as, there are today. We did not have any video games or, computers, so you just found whatever you could to entertain yourself.

It came to pass on this sunny summer, Saturday morning, my best friend who everyone nicknamed Jack Rabbit; because he could out jump and out run anyone in the entire town. However, today Jack Rabbit and me we went down to the railroad tracks to play on one of the boxcars. This was of course a place we had been told not to go to.

But, we were almost nine years old; the box cars look like a fun place for us to play. Well, as we made believe we were a couple of old Ho-Bo's who had come here on a long journey, the boxcar which we were playing on made a tug and Jack Rabbit and I lost our balance and fell to the floor of the boxcar, the next thing we knew the boxcar was moving. Then, as the boxcar begins to move a little faster, we were now aware the boxcar had been hooked to the engine that pulled them. Our now making believe we were a Ho-Bo's was no longer making believe at all, we were on a real hobo journey. It did not take the engine long to pick up speed and we were moving down the track at what seemed to a couple of small boys' a hundred miles an hour. Our little town was fading quickly behind us, as we looked out the big open door and we had no way to jump off the boxcar, even if the train was going slow enough to jump there was not a place to jump, as there was nothing but cliffs and large jagged rocks. We were in a lot of trouble and in more ways than we knew. I think Jack Rabbit wanted to cry and to say truthful I did as well, but I was not going to tell Jack Rabbit nor was he about to tell me. This was just something we would not let each other know. Now, since we had not made it home for our dinner at noon, and granny always had dinner ready and on the table at exactly noon every day. Sometimes, when we went off to play granny would fix Jack Rabbit and me couple of peanut butter and jelly sandwiches, and we sure were wishing we had a couple of those sandwiches right now, because, we were both beginning to get powerful hungry.

We had no idea where we was at, and all we could see as we looked through the open door of the boxcar was unfamiliarly woods. We had been on the train all day and the darkness was now beginning to enclose around us, and Jack Rabbit said, 'Lone Wolf, that was my nickname, I sure wish we had a flashlight.' Well, I said, 'I wish we did too.' We could hear the train blasting away on the lonesome sounding whistle through the dark night, we could hear the clatter of the big iron wheels rolling across the railroad tracks, it sounded as if we had not slowed down once since we left out little town.

Frequently we would pass a crossing where the traffic had to stop and wait for the train to pass. We could hear the warning signal cling, cling, cling as we passed hurriedly by. Sometimes during the night Jack Rabbit and me decided there was nothing we could do and we had just as well lie down and go to sleep in some straw in one corner of the boxcar. Sleep was difficult for the both of us tonight, for me all I could think about was what granny thought happened to me. The train that Jack Rabbit, and me had been playing on was near a river, I thought that if anyone had seen us there they may have told granny, and then granny and Jack Rabbits mom may be thinking we had fallen in the river, and they were likely here right now dragging the river looking for the two bodies of two nine year old boys'.

They could also be thinking some old ho-Bo had kidnapped the two of us. I knew granny by this time crying and wringing her hands for me saying, oh 'I just know that something bad has happen to my little boy." Sometime during the night I had fallen asleep when something caused me to become awaken, I noticed the train had at last stopped. I laid there and listen; I wanted to make sure I was not dreaming. Then I shook Jack Rabbit and said. "Get up and let's get off of the boxcar." Jack Rabbit sprang up wiping sleep from his eyes and we wasted no more time to jump off the boxcar. The first thing we did after jumping off was hide in some nearby brush to make sure we had no one had seen us get off the train. After, about fifteen minutes we decided it was safe enough to leave our hiding place and go in the direction we thought was home. As the two of us begin waking along the tracks toward the back of the boxcars, we figured this must be the direction. We also, know it had to be a very long way back home.

We had been on the train now since just before noon the following day, and now it must be around eight- O'clock the next morning. It seemed as if Jack Rabbit and I had walked at least a hundred miles. As most nine year old boys' did we, were famous to not often wear shoes to play around town in, and we had no shoes on today either, and the hot rocks which lay between the rail road track were beginning to make sores on our feet. After what felt as hours of walking and we had not seen one house. Our stomachs were now on empty and making growling sound. Then, after we had walked what seemed the second hundred miles, my feet felt as if they weight a ton when at last we looked up and saw something which looked like buildings ahead of us. We wasted no more time as we took off running toward the buildings just as fast as our weary legs and bare feet would carry us, and sure enough, there was something here all right. However, we had forgotten one thing; it was now a Sunday morning, and none of the little country stores here were open. Everything here closed to observe the LORDS day. Therefore, we started walking exhausted, starving, and almost too weak to go much further. Then, we saw another remarkable sight. Sitting here out in the middle of nothing else around was a beautiful white two story house. Jack Rabbit and I broke out in a run to get to the front door and knock. However, we knock, and knock and knock some more and no one was at home. Again, we had forgotten it was a Sunday and it looked as if everyone around here went to Church on Sunday. Now, what are we going to do jack rabbit asked? Well, I knew that either one of us had enough strength to go any further, or further more we had no clue as to where we were?

Having no other choice the two of us just sit there on these people's front porch. We decided we had just as well sat here and wait until someone comes home however long it took. I remembered granny telling me that there was this man in the Bible in the book of Matthew: 3.4 {KING JAMES} This Man named John ate locust and wild honey. 4. And the same John had his raiment of camel's hair, and a leather gridle about his loins, and his meat was locusts and wild honey. I was thinking that might taste good right now, except we did not have any honey or locust to eat. While, we were waiting, I told Jack Rabbit, I was never going to play on another boxcar unless I had me some peanut butter and grape jelly sandwiches with me'. Jack Rabbit said, 'he was never going to play on another boxcar again even if the boxcar was full of peanut butter and jelly sandwiches'.

I suppose we must have sat there for about three hours when someone at last pulled up in the front yard, a big man got out of his car first, and then, his wife and five children got out after him. This big man comes walking up towards Jack Rabbit and me, where we were sitting on his front porch.

He looked as big as a mountain, and he had a mean look on his face. Then, he said, looking mostly toward me and with a deep and angry voice. "What are you two boys doing here on my porch?" "Who are you?" "And where are you from?" He said, "Don't lie to me boys, because I know you're not from around here, cause I know everybody from around the parts of these here woods for fifty- miles." He said, "I even knew everyone's dogs and their cat's name." I thought he must be a smart man to know all of that. I wondered if he might be related to old Hobo Joe. I remember old Joe sure knew something about anything you wanted to know? He asked, "Well, are you going to tell me where you are from?" Well, I was thinking if he could just stop talking long enough, I could answer his questions. Then, finally I interrupted him and said, "Sir, everyone just calls me Lone Wolf, and my friend here they call him Jack Rabbit sir." "We are here from a little town in Arkansas." I said, "We don't know where we are now, but we sure are hungry, and we could work in the yard if he would just give us something to eat." Well, then his wife interrupted and said, "Stop harassing these young boys lumberjack." I guessed this was his nickname as well. However, she said, "They had plenty of fried chicken and biscuits left from dinner that you boys can have."

Oh boy did this ever sound good my mouth was watering so. I must have looked like a hungry slobbering old wolf in some ones chicken coop. Then, Mrs. Lumberjack took us and showed us were we could wash some of the dirt of our hands and face from being on the train. They had water that ran inside the house and at granny's I had never seen this before, because we had to go outside and pull our water out of a deep hole with a rope, then carry the water into the house in a bucket. However, Mrs. Lumberjack said, "she understood that we never knew how this inside water worked." Mrs. Lumberjack then showed us how to work the hot and cold water, so we could wash up. Then, after we were all clean, we sat down Mr. Lumberjack did the same thing that my pa did at home he ask everyone to bow their head and he told the Lord that they were thankful for the food we were about to partake in. Mrs. Lumberjack had fixed next to my granny's' the best-fried chicken, mashed potatoes biscuits and gravy' I had ever eaten. Then, after we had ate and was so full I thought I might pop, Mrs. Lumberjack said, "Now you boys do not have to work to pay for you dinner." She said, "You know you boys are a long way from home to be a couple of boys your ages." Then, we told her how we come to be here, by playing on the boxcar back in, Arkansas. She said, "Well boys, this is not Arkansas that you are in, you are in the state of Missouri right now". Now, to a couple of small boys are age that sounded like we had traveled a million miles. Jack Rabbit and I talked over our situation for a while and we said, "We both sure was tired of trains, but since we both had a full stomach we guessed we could catch another train that was going back toward Arkansas." Then Mrs. Lumberjack said, "No way would she let us get back on another train." She said, "You boys are about two hundred miles away from your hometown. "She said, I will speak to Mr. Lumberjack, and he would take us back home." Well, after Lumberjack said, he was going to take us back home Jack Rabbit and me loaded up in the back of Lumberjacks pickup truck. Then, before we took off Mrs. Lumberjack come out to the truck and handed me a brown paper bag. She said, "Now this is just in case you boys get hungry on the way home." After we had gotten down the road, apiece I decided to look inside the bag. There was more fried chicken, and a little something extra, two big slices of homemade apple pie. Jack Rabbit and I ate that fried chicken first, and then we ate the apple pie so fast it looked as if it had vanished before our very eyes. I guess it must have taken Lumberjack about four hours and we were back in our hometown once again.

23

Happy Reunion of the Two Ho Bo's

When Lumberjack got Jack Rabbit and me back to my grandparent's house, my granny saw me get out of the back of the truck through her living room window. Well, she come running off the front porch and across the yard as if she was running like someone was chasing after her, she was crying and saying at the same time, praise the LORD boy your safe. Lumberjack got out of his truck and introduced himself and he told my granny and pa not to go to hard on me, as I had learned a powerful lesson from all of this, granny, promised, and said "They were just thankful that I was ok, and they could not thank him enough for taking care of me and getting me home safely." Lumberjack let Granny fix him something to eat before he started back home, and this would be the last anyone would ever hear from, Mr. Lumberjack. After, I told granny the story of how Jack Rabbit and I met Mr. Lumberjack and his family, granny thought this was somewhat of an unusual thing to have happened. Granny tried after Lumberjack went back to Missouri to see if there was anyone with the name, he gave her, living in the area that all of this happened at? Granny always ended up with the same answer, no one had ever heard of anyone by that name living anywhere around that part of Missouri, granny even notified the sheriff. Even the sheriff told granny the only thing that was in this area was forest and wild animals. After Mr. Lumberjack had left, granny walked Jack Rabbit home and explained everything to his mom about what had happen to us. It would always remain a mystery of what happened on this day, that a family who lived in the forest alongside a railroad track, feed Jack Rabbit and I. Then, it was as if there was no trace of anyone living there? Had this been real or, was there something else going on? Granny said she believed that GOD'S had put angels there to take care of the two of us. She said, the Bible talked of them in many places for instance in the book of. MATTHEW 18:10. {KING JAMES} Take heed that ye despise not one of these little ones; for I say unto you, that in Heaven there angles do always behold the face of MY FATHER which is in Heaven.

"Our concern for children must match GOD'S treatment of them. Certain angels assigned to watch over children, and they have direct access to GOD. These words ring out in cultures where children are ignored, or aborted. If their angels have constant access to GOD, the least we can do is to allow children to approach us in spite of our far too busy schedules."

24

Summer Ending

The rest of the summer for Jack Rabbit and me, was coming to an end, and we had went through reasonably thrilling summer for two nine years old boys. We would have a pretty good story to tell everyone of our summer vacation when school started back. We would most likely have one of the best stories of all to tell about our summer vacation riding the boxcar to Missouri. Fall was here and it was once again time to start back to school. Granny had been busy on her old treadle singer sewing machine through the summer making me new school clothes. I believe my granny was just about the best clothes maker there was anywhere in the entire country at making clothes. There was not a piece of clothing which my Granny did not know how to make. My clothes always looked as if you bought them right out of the store. I guess about the only time I ever had store bought clothes was on Easter Sunday. Pa and granny would always each year just before Easter pay someone to drive the three of us some fifteen-miles to the nearest city with a big clothing department store and buy me a new suit to wear to church. Granny had made me three new cotton shirts and three new pairs of pants for the school year. Then, there was this item of clothing I wish granny had not learned to make, and this was a mohair sweater or, some people called them a wool sweater. It was warm enough alright but, I hated to wear it because it made my skin itch and tingle all over, and I had to scratch all the time I had this on. But, at the beginning of each new school year granny and pa bought me a new pair of shoes before school started, of course in those days a kid never cared much for new shoes, as we had just as well go bare foot.

25

Another Winters Splendor

It was now the winter of 1961. Being nine years old and in the first grade made me look as if I was not to smart? Even though I really never believed it was entirely my mistake. They would not let me start to school until I was seven this put me behind a year, then, my dad came to took me out of school in the middle of the year and moved me to another school. However, as the new school year begin it was not as bad as I first imagined it would be. And, besides, I didn't have any say to the issue. As the winter was upon the little town it was near time to see our first snow of the year, I believed it would be as the pictures I had in my mind of the past winters here with granny and pa. Once again, I was so excited for that first snow to fall so Pa and I could go out and build an even bigger snowman than we had built in the years past. Our first snow was earlier this year than they had been in years past. Our snow fell on Christmas-eve night and it was indeed another enchanting picture as if it had come out of a storybook. Once again, pa and I went out and we did build the biggest snowman ever. Again, it had everything as the last year had a corncob pipe, a carrot nose button eyes right down to granny's hand knitted scarf.

I always believed pa was most likely the best snowman builder there was? The huge snowman always looks as if it were going to start to talk at any time.

26

What's in the Big Christmas Box

I suppose Christmas has always been the most exciting time of year for just about any kid wherever they have Christmas. Once granny told me that in some places of the world they did not believe in the celebration of Christmas, and in these places the kids there did not get to have any great gifts to open on Christmas morning like we did here in America. I sure was glad I lived in Arkansas, a place that believed in Christmas. This was a special time of year that not only did we get really neat gifts, but also we had many different things we could have to eat. Granny always fixed ginger bread cookies, apple pies, pecan pies, and cakes. There were all sorts of different kinds of fruits like apples and, oranges to eat and we could eat as much as we wanted.

However, the best thing about Christmas morning for me was after everyone had eaten their breakfast, and pa had built a good fire in the old pot belly stove, and everyone had gathered in the living room around the decorated tree. Everyone would sit and wait for their name to be called to receive their present. There was this one Christmas, I remember most of all, because of the joke some of the family members played on poor old pa. My Aunt Annie, the one who most of the family never had much to do with, because of her being different, because she was half-Indian and some of the family thought that shamed the family. However, Aunt Annie gave me a real pair of Indian moccasins, a real looking tomahawk and a bow and arrow that was not real. Granny and pa gave me a new pair of store bought paints, and a store bought shirt, a sweater, that was not made of wool, some mittens and a pair of galoshes for when I went out to build a snowman. Pa gave me my first real pocket knife and I remember pa telling me this knife is for whittling on a piece of wood, and it is never to be carried to school for any reason. I would later be sorry I had not listened to pa's instruction about leaving the pocketknife at home. I do not remember everything everyone got this year, but I do recall what the family done to poor old pa that year. You see pa had the biggest box of all sitting beside the cider tree. The paper wrappings on it were the most beautiful of all with a most beautiful green bow tied around it. Pa would keep saying, I wonder what anyone could have bought me that would take such a big box to put it in. Pa's patience was about to get the best of him, he was becoming as bad as us kids about wanting to open his present, and the family keep making him wait until the very last one to open his big present. Well, at last someone said, ok granddad you can open you present. Well, pa begins to ripping and tearing the paper off that big box like one of the kids. Then, when he had pulled all the paper off, there inside that box was another box just one size smaller than the first one, and this box had more wrappings of pretty paper. Over, and over again, and then when he had unwrapped eight boxes inside the other he come to the last box, and it was a small match box. Well, now pa said, 'he can't imagine what could be in a box that small box'.

Now, pa un-wrapped the small matchbox, and inside the matchbox after, all the work, he had done there was an old chicken bone in the box. Well, everyone but pa found this to be humorous, and everyone was laughing so hard that no one had seen when one pa's son's went out to the car and came back with still another box wrapped with more pretty paper and said, "dad this is your real present". Of course, after this, pa expected that something might jump out at him, but as he carefully pulled away the paper this time to open the box, we all watched tears of joy pour from pa's face as he found the most beautiful gold pocket watch you had ever seen before. Pa carried that gold watch wherever he went, until the day the LORD called him home to be with HIM.

27

My Pocket Knife and the Hair Cut

It always seemed if something terrible was going to happen to anyone it would undoubtedly happen to me. Our class had about twenty students, I would imagine fifteen were boys' and the other five were girls. I had the bad luck of having a snobbish little red headed girl sit just in front of me, all the kids said, she was the teacher's pet, because she made the best marks of anyone on her paper, everyone just called the little girl, Red. I would have to admit Red did have the prettiest red curly hair I had ever seen. Red's mother always kept her hair put in two pigtails. Now, this hateful little girl was always tossing her hair back on my desk, and this was starting to become a nuisance to me.

I had asked Red to stop more than a few times, but she just ignored me. She actually said, that she could not help were her hair went. Well, one day I took to thinking I had put up with all of this I wanted, so I was sure I could resolve this and I took it upon myself to help Red with her problem, seeing as she says she didn't have to, and she could not help where her hair went. One morning after the teacher had taken roll call, she started as always throwing her pigtails back on my desk. I ask her one more time to please stop, and as always, she said, 'she did not have to.' I became raged with anger over this.

However, this morning when those pretty red pigtails was just laying there on my desk I gently pull out my Barlow pocketknife the one which my pa gave me for Christmas; this was the pocketknife which pa told me not to ever carry to school, and that it was for whittling on a piece of wood only. Today, I had disobeyed pa's orders, and I would later accept full responsibility of bringing the pocket knife to school. Today I would use my new pocket knife, for something besides whittling on a piece of wood. I would use it to cut off a pretty red pigtail. I opened my Barlow knife; then I smoothly took hold of one of those pretty red pigtails with one hand, and with the other, hand I cut off one of Reds pretty red pigtails right at her head. Red thought I was just pulling her hair as I had in the past; she had no ideal I had just cut one of her pigtails off. I took the piece of pigtail and hide it inside my shirt. I was trying not to laugh out loud as to draw attention to what I had done to Reds pigtail, but it was so funny that she had not noticed; and because she kept throwing her hair around thinking, she had both pigtails on my desk. The incident become so funny, I burst out into a laugh and then the class caught onto what had happen and everyone begin to laugh, at last she realized what had happened and she burst into tears. The teacher asks me were the piece of hair was. Well, the hair was starting to itch against my bare skin underneath my shirt, so I pulled out the pig tail which was about a foot long, and handed it to the teacher. Just then, another one of the class comedians announced that maybe Red could use some scotch tape and tape the pigtail back. The teacher told everyone to silence their laughter or, everyone would be going to the principal's office with me. The teacher said, 'there is nothing amusing about this,' he also said, 'Mr. Lone Wolf, is in very severe trouble.' I guess this was at the high point on my list of thoughtless things I had ever done in the past. I could just imagine what pa was going to do to me. He was going to forget, to remember when to stop beating me with the big leather strap. The teacher told me to go at once to the corner of the room and he did not want to see my face for the rest of the day. It seem as if the day would never end, all I could think of was the pain I was going to be in when pa found out about this. I was thinking what Red's dad was might to do to me. I had myself in one of the biggest fixes I had ever been in. I was thinking maybe, I could go back to the railroad track and hop on another train that would carry me a million miles away from here? I thought maybe, I could run away, join up with a circus, and disguise myself, as a clown, and no one would know whom I was? My mind was so baffled. Finally, the last bell rang and the kids ran out of the class, all but me, and I was still standing in the corner looking at the wall. I could see the teacher from the corner of my eye as he started walking back to where I was. My teacher was a large man who walked lamely because the Germans shot him during the attack of Pearl Harbor, and his use of a prosthetic leg made a noise when he came toward me. He handed me an envelope, which he had placed a piece of paper inside, then he said, 'make sure you're granny and Pa gets this.' He said, 'he would be expecting an answer from them.' Well, I first thought about just letting the letter accidentally fall from my books on the way home, or I would just plain forget to give granny the note, but he said he expected an answer from them. I was unusually slow today walking home as I kicked a tin can along trying to help me thing on what to do. I never knew what the teacher had written on the piece of paper, maybe it was nothing about what had happen today with Reds pigtail. I thought about opening the letter then if it was something bad, I would make a decision from then on what to do, but that would just be more trouble, and brother I had enough of that already.

28

The Punishment

All of this because of a snobby little- red- headed girl with pigtails who just had to continue to throw them back on my desk. This was all her fault. However, I was overdue getting home today and I knew granny would soon come looking for me. I had stopped to talk too just about everyone along the way home today that I could, even some that I never cared for, and sooner, or later I had to come home, and in about two more hours, pa would come home as well. When, I came through the front door granny ask, "Son what took you so long coming home today?" "I was getting worried about you." I said, "I was just thinking about stuff granny." My heart was hammering so hard it was hurting. Then, I "asked granny, do they ever send kids to jail? Granny asked, "Why, you would want to know something like that son?" Well, I said, "The teacher told me to give you this note, and I think it might be about something I did at school today." I wished I could have fainted when I handed granny the note from my shaking hands. Then, as she opened the envelope she instantly said, "Oh LORD, be with this child. Would you look at this?" I think she must have been talking to the LORD, telling HIM to look at the note. I thought she was going to call the LORD down from Heaven to discipline me for what I had done, and actually, right then, I would rather had the LORD come to punish me. Well, pa came through the door and he looked past his usual tiredness today. His face was sweaty and dirty. Then, pa went to the washbasin to wash off some of the dirt, and granny fixed him a glass of iced tea. Then granny said, "Dad, I want you to promise me something here and now, and I mean you had better keep your promise." Well, I do not know how pa already knew that I had done something but he said, "Ok what has the boy done now, mother?"

Then granny asked pa again? "Do I have your promise that you will listen to me?" "Yes, mother, I promise pa said." Well, the boy was sent home today with this letter, then granny give pa the note, I thought my heart would stop now for sure. Pa never said a word; he takes hold of me by the arm and started pulling me to the woodshed and on the way through the door, pa grabbed the whipping leather. Pa had someone come and build a new woodshed after a tornado blew the old away. Sometimes I wondered if the woodshed was for keeping the wood for the old potbellied stove dry, or was it more for the thrashing I got. The leather was hitting my bare legs, my back, my buttocks and I was squirming in every direction trying to get loose. Then, I faintly heard granny calling out to pa "stop; I could hear granny saying 'oh dear your killing the boy dad she would say, stop!'"

Finally, pa came to his right mind and the whipping at last stopped. I just laid there all curled up in one corner of the woodshed, crying and this cry was not pretend, as I had planned for it to be. I was hurting something awful. My legs, and back, and my buttocks looked like I had caught some awful sort of disease with all the welts that was on them. Granny picked me up and carried me into the house, and began putting ointment over my welted body. Pa kept saying repeatedly that this beat anything he had ever seen. Pa said, "he didn't know what they were going to do with me, he said, to granny we take the boy to church, we teach him right from wrong, and just look at this mess". I don't think I could ever recall seeing pa this railed up. Where have we failed at mother?" Then, pa said, "I wished a million times over I had never given you that pocketknife". He said, "I told you that the knife was to never be taken to school, that it was for whittling only."

Then pa, ask, "Where is the knife?" With my trembling hand I pulled the knife from my pocket and with pleasure handed it to pa,

Granny spoke up and said, "We had to offer to have the little girls' hair fixed as best that could be, and to offer our apologies for what I had done." Pa said, "They should go right then, and take care of this, and that I was coming along, and that I had better sound like I mean it when I apologize to the little girl." We walked about a mile to where Red lived, and pa knocked on the door with a knock that sounded like he was trying to bring down the house.

I was beginning to think after pa had knocked on the door for over what seem ten minutes maybe, no one was no one at home. Then, just as we were about to turn away and walk off, the front door open and there was little Reds' dad, and you could see that he was fuming mad. He said, 'just wait until see what a mess my child's hair is in because of that boy of yours.' Well, we walked into her room where Red was lying with her head pushed down into her pillow, and she was bawling out, still from the pigtail I had cut off earlier that morning.

I thought, Red should have stopped crying before now and she was taking this much too far. Then little Reds' dad said, to my granny and pa, "See this, just tell me what can we do about it," she has had her hair all of her life, it has never been cut. I was thinking well, it's been cut now, but I kept this thought to myself. Granny spoke up and said, "She and my pa would pay for whatever was needed to be done to fix his daughters hair." Then, Reds' dad said, "There is nothing that can be done that will fix this mess, her mother will have to cut the other piece of hair off." Then, pa looked down at me and said, "Boy you had something you wanted to say." Yes, sir I replied. I then, looked down at Red still lying there with her head shoved into the pillow and still whining and even though she would not look up towards me, I was trying to make an effort to make a tear appear to be coming from my eyes, so it would look as if I really meant it. I said, Red, "I'm really sorry for me cutting your pigtail off, and I wish a million times, even more, I had never seen that old pocketknife." I said, "I wished pa would take it and throw it in the river." Well, this part I never truly meant it. I was really hopeful pa would give it back to me after all it was my Christmas present. I sought to believe from here on, that I was over getting myself into so much trouble, at least for a while.

On our way, back home pa and granny never had a word to say to one another then, as we entered the house pa told me to sit down that he wanted to talk to me. Something inside me was saying, telling me, not only did your mother never love you and did not ever want you, now you have no family at all who loves you. I had heard of homes for children, who did not have parents of their own, and these homes were orphanage intuitions, and I could imagine this was a place which I would be going to living at. My suspicion was telling what I already know pa was going to say.

we love you, and wanted the best for you, but your granny and me don't know anything else to do but to put you in the orphan's home and maybe, someone will adopted you.

I was thinking about what pa said, of taking me to Church and trying to rise me up proper. Well, pa started out his talk with me. Son, what have we done wrong? We don't have much money, but we have given you all the love we have, we don't go hungry, and you have clothes to wear and a roof over your head, I am sorry this is all we have to give you. Your granny and I have tried to teach you about GOD and to grow up to be a respectable man someday then; just like that pa ended his talk to me. The next morning granny got dressed up and put on her finest clothes that she had and went to my school and talk for a long time talk with my principle, granny confidently promise the principle I had learned my lesson from this and I had been punished for my deed and that nothing else like this would ever happen again, if he would let me back in school. He did allow my returning to school the next day. However, I had to sit with my chair facing the wall at the back of the class for the remaining of the school year, and the little redheaded girl who was missing one pigtail now transferred to another state, after her mother cut the other pigtail off. Pa was right when he told me you should have ask the teacher to have moved you if the little girls hair was bothering you. I did know better, and it was true that Pa and granny were raising me in a Christian home, to love and obey GOD, and to study and mediate on HIS word daily. As a child, I had been abandoned and unloved by my mother, but still what I had done was no excuse for my behavior. I would be an adult before I would be able to understand the full meaning of my repentance. Today, I can look back in wonderment of what would have happen to me had my grandparents not loved me and wanted me, if they had not chosen to accept this responsibility it would likely have been the orphanage institution, and life would have taken a much different direction.

I learned something from 2. Corinthians 7:10{KING JAMES}

C.10. for GODLY sorrow worketh repentance to salvation not to be repented of: but the sorrow of the world worketh death. 11. For behold this selfsame thing, that ye sorrowed after a godly sort, what carefulness it wrought in you, yea what clearing of yourselves, yea, what vehement desires, ye what zeal, yea what revenge! In all things ye have approved yourselves to be clear in this matter.

12. Wherefore, though I wrote unto you, I did it not for his cause that had done the wrong, nor for his cause that caused the wrong, but that our care for you in the sight of GOD might appear unto you.13. Therefore we were comforted in your comfort: yea and exceedingly the more joyed we for the joy of Titus, because his spirit was refreshed by you all.

You see being truly sorry and truly repent before GOD for our wrong GOD is always there waiting with open arms to forgive us any sin. I was at this moment reminiscing on a time that I had asks granny and pa to let me sit in the back of the Church with the other boys my own age instead of sitting between the two of them. Pa agreed that I could do this starting the next Sunday. Well, Sunday come around and as soon as my Sunday school class was over. I met out in front of the Church where in those days the kids played, all the grown men, including the preacher we had at the time gathered to have a cigarette break before Church services started. I made myself noticeable to pa on purpose, and I saw that he had acknowledged that he had notice me. Well, as soon as the bell ringer for that Sunday began ringing the bell to let everyone know it was time for the services to begin everyone went into the Church. However, this would be my first Sunday which I would not have to follow behind pa to sit between him and granny. Pa went down the aisle toward the front pews pa and granny always sits in the same pew every Sunday. Everyone, seen to have his or her own seat every Sunday as well I believe if any newcomers had taken a regulars seat they might have been asks to move.

Well, after pa went to where granny was seated I filed in behind him and sit on the last row of pews and on the outside next to the isle. As soon as the singing was over and the preacher had been about fifteen minutes into his sermon I noticed Pas' head nod as if he was dozing off to sleep, and I figured this was the time to make my great sneak out the back door. It was almost too easy why I had not thought of this brain storm before. Well, I quickly ran down to the creek which was only about a half mile from the Church. Since, I learned early to take a smoke from time to time and enjoying it, I had hid myself a corncob pipe and some pipe tobacco under a rock. After locating the hiding rock and reaching under it, I pulled my pipe and tobacco and some wooden matches. I was now lying in the tall thick grass and listening to the creek water run over the rocks enjoying the sweet pipe tobacco. I must have been in too much of a hurry to return to the Church and puffed on the corncob pipe to hastily because when I stood up to leave the whole world around me was moving as if I would spin right off the earth. Well, when everything stopped spinning I hurried back to the church just before the last amen and the preacher had dismiss everyone I was waiting outside when pa and granny come walking out. Since, neither pa nor granny ever owned a car, and you could walk to any place in town you needed to go anyway there was no real need for them to have one. That Sunday after we had returned home and I had changed from my Sunday clothes to my play clothes and we had set down at the table for our Sunday dinner of fried chicken mashed potatoes' with gravy and corn on the cob, chicken was every Sunday at granny's house for some reason. Well, pa had said the blessing over the food as he always did and as we were eating pa caught me off guard and ask me how I enjoyed sitting with the other boys today. Quickly, I thought, "I liked it pa I said." "Good pa said," oh by the way what was it that the preacher preached on I plum forget pa said." "Oh, it was the pulpit pa, I said." Well, that was not the correct answer believe me.

That was not the question boy, what did the preacher preach about, now, of course since I had not been there I did not have even a clue. "I don't know pa I answered. "Why, weren't you listening from where you were sitting?" "No sir" "Why not, Pa exclaimed!" "I was not in church pa." "I see pa said, and were where you boy"? "Well, Sir I went down to the creek there I have a corncob pipe with some pipe tobacco hid and this is where I was." "Ok pa said, beginning next Sunday you start back to sitting between your granny and I, and we well have a walk to the creek after dinner and I will take the pipe." I never learned how exactly it was that pa knew I was not sitting on the back row with the other boys? 'That was the last time I was trusted to sit with the other boys for as long as I lived with granny and pa. Now, I was going to be surprised again today at what pa would have to say. Pa said, 'boy I'm sorry about giving you the hard whipping I did earlier, However, you have to learn right from wrong or, your goanna end up in some trouble someday that your granny and I will never get you out. I believed I learned a lesson that day, and I never enjoyed watching a woman get her hair cut after the day of the whipping.

29

A Runaway Boat

Old man winter was for another year forgotten and another school year was at last over and I had graduated to the next grade. I would move up into the second grade at the starting of the next school year, I couldn't imagine what I would have done if I failed again this year? I would have passed my first year if my dad would not have taken me out in the middle of the school year? And, of course there was the fact I was not allowed to start school because of my birth date. Nonetheless, it was the time of year, every kid looked forward too, summer vacation and this summer would without uncertainty be the most thrilling summer vacation I could have ever had. My friend, Jack Rabbit and me only thought the year before had been thrilling when went on the hobo journey with our train ride was exciting. We were in for a terrifying time this summer.

As I said, before one could never imagine Ole Huckleberry himself would have got himself into any more of a chaos then Jack Rabbit and I was always getting into. Jack Rabbit and I were looking forward to our summer vacation, and as we were looking for something to do on this bright summer morning. W started off today by walking to the river, of course the river was a place we both knew we had been given strict instruction we were never go there. If only we had listened to the advice but, then on the other hand, we were both a couple of curious kids. As we were walking along the riverbank we out of the blue came upon an old wooded boat that someone had left on the bank of the river tied with a rope. Well, we thought it surely nothing could be wrong with our sitting in the old boat, and what could it hurt while we were just sitting in the too make believing were a couple old Vikings on some far away ocean, going off to a strange land fighting and taking gold and valuables from other ships?

We also imagined it would be more fun if the boat was actually sitting in the water, so the two of us pushed the boat from the bank out into the water after all it was tied up with a rope. Next, as we were making believe, we did not notice the rope which had broken loose from being tied to a tree we were drifting down the swift current of the river. Well, the two of us were now in a real jam, because Jack Rabbit or, I had not learned to swim yet and there were no life preservers in the little wooded boat? We also, did not know if the fast current of the river was going to slow down or, worse yet if it was going to get even faster as we drifted downstream. We were both fighting with all our strength using the wooden boat paddles to get the boat over near the banks of the river but, the current of the river was much too swift for two little boys like us. The little wooden boat went into a spin, and around and around out in the middle of the large river we were spinning. I could see large boulders sticking up out of the furious river. I knew that if the little wooden boat was to crash up against one of the boulders that it would break apart into maybe, a million pieces and the river would swallow both of us in the swift current. After we had spun around for at least a good five minutes just missing boulders on either side of us, we had become dizzy, and the whole world looked as if it was turning around. We begin to yell as loud as we could help! Help! Help! However, there was no one around for miles to hear our call for help. There wasn't anyone out here. There was nothing but water and rocks along the bank of the river on both sides of us. It seems that the further we went down the river the faster the current was getting. Jack Rabbit and I was trying with all our strength to us the boat paddles to get the boat over against the bank, but the current was too swift for us. We begin to hear a new sound, which sounded as if thunder was coming out of the water just ahead of us. Then, as we looked ahead, we could see the river was coming to a fork. The thundering sound was coming from a waterfall which was only about a hundred feet ahead of us. After struggling, the rapids and surviving through this, now it look as if we were going to be toss over a monster of a waterfall drowned and crushed by the rocks at the bottom. Then, just as we come to the fork in the river, we lost one of our wooden boat paddles, it went one way in the fork, and the wooden boat drifted off to the other side. Then, before our eyes, the boat paddle dropped out of our sight as it went over the waterfall, we had safely floated the other way. We were safe; at least we had not gone over the waterfall. Just now my attention was thinking of what granny had taught me about angels, and I supposed we must have had at least one of those angles with us today. We were now away from the thundering sound of the waterfall, the current of the river had slowed, and the river had widened until it looked as if we were out on the ocean just drifting slowly and calmly along, having nothing to motor us except the gentle wind and a now gentle current from the river.

I question myself how two boys who were just a little more than nine years old could get into so much trouble as Jack Rabbit and always managed to get into? Sometimes, the little boat would drift up against the bank of the river but we could never catch hold of anything to get a good grip that we could hold onto, as the rocks were slippery with moss. I was thinking to myself, this is even a bigger mess this time then when Jack Rabbit and I were two hobo's on the train ride. I guess we must have drifted for more than four hours. The river was so large it now looked as if we were lost on the sea some place. The little boat was just moving along by the gentle pushing of the wind. Then, the sun begin to set behind the cliffs of the huge rocks on either side of us, it was going to be dark soon, and since no one had found us by now, it was unlikely anyone would find us during the night. Jack Rabbit and me had not eaten all day, and again, this brought back memories of our train adventure when we were both hungry enough to have ate a bear. Then, there were the nice people who we had met along the train tracks who fed us all that fried chicken, mashed potatoes and gravy and even apple pie. Whether, or not these people had been angles we never learned, however we did learn that these people never lived were this happened.

But, for now I sure wish we could meet anyone out here, real people or angles, as long as they had some food. I was wondering if the two of us would ever learn to carry along some peanut butter and jelly sandwiches when we left the house, because we were always getting our self into jams and was always needing food. I told Jack rabbit that as soon as the man who owned the boat came to the river to use his boat, he would see it missing and then he would send someone looking for it. We both understood, it could likely be days' or, maybe even weeks before the man would come back to check his boat, and by then we would have starved to death. Now, as darkness begins to set all around us we were two frightened little boys out here on a river alone. If there was anything good about tonight it was the moon was shinning so bright it looked as if an angle was holding up a bright light over the river. The huge river looked as if it were one gigantic piece of glass now, it looks as if you could step out of the boat and walk across the water to the shore. I remembered granny telling me the story of how JESUS walked on water, but we were not JESUS and we could not walk on water, and JESUS did it through faith in HIS FATHER, I had not yet learned that faith?

So, as we just lay there in the bottom of the boat drifting downs the river we gazed up at the skies. The skies what looks as if there were a t least a million stars, I could ever remember seeing. Then, as Jack Rabbit and I laid there we tried to count to a million stars before we fell asleep, but of course either one of us could count to a million. It was peaceful here tonight on the river and we thought this might not be all bad if only we had just had something to eat? Occasionally, we would hear a big ole fish jump up out of the water then fall back into the river on its belly. Listening to the big fish jump out of the water and then land on their belly, reminded me of the story that granny had read to me from the bible about a man name Jonah, who had disobeyed GOD. {KING JAMES}. 1:15, so they picked up Jonah and threw him into the sea, and the sea ceased its raging.

17, now the LORD had prepared a great fish to swallow Jonah. And Jonah was in the belly of the fish three days and three nights. I sure was hoping that GOD was not planning on having another great fish such as this to swallow the two of us.

Then, there was the cry of a lonely wolf somewhere in a distance in the cliffs. Then from fatigue of our struggle from fighting the currents earlier in the day, sometimes, during the night we both went to a sleep. The next morning when we awoke the sun had begun to rise; the little boat was now just sitting out in the middle of the river as if a giant magnet was holding it to one spot... I believe we must have been missing now for over seventeen hours, surely someone was out trying to find us? Then, we become aware of something down river about a fourth of a mile away. There was another boat, and in the boat was a man pulling on a string that was tied to both sides of the banks of the river, and this line had a bunch of hooks on it, and on those hooks was a bunch of mouth-watering fish. I believed by now Jack Rabbit and I could have eaten one of those fish raw. Jack Rabbit and I began to shout out as loud as our fragile voice could yell Help! Help! Help! Just then, the man heard us and stopped what he was doing. This man had a motor on his boat, so he dropped the line with all the fish on it and came to us. As the man pulled, along side of the little wooden boat, which we had been in for now over seventeen hours, he grabbed the side of the boat and said, "What in the thunder is wrong here?" "What's all the shouting about?" "Where is the blonde-haired man that was in the boat with you, when I heard you yelling?" "'There has been no man with us sir I said.' Yes, I seen big tall blonde-haired man in the boat with you, I'm sure I did, but now I don't see him". Sir, we have been along out here since yesterday when the rope broke loose from the boat back up the river." "Well, are you boys ok?"

We told him the story of how we had been playing in the boat and somehow the rope broke loose and we had been drifting since the day before. After we explained our story to our rescuer, he said, "Well, you boys have came across some rugged country those rapids back up the river are pretty tough to come across, plus there is some tough under current all across that part of the river."

"You boys are lucky to have made it through there." Well, granny had taught me not to believe, in luck but to believe in the LORD, and that we all had angels assigned to us. The man said, "You boys have floated over twenty-five miles from your home." Well, he said, "you boys might as well call me Catfish Bob that's what everyone in these parts calls me." Catfish Bob said, "I am called this, because I fish for a living." And that was what he was doing when we seen him, he said he was running what was called his trout lines. Catfish Bob took a piece of rope from his boat and tied one end to his boat and the other end of the rope he tied to the little boat we were in and pulled us down the river about two miles to a boat dock, to where his truck and boat trailer was. Catfish Bob was a very huge man, and after Catfish Bob, had pulled us down the river to a boat ramp where he had left his truck and boat trailer he loaded the little wooden boat in the back of his truck and told us he would take us back home. Well, as we were riding home, I told Jack Rabbit we sure were in a mountain of trouble this time when we got home. This was the biggest thing the two of us at least up until now we had ever done. Catfish Bob said, he use to be a little boy once himself and he imagined everyone should keep in mind that we all were at one time or another little. He said, "Boy's as soon as I get you home I will speak to your parents and tell them, the same thing. I said. "Catfish Bob, I ant got no parents, just a granny and a pa". Catfish Bob said, "What happened to your parent's boy did something happen to your ma and pa"? Then, when I told him how mom never wanted me, through her pregnancy, and how she made dad make me go live with my granny, and pa. Then, catfish Bob ask Jack rabbit about his ma and pa, and Jack rabbit answered and said, "I want got no pa, just a ma, my pa dead when I was just a baby." Catfish Bob took out his handkerchief and pretended to blow his nose but, I think he was crying and he rather not let us know that he was wiping his eyes. Well, it sounds like the two of you are loved very much to me catfish Bob said.

I guess we had driven about thirty minutes, when Catfish Bob asks Jack Rabbit and me if we could use something to eat, and of course we could, we where both so hungry we could have ate something killed and left on the side of the road even some of those raw fish Mr. Catfish Bob had.

Well, ole catfish Bob stopped at a little country store and bought some bologna, potato chips, and a bottle of cola., and as hungry, as Jack Rabbit and I were, this was almost as good as the fried chicken was when we took our hobo, train adventure. I told, catfish Bob about Jack Rabbit and I, and our adventure of the train ride, and that we had been missing for a day and a half, but this time I was sure pa and me would be visiting the woodshed. The more I thought about it and the closer Catfish Bob was to getting us home the more I was wishing catfish Bob had not found us. I was wishing that Jack Rabbit and I did not have to go back home until we had grown up. Since, we had stopped along the road to eat our sandwiches, it took us about an hour and an hour to drive back home. My heart was thumping away so hard it sounded as if someone was playing war drums inside my chest. After we drove into town, Catfish Bob said, "Let's go to the river, and put the boat back and then, we'll go to your grandparent's house". Catfish Bob was trying to put my worries at rest which was obviously showing from all the squirming around in the seat I was doing, when he reached over, and patted my knee, and said, "It's going to be all right you'll see." Well, catfish Bob unloaded the little wooded boat back at the river and tied it back up in the exact place Jack Rabbit and I had first left.

Then, as we drove down a hill which led to granny and pa's place, I could see from a distance of about a quarter of a mile away, that now more than anything, I wish I could wait and come back after I was a grown-up. The front yard of granny and pa's house looked as if the entire town was there. I could see the old sheriff car sitting in front of the house, we never actually had a sheriff but often the sheriff from the next town which was about twenty-miles away would come to town. Jack Rabbits mom was there as well, it looks as if the entire neighbor of four hundred people was at granny and pas, place. It turned out that the old man who owned the boat we had been in was there as well. When we pulled up in front of the old house I seen granny standing there crying her poor old eyes out, she was wringing her hands around and carrying on, everyone was coming up to her and Jack Rabbits mom, hugging them both and everyone was crying together. I first thought maybe, something had happened to my pa, but this was all for Jack Rabbit and me. Someone told granny they had seen Jack Rabbit and me playing near the river the day before and had told and of course, everyone was thinking bad thought that the two of us had fallen into the swift river and carried away by the fast current. Then, the man whose boat we had been in, had reported it missing after he found out that two young boys' were missing and everyone sort of put the two things together and had assumed, we were both drowned. The old sheriff said, 'since the rope that was tied to the boat looked rotten it likely snapped loose by our weigh. He said, the boat had probably tipped over in the rapids somewhere down river. The old sheriff told granny, he would get a team of rescue people to start dragging the river at once and they would not stop until they found us. Now, when old Jack Rabbit and I got out of catfish's truck you would have thought everyone in the front yard had seen two ghosts. Now, there was more hugging, and more crying going on. I guess Jack rabbit and I had caused more excitement this day, than this little town had ever seen before. Now, the real odd thing about all this was, the man who owned the old wooden boat that Jack rabbit and me had been missing in said, he did not see how we could have stayed out there for a day and a half in his old boat, he reached to scratch his near bald-head and said, "He had left the boat on the bank because it had five holes in it, and would fill up with water in an about fifteen-minutes". However, the odd thing about this was the boat was just as dry as powder the whole time we were in it we even slept in the bottom of the boat, and not once were there ever any water in the boat. Catfish

Bob had walked up to granny and explained to her how he had found us. He said I really did not know how they ever survived those rapids. He told granny that a strange thing had occurred when he first spotted us, he said, he had seen three people in the boat with us, but when he got to us, there was only the two of us. He told granny and pa that he believed we had already had our punishment after what we had come through. Well, I had turned around to say thanks once more to Catfish Bob for rescuing Jack Rabbit and me but Catfish Bob seem to have vanished without anyone seeing him leave.

30

The Old Abandoned Jail

At one time, in my little town we had a need for a jail. For some reason
the jail had been abandoned for many years, and the little town no
longer had any use for it. In fact, we never had any police in our little
small community. The town did have one old man they call the town
constable, and you would not often ever find him, when there was
an occasional to have the law for something, and this was usually
someone needing to get a cat down from a tree or something like that.

Our town was sort-of –a copy cat of the show of Mayberry. I
remember the constable had a Volkswagen for his police car; anyone
of us kids could have out run him own our bicycles. However, our little
town had this old one-cell rock jailhouse. The old jail had not been in
use for many years and all the windows were missing however, it did
still have all the bars. In addition, to it looking as if it would fall over
at anytime, you could still lock someone in there, if you had a padlock.
The townspeople wanted the old building torn down as everyone
said, 'it was an eye sore to look at.' One day my friend Jack Rabbit and
I were making believe we were the sheriff and deputy of the town. We
decided that we needed a prisoner. Well, we had a kid that everyone
called Cotton. Now Cotton was just a little younger than Jack Rabbit,
me so we took Cotton and told him we had to lock him up for while,
and we would come back later to let him free. So, Cotton wanted to be
accepted as our friend and he readily said, ok. Now, everyone called

the kid Cotton, because his hair was as white as cotton. After we made our arrest and put, Cotton in jail and locked it with a padlock, which belonged to Jack Rabbit, the two of us went off to play and, we forgot about having Cotton in the old jail. We played all day, and then as it had begun to get dark, when little Cotton had not come home his parents began to worry and come out to look for him. His dad and mom come to granny and pa's house asking questions if they had seen him Well, I remembered then, that Jack Rabbit and I had forgot about locking him up in the old jailhouse.

I was afraid to say anything about what I knew, because I also knew as soon as I told, pa he and I would be going to back the woodshed again. That old woodshed was of course a place which all most every parent owned, and it was a sort-of private and special place for the parents to take their kids to that conducts badly. Well, I wasn't in anyway excited about going back to the woodshed again. This place was becoming a familiarly place for me. Therefore, I kept quiet, but in the meantime, However, I hated the though oft Cotton having to stay locked in that old dark jailhouse all night. I imagined how it might be frightful being there all night by yourself, and more than ever if you were a little person such as Cotton was. Shucks, it would have even frightened me, and I was now just over the nine year old mark now. This was another reason I knew pa would take me out to the woodshed, I knew pa would say you, should have known better to pull such a thing as this. Pa was a firm believer in every word in the Bible. Some words seem to have more meaning than others did for pa. Such as in the book of Proverbs: 13:24. {KING JAMES}. He that spareth his rod hateth his son: but he that loveth him chastenth him betimes.

Pa was a firm believer of this passage of the Bible. Now, I did not know what to do about getting our little friend Cotton out of the old jailhouse and at the same time, spare Jack rabbit and I the pain I knew would be upon the both of us when they learned where he was and how he came to be there... I found myself in a real mess once again, this time I did not know how I was going to get out of it.

Jack Rabbit and I both had strict rules about leavening any place away from the house after dark, I we could not sneak off later and go back up to the old jailhouse to let Cotton out and, another bad thing about this was we forgot there we never a key to the padlock. Then, there was another rule in the Bible. Job 31:6 {KING JAMES} let me be weighted in an even balance that GOD may know mine integrity.

Well, I was about to find out if this honest policy for me was everything the Bible said it was going to be. By now the little boy's mom who was now sobbing saying repeatedly she just knew something bad has happened to her little Cotton. Well, I could not let it go on any longer and as they were walking off, and again with my heart pounding heavy inside my chest I spoke up and said, "I know where Cotton is." "Where, the dad asks?" "Where is our boy is he ok?" "Where is he?" Cottons poor father and mother were in tears. "Why have you not said, anything about this boy?" "Tell us where to find our boy!"

Well, sir, I said, "earlier today when Jack Rabbit and me were pretending we were the sheriff and deputy we pretended we needed a prisoner and we had to arrest Cotton and lock him in the old jailhouse with a padlock of Jack Rabbits' and we forgot to go back and see if we could get him out."

"Where is the key to the lock boy, Cottons dad asked?" "Give us the key so that we can go let him out, he must be frightened half to death by now". "Well, sir we don't have no key." We just had the old padlock sir, I said." It was now that time to start a concern about this honesty policy of granny and pa's, because I could just about see blood in pa's eyes. Pa looked at me and said "Boy, what is the matter with you?" Then, after everyone had finished yelling, Cottons dad said, 'we have to find someone with a hacksaw to cut through the padlock." Then, after pa and the little boys' dad went around to what seem ever neighbor house in the town they at last found someone who had a hacksaw and went off to cut cotton out of the old dark jailhouse. I was glad the poor kid was not going to have to stay there all night there, and sure enough when they got to Cotton he was frightened something awful. However, in the mean time while they were freeing Cotton from jail I was thinking on how to stop some of the pain when pa comes back and we had gone to the woodshed. Then, it came to me to put on some extra clothing, then when pa went to whipping me with that strap of leather I was going to pretend that it was hurting something awful, crying and taking on so, that maybe he would think I had, had enough and would stop whipping me. Well, pa after pa came back home from helping free Cotton from jail it look now as if his eyes were shooting darts out of them. Granny told pa he should wait a while until he was relaxed before we went to the woodshed. Pa said, "The boy has to be punished mother". Pa always called my granny mother for some reason," and ma always called Pa dad, "Why that poor kid was scared half to death." He told ma. Well, granny kept pa drinking coffee trying to calm him down, but the longer I had to wait to go out to the woodshed the more nervous it made me. I just wanted to get this over with. At last, pa called me into the room with him and granny and said. "I have decided to let you think about what you have done tonight, and tomorrow I will let you know what your punishment will be." Well, this was not what I was expecting at all, I never wanted the whipping, but I wanted to go ahead and get it over with, I did not want to have to lay all night and think about it anymore, and besides I already had my pants padded for this. However maybe, this would work out after all, maybe, pa would forget by tomorrow. Then, the next morning, as granny was preparing pa's breakfast as she always did everyone seem to be in a happy frame of mind this morning. Then, just as I thought pa had forgotten about the night before it happened, pa was drinking his coffee when he called for me to come in to where he was.

I started to get a tear in my eye, and show pa some remorsefulness for what I had done by locking little Cotton in the old jail, and that I would never do such a foolish thing again. Pa said, "Part of the punishment was for you to worry through the night as the little boy was worried." I believe you are ashamed of what you did. The second part of the punishment is your going to stay locked all day in the woodshed. I was somewhat puzzled about the way pa was going to be punishing me. However, when we went into the woodshed pa said, here is some water and peanut butter sandwiches for you to eat today. As pa turned to walk out he said, 'someone would be back this afternoon to let you out." This, will give you a chance to think about how Cotton must have felt having been locked up all day. Then, pa turned and walked out the door. Then, this peculiar feeling came over me as I listened to pa put the padlock on the door of the woodshed. It was then I believed I knew how little cotton must have felt when we padlocked him in the old jail cell, and left him there all day.

As I sat there, throughout the day I was hoping that pa had a key, and that he would not have to go from neighbor to neighbor looking for another hacksaw to get me out. I cried from a broken heart, because I didn't think anyone loved me. I thought about how I felt about my mom not loving me and the way she had treated me, the way she had rejected me and had never showed me she loved me, now I felt that maybe granny and pa had as well stop loving me. I thought about my friend Jack Rabbit if he took the whipping or, what had his mom gave him for his punishment in his part of what we had done. I imagine I must have sat there until around noon when I ate my first peanut butter and jelly sandwich, then I feel asleep. I dreamed about Cotton locked up in that old dark jail. When I awoke, I heard someone unlocking the padlock. Then, as pa stepped inside the woodshed, he said. "Well, son, how did that feel?" I told pa I was sorry for what I had done, and that I would apologize to Cotton for doing this to him. Pa said, "Ok this was your punishment I wanted you to feel the same thing that little boy did." However, after the day was over, I realized that this was after all better than the whipping; I realized I had done something very bad and I deserved some kind of punishment for my part.

31

The Tornado

Just before the sunlight hours were setting today, a storm began to build in the West and the clear blue skies began to fill with thick dark clouds. Thunder begin to shake the ground and lighting came out of the dark clouds, with a long tail behind which touched the ground. Pa said, "Once when he was a young man he was in a storm and the lighting struck him and it had affected his hearing." I was thankful I was not still in the old woodshed when this storm came up. Granny said, "This is going to be a bad storm and we needed to get blankets and go to our neighbors storm shelter." This shelter was a huge place built with cement under the ground they had kerosene lamps so when the lights went out we could see. Now, granny, pa, and I along with the neighbor's family of three all went down in this underground shelter for protection. We had not been down in the underground for more than three, or four minutes when we begin to hear something that sounded like the freight train that Jack Rabbit and I had been on and we had listen to the blowing of its whistle.

We could hear the cracking and breaking, of the beautiful tall tree's that seemed to reach the sky, it was the most awful thing I had ever heard before, then after a while the man who owned the shelter, who everyone called Crosscut said, "He thought it was safe to come out." Then Mr. Crosscut walked up the steps leading up from the ground, and pushed up a door out of the ground and there was the sun shining down into the hole in the ground where we were. It was still raining, but Mr. Crosscut said, 'the storm has passed and it was safe to come out.' Well, everyone came out of the shelter to see a sickening sight. The big tall tree that had once stood shading our houses were broken half into, some were lying over on the ground, some were blown through people's houses, and there were even trees' in our yard that wasn't from around where we lived. There were parts of people's roofs missing, and only parts of their houses left, people were crying and hugging each other, saying what a horrible thing this all was. Granny was praying that no one lost their, live from this storm. The old house we lived in was still standing. However, there was something missing here at home and that was the old woodshed, the storm had blown it completely away leaving no sign that there had ever been a woodshed on the property. I was just thankful that Pa had let me out before the storm.

The next day the entire town was out helping one other clean up the mess the tornado had left behind. People were praising GOD that not one life was lost, and only a few people were hurt. Then, as I walked by the place where the old rock jailhouse once sit, the one which Jack rabbit and I had locked Cotton up in only the day before, I was surprised at what I was looking at. The old rock jailhouse that had been standing for so many years was now just a big heap of rocks piled on top of each other. The tornado had blown it completely down into one big pile of rubble. Well, if anything was good about the tornado for anyone in town, it was that now the townspeople at last had what they wanted for years, the old eye sore was at last gone. Of course, no one could have been any happier about the old jail being gone than Cotton was, because now, no one could ever lock him up in that old jail again.

32

The Science Teacher

Our summer vacation from school was over and a new year of school was starting, I remember one of my teachers. She was a little old woman who looked to have been at least one hundred years old and as well looked in poor health. She spoke with a squeaky voice and this is what we called her.

Mrs. Squeaky came to class one morning, and ask for everyone to take their seats, and for the class to come to an order. However, I decided this morning I wanted to be the boss. This was during a time when our classrooms did not have air conditioners, and it was a hot stuffy morning. Therefore, I unbuttoned my shirt exposing my bare bony chest. I pulled off my shoes and prop my feet up on top of the desk, then topping everything off, I pulled out a cigar from my shirt pocket and placed it into my mouth. Well, Mrs. Squeaky did not share my humor this morning. She said", I was to make myself respectable for her class, and at once." "I then ask, and what if I don't?"

The next thing I remember was the little frail old woman was at my desk beating my bare foot with a wooden rule. Once again Mrs. Squeaky told me to put my shoes back on, and to button my shirt and to remove the cigar from my mouth. Well, my classmates found this much funnier than I had, as everyone was laughing so hard, that most of them had tears in their eyes; some had even fallen to the floor laughing. I as well, had tears in my eyes but it was not because it was funny anymore, but because of the pain I was now in from the wooden ruler pounding my bare ankle. I was more than graciously relieved to do as she had instructed me to do as long as she stopped beating me with the wooden ruler. Shortly, after school had started that year, Mrs. Squeaky decided to retire from her teaching as a science teacher. I often believe her retirement came because of class clowns as me become more than she could take.

33

Twenty-Five Cents

My next science, teacher was a male teacher and he was not one to consent with me or anyone else who were strong-willed enough to have a bad behavior. He believed like my pa believed and that was the verse in the bible about spare the rod. Proverbs 13:24 we only knew our new teacher by Mr. J. Mr. J kept a piece of wood in one corner of the room. It was carved out into a wooden paddle that was about two and a half feet long, by, two and a half inches thick. Mr. J called this piece of wood his thinker. Of course I was the first one in the class to find out exactly what the thinker was for? Mr. J did not accept the same things that Mrs. Squeaky did. When Mr. J told you to do something he meant to do it and to do it, in his timing.

If you got your name written on the blackboard five times during class, for talking you either, had to stay in during recess and do your homework assignment, or you had one other choice you could take five licks with the thinker and get your name erase from the blackboard and you could go out with the rest of the class. As you perhaps would know, my name was the first to always on the blackboard, and I always choose to take my five licks with the thinker and go out with the class for recess.

I believe I had at this point built up possibly some callus on that part of my lower body?

Mr. J, also, had a son who sat in a desk behind me, and every recess

93

just before the bell rang well, my name was always on the board, Mr. J's son would tap me on the shoulder and whisper, "I will pay you twenty-five cents if I would let my dad give you the five licks with the thinker." Well, I thought this is too good of a deal to pass up, because I was going to do it anyway. My granny and pa never had twenty-five cents to give me every day for spending money. Well, I thought a boy could get rich this way. I took my five licks with the thinker and at the same time made twenty-five cents to spend at the candy store during recess, and for twenty-five cents, you could buy a large baby Ruth candy bar, a cup of coke, a bag of lays potato chips and still have money left over. This was working out great, at least until one day when the recess bell rang and my name was the only one on the blackboard, as usually the teacher dismiss discharged everyone to leave. Everyone except me and this time his son. Now, Mr. J's' son spoke up and said, "But dad my name is not on the blackboard." Oh, "I know, replied Mr. J, but we're going to see if you still want to pay Mr. Ken here to take five licks after today, after you get five licks with the paddle." Mr. J explained that he was wise as to what had been going on. Well, my good paying job I had ended that day.

34

Scary Wooden Coffin

Other than the old rock jailhouse which the tornado blew down there was one other old building the townspeople said, they wished the tornado would have blew away as well, It too had been standing around for a number of years, and it was in as much need of someone tearing it down as the old jail had been for so many years. This old place was a huge old building standing almost in the centre of town. The old building had at a time served as a funeral home in our little community. It was an old eye sore of a building which was falling down brick by brick. Many of the window panes were broken out and, on the inside it had a collection dust and cobwebs. Through a big picture window that was partly broken, you could see an old harp standing beside an old wooden coffin. Well, I had never heard anyone play a harp before, so I did not know exactly what a harp would sound like.

Some of the town's folks made claim, that "under the wooden coffins lid, there was a piece of glass which, and you could actually see an old dead man lying there and he looked just the same as the day he was put there over fifty-years ago". Well, I never cared to go inside to look under the lid, so I just took everyone's word as it was the gospel truth. I was never even overjoyed just to walk past this old creepy building. Even if it was during the daylight hours, I always crossed over to the other side of the street just before I reached the old building so I would not have to go past this frightening old place.

People said, the old dead man in the old wooden coffin had owned this old building while he was still alive and this is where he wanted to lay at rest when he died, and he never wanted anyone to disturb him, and I always thought his words should be keep with respect. I was still trying to know why everything always had to happen to me as it did, but today I had unintentionally played to long with my friend Jack Rabbit today and, the sun had almost set, and it was beginning to get dark I was to always be at home before it got dark. Well, I had to come right past this old building with that old coffin in it. Now, as I was in a hurry to get home I thought, if I ran past the old building, it would be ok. The wind had just begin to blow strongly and was making a howling noise that sounded so lonesome that it was making cold chills run all over my body. I had not until it was too late realize I was right in front of the old building with the creepy old wooden coffin with the old harp sitting there? Just, as I was walking in front of the big partly broken out picture window I seen something that made my hair stand up, my skin begin to crawl, and I was frozen stiff as a statute. I wanted my feet to move but they would not go anyplace. I stood there not being able to move as if someone had glued my feet to the spot where I was standing. Next, I saw a lighted candle on a table next to the old coffin; and the wooden lid looked as if it was half way open at least open enough the old man in there could get out if he had wanted to. Then, I was sure I heard for my first time someone or something was playing that old harp, and believe me, I never wanted to hear it any longer than about five seconds, when my feet begin to move again, and I was off moving faster than lightening. I do not think any kids' feet ever moved as fast as mine did this night, I think I could have out run my friend Jack Rabbit and he was the fastest kid in town. The more distance I was putting between me and that old building and nothing was chasing me or, least nothing was getting close enough which I could see from looking over my shoulder, and the closer I was getting to granny's house the more I was thanking the good LORD above.

When I came running through the front door with an ear-piercing scream, granny said, "Havens sake boy, what's the matter with you, you look as if a ghost was chasing you!" Well, granny never knew how close to right she was about a ghost chasing after me, except I suppose I must had out run the thing. By now, I was completely out of breath and I went to try to tell granny about the old building up town with the old wooden coffin in it. Granny I said, "I don't think they put enough nails in the lid to hold the old man in there, because the lid is partly moved away, enough that the old man can get out." "Heavens sake boy what were you doing up there messing around that old place for anyway?" Well, I told granny, "I was not up there messing around on purpose, but I had stayed at Jack Rabbits to long and it was starting to get dark when I had to come right past that old creepy building."

I said, "granny that's when I come past the broken window and I saw a lit candle sitting on the table next to that old coffin and the lid was slide back enough that the old man could get out." "Then, I heard the harp playing granny." Well, granny said, "This was impossible, she said, "Dead people cannot get out of their coffins." Well, "I said, granny someone should go there and take a look and see." Granny said, "She would go the next morning and show me that the old man had not been out of the coffin." I said, "Granny why don't we just let it be, and let someone else worry about this?" The next day came around much faster that I wanted it to, but I did want to make sure the old man had not been out of the coffin the night before. Before, granny and I left to go look in the old building I suggested that we stop and pick up my Aunt Annie, who was part Indian to go along with us. I knew if that old man was out of his coffin he would not dare mess with my Aunt Annie. My Aunt would have fought a grizzle bear for me, and I believe she would have won the fight.

Therefore, Aunt Annie said, "Sure she would come along." Well, the old building was even creeper inside than it was from the outside. There were dust and spider webs all over everything in here, a perfect place for the old man to live. When you walked across the old wood floors, they made a squeaking sound that made your skin crawl. I was wishing I had not even suggested we come here. I just wanted to hurry up and look to see if the wooden lid was still nail down, and then I wanted out of here. We were at last up close enough that I could look to see that the lid was still in place. I did tell granny that someone should put more nails in the lid just to make sure. Granny said, 'there you see that old man hasn't been out of the coffin since the day they put him in there".

35

The Screen Door Incident

I think when you are a small boy or perhaps a small girl, people just always look to be old when you look at them, and even though I am older now than my grandparents was when all this took place. However, I took the ideal one day that I was big enough that if I never wanted to do what pa told me to I never had to, and he was getting to old that if I decided to run he could never catch me.

Of course I was forgetting the reality that I would need to come back? I remember this day vividly,

I was in a hurry today to get outside so I could play, and one of pa's rules was not to slam the doors at his home. Well, as I ran out the front door I forgot this rule today and I by accident let the door slam shut. This, never set well with pa who had just happen to be sitting nearby, so he called me back and told me to shut the door as it should be. This never set well with me having to interrupt my importance to get outside, and having to come all the way back just to shut the door over again, by pa's dumb rule. When, I come again to close the door as pa called proper, I grasp the screen door and with all the power I had inside of me, I toss the screen door shut. This made pa furious with anger, I had not seen him with as much anger since I had cut little Reds' pigtail off. Pa jumped straight up from his sitting chair to seize the switch from over the door and before he had time to take the switch down, I had broke into a run that was faster than when I believed the old man in the coffin was after me from his old building. I could not believe an old man could ever run as fast as pa could. Why, I could out run just about any kid in town other than Jack Rabbit, but as I was running, I could sense something stinging the back of my naked legs, when I turned around to get a closer glance, it was pa with that big switch from over the door hitting me. I think he would have whipped the skin off me if, granny had not stopped him. I was more than ready to go back and close the door the proper way. I also, from that day on never forgot pa's rule about the slamming of the door.

36

Mom Moves to Granny's

Even though pa gave me many whippings, as I was growing up as a young boy, I really think his believed the verse in the bible about spare the rod and spoil the child to be his most favored verse of the entire bible. I understand he did it out of love to teach me right from wrong in order that I might grow up to be someone to be respected. I know my granny and pa was well respected people in the town, not one person would have told you anything bad about them. I was now growing up fast and now it was a time which my mom and dad, was not getting along to good and mom decided that she my sister and brother would move back to Arkansas to live, and of course, she would had no place to stay when she got here other than with granny. I guess mom must have looked for work for, about a month when she at last found a job as an assembly worker in a factory about fifteen miles away. I had lived with granny and pa now most of my life, in fact since I was just a baby. Granny and pa were the only mom, and dad I knew. They had always been there when I needed someone, they were there when I was sick and when I was in trouble, even though I though pa would beat me half to death once, or twice for misbehaving they were the only parents I knew and loved. Well, mom came to granny and pas and, mom did find a job and started to work, she was now moving into her own place and because mom did not have a sitter for my younger sister and brother. Mom told granny, I would be coming to live with her."

I knew why, I was coming and it was not something complicated to figure out even for a boy of my young age who was now ten years old could understand the reason. I knew she had never wanted me; this was why I had been with my granny and pa all these years. I knew this even before I was born, I could remember the feeling I had while she was carrying me in the womb, I could even remember the rejection after I was born. Therefore, I knew she only wanted me for something else, and it was not because she just started loving me. Every feeling I had, about this was right, mom did not want me along because she started loving me, but she needed someone who she could us to watch my younger sister and brother while she ran all over the countryside. It all begin within the first weekend after moving out of grannies, that mom come in from work on a Friday afternoon and said, she needed to go sit with a sick friend over night, and that we would be ok at the house. It was the following Monday afternoon when we would see her again. Her excuse was that her friend was much sicker than she first thought. The following Friday when Mom came in from work it was the same thing all over again she said, this time she was going out for a while to visit with some friends, it was the same thing all over again it was Monday afternoon when she came home. This time her excuse was that her friends lived a long way out in the country and her car broke down and they did not have a telephone for her to call anyone to come and get her. This went on every Friday, and it was always Monday before we would see her again. Then, it started becoming a week at a time before we would see her. I was having to bath, feed dress my little sister and brother, I was trying to do a grown ups' job in a ten year old boys' body. I had learned to cook a full course meal, when mom would be gone for days' at a time. I had to stay home from school to take care if my sister and brother. Then, there were times the three of us would hitchhike a few times thirteen miles away to granny's house, because there would not be any food at home to eat. When, granny would ask mom where she was during these times and why she was leaving us along, mom always had a ready explanation to give granny; however, I do not think granny ever believed any of her lies. My rebellion to stay at home while mom went on her weekend outings was becoming a nuisance and I imagined that mom thought it was best if she conceded to let me return to live with my grandparents again. I had somewhat of a guilty conscious that my sister and brother would stay behind but at least mom did show the two of them some affection.

37

A Visit to Investigate Mom

Someone called my dad in Missouri about our mom leaving the three of us along for days' at a time. Of course I never really knew for sure, but I always believed it might have been our granny who had made the call to our dad. It was another weekend and as each time in the past mom came in from work on a Friday after work and said, she had to go out for a while and would be back later." We knew it would be Monday before we would see her again. However, this weekend dad showed up around ten P.M. Friday night, mom was not at home and when he came in to find her not at home, and the three of us were there alone he near hit the ceiling from being so raging mad. Well dad put the three of us into his car and we begin to drive around looking for mom, then around midnight dad drove to the Arkansas Missouri state line and there was mom's car just sitting out in plain sight. Mom was in a bar and so drunk she couldn't have found her nose on her own face, much less her way home. After dad paid someone to drive mom's car home I believe this was the worst fight I had ever known dad and mom to have. Dad stayed until Sunday morning and all the close family members meet at granny's house to see dad off. I remember this morning, it was a light rain which later had turned into a down pour dad had begin drinking beer, and whiskey as soon as he had got out of bed that morning. I guess dad had been gone around three hours when an Arkansas state Trooper came to granny and pas' door, and approached my granny and ask if she was my dad's mother?

Granny said, "Yes sir, I am! What's going on?" Joking granny said. "Am I being arrested officer"? Granny knew she had never done anything wrong in her life to be arrested for. Then, the police officer said, "No madam, I'm afraid I have somewhat horrible news, your son has been in a serious accident just over the Arkansas, Missouri state line." The police officer went on to say, "There was fatalities in this wreck, and your son is in very critical condition." Granny's face turned as white as the first snow I remember seeing. Just then, she fainted falling to the floor. After the police officer worked to get granny revived the officer gave granny and pa the name of the town and hospital where my dad was at. The police officer said, "You should go there as soon as you can madam." Well, after granny recover her consciousness, she, went to my Aunt Annie to have her stay at her and pa's place while she packed some clothes into a suitcase and pa went to find someone drive them to, Missouri. Pa went at once to look for someone to take them to Missouri to where dad was. Having lived here in the little town for the better part of their lives pa was only gone for a few minutes when he returned with one of the local merchants to take us to Missouri. Granny packed a few things then she would stop to cry for a while.

Granny and pa had lost a daughter in a car wreck when she was only in her twenties after, a drunk driver crossed over into the lane she was riding in a car and killed her instantly.

Now grannies elder son was in a serious condition from car wreck, I suppose it was enough to make a body break down. After granny had called mom she said, she was sorry to hear about this but still she could not get off work to go. I guess we must have traveled about three hours when at last we had arrived to where dad was in the hospital. Even for a young boy as I was at the time I thought this was rather strange that my mom would not want to go see my dad? After all they were still married at the time. It looks as if the closer we got to the hospital the more granny, would break down. I dread to see what my Bud looks like she would say, for some reason she always call dad Bud, even though this was not his name. Well, we were at last at the emergency room when the nurse stopped us and explained I was not allowed to go to my dad's room, but it never took granny long to talk with the nurse and, she agreed to let me go in as long as I never upset my dad. I later wished I had stayed out in the waiting area when I looked at dad lying there. Dad's face had deep cuts across it with pieces of his skin missing and parts that the doctors had sutured back together, his face was black in places and blue in other places. Both of dad's arms were in cast and both legs were in cast a well. Granny went to talking to dad, but he could not hear a word she was saying because he was in a coma. Now, both granny and pa were crying, and the nurse said, "She thought it was best if someone took me out to the waiting area". I guess this turned out to be much worse than what anyone had been ready for. Pa told granny that he had better take me back to my moms and that he would return in a couple of days on the bus. Granny told pa to contact their preacher and have the church to start praying as soon as he returned. Before we had left the room, I heard granny reminding the LORD, of HIS word in the book.

ISAIAH 53:5{KING JAMES}. But HE was wounded for our transgressions; He was bruised for our iniquities: the chastisement of our peace was upon Him; and with his stripes we are healed.

ROMENS 4:17 {KING JAMES} {As it is written, I have made thee a father of many nations]. Before him whom he believed, even GOD, who qucikeneth the dead, and calleth those things which be not as though they were.

1 PETER 2:24 {KING JAMES} Who HIS own self bare our sins in HIS own body on the tree, that we being dead to sins, should live unto righteousness by whose stripes ye were healed.

I have never understood why people when they pray needed to remind the LORD of something HE already knew. I never knew that GOD could ever forget anything? After, pa brought me to moms; he wasted no time getting back to Missouri to be with dad. This time however, pa had to ride the greyhound bus back to Missouri. By the time pa returned, the miracle, which granny had been praying for, I assume had taken place. Dad had come out of his coma, and was sitting up in his bed and was recovering remarkably well. The doctors who put dad back together said, they had never seen anything as remarkably as this before, granny said, "It was because of the prayers." Granny believed this. "GOD'S word says in ISAIAH 55:11 {KING JAMES} so shall MY word be that goeth forth out of MY mouth: it shall not return unto ME void, but it shall accomplish that which I pleas, and it shall prosper in the thing whereto I sent it.

The doctors told granny, if her son continued to recover this way he could go home in a day or, two Well it was about three weeks before dad was released, and pa and granny's friend drove back to Missouri to get the three of them, but then an unexpected thing happened.

Just as dad went to walk out of his hospital room there were three Missouri state police officers waiting just outside the room. They handcuffed and arrested dad on the spot for involuntary manslaughter. The state of Missouri had filled charges against my dad for the fatality in the wreck.

Now, dad was recuperating from his injuries in the Missouri county jail. I guess he must have been locked up for around two weeks, and when his hearing came before the jurors dad was found guilty of involuntary manslaughter and was sentenced to prison. Another prayer was about to be answered however for dad, just as the sheriff's deputy's were putting the handcuffs back on dad, the wife of the man who had been killed in the wreck was present in the court room, at which time she rolled her wheelchair out into the isle of the court room and ask permission to addressed the court. The old Judge give the woman permission to say what was on her mind. She said, "You're Honor, "my husband was a dedicated preacher, and we were coming home this day the accident happened from a sermon which my husband had just preached." "'I have been left a widow; and left in this wheel chair for the rest of my life; I will forever have nightmares of looking over at my husband that day and seeing his head had been completely decapitated from his body." Both this man and my deceased husband were on the wrong side of the road, the roads were slick from the rain that day. But putting this man in prison for this accident will not bring my husband back nor, will it get me out of this, wheelchair. I do not wish for this man going to prison. After hearing the woman's testimony, dad was immediately released. The Judge ordered the deputies to remove the cuffs from dad, and he was a free man. Granny, pa, and dad give the woman a hug and told her that words could never say thank you enough, and that they were so sorry for all she had lost. Dad was still going to need many months of rehabilitating. Then, when the cast could be removed from his arms and legs, you could see more ugly cuts from the wreck. However, dad seemed to heal quickly but become discouraged with not being able to work. Once again, dad decided he would move to another state to find employment where he could make a living. This time dad chooses St, Louis, Missouri. Mom had been living with granny during dad's recovery, and now she was going to move some thirteen-miles away after dad left. Things did not change with mom either. As soon as dad had left for St, Louis, and we had moved out of granny's house it was the same thing all over again. We would see mom for a while in the afternoons when she would come in long enough to bathe, and then as soon as Friday comes around we would not see her again until the following Monday afternoon. This went on for the next several years school was becoming a big problem for me especially since I was much older than the other kids were in the seventh grade.

38

Mom Gve Her Custodial Rights Away

Dad once again got word that mom was hanging out in the night clubs and leaving the three of us sometimes for a week at a time. There had been many times the three of would need to hitchhike thirteen miles to granny's house, because we had not seen or heard from our mom and there was nothing in the house to eat. This, time dad come to Arkansas he said, it was the last time, because this time he would clear this situation up, with a divorce. I can remember the morning in the courtroom when the Judge told mom she would be awarded custody of the three of us. Why she had been given the award no one ever understood? However, mom stood up in the court room and told the Judge that she did not want the custody of us. She said, she could not take care of us and did not want the responsibility of having to raise the three of us she told the Judge the court could do whatever they needed to do with us?

Then, our dad stood up in the court and told the Judge that he wanted us, I thought at the time this s was good at least it was better than having to go live in an orphan home. However, as it would turn out I would have rather lived in jail for the rest of my life; this was not going to be a good thing for the three of us?

As time went by, I was wishing our dad had said that he as well did not want us. After we returned to St. Louis, Missouri we would learn dad was not only engaged to marry another woman, but she was already living with dad, and what made it worse for us this woman dad was marrying was also an alcoholic. Dad took my brother, and sister, and me to Missouri as soon as the court hearing was over.

39

Evil Step Mom

Upon arriving to our new home in Missouri to live with dad and our new step mom to be who was blind drunk when we walked through the door for the first time to meet her. Dad said, "This is going to be your mom and from this time forward you will call her mom and you will respect her as your mom in every way!"

Well, I could see what our future was going to be like. Our new step mom to be also, had a newborn baby girl that was two months old, everyone suspected that the baby was my father's child and that would now make her not our step sister but a blood half sister? No one ever really knew if this baby was my father's child or not and since both my father have deceased I expect no one will ever know could, but as it was I could already see the early warning sign here. I was going to be not only a babysitter for my own sister and brother I was going to be a free babysitter for an infant stepsister.

My sixth sense was right on the mark, every day dad went go to work and our step mom to be would be staggering drunk by high noon. If we had misunderstood anything we were told to do that day step mom would tell, dad, and dad would give us the thrashing of our life he would beat us with-in an inch of our lives. Our dad being a man with a built as big as a bear sized man swinging the quarter inch strip of leather would cut deep into my skin, each time the leather hit me it made deep cuts into me, These beatings' become expected everyday for us. Dad married this alcoholic woman, and one more time dad told the three of us, that we would respect her as our mom or we would be beat. Even though I had become a regular babysitter, I guess there were some advantages of my now going on fifteen, I had learned from having responsibilities that I could take care of myself if I need to. Our new stepmom also, had a young son about the same age as my biological brother and two teenage twins a boy and a girl who was about the same age I was? These two twins lived with their biological father.

The twin son was drafted into the United States Army, sadly and not long after he had served his time in the Army he unfortunately drown in a fishing accident. It would always remain a mystery to myself as to his death as an accident by drowning as he was a man of 6'3" inches in height and he had drowned in 6' of water. It look to me as if he had only stood up 3" of his head would have been out of the water?

Then, the fate struck again as the younger son died with a brain tumor. The daughter, who was near my own age was, I believed to be at the time was the most beautiful woman in the entire world. Oh my how I had fallen instantly in love with her, when she and I would see each other I felt as if I was walking with my head in the clouds. But, she was my soon to be step-sister, which would not have troubled me in the least, love was love. However, as time went by she moved in her direction and I moved in mine, it would take many years for me to forget this first love which I believed to have been an angel. However, each time the beating from dad seem only to get worse, each day dad come home after work, and our new mom would make up some of the most ridiculous lies to tell dad that we had said, to her that day, which we never. Dad would call the three of us in and tell us to apologize well, we had to make our choice, either make an apology for something we had not done, or get a beating. Most of the time, my little brother and sister would say they were sorry mom and spare the torment from the beating dad would surly give if they had not apologized. For me I had taken about all I could take, and I had to come up with a plan. I knew if I did not do something soon dad would get drunk some night, start beating me with the leather strap or a plastic ball bat, and forget to stop, until he had kill me. My grades in school had become so bad I had already dropped out of school. I had gone to work as a gas station attendant pumping gas and at a reasonable wage for a fourteen year old boy. I was paying dad for my room and board and had turned into an alcoholic myself; I had actually been born an alcoholic mom drank while she was pregnant with me so what went into her blood came into mine as well.

The rest of my money went to support my drinking habit. Our new step moms continual lies to dad every day after he came in from work, lies that we had called her a bad name or that she had asks us to do something and we refused to do it, and dad would bring out the leather strip. This piece of leather was about four, foot long, and one inch wide and about a quarter of an inch thick, and with dads' muscular build when he laid the leather against my hide, it tore chunks of meat from my body, and blood would run down the length of the tear. There had been some beatings when I thought I was going to collapse into unconsciousness. I needed to put a plan into place, and soon, I had managed to save thirty- two dollar this would not last long. I had to try harder, but I needed every situation to be exactly right when I left. However, I had to leave or dad would kill me with one of the blood, bath beatings. Somehow, I was able to keep control of myself and had made another year. I was now fifteen years old, the beatings were not as regular as in the past, but I was still getting them. Most of the time dad and my step-mom were so drunk they never knew I was even around. I was as well doing my share of drinking now and no one even noticed it. Dad quite his job and went to work at another gas station the boss fired me because of being too drunk to come to work. I had however put back seventy-five dollars now to leave on, and I had my plan all in place now. I would wait until the next time dad and step-mom passed out from being drunk and I would leave in the middle of the night to go to Arkansas and live with my granny and pa.

40

No More Beating

This was the night I had waited for so long for. It was a Saturday in mid August 1968, dad and my step-mom had been drinking since Friday afternoon; both had passed out at around ten O'clock on this Saturday night. I said good -bye to my little brother and sister, and put a few of my clothing in a pillowcase, along with about a days' supply of food that consisted of a can of pork-n-beans, saltine crackers, potted meat, a can of coke and a Hershey's candy bar for desert. I was hoping to have a golden thumb for hitching all the way to Arkansas as I walked down the gravel driveway of my dads' house. I would have to walk about four miles through the city limits before I would reach the interstate highway. From, There, I would need to exit onto another interstate highway for about fifty miles east and then, to highway 67 S. This was an old highway; and it was a less traveled highway, that would run for the rest of my trip of about one hundred and fifty-miles. Houses out here for the next one hundred and fifty-miles would be only a few, about one house every twenty-miles or so, apart from the other. When, night came, the road becomes almost deserted with any traffic, I knew of only one business out here, a gas station and a good restaurant that served up good home cooked meals, I would have to keep walking past the restaurant as I had limited funds.

I expect I had walked about a mile when a car pulled up beside me and asks if I needed a ride and I said, sure, I am going to the interstate.

The man looked to be in his early twenties and was dressed, he said, "Jump on in I can take you there." After we had drove about a quarter of a mile he reached over and put his hand between my legs and said, "before, I take you to the interstate would you for like me to show you a good time?" Well, I had to think fast and just then, the traffic light changed red, and before he could think about grabbing me, I leaped out of the car and was running in front of cars which had stopped ahead of us. I could hear him yell from his car, "Hey come back I was just teasing." Somehow, I manage to lose him in all the city traffic. I thought I had trained myself better than this. I would have to learn from now on, how to be a better judge of a person's character than this. The rest of the way to the interstate I walked and by now, it was getting late and most likely, no one was going to stop and give me a ride. I walked until sometime around four a.m. The skies seem to have opened up and it was coming, a downpour of rain. I was soaked to the skin by the time I walked far enough to come to an overpass on the interstate. I crawl up toward the top of the overpass and here it was a flat slab of cement about the length of twenty-five feet in length and about eight –feet wide. Well, here I could sleep without having a fear that I would roll off. As I lay here listening to the rain, it brought back memories of the time I was living with my grandparents as a toddler when it rained, how I enjoyed listening to the rain pat softly on the house's old tin roof. The walk this far and the rain failing was causing me to become sleepy. It was dark from where I was, but I could still see the traffic on the interstate below. This position gave me a good lookout to some extent it was like a fortress. My undisturbed sleep ended with the sky's having mostly cleared and a bright eastern sun was coming peeking through the few clouds that were hanging around. I knew from the sun that I was going in the right direction and that my next turn would be to the South East, then straight south to, Arkansas.

41

Mysterious People

I must have walked about five miles when a station wagon pulled over to the shoulder of the interstate, I into a broke in a run to get to the car. A woman rolled down the window on the passenger side. As I approached the station wagon she asks, "Do you need a ride young man?"

"I replied yes" I open the back door and seated myself in the back seat.

After, I had settled in with my pillowcase with my few clothes the man driving turned about a half of a turn in the driver's seat, stuck out his hand to shake mine, and said, "Everyone calls me the Wildman," and I could tell right off, why anyone had gave him that name. His long blonde hair was sticking out in every direction from his head. The wife's name here is Rose like the flower man he said, and this was a very good name, that matched her very suitable. Her face was as pretty as a hand painted porcelain doll, her cheeks were the color of a rose with dew on it opening on a spring morning. Then, there was the little person sleeping between Wildman and Rose. We call the little one here Taters, because he loves' to eat potatoes Wildman said!

Well, Wildman said, "Now that you know our names, who would you be, if I could ask?"

Lone wolf," I said," "Ok Lone Wolf where are you headed for man?" "A small place in Arkansas, I replied," "Will, I never heard of it man, but we can help you out Lone Wolf until you get to highway 67." We had driven about fifteen – miles when I could hear a strange noise coming from my stomach. I remember it had been more than twenty-four hours since I had, last had a bite to eat. I ask, Wildman if it would be all right if I ate my Hershey's candy bar and drink my can of warm coke in his car?

He said, "Well, I don't mind at all, but would a good cooked meal sound better to you than a candy bar, and a can warm of coke?" "Oh, yes sir, it would, except I ant got no money. "This will be our way to bless you, Lone Wolf you are our guest today." And, you can leave out the sir part, just plain Wildman. At last, we come to a billboard sigh that read home-cooked meals exit one mile ahead. Well, sometimes when I think back on this day I wonder if my stomach though my throat had been cut I was so hungry. After we sat down in the restaurant, Wildman said, 'now Lone Wolf you don't be shy and order anything on that menu you see and want." I could not remember when the last time was I had smelled such good food. I would guess it was the last time granny had cooked for me, because at my dad's and step-moms house, usually the main meal that was served was cold sandwiches or frozen dinners. There was so much food on the menu that it was not easy for me to make a pick from. As I was looking at the menu, I glanced over at the people seated at table next to us and when I seen what they were having, I was certain of what I wanted the exact same thing this person was having, a chicken fried steak with mashed potatoes and gravy with hot biscuits, French fries, a salad and iced tea. Well, while we were drinking our tea and waiting for our food. Wildman ask, "Lone Wolf, you look young to be out here on the road all alone mind telling me what's going on". "No, sir I said. Please forget the sir, Well, I guess I don't mind, then I started from the beginning of mom rejecting me and I finished the story with where I was at to this point".

Our meal came as I was telling my life story to Wildman and Rose. I had never seen so much food on anyone's plate at one time in my life. The chicken fried steak I ordered looked as if I had ordered the entire cow, there was at least a half dozen hot biscuits and I was glad that little Taters enjoyed potatoes because he would surly need to eat part of mine. Wildman ask everyone to bow our heads and he, reminded me of pa when it came time to eat. Pa never missed saying thank you to the LORD and, that we were so thankful for the food we had to eat. Except, I guess Wildman's prayer was different from what I had listen to pa pray. Wildman, Rose, and I all held hands, and then he looked up towards the ceiling and said, "FATHER we are thankful for these provisions and our new friend. Amen." I could taste the meat before Wildman had said, amen. While I was eating and being gluttonous with my food, Rose sat looking peacefully taking small bites of food to her mouth as if she were a bird eating; Wildman mostly spoke for the family. He said they were coming from Rose's grandmothers funereal. Well I said, 'I am sorry to hear that,' Then, Rose at last had the chance to speak for herself, when she said, 'That's kind of you Lone Wolf to say that.

I felt as if I were holding everyone from leaving as, I was having a great chore in getting all the food down, but I was for sure going to have the plate as clean as if it had been washed before I left. At last, my plate was as clean as a whistle and I imagined I might explode at anytime.

After we had all climb back into Wildman's station wagon, I felt as if I had weighted the wagon down after the meal I had just finished. We were headed back down the road. Twenty-five miles more and what seemed to be an oddly matched couple Wildman, Rose and little, Tater would be letting me off at the next exit, and they would be going on to their home. I learned in that next twenty-five miles that why my instinct was right about Wild man and Rose. Wild man was a preacher and Rose was a veterinarian, I thought from the beginning of the trip when I first met the two they were peculiarly in their match to each other. The twenty-five miles seem to pass hurriedly and Wild man had found a place we could all get out of the car and shake hands and say good -bye properly. Then, just as I was picking my pillowcase of clothes up to walk away Rose reached into her purse and handed me a ten- dollar bill, she said, "You may, need something before you get to

Arkansas, please take it". Big tears welled up in my eyes. I stood there on the side of the road for the next sixty-seconds watching the station wagon until it had disappeared out of sight. I now had a hundred and fifty miles to go.

42

A Hundred and Fifty Miles

I expected from the amount of daylight in each day, that if I would need to walk the full trip to Arkansas, I could walk around fifteen-miles a day, and at that I would walk there in about ten days.'

I was hoping however walking the one hundred and fifty miles would not be necessary. I had been out here on highway 67 now for more than three hours and I counted fourteen cars, none of which had notice my golden thumb as I had expected everyone to see when I started out. Now, as the sun started to set today, all I could think about was getting to granny's I was thinking to myself if dad had called granny and told her that I had left and I was probably coming there. I expected he told her he would be there to return me back to, Missouri. Then, as my hours of walking brought me into the night I was in what looked as if I was in a wilderness, there was not a light from a house or a business to be seen; I had not seen the lights from a motorist since it had become dark.

It was for me a bit frightful out here in the middle of what seem to be nowhere. I begin to whistle a made up tune, as I walked along then, after whistling for a while I would sing aloud just in case there was any wild animals in the close by woods, I thought my noise would alarm them and frighten them away from me, especially the signing. I had walked all day and it was must be around midnight.

I had just finished walking to the top of a hill, when from a far distance I could hear the whine of an engine starting to climb the side of the hill I had just walked. It was the sound from the engine of an eighteen-wheeler. At last, I was not the only person out here on this lonely road. I stood here at the top of the hill and looked back to see if I could catch the glimpse of the trucks headlights. Then, all of a sudden, I could see a dim light from what looked to be about four miles away, two lights were visible and then when the truck went around a curve and down another hill, I would lose sight of the headlights. I could tell the truck was getting closer as the roar from the engine was getting louder after, what seemed at least thirty-minutes of waiting, I could see the big rig indeed it was an eighteen- wheeler alright. However, would the driver see me in time standing in the dark, and if he did would he risk stopping to pick anyone up without being able to look at the person?

As the big eighteen- wheeler came to the top the hill and I throw my hands up high above my head and with my thumb stuck back high into the air, my heart was pounding rapidly. I did not want to spend the night out here in the dark. The big truck engine did not sound as if it was slowing down I guess the driver had not seen me standing here in the dark after all. Or, maybe he seen me all right, but was not willing to risk picking up a stranger at night, so I would have to make the best of my circumstances and keep walking and sing a little louder. Then, all at once, I listen to the air breaks from the eighteen-wheeler come on and I broke into, a run as fast as my feet could carry me, I had never ran at such a speed before. When I reached the big truck I climb up the steps and opened the door and an overhead light come on, and there sit a man as big as a mountain. He looks as if he had never shaved in his entire life as his beard was as thick as a grizzle bear. He did not say a word but instead, when I stepped up into the cab of the big rig he gave me thumbs- up signal as to say its ok climb on in pardoner. Well, I gave him the thumbs up signal right back. The huge man had a sort of grin on his face and pointed to a clipboard with a piece of paper fastened to it. Well, I had closed the door and the light in the cab light stayed on, and the big man was now pulling off shifting through the gears. When,

I began reading what was on the paper attached to the clipboard I read these words. Hi, my name is Ridge Runner, I don't have a voice to talk to you with, so unless you know sign language we will just have to try and, make the best of this trip with writing notes to each other. Well, I had never learned sign language. After Ridge Runner went through the gears I think about seventeen I counted, he took the clipboard and wrote. "Do you mind telling me what your name is son." Then, I took the note pad and wrote back my name is "Lone Wolf sir." Again, he wrote, "where are you going Lone Wolf?" He handed the note pad back to me, and I wrote back on the piece of." Arkansas." Well, I seen another grin came across Ridge Runners face, and he wrote another note that said, "I can take you with in fourteen- miles of there." Then, he turned the paper and wrote, we should be there sometime around four or five O'clock in the morning. I made a nod with my head that this was ok by me, then, he pointed to something behind the seat, and I did not know what he was trying to tell me. Then, he pointed again, when I turned to look at what he was trying to show me I seen that the big truck had a bed and when I realized what he wanted he nodded his head. Well, since we could not communicate with speech and I was tired I crawl back on the bed and went fast asleep. My next awareness of anything was ridge runner shaking me and handed me another note that read you're here. I rub the sleep from my eyes, then returned to the front seat, and looked around, and he was right I was in a town in Arkansas; I was only about fourteen-miles to granny's house. Well, I stuck out my hand to thank Ridge Runner for the ride and for letting me sleep in his bed, Ridge Runners just gave a nod with his head to say you are welcome, and I stepped down out of the big rig. Then, as the big truck was pulling away, I noticed an unusual sign on the back of Ridge Runners' trailer there the words written in big bold letters read. HEBREWS 13:2{KING James} Be not forgetful to entertain strangers: for thereby some have entertain angels unaware. Strangely enough this was now my third time to encounter a strange experience were someone had helped me, and it always turned out that the person who had actually helped was someone who only, I had seen and talked too. However, after every incidence it would jog my memory of scriptures of when granny would read to me from the bible about angels. Here again was one of those times that brought to my memory of the scripture in the book of. St. Luke 4:10 {KING JAMES] for it is written, HE shall give you charge over thee to keep thee:

43

Dads' Call to Granny

I could see from a clock hanging in a local business that it was five-thirty a.m. If I should have to walk the entire fourteen miles to granny's I believed I would walk up on the front porch of granny's house in about eight hours. Now, if dad had not call granny and told her I had run away from home and I likely was trying to reach her and pas' house she had no way of knowing I was coming, and she sure would be surprised when she seen me walk up in the front yard. I could hear her voice call out land shakes boy, what on earth are you doing here? My next thoughts were what if dad is already there waiting on me to show up. However, me and my golden thumb which I started out with was not having any luck with so many rids and I walked the entire fourteen miles without any one stopping to ask if I wanted a ride. My estimate about the time I would arrive was not that far off from where I had figured it. It took me almost twelve hours to walk. I had stopped once along the way to eat some pork n beans, and crackers I had stashed away in my pillowcase with my clothes when I left dads. When, I caught the first sight of granny's house I did not see dad's car sitting there, this relieved some of the heaviness that was pressing against my chest. Then, I took in a deep breath and double my fist and knocked on the door, granny heard the knock and quickly opened the door. Granny's first words no less than I had expected, when she seen me was, "praise be boy you are safe." Then, not to my surprise granny said, "Son, your dad has called me and asks me as soon as you show up for me to call him." Granny said, "you know I have to call and let him know you are here.' Well, granny made the call to my dad and his advice to her was that I had best stay there when he get there to retrieve me. I guess dad left as soon as he finished the phone conversation with granny, because in about four hours from the time granny had talked to him on the phone dad was walking through the front door of granny's house. Of course, dad always drove as fast as the speed odometer registered on any of the old cars he ever owned, for dad that was what it meant to do. If it read, 150 mph that was how fast he drove. I would have thought that after the car wreck which dad had been in earlier, that had near took his life, and it had taken an innocent man's life and leaving a women a widow and crippled for the rest of her life would have frightened dad enough that he would never drink and drive again. At least it should have put enough fear into him that he would slow his speed down. Well, in the mean time before dad arrived to take me back, granny had dinner ready and a dinner it was. It brought to mind me of the meal I had eaten, with wild man, and his wife Rose the day before. Granny served up some fried chicken, mashed potatoes with gravy, hot biscuits, corn-on –the cob and iced tea. The next four hours passed quickly, dad walked into the house, and there was a strong smell the whiskey on his breath as soon as he come through the door. He looked over at me, pointed his finger, toward me, and just as he started to tell me what was about to happen to me, granny interrupted his speech, and said. "Listen, Bud, this was a nickname for my dad that granny called him. She said, "If I hear that you have laid one finger on this kid I will come personally to Missouri, this child has enough marks on his back he looks like a zebra, so I would advise you not to put a hand on him ever." I guess dad understood granny was serious because he told her that he was not going to put the strip of leather back on me again. I was only hoping that he was not telling granny this and then as soon as we arrived back to Missouri he would half kill me this time. Dad ate a small amount of the dinner granny had fixed and said, we had best pull out, but since it was now after midnight granny talked him into staying the night, then getting up and leaving at first light. Morning come sooner than I wanted it to, mostly because I never wanted to go back. I knew in my gut that I was going back into the same old thing, nothing had changed with Dad and my alcoholic step mom, and she would still have the same old lies to tell dad every day after work, and out would come that strip of leather. However, I never seemed to have had much of a choice at the time. Granny fixed us a breakfast of bacon and eggs, homemade gravy and biscuits.

Granny hugged me and, dad and she reminded dad one more time the he had best not put the leather to me for this dad once again, promised granny he would not. We had no more than left sight of grannies house, that dad reached under the driver's seat and pulled out a fifth of Yellowstone whiskey. Dad had not said, a word to me all this morning and we had been driving around two hours, and we were now at about at the half way point of the trip. Dad had been swerving on and off the road after about the tenth swallow of the whiskey and he was in need to ease himself of all the fluids that was inside him. At last, there was a billboard sign that read open twenty-four hours for your convenience, fresh coffee, clean restrooms, and good home cooked meals. Well I knew dad was not interested in anything other than the restrooms, so he pulled into the parking lot and slid to a stop in front of the restaurant door. After dad had left the car and while he was, visiting the restroom a thought came to me. From the way, dad was weaving on and off the road and driving at speeds' of sometimes over a hundred miles per hour, I thought for my safety maybe, I should get out while he was relieving himself and walk off into the nearby woods. However, would dad leave it at this and go on without me, or would he call the local law enforcement and have them search the woods until I was located. Then, before I could reach a conclusion dad came walking back from the facilities, and we were once again running off, and back on the road at over a hundred miles per hour again. I wondered where the police where, when you needed them. Well, at last the trip was over was and by the grace of GOD we had made it back and was in the driveway of dad's house safe. Still, in all this time since we had left grannies, house in, Arkansas, dad had not spoken one word to me nor had I said a word to him. It was as if I had been a mannequin sitting in the passenger seat along side of dad. Dad got out of the car and started walking towards the door and I picked up my pillowcase of partly clean clothes and partly dirty ones. I turned and looked back down the drive from dads' house and the thought occurred again, you should just turn away and run again. I was going too later learn that I should have to listen to my sixth sense. Nevertheless, for now I needed to reorder and put together some better thought out plans before I left again. I wasn't sure how long this would last, for the rest of the day, over night or when things would blow up, but they would, and I knew it. It wasn't if, it was when. For now, I would do everything in my power to make this work out, and I needed more money as the last of what money I had I had spent. The next day I had found a job working at another gas station pumping gas. I would come in from work each day bathe put on clean clothes and go out to find someone who would buy liquor for me, and this was never a difficult task. I would stay away from home until late hours of the night; I knew dad, and old step mom had drunk until they had passed out. And, as long as I was paying them room and board to stay there I was never ask any question about what time I had come in the night before I guess I could not see that I had become an alcoholic as well and at a very young age. Somehow, I managed to continue this up for the next two weeks at which time my boss handed my paycheck to me and said, 'you're fired.'

44

Meeting Hobo Joe

I knew the minute, I told dad and step mom I lost my job, and there was no money for me to pay my room and board I would have two choices, one would be find another job and quick, or move out.

I decided that in my best interest not say anything and just wait until both had drink enough to pass out and one more time I would put some things into a pillowcase and go back to Arkansas. The waiting wasn't long. That night both of them had drink until they passed out drunk. Again with my pillowcase as my suitcase, I put two white tee shirts, two pairs of under shorts, two outside shirts, two pairs of jeans and two heavy pairs of socks I had always heard that your feet was the most important things to care for. As well as this, I put in two cans of, potted meat; two cans of Vienna sausages some crackers and an orange crush soda pop. Once again, I told my little sister and brother bye and I was on my way back to the interstate. It always seem that it had to be at night when I needed to leave, but I figure this might be the best time as it would be easier to hide from view of police, if I need too.

I looked at the clock on the wall just as I walked out the door and it was ten minutes past mid-night. The walk out to the interstate through the city about four miles would take me about an hour and a half then I would put that golden thumb out once again in hopes it would work with getting a ride as far as one could take me. After I had walked about ten miles down the interstate, I remembered the last time I was on this interstate; I had noticed a railroad track, which ran alongside the highway. I slipped off the interstate and walked about three hundred yards and I was on the railroad tracks. I sit down on a rock, which was about four foot from the track and I waited. I was not here for more than thirty-minutes when I could hear the whistle from the train coming around a curve, the train was moving at a snail pace as it rounded the curve. I hide behind the rock and then as soon as I could see the lights from the engine I waited until I had counted twenty-five box cars on the train that had passed me.

I knew the engineer could not see me from this far back; I threw my pillowcase through an open boxcar door. I took a firm hold of the ladder on the side of a boxcar and was holding onto the ladder with both hands, I threw one leg into the door and was trying to let go of the ladder until I could get the rest of my body into the boxcar. Then, my heart almost stopped. Just, as I pulled my left leg through the opening of the door I felt, someone take hold of my ankle and began to pull me into the boxcar. Then, after I had been pulled into the boxcar I sit looking at the nastiest looking man, I had ever looked at in my entire life. I thought wild man's hair was Wild when he and Rose had given me a ride, Wild man's hair would have been neat compared to this. I had now moved slowly to the far end of the boxcar away from this nasty looking man that was here on the boxcar with me. He had two teeth left in his mouth, and both of them were green as a cucumber. His hair looked as if he had not put any water or a comb to it in months; it was in a matted and knotted disorder. The clothes he had on looked as if he had worn them all his life without pulling them off once in all his years to wash them, the unpleasant smell that was coming from the old man body was causing me to become nauseated. He looked at me for a while and said, "Hey kid, my name is hobo Joe." "How about you, you got a name boy." Yes, sir "I replied everyone just calls me Lone Wolf. Well, Lone Wolf." "Where you headed?" "Arkansas I replied." Then, old Joe begins to laugh and I thought that maybe, I had run into a crazy man. Well, after Joe had laughed hysterically for a while he said, "Boy, you ant goanna get to any Arkansas on this here train, this train is going out to Colorado." Joe said, "You might, as well take it easy Lone Wolf, this trains going to Colorado to pick up a load of coal." "The only time this train stops is to let another train pass in the opposite direction and to switch tracks." Then, Joe said, "You don't look like any hobo I seen before and he said he knew most of the hobos out here, what brings you out here?" Well, I begin to tell old Joe about my life, and I even showed him the lash marks from the leather strip dad had put to me so many times. Joe said, "Well that's too bad that a fellow's dad would do such a thing to their own son." Joe said, "You stick with me boy, and I'll show you all there is to know out here." "I have been out here for going on ten years now." Joe told me, "he knew everything thing there was to know about the hobo life."

He told me the reason he came out here to live this way was that his wife had divorced him and took everything he had, and then put him out into the streets. Well, ole Joe seemed to be all right, other than he sure could use a bath in the worse way. Joe said, "It was about eight hundred miles before we would reach Colorado and that as soon as the train stopped to wait on the West bound train we could hop off and run into the woods." Joe asks, "If I had any money on me that he could sure use a bottle of Morgan David wine?" I said, "I have a few dollars on me." At last, the train stopped where old Joe said it would. After the train had come to a stop old Joe and me jumped off the boxcar and ran out into some nearby woods that were near a river. I had taken notice of how old Joe was walking with a stiff leg, and I ask him what happened that made him walk stiff leg like that, he said "an enemy shot him in the leg during the war."

I had heard about people who had been in the war and they did not care to talk much about it with anyone so I just left it at such. It was just about sundown, and Joe started a small campfire. Then, as we sit around the fire Joe was smoking roll your own cigarettes and he asks if he might smoke one of my ready rolled cigarettes? Anyone listening to Joe talk would imagine Joe was some kind of philosopher, because Joe could tell you something about every matter you could think on to talk about. He told me about when he was a truck driver, an air plane mechanic why hobo Joe had even worked for a doctor once. Maybe, Joe had all this learning from being aged, I never rightly knew how old Joe was, he never told me his age, but sometimes a person has wisdom through age. I remember granny telling me the story of King Solomon in the bible maybe, old Joe had done the same thing and ask God to give him this great knowledge that he seem to have? The following morning around Ten O'clock Joe said, we where some place just outside a town in Kansas. Joe said, I he would help me to put up a lean- to and then for me to give him enough money to buy a fifth of wine and he would walk back down the road about two miles to a little town, he knew which sold liquor. I said, "Ok," I was wanting a good stiff drink myself. Well, Joe collected two long pieces of sticks, and then Joe took out a pocketknife that was sharp enough to shave with. Next, Joe cut about ten or so notches on both of the long sticks. Then he gathered ten small sticks about four foot long, and laid them across the notches, to finish Joe gathered some limbs that had green leaves on them and laid these over the whole thing, Joe said, now at least this will give us shade, and he was right it was cool and shaded under all this. Well, I give old Joe a ten-dollar bill, and after he put, up the lean to he left to go to town. I thought after old Joe had gone just how dumb a thing that was to give a total stranger a ten-dollar bill and look forward to them to come back with anything. I suppose I had waited for at least three hours when it struck me that old Joe was not coming back with the wine, or any money. Then, as I set there wishing I had not give him my money I heard the leaves behind me rattle, and when I turned to see what, or who was coming up behind me it was old Joe. Joe explained the long delay was because he had to tiptoe around and return another way back, because the law had took notice of him, and they did not take much to hobos in the little town Joe said. Ole Joe opened the bottle of Morgan David wine and took a big mouth full then passed me the bottle. I looked at Joe, then at the bottle of wine, with Joe looking so stomach turning and those two old dirty green teeth made me near sick, and I never wanted to put the bottle to my mouth after Joe had just put it to his first, but I did want a drink powerful bad. However, after I considered this for about a minute I reckon the alcohol would kill any germs and I took a mouth full of the wine, and passed the bottle back to ole Joe. I remember drinking around half of the fifth when I had become sleepy and Joe said, he would watch camp if I wanted to get a quick nap. I was somewhat exhausted, the wine had gone immediately to my head, and I went into a deep sleep. After, some few hours of sleeping I rose from where I had been laying and looked around to see if Joe was asleep some place but he was nowhere at our little campsite. The Jug of Morgan David wine was not here nor was old Joe. I emptied my pillowcase out onto the ground to get my money from a sock that I had put out of sight. I guess while I had been drunk I told old Joe where I had put my money, or he was just that smart because my money was gone as well. Old Joe had not as much as left me a paper dollar to buy a pack of cigarettes with. I remembered old Joe said, the reason he walked with a bum leg was that he had been shoot up in the war, I believed now that too was a lie, and most likely someone shot him for stealing instead. I was in a genuine predicament as what money I had jammed back in my sock was every cent I had to my name. I only had a few crackers-left one can of Vienna sausage. I could not help but too wonder why old Joe did not take my food as well. I really would not have believed old Joe would have done such a wicked thing to another human being that was down on his luck. I suppose this was one of those things that Joe said; he would teach me all there was to know about being a hobo? This was one of those lessons you learn out here on the streets.

I was going to learn to stay alive the best I could. I had one thought to come to mind and, that was to call granny and ask if I made it back could I stay with her and pa. Well, I felt around in my pockets and found a twenty-five cent piece that I could use at a pay phone to call and see if granny would take a collect call from me. Then, as I started out of the campsite that old Joe and me had first come to, I seen old Joe had left something behind after all, and that was his old ragged coat. It was not much but at least it was something to keep the wind off and besides old Joe had a secret pocket stitched on the inside of it so that he could slide things in there without anyone seeing him. Well, I bent down, picked up the old ragged coat, and tossed it over my shoulder and started walking toward the little town that Joe had went to get the wine. I was remembering that old Joe told me when he first came back from town that the law was not kindly to strangers in their town. Maybe, I could tiptoe in to make a quick phone call from a pay phone before anyone noticed and stopped me to ask any questions. Slipping in was easy enough and I located a phone without being seen by any law as Joe had made such a commotion about. I dropped my twenty-five cent piece into the slot and listen as it made a ding sound then, I dialed the O for the operator, and a voice came on and said, "Operator may I help you?" "Yes, I would like to make a collect call to the number, and then I gave her my granny's number." The phone begun to ring one, two, three, four, five, six, seven times, the operator came back on the line and said," I'm sorry but there don't seem to be anyone at home". The phone was still ringing as the operator was speaking; it was on the ninth ring I heard a voice on the other end of the line say, "hello." It was granny's voice. The operator asks will you take a collect call from, then the operator asks me to say my name, and I said, Granny it's me Lone wolf, granny's first words were. "Thank you GOD this boy is ok?" Granny I said, I'm in trouble could I come back and stay with you and pa until I find some kind of work to do?" Then, my heart sunk lower in my chest that I had ever felt it go before when granny gave me her answer. Granny said, "Son you know your pa and me love you as if you were our own, but your dad has called again and told us everything, and under the circumstances we don't think it is a good idea for you to live with us." "Your pa and I are getting to old to be raising children, granny said." "We still love you and we will always pray for you."

45

My First Time to Steal

The statement we will pray for you had become such a familiarly saying from people over the years that it all most caused me to be sick. I never understood why GOD expected people too offer only a prayer for someone, when they could actually help you. I thought the bible explained this as in reality to giving not only offering a prayer? MATTHEWS 19:21{KING JAMES}. JESUS said unto him, if thou wilt be perfect, go {and} sell that thou hast, and give to the poor, and thou shalt have treasure in heaven: Come {and} follow me.

There was nothing more to say. Granny and pa were undoubtedly finished with me as well

I was on my own. I was without any family at all, and I would live out in the big world alone, as best as I could. I hung up the phone after telling granny that it was ok, after all I was a big boy now, soon to be sixteen years old. The phone retuned my twenty-five cent piece I had deposited for the call to the operator, but twenty- five cents was not going to buy any food, or wine or cigarettes. Having GOD fearing, and GOD loving grandparents too raise me in a good home, with granny reading to me from the bible and teaching me to pray each night, I never imagined granny saying no to me? Nevertheless, as a mother, bird knows when to push her young babies out of the nest and let them fly on their own, granny must have knew that it was time to let me fly on my own. However, because of the teaching I grew up with I knew stealing was something that was about the worse things anyone could do. But, I was desperate, old Joe had taken every cent I had with the exception of the twenty-five cent piece and the dirty scandal would have taken that as well, had he have found it.

After leaving the pay phone, I started walking; not knowing where to go, and then it came to me. Someone in a discussion had told me if you were sixteen years old; there was a place in Illinois that hired people at a canning factory. I begin adding up how much time I had been out here, and I figured I was now at least close to being eighteen or, I thought I was anyway. So, I had to learn how to go from Kansas to the state of Illinois? I quickly learned I need to hitchhike northeast. I only hoped I would not need Identification for the job because I did not have even a driver's license? But, I did look much older that what I was. I reckoned I looked like I might be already at least in my earlier twenties this was something that I accounted for the life I had lived up until now. I was going to need something to eat to give me some strength for this trip of about six hundred miles, and I wanted a drink of wine as well. It now being the middle of September, and it was a late afternoon I was not going to draw to much attention if I put on the old ragged coat that I had of old hobo Joe's, the one with the secret pocket sew up on the inside. I had learned, wrong from right my entire life, granny and pa taught me the golden rule in their house. However, I always seemed too do the wrong thing. Nevertheless, as I walked I had not remembered when the last time was that I cried, but my face was getting wet from tears trickling down my face.

Once, again I was praying asking GOD who never really seemed to pay much notice to me. I ask GOD, why my mother never wanted me, but as all the times before HE never answered me or, maybe HE was answering and I just wasn't paying attention?

The first store I come to I walked in took a grocery basket, and began walking up and down each isle as if I were shopping. I would nod a hello with my head to this person in the isle and then too another trying not to create any suspicion. As I passed the bananas, I picked up a half green one and slipped it inside my pocket, then a green apples, a block of long horn cheese, and leaving room for a pint of Morgan David wine, and three pack of Winston cigarettes. Now, to put the last touches on my plan, I had to put some items in my basket, things' such as a quart of milk, a can of mushroom soup, a box of crackers. Then, I pushed my basket to the check out and after the cashier rang it all up, she told me the total I reached to my back pocket as if to pull my wallet out to pay, when I exclaimed with an expression oh no, "I have lost my wallet." I felt around in every pocket I had, making believe to search for something I knew was not there in the first place. Well, after a full minute of making believe I was looking for my wallet I said, 'I'm sorry to have caused this trouble.' The checker said, "That it was all right and said she hoped you find your wallet." I said, "Thank you," and left the store with my stolen items hidden away inside the secret pocket of old Joes' tattered coat without anyone knowing it. The old ragged coat Joe had left had served for some use after all. However, it was getting too late to leave and I decided since it was not but a short walk back to where old hobo Joe, and I had camped out I would go back there and spend the night under the lean to. Not a leaf had been turned while I had been gone. I crawl under the lean to and took the bottle of Morgan David wine from the inside pocket. After the first chug-a-lug, the wine was as if a new reviving came to me when I swallowed my first mouth full of the grape wine, then I bite off a chunk of the cheese.

After my feast of wine and cheese, it had filled the empty space in my stomach, and I smoke two cigarettes to top off my meal. The wine had relaxed me enough, that sleep overtook me, and for the rest of the night anything could have carried me away without my knowing of it.

46

Arrested

It was an early September; mornings the sun took its first peep from underneath my lean- to and I awoke with a hangover which I thought I would surly die from. I recalled Old hobo Joe, told me when this happen to him he did what was call "hair of the dog," to cure this he just another drink of what gave him the hangover in the first place. Well, I never had anything to lose, so I shuffle around looking for some of the poison I had drank the night before. I found enough for four good drinks, and I turned the bottle up and took as much into my mouth as I could hold; enjoying the flavor of the grape taste before I swallow it. The first drink taste good so I repeated this over again until, I had finished the bottle, and it did seem too help the hangover as Joe ad told me it would. Now I needed to break camp and leave before someone took notice and turned it in that a hobo was homesteading here. I had walked almost through the city when a sheriff's deputy pulled along side of me in his cruiser and rolled down his window. "He told me to stop." Will, I knew I could not out run the deputy's gun, and besides if I ran he would think for sure I had done something and arrest me.

After the deputy got out of his cruiser, he did not look much older than I was, he asks, "boy what's in the pillowcase?" "Just a mix of some dirty clothes, and a few clean ones sir, I said!" "Empty everything out on the ground, the deputy ordered me!" The deputy was not talking in a friendly tone of voice. He was not asking me he was making demands. Well, I started to untie the shoelace that I had the opening of the pillowcase tied with, and the deputy said, "Hurry it up boy; I don't have all day to be trouble with you." Now, my hands were shaking, partly because the deputy was causing me to be unsettled, and partly because I was in need of drink of wine. At last I had emptied all my clothes both clean and dirty ones out onto the sidewalk, the deputy took his boot and kicked through everything lying there on the ground. Then, he started to ask personal questions such as, "Where are you from boy?" I never know that one person could own a town, but he ask me "Why are you here in my town boy?" The interrogation by the deputy was causing beads of sweat to break out all over me and then he asks, "Why are you sweating so boy?"

"Are you on some of that dope boy?" "I bet you're one of those hippie dope boy's, and we don't put up for dope in my town." Then, the deputy orders me, to turn around and put your hands behind my back!" "What about my clothes sir, I said!" This is all I own. "Are you resisting an arrest boy the deputy asks?" No sir, I just need my clothes I said.' After the handcuffs were tightly around my wrist, the deputy shoved the clothes, which were, now scattered every place on the sidewalk back into my pillowcase and put them and me into his car. Why are you arresting me I Asks as we were on the way to jail"? Suspicion this will be enough to keep you in jail for the next seventy-two hours. The drive to the jail was only about fourteen blocks away. After, the deputy took me from the patrol car and inside the jail there sit the town's old gray-headed sheriff. The deputy informed the sheriff that he had a real smart one here. Well, the old sheriff asks the deputy what has this here boy done? The deputy said, "Sheriff this here is one of them hippie boys." He said, "I figure he is on some of that dope." "He has no ID on him, and he claims he is on his way up north to work at some cannery, but I think we should keep him around until they have checked out my record."

The old sheriff said, "Put him in a cell." I spent the rest of the morning just sleeping, when they brought my lunch, I pretended I was asleep and left the tray of food sitting in the floor until they came back around and picked it up. The next morning I did the same thing at breakfast, and again at dinner that night. The old sheriff said, "Listen boy we don't care if you never eat, that ain't goanna get you out of here any sooner." I never troubled myself to answer him, and he walked away. The third day I had still declined to eat breakfast again. Then, at lunch that day when they came around with the food tray it did look good today. Today, the food tray was loaded with, roast beef, mashed potatoes with gravy, green beans hot rolls and ice tea. Well, I was still so raged with madness from being here without any reason; I take hold of the tray of food and tossed it to the floor.

This caused the old gray-headed sheriff to show his bad side of himself. He said, to me. "If he could get by with it he would take me out of this cell and whip me to an inch of my life, he said, my poor old wife cooked, and slaved over a hot stove all day to cook that meal for all of you losers, and you have no respect for anything!" Well, I had to reply. I said, "Mr. Sheriff, take, a look at my back. I turned around and pulled up the tee shirt I had on and said, look at the marks on my back, left from a quarter inch thick strap of leather that my dad used on me when I was at home and I said, "Mr. I have already been whipped within an inch of my life." Then, I finished by saying, 'I never ask your wife to cook anything for me, besides you know you have nothing to keep me here for any way'. Well, the old sheriff said, I apologize for losing my temper. Then, he told the deputy to take me out of the cell, and escort me to the city limits. He turn to me and said, boy listen to me. "I don't want to ever see you again". The deputy did as the old sheriff told him to do and took me to the outside of the city limits and let me out. Then, just as I was walking away, the deputy said 'hey, that old sheriff meant what he said, about not wanting to see you back in my town again'. This time I never answered instead I just kept walking. By the time I turned around to look behind me, the deputy was gone. It was now two O'clock in the afternoon when the deputy let me out and I was walking east on an unmarked highway. I was trying to think in my head the best way for me to go, I would hike back to Saint. Louis, Missouri and from there I would head up north to Illinois.

47

Frank and Jack

Just then, a big gray Buick passed by me traveling at almost the pace of a turtle. Then, only a few yards in front of me the Buick came to a stop right in the middle of the road. I did not need to run to the car because it stopped so close, I could lay a hand on the back bumper. I walked up to the passenger window when a woman rolled down her window and asked," Young man do you want a ride?" "Yes, thank you I said." I opened the back door and climbed in the back seat of the cleanest looking Buick I had ever looked at. The Buick was a 1968, with only twenty-thousand original miles on the odometer, you could still smell the scent which a brand new car had too it.

After, I got myself seated in, and we were driving down the road again still at a turtles pace, the woman driving said, my name is Frank and this here is my twin sister Jack." I thought this was out of the ordinary names' for two women, but, then Frank said, our daddy was hoping we were going to be boys' He was going to name them Frank and Jack. So this is where the names Frank and Jack come from." She said; "just call us Frank and Jack young man." Well, I learned next that these two twins were seventy-five years old, and the two of them just traveled all over the United Stated looking at everything they could.

I had not yet took a close look at either one of the old woman's face, but from behind they, both looked tall and slender, and both had long hair and as white as cotton, which they tied up in a bun on

140

top of their head. Just listening to their voice, and looking at them from the back seat, you would not have known they were more than twenty-years old, the way the two of them was carrying on. Well, so far, Frank had been doing all the talking, when Jack interrupted her sister and said, "Frank why don't you let the young man have a change to say something, we don't even know his name." "Everyone calls me Lone Wolf, I replied." And, "where might you be from Mr. Lone Wolf "Jack, ask me?" Well, "I suppose I'm from every place I said." "I've got no real place to call home ma' am." "Don't you have a family some place Mr. Lone Wolf, Frank asks?" "None that welcomes me ma'am I answered." Without going into great length of telling everything, I said "I was an unwanted birth and my grandparents raised me". "Then, a few years ago, my dad and mom divorced and I went with a sister and brother to live with our dad and an alcoholic step mom, who made my life miserable." She would make up lies to tell our dad, and he would use a strip of leather that cut and tore my skin so that, even today I wear marks to remind me of the beatings. Oh, that's "a most horrifying thing frank said"! "Why, I don't blame you for wanting to get away from that." At last we had switch now to talking about the two of them instead of me. I learned that, Frank, had retired from a career of teaching, and Jack had retired from a career of nursing. The two anxiously waited for their turn to tell about how they had been raised own a farm and, with their daddy and mommy both working as much as sixteen hours a day in the fields too put food on the table, and too see that they received a recognized education. From time, to time the conversation would switch back to me again and I would do my best to get around my turn, and open the attention back on them without either of them recognizing what I had done, a little piece of psychology I had picked up along my travel. While the two of them talk, I was partly listening and partly wondering if I could make better time if I ask to get out and walk, because I imagined we must have come about fifty-miles, and we were still moving at the same turtles pace when I got in the car. What should have taken about one thirty minutes to travel had taken over an hour and a half now. A few times in our going down the road I thought we had actually stopped in the road.

If the map in my head was accurate I was now just over three hundred miles to, Missouri and judging from the speed Frank was driving it was going to take at least eight hours to get there. I guess there was one thing certain about Franks driving, and that was she was not going to be stopped and citied for breaking any speed limit. I estimated the time when Frank and Jack picked me up that it was around two O'clock. I noticed this from a clock in the dashboard of this magnificent looking machine. I knew however that soon enough we would part and go on our individual ways as I we would say good-bye to each other, and wish each other a safe journey. Right now, I was wishing I had bottle of Morgan David, hid away in my inner pocket and could take swallow. I learned from their stories about some of the cities they had visited I hoped someday to see as well, such as the empire state building in New Your City, then there was the White house in Washington D.C. Then, when they told me how much love, there was in their home when they had grew up with a loving mom and dad on a farm in a little community of Oklahoma not only captivated me but also, made me wish I could have had just a fraction of this type of love from a mom and dad. Now, with the cool September wind blowing through the open window, and with Frank and Jack talking, telling one story, after another, I had fallen off to sleep, only to have been awakened by Jack saying we made it. I wiped my eye with my fist and looked at the dashboard clock once, again and it was fifteen-minutes after eight. Frank asks me, "If there was any precise place I would like them to take me," and I replied, "No just any place will be ok." I thought I could hold up under one of the overpasses for a night's sleep and get a fresh go at the first light of day. I did not want to go back to dads' place again. Frank pulled into an all night gas station to top off her gas tank and after the station attend came out to fill their car we all embrace each other with a hug and wished each a safe journey, Frank said, "Young man you have touched our lives". Jack reached into her purse pocket and handed me a ten-dollar bill. As I was walking off into the cool September night toward the busy interstate highway, I turned once to look back and I noticed that Jack had taken a hankie from her purse and was dabbing her eyes. I would remember the two old twin sisters always. My walk to find an overpass too sleep under, was only a mile walk, and I crawl up to the top of the flat cement under the bridge, and lay there on my pillowcase as a pillow, while having a smoke before sleep.

I still had a long journey ahead until I would be in Illinois, so a good night's rest would do me good.

I used my pillowcase as a pillow, propped up against a beam of cement support under the bridge and as I counted all the cars passing by below me I quickly fell asleep wondering where everyone was going. It seems as if I had shut my eyes only for a moment and the dawn arrived I took up my pillowcase, and slid down the cement embankment, and started walking down the interstate with my fist doubled and a thumb stuck up high in the air for a passing motorist to notice and hopeful someone would aide me with a ride. There was one thing about walking; it gave me plenty of time to think about my past, and about my future. I had now turned out to be no more than a common thief. Going to jail would have disgraced my Grandparents to no end had they know. Either of them had never as much as taken a stick of firewood from anyone without paying for it, and I was taking anything I could in order to survive. My pa would say work for it, or do without.

48

United States Marine Corps

I had walked about three miles when a green Pontiac with unusual tags which had the words. United States Government stamped on the plate. My first thought of seeing these tags when the car had pulled off the road waiting for me was to turn and run as fast as my legs would carry me back in the direction from which I just come. As I have mentioned before, one should always go with that first intuition, but once again, I went against my feeling. I walked up to the green Pontiac and a man rolled down the passenger window and asks, "Would you like a ride young man?"

Yes sir, "I replied." "Get in, a man in a Marine corps uniform with many strips and medals hanging from his chest said." Wow, this was a beautiful uniform to look at. "My name is Sergeant Scar," 'And, your name is, he asks?" "People just call me Lone Wolf sir, I replied."

"Where are you headed, Lone Wolf, the Marine sergeant ask?" "I am going up north to Illinois looking to find work at a canning factory." "I see, was his reply." "Well, what would think about a real job, a career in the United States Marines?" "I'm a recruiter for the United States Marines he explained." I looked over at Sergeant Scar, and I did love that uniform, I don't think I had ever seen a prettier uniform in all my life. His blue trousers with a red strip that ran from the top of the trousers to the cuffs and a brown shirt that if he taken it off it would have stood up all by its self. His shoes were shinned so that you could have used them for a mirror to look at yourself with. He looked tough enough that no one was about to try and take him on, in a fight, and I liked that idea of having my body put into that kind of shape, and never again would anyone beat me the way my dad had in the past. Well, I never hesitated to answer, and I ask "how?" Then, Sergeant Scar asks me how old I was?" I had not thought about my age in so long I had almost forgotten, it took me a minute to calculate and then I said, "I'll be eighteen in a few weeks' sir."

"Good, Sergeant Scar replied." "What about high school, did you finish?" "No sir, is that a problem I ask?" "Not if you can pass the GED the Marines will give you too get in." "Thank you can do that Sergeant Scar asks." "I can pass it, sir." "Good he said." "I'll take you to my office it's just at the next exit." The Sergeant reached into a briefcase next to him and pulled out a stack of papers that look more look a short novel and said, "Start answering the questions."

Well, by the time I had finished answering everything in the stack of paper, I felt as if I had already taken the GED. Then, we arrived at Sergeant Scar's recruiting office. He said, "Come on, and I show you a film about how the Marines train boys to become men in twelve-weeks." "You will be a lean mean, walking machine after you finish the twelve weeks of training". Now, that was what I wanted to hear. After, watching the film I said, "I'm ready." I felt like I could right there before having any training rip a grizzly bear apart. "I said, I want to be a Marine sir', and sergeant Scar said, 'you are ready private Lone Wolf." "There are only a few more things we need to do, and one is you will need to come back to my office first thing in the morning and I'll take you down town to the Marine Corps headquarters where you will take the GED exam. If you pass that, next comes the physical, and then you will be sworn in." What next, "I ask?" "Then, in two weeks when you turn eighteen, you're on your way to the Marine Corps basic training camp in San. Diego, California". Well, I had a problem which, I had not told Sergeant Scar, I did not have a place to stay for the next two weeks. I did not have money for a motel, ten-dollars to my name that was a gift from Frank and Jack, and I needed a drink of wine and in the worse way. I only had one option and that was to call my dad, after all, it had been a long time, since we had seen one another, maybe he had changed. At least I was big enough now that I didn't think he would try to use that strap of leather on me, and besides, maybe he would respect the fact that I was going into the United States Marines too serve my country.

"Ok, sir, I will be here first thing the following morning." I walked out of the office and went straight to the first liquor store I knew that would not ask for any ID. After buying a pint of Morgan David wine and had it wrapped in a brown paper bag so that it might not attract much attention.

I started walking to find a pay phone, and sipping on my Morgan David wine, I could almost see myself in those dress blues, the ones with the red strip running down the side of them, and wearing that neatly pressed brown shirt and my shoes polished so that I could see my face in them. My thoughts had taken me so far away I had walked right past a pay booth telephone. What was I going to say to dad when he answered the phone? What was he going to say to me? I had assorted feelings going through my head, but I had to do, this. I wanted to be a Marine; this was something I would never have another chance to do. Anxiously I put twenty-five cent into the slot, and rang dads' number. To my surprise, dad answered and said, "Hello." I think dad said, "This is the mule barn." Dad was a bit of a joker sometimes especially after he had a few mixed drinks.

Hello, "dad it's me." "Dad said, me who?" "It's me your son." "Where are you boy, in jail?" "No, I'm in town for a couple of weeks, I just joined the Marines dad, and I need a place to stay for two week when I turn eighteen, just until I get my orders, dad can I come home and stay for two weeks please, I asks?"

There was silence on the line and, I thought he might have hung the phone up, but I imagine he was asking permission from my step-mom then he said, I suppose". "I said, thanks dad. I hung up the phone." As I started my walk towards dads' house still sipping on my pint of Morgan David wine, wrapped in the brown paper bag, I was asking myself had I done the right thing? Did the Marines mean so much that I would go back to a place where I had been beaten with leather until a few times me near lost consciousness. A voice in my head kept telling yes. I kept walking and the closer I got the faster my feet seem to walk, and soon I was walking up dads' driveway. As I approached the door in front of the house, I took in a deep breath, exhaled the air slowly, and knocked on the door. I had only knock once on the door when, I heard dads voice say, "The door is open". Well, as I step through the door everything was as I could remember it as it was when I had left. The kitchen table was sitting just inside the door as it was before. Dad and my step-mom spent all their time drinking glass after glass of Yellowstone whiskey, there at this table. As I came in dad stood up and surprisingly reached out his had to take mine and shake it, I had never remembered dad doing this before. However, nothing seemed to have changed, much as dad and step-mom were both, blind drunk. Dad pointed to an empty chair and told me to sit down. Then he started the conversation by saying, "So you joined the Marines did you?" "Yes sir, "I said," "Saying sir to my dad was a change, but I thought I had better get use to the change. "Well, your step mom and I both wish you the best, dad said." Sure, I thought, as I looked over at my step-mom hardly able to hold her head up. And, then with a struggle to raise her head and mumble her words ask me, "Why would the Marines want you?" "I thought they took only a few good men she remarked?" Then, dad interrupted and said, "That's' enough." While dad and I was talking about where I had been the past year or so step-mom interrupted again, and said, "lets see if you're a man, have a drink with your old dad and me." Well, this suited me. I had finished the last of my Morgan David just before I come up the driveway. So I said, "Sure, I can handle that", and dad poured me about a half of glass of the Yellowstone whiskey into a glass and filled it the rest of the way with coke. As dad and step mom talked I finished my first glass in less than four minutes and was sitting with an empty glass, when dad ask, I guess you could use another one? Sure, "I said." Two hours passed, dad had served me six glasses of whiskey, and I did not feel close to being drunk. The fifth we had been drinking from was empty and dad said, "We needed to go to the liquor store and buy another bottle." Dad had talk with me more over the past two hours than I could remember him talking with me my entire life. He said, so I guess we are elected to go" and dad pitched me the car keys and ask, "You do know how to drive a car"? "Yes, I can drive dad." I said, "I have know, how to drive since I was around twelve-years old except I don't have a drivers license." Dad went ahead and let me drive his car to a liquor store about three miles away. After the trip to the liquor store and back, I learned that at least there would be one less person to drank, on the new bottle of whiskey, as step-mom had passed out on the coach in the room next to the kitchen. Dad and I continued to drink and talk for another hour when he had to give up and went to bed, and left me to drink all I wanted. I thanked dad for letting me stay before he had go to bed, and we said our good-bye that night. Drinking seen to come like second nature to me, and, after all one has to remember I was an alcoholic from the time mom conceived me, she drank and smoked marijuana through the nine months of carrying me inside of her, everything that went into moms' blood went into my blood.

Now, the following day would be a day for my medical examinations I decided to go to bed as well. I arrived at the recruiters' office the next morning and I was waiting on him to show up.

Sergeant Scar and I drove to the downtown area of St. Louis, Missouri to the Marine Corps headquarters where I took an all day written exam. At the end of the day, and all the test were graded, I had passed every test. The next morning I was to report for the Physical examination. Well, after I come in that day too report too dad that I had passed the written exam and that the next day I was going to take my physical we had another night of celebration. Again, both dad and step-mom had passed out way before I had even begun to start felling anything. The following morning Once again I was waiting in front of Sergeant Scars' recruiting office waiting for him to take me to the down town marine headquarter.

The physical examination took most of the day; I had never been check by so many doctors and given so many shots in all my life. I was ask to bend over and touch my toes,

A hearing test,

An eye test,

Then probed,

Stuck with needles,

A doctor put his finger in my gentles and told me to cough. I would now, understand why they called the Marines the few and the proud. I was thinking just the exam itself would kill me. Then, the end of another day and, the doctor read the outcome of my physical, I had passed everything. Now, the only thing left was to get me sworn in. The next two weeks went by hurriedly and it was at last time for the swearing in.

This was done in a room with about fifty other Marine recruits, after this was finished, I was told you are no longer a civilian; you are the property of the United States Marines corps. You will do what you are told to do, when you are told to do it, do you understand that you scum bag maggots the Sergeant shouted at the top of his lungs!

Every Marines in the room yell back at the top of our lungs, "Sir, yes Sir!" Then, while we one further instruction officer sitting behind his desk said, I need four volunteers to for Parris Island South, Carolina. Well, everyone had watched the film through the course of recruiting, and everyone had heard about Paris Island. No one here today wanted to go to P.I. This was known to be one of the toughest and meanest places the Marines had, to take your basic training. So, not one new recruit volunteered for P.I. Then, the officer said, "Oh, it looks to me like what I have here is a bunch of smart ball players, who wants to play hardball with me." Well, we were no match for him.

He said, "So this is the way you want to play?" "If you remember maggots just minutes ago you were told that you now belong to the United States Marines, and that you will do what you were told, when you were told to do it." Then, he took his index finger and pointed to the first private in the first row and said, you are going to Paris Island, private! Then, he pointed to another, and said, you are going to Parris

Island private! And, a third time, he pointed his finger at another private and said, you private will be going to Parris Island then to the fourth and lastly, he pointed his finger to me and said, you private, that would be me will be going to Parris Island.

Well, my orders in my hand said, I would be going to take my basic training in San. Diego, California. Just then, my recruiter walked into the room, Sergeant Scar that was. So, I approached him, and advised him that my orders said I was to report to the base in San. Diego, California. But, now this officer said, I was to go to Parris, Island South Carolina. Well, Sergeant Scar, who had been particularly nice to me through my recruitment said, "private have you been sworn in yet? "Yes sir, I replied!" Then, he was in my face yelling you are a marine now private you will, go where the marines decide to send you to take your basic training, you will go take your training with the devil, if they tell you too."

I knew from this day on, I should have listen closer to my intuition, because this was not going to be the career I first thought it was going to be. I imagine there must have been a least a million ideas running through my mind at this time, things like just get up and walk out, protest this to someone else, but who? Well, after sitting here for over an hour fearfully going over what to do, four more Sergeants' came running through the room screaming at the top of their lungs move it! You scumbags get out of my room and onto my bus Move it! Move it Move it maggots. Well, all fifty of us was trying to get out the door at once shoving and pushing trying to do what were told to as fast as we could. Just outside the building was a big bus that had THE UNITED STATES MARINES written on the side of it. Everyone loaded onto the bus, another Sergeant drove about four miles to the Saint Louis international airport. The Sergeant who brought us here took us to the gate where we would load onto the airplane and then made a speech that was clear and precise. "Listen up you maggot's, you had better be on that plane when it leaves, because if you don't report to your assigned post and, they send me after you, I'll bring you back in a body bag, you understand me you scum bags?" Then, all fifty of us yelled at the top of our lungs, "Sir, yes Sir!" Of course his choice language was more forceful. The next three hours waiting for our delayed plane to arrive at the Saint .Louis international airport finally taxied up to the departing gate. I had never before had such feeling. My heart that had just been thoroughly checked and was declared I was in perfect shape was now skipping beats. Today, as I walked toward the passenger terminal to enter the big seven forty-seven jet, this would take me to my first stop in, Georgia. From here, we would transfer to another airline that would pick up even more recruits and from there to an Island. When, our plane landed there, the Marine Corps would pick us up and take us to the Island.

Again at least a millions thoughts were now going through my head, so many that, I could not decide on which to choose from. Should, I jeopardize my life by not getting on the plane here in Saint. Louis, and have the tough looking Sergeant come after me as he said he would. However, he did point out in his speech, that if he had to come looking for any of us who had decided not to board the plane, he would come look for us, and bring us back in a body bag if this was necessary.

Was he for real, or was it just a speech to be humorous, and scare a group of green horn Marines? I had learned by now how to read people somewhat, but he had a different face, one that I could not make out if he was telling the truth or whether he was just joking, at any rate it was something I was not at this time ready to risk. I was on the plane, and I had a window seat just behind the right wing.

Looking out the window as the big seven forty seven increase speeds of over a hundred miles an hour down the runway and then the big shinny metal bird lifted from the ground into the air.

This was my first flying experience I had ever had. I had been on many hallucinatory flying trips, and being in places which I was not really at, on some of the drugs I had used in my past, but this was a reality flight. Sometime during the flight, I had fallen asleep I had a dream about the time when I was back on the train with old hobo Joe. Then, my dream was interrupted by the pilot announcing over the intercom that we were approaching, Georgia international airport, and those going to, South Carolina would change airlines here. After, the Ozark airliner had taxied up to the terminal I had walked to the Delta airlines. Waiting for my next flight out, I was still struggling with making a break for it and running. After all, I had experience of being a hobo; I knew the ins and outs of living on the streets. I imagine I could evade capture for at least a year.

It look as if as if every time I was about to carry out my plan something would disrupt it.

Just as I was about to pick up my personal belongings the announcement come over the loud speakers of the terminal that the flight to Charleston, was boarding at gate 5. When, I looked up

I was sitting in front of gate 5. This was the last chance; I would have the opportunity to run or to stay. Will, I go AWOL, or get on the plane to Charleston with the rest of the recruits and go to the airport in, South Carolina, and from there onto another marine bus which would carry all of us to the Island, Paris Island the Marine Corps toughest and meanest basic training camp there was. Then, as the words went through my mind again, from the sergeants speech about him having to come find anyone of us who decided not to arrive at our assigned destination, I concluded too end the trip at the Marines corps basic training camp at parries Island, south, Carolina. At last, we had landed in South Carolina and the Marines had picked us up on their bus.

As we were driving to the Island, I was thinking this is my last freedom for the next thirteen weeks. I am now the property of and belong to the United States Marines. At last, I was here on parries Island. Now, standing just outside the bus were two drill instructors one a senior instructor and his assistant. Both, of them were yelling at the top of their lungs, so that they could have awakened the dead. Get off my bus you maggots, move it! Move it! Move it! Move it. Get on my foot prints. The senior instructor said I am going to be for the next thirteen week while you are here your mommy and your daddy. My name is senior staff sergeant bull dog. This is my assistant; his name is assistant staff sergeant Saw shark. By the time you finish this thirteen weeks if you finish you are going to feel as if you had been bitten by a real bull dog, both old bull dog and a shark ask do you hear me? There were hundreds of yellow foot prints painted on the deck. The senior instructor was yelling at the top of his lungs, what had he done to the marines that they were sending him this to make marines out of? He told his assistant old Saw Shark that the United States marines, was trying to ruin his career.

We were trying to unload as quickly as possible from the bus, onto the parade deck on those yellow foot prints standing at attention, or as best we knew how to stand at attention. The senior drill instructor Bull Dog come running up to me and with his nose touching my nose and with his rounded stiff hat that was poking into my forehead, yelling in my face, where did they send you from? Sir, "I come here from, Missouri sir." I believe that was my first of many mistakes I would make. Sergeant Bull Dog said. "You're not an eye, you are a private!" He said, to assistant Saw Shark holy cow would you just look at the rubbish the Marines is sending me these days?" "How in creation, am I supposed to make Marines out of this?" He told Saw Shark, "he believed his career of twenty years was finished." Then, he ask me," what are you doing here private in my Marine Corps?" Sir," I want to be a Marine sir, I replied!" That mistake again, that I word is understood as your eye, and you are not an eye but a private.

Well, after I had answered his question and told him I was from Missouri, he pulled off his perfectly rounded hat and tossed it onto the ground and said, "the Marines is trying to ruin my career, they have sent me a Yankee from the show me state". Then, after he picked up his hat from the parade deck, he said to, Saw Shark his assistant, this has to be the worse bunch of recruits he had seen in all his nearly twenty years career. He told his assistant, "It is not possible to turn this bunch of sissies into Marines?" Well, after I had been on the plane and in airports, waiting on transferee it had been about thirty-six hours since I had been asleep. Now, after unloading from the bus and standing here for two hours with two instructors yelling so that you would have imagined they would lose their voice, or I was going to lose my hearing. It had begun too rain and the two instructors did not seem to notice. At last, old Bull Dog said, "We are going to march to a building called the receiving barracks and here you, will be issued everything you would need". Then, he gave us a list of things that we would get.

Toothbrush,

Shaving cream,

Razors,

Bath soap,

Under shorts,

Tee shirts,

Fatigues,

Bucket,

Scrub brush. The list went on; all of this went into a bag called a sea bag. Everything must have weight in at around twenty-five pounds. Then, last but the most important of everything the Marines issued us was the M16. This was a powerful weapon, your best friend, and you would not call it a gun. It is not a gun and you better remember it, this is a rifle it is used for killing. After, gathering our personal items and stuffing them all into the sea bag we tossed the bag over our shoulders and as the two drill instructors were yelling for us to move it we ran with our heavy gear toward our barracks. I watch as big masculine young men fell to the ground from exhaustion. The next stop was the barracks where would live for the next twelve weeks. Well, old bucket mouth Bull Dog, began yelling again put this gear into your footlocker and do it now, move it, move it move it.

At the foot of each of our bunk was your own personal footlocker. Sergeant, Bull Dog, said listen up maggots you are no longer civilians you are now the property of the United States Marines, for the next thirteen weeks, you will not do the things you did before today. From today, you will do as you are told, when you are told. Everything you do you will ask permission first? From today if you need to scratch your elbow you will loudly address me; Sergeant the private request permission to speak sir? If I say permission granted then, you may tell me your request? Sir, Private Yankee request permission to scratch his elbow sir! If I say permission denied, private you better not scratch your elbow, I will catch you private and I will make your day miserable, your platoon will suffer along with you and they will make your day miserable as well.

Next, we were ordered to the barbershop where we would receive the worse haircut you could ever get. I could have given myself a haircut as good as this. The Marine barber asks me, "private how you would like your hair cut today?" I said," Just a little off the sides Sir." He ran the clippers across my head about three times and said, "Step down. Then, he called for next private"! When, I looked in the mirror, my long blond curly hair had all vanished leaving me totally, bald. Everyone who had come in here now looked the same not being able to tell one from the other. Now, after getting back to the barracks the instructor was giving us our schedule for the following days lay out. He said you "will fall out, of bed at four a.m." Bull Dog continues, "We will go for a short hike of fifteen miles." "We will do this before breakfast; we will turn around and run back the fifteen miles until you have fallen out if you make it back, then you can go have breakfast." "Do you understand me maggots?" "Ok, move it!" This turned out to be a very common word for Bull Dog and Saw Shark. We would do all of this with our backpacks pulse our M16 over our shoulders. Then, when we return, and put everything up, we will go to the mess hall for breakfast. After, breakfast we would meet on the parade deck, each morning. Bull Dog said, "You will think by the end of the day you had body parts you never knew you had. Push-ups, climbing a rope that reached about forty feet, climbing over walls, crawling under barbwire on our backs, crawling through mud holes, and the list went on. All the time we were attacking each task the two instructors were coming up to me putting their nose in my face yelling and looking at me with eyes that would have melted steel.

49

A Big Mistake

Then, I made my second big mistake. Old Bull Dog ordered the platoon to remove their rifles that were chained with a combination pad lock at the end of our bunks. After taking too long with unlocking my combination, Bull Dog came running up to me again with his ugly face pressed in mine and ask, "What's wrong with you private, can't a Yankee do something as simple as open a combination pad lock?" This is when I made the biggest mistake of all when I said, "sir, the combination is stuck and the private cannot get his gun off the bunk sir." I could see his face turn red, his face blow up so that it looked like a toad frog, and I thought he would explode at any time. He began yelling, this is not a gun? "You will never call it a gun again; this is a rifle or the M16." It is the most powerful weapon there is. "Is that clear private maggot?" "Sir, yes Sir, this time I yell so loud I thought I would lose my voice from laryngitis." Next, old Bull Dog said, "Private turns your covers back on your bunk, place your rifle with the barrel lying on your pillow, and cover it back up with you covers." Then, I ask another dumb question? Sir, if my rifle is in my bed, where will the private sleep tonight Sir?" Then, he went to his quarters, brought back a flimsy old wool blanket, and pointed to the floor next to my bunk. There, "He said, you will sleep on the floor." And you had better pray that there is a GOD in Heaven, and that HE does not let anything happen to my rifle!"

I had moved so far away from any GOD, and the teaching I grew up with I could never think about finding it even a little possible that there was a road back to GOD for me? I questioned maybe, GOD could not even see, or hear me anymore. I could not picture any communication

Between me and GOD. I just imagined I had been disconnected from HIM altogether? Well, I knew now I had made one of the biggest mistakes I had ever made before, but I had myself into this spot, I would have to get out somehow. The following morning I was awaken by the sound of someone playing a horn, just outside of the barracks, I was going to learn shortly this sound meant reveille. It meant you better roll out of the bunk and come to attention.

Old sergeant Bull Dog and sergeant Saw Shark both come running through the barracks kicking over trash cans pulling covers off everyone turning over some of the bunks even with people still sleeping in them that was not out of bed and standing at attention. Today I believed I would never live through a longer day than this one had been. I recalled today Bull Dogs telling us that we were going to have parts on my body that we never knew we had and he was correct. When the day had finished, I was not the only one who was having the same thoughts about how to get out of this mess. Day after day, it was a little worse than the day before, it went on until the fifth week, when I had decided on a plan. If Gomer Pyle had not been discovered at this point in the sitcom called Gomer Pyle USMC, I could have been the star of this show instead. Well, in the military they use something called cadence I guess you were not suppose to understand what was being said, just do it anyway. Today, we went out onto the parade deck too drill with our rifles and old Bull Dog, senior drill instructor "called right shoulder!" That, meant he wanted us to put our rifle on our right shoulder, and of course I knew this, but instead, I put the rifle on my left shoulder. When, Bull Dog called, left shoulder, I would put it on my right shoulder. Of course, this did not set well with Bull Dog. He came running up to me with his ugly face in mine again, yelling Yankee, don't you know your right from your left?" I answered "I guess not sir!" I used that I word again and that as well did not go well with Bull Dog. I continued to carry out the same act with any instruction. When were marching and old Bull Dog called out to the battalion, to turn to the right, that meant he wanted his company to turn and march to the right, well, I again I knew the difference but, instead would go to the left, if he said about face, instead of turning around with the rest of my battalion I would keep marching forward. Then, Bull Dog asked me one day, which direction north was. I pointed toward the west. I continued these foolish and dim-witted acts up until one day Bull Dog said, I needed to see the company commander, which I did, and the commander told me," I don't think you belong in the United States Marines private." The commander asks me, "how do you felt about this," and I said, "I agree sir." His next suggestion was a discharge a discharge called honorable discharge under general conditions. I was not sure what exactly it all meant, and it really did not concern me much, as long as it said, some place that it was honorably discharged. They took me from my platoon and relocated at once to a new location on the base where I would wait for all the necessary paper work to clear. This was going to be about another three weeks. After, I had time to think about the crazy act I had just pulled off and by the time I waited another three weeks I could have finished my, twelve weeks of basic training, and went home in one of those beautiful blue uniforms I had seen sergeant Scar wearing on that day he had given me a ride. However, now I would not receive the dress blues' uniform as the Marines referrer to, instead I was going home with my civilian clothing and two hundred dollars in my pocket. What's more, I was not going to prove too my parents or most importantly myself that I was good enough for the United States Marines.

I thought about the constant drilling and yelling from old Bull Dog and Saw Shark being in my face constantly, I realized this was a part of molding all of us into a hard core Marine, and the more I thought about it, I realized that I could have adjusted too that type of training. However, the problem I was having with the Marines was not the Marines, and it was not that I could not do it, but I was going to stay here for the next thirteen weeks without a drink of alcohol and my body was trembling, for a drink. Then, my second excuse was I was going to have only three cigarettes a day and that would be by permission only. I did not believe I could live with these rules for the next thirteen weeks. I had lived by my rules most all my life, and making such an adjustment now at eighteen was unthinkable. I had settled into my new barracks with other new recruits that had as well made up the crazy act as I had or, some of the recruits had went to more extremes, such as cutting their wrist with a razor blade. A long three weeks of which appeared to have been six months was at last over and I was given my Honorable discharge and, my pay check for the month. And a bus ticket back too, Missouri. I wonder why the Marines flew me out here on two different airlines, and now I was going to take a Greyhound bus all the way back to Missouri, this would take several days by bus. However, it came time to leave the base and a corporal carried me and nine other recruits who had not made the Marines to downtown Charleston, South Carolina bus station. I knew in my gut if I had ever made a mistake in my life, this was it. I had an opportunity here to prove I could be somebody. As everyone sit waiting on his bus to arrive to take him to whatever part of the country they was going to, I wondered if anyone else was feeling the way I was right now. I could scene something inside of me wanting to pick up a phone and call the Marine base and tell them, I made a mistake, that I had just been putting on an act and if you will let me come back I will be the best Marine, the Marines has ever seen. But, not making that call I would regret for the rest of my life. I cannot count the times that I have wished I would have not played that dumb act, and made the Marine I joined up to be.

50

Back to the Street's

I had always had a weakness inside of me of wanting to put the blame of my alcoholism on someone or something else other than myself, which had already ruined my young life at eighteen years old. I blamed most of my being an alcoholic, on my mom. I always believed if my mom had only show she love me and not have drunk through her pregnancy with me would I have turned out to have been anyone different than, what I was at the time? I could not accept the fact it was my own choice and it was me that was at fault. Nevertheless, I was on a greyhound bus and was arriving in, Georgia, when the bus driver announced to everyone this stop was a transfer stop and everyone needed to get all their personal belongings and exit the bus. After finding my gate for the bus to, Missouri I was told it would be a four-hour layover until I could get my next bus to Missouri. I thought since I had a four hour wait I may as well look at the city. As I begin walking looking into all the shops that were side by side, the city seem to be jammed with people. There were signs that read totally nude bar with gorgeous young woman. Now, I started having that strong-will for a drink of alcohol again. I walk inside a tavern with all the intention of only having a couple of drinks while I waited for my next bus. The bar tender never ask me for any form of I.D.

The fifth hour passed and I was, not back at the bus station. I knew the bus was to leave after four hours so. I had missed my bus to,

Missouri. One of these gorgeous women working here had sit down too accompany me and ask if I wanted some company, and could I buy her a drink. Of course I wanted some company. I was a young eighteen year old man. Well, after a couple of drinks with her plus the ones I had already drank I was feeling pretty good, and had not notice she had put her hands onto my pocket and had taken from me of all but twenty dollars of my pay from the Marines. The only reason she never took this was because I had put this twenty dollars inside my sock for some reason. At midnight the owner of the tavern asks me to leave; he said, "I was too drunk for him to serve any more liquor to." Stumbling out the door and onto the streets of a strange city and not realizing at the time my money was all gone but twenty dollars to my name. I had somehow walked to a motel and, to tell the truth I could not remember coming here. it was the next morning when I realized I had paid fifteen-dollars for a room and I only had five dollars left. This was not even the serious part yet, I had, as well lost my bus ticket. This was indeed a problem; I did not, have enough money to pay for another bus ticket to. I was getting hungry and of course I needed another drink too begin my day there seem to be no other choice but to hitchhike at least I had some experience with this.

After I had left the hotel room my first stop was at a grocery store and when the Marines had discharged me they put me back in civilian clothes, and one of the things I still had was the old ragged coat that old hobo Joe left when he disappeared with what little money I had.

I believe once you have learned a skill, you can never put it entirely out of your mind. I walked into the store, and took a grocery basket as I had done in the past, and started up and down the aisles putting things into it, I knew I was unable to pay for but, I had to make it look as if I was shopping. When, I come to the wine, it went into the secret pocket of the old ragged jacket that once belonged to old hobo Joe. The same thing with two cans of Vienna sausages, two cans of potted meat and two packs of cigarettes. I put a quart of milk in the basket, a loaf of bread, a pack of bologna, and an onion, then when I went to the checker and she rang everything up I reached for my wallet and said, "oh no! I seem to have left my wallet at home." Once again, another checker said, "it was no problem, she would have someone put the things back", and I walked out of the store with enough supplies to last another day, or two after leaving the store I walked most of the day, which was about twenty-miles out to the interstate. I decided since I would be embarrassed for my being rejected from the Marines not to return back home, especially, since I remembered old step mom asking me back when I told dad and her I had enlisted in the marines, she remarked why would the marines want you, I thought they only wanted a few good men? I would go back to my first plans before old sergeant Scar had gave me the ride and recruited me into the Marines. I would head back northeast again too Illinois and go to work at the Del Monte cannery. I was hoping this was the canning season. It was now late December the temperatures in Georgia, was cold at nights, and more than ever with only the flimsy coat of old hobo Joe's.' As I was walking Northeast, I would need to put on two pair of jeans, along with two pairs of heavy socks and use a pair for socks for gloves to keep my hands warm. The days were also getting shorter and night was closing in quickly. I was in sight of an overpass and it seemed as good as place as any to crawl under and spend the night. As I sit under the bridge, I drink from the bottle of wine I had taken from the store that morning thinking it might warm my blood and I could get a proper- night's sleep. I must have awakened twelve times during the night with the passing traffic below me honking their horns and emergency sirens passing by, each time I woke I would reach and take a mouthful of wine too warm me for another twenty or thirty minutes. The long sleepless night at last ended and I was walking interstate again hoping my golden thumb would charm someone to stop and give me a ride, even if it was for no more than twenty, or thirty miles it would help and certainly I would be grateful for it. Some states I would no more than put my thumb into the air and someone would stop and give me a ride. I well remember when, the two old twins Frank, and Jack who was not afraid to let me in their car and took me all the way to, Missouri. Then, I was recalling another time when Old Wildman, and his wife Rose and their baby Taters picked me up and bought me the biggest chicken fried steak I had ever seen.

51

Drugs and Stolen Goods

It looked as if the people here in the south were a little hesitant about stopping for strangers on the road. I had walked almost into, Tennessee I had my golden thumb high in the air when I seen a Volkswagen bus painted with all sorts of different colored flowers from the front bumper to the back bumper. The drivers pass me and pulled over to the side of the interstate, I broke into a run with my pillowcase over my shoulder and ran to the bus waiting for me. When, I open the door, enough smoke came out that; I thought the inside of the van was on fire. Inside the bus sit a young man looking to be in his early twenties, and he said, "Jump in dude." Music from an eight track tape player with heavy metal music was playing through eight stereo speakers' the music was so loud I did know how he could concentrate on driving and listen at the same time. After, I had a minute to take a better look at this person who was caring enough to give me a ride, I seen he had long black hair that had been weaved into a long pigtail, he had earrings in both ears and tattoos that covered both of his arms and a full beard. He reached out and took my hand with a handshake I was not familiarly with when he went too twisting his hand in mine, and pulling on my thumb, I just tried doing, what he was doing.

Next, he said, "The name is Roach man, what is your tag?" I had to think for a minute about what my tag meant then I said, "Lone Wolf the name. I answered." "Lone Wolf you want to smoke a joint man, he

163

asks?" "Sure, I replied." Roach ask "where you headed to man," I said, "I'm going up north to Illinois; hope to go to work at the cannery." Roach said, "I have a better idea, why don't you come further north with me, I am going up to Michigan to work on a fruit farm up there they pay you more money than the cannery does." I thought about it only for a few minutes and said. "Sure why not." I had no place that was home for me. Roach turned off onto interstate 75 this would take us right into the state of Michigan. Roach said, "This was where most of the fruit farms were." Finally, Roach turned the stereo down to a medium level that I could recognize the sound of him talking, and I could talk without an ear shouting talk. I guess Roach forgot that he had already asks me if I wanted to smoke a joint, but he ask me again, hey man want to get high, and I said, again, "Sure, why not." Then, Roach said, "Reach behind the seat and look in the cigar box, and get a joint out." I pulled out the cigar box, put it in my lap, and open the lid, and it had about ten of the largest marijuana cigarettes I had even seen, they looked like King Edward cigars.' Roach said, "Fire one up man." I took the marijuana and lit it from a wooden match that was in the cigar box, and inhaled as much as my lungs could hold. When I released the smoke, I coughed and Roach said, "This is some first-class stuff man." 'Acapulco gold comes from the old Country down in Old Mexico."

Roach drove all day stopping only at rest stops to use the bathroom, or to stop and get gas in the old Volkswagen. He drove through Tennessee, and Kentucky we had almost come through the state of Indiana, when I could hear sirens behind us, I bent over to look in the outside mirror of the bus when I seen flashing lights. I said, "Roach I think the police are behind us and they want you to stop." Roach said, "That's that was just his luck. I have all this dope in here and a few things that are not mine; Roach said, he supposed he would be going to jail." I was watching out the mirror when I seen two police officers walk up to the bus, one on Roaches side, and another on my side. The officer took his flashlight and tapped on the window for Roach to roll down his window and the officer on my side did the same. When, Roach and I rolled the windows down as we were instructed all the smoke from the marijuana we had been smoking went rolling out of the bus it looked as if we had the bus on fire. The officers went to backing away from the bus, and swiping the air with their hands trying to clear the smoke away from them. The police officer on the drivers' side asks Roach, "Have you boys' been smoking a little wacky weed tonight?" At this point, there was not much use in lying because they knew what marijuana smelt like, and both of us answered yes. Then, the officers said, "Were going to need to search the bus." Just then, two more police cruisers pulled up one behind us and another in front of us. We were completely block even if Roach had of wanted to try and make a run for it. They put Roach in handcuffs, first then put cuffs on me. Then, after they look through the inside the old Volkswagen bus, the officer said, "You both are under arrest for illegal possession of drugs, and possession of stolen property." As it turned out old Roach had never had plans of going up north too work, but too sell fifty pounds of marijuana and twenty stolen car stereos. After, we were taken to a jail in Indiana they put Roach in one room, and me in another. I was asks if I wanted a cup of coffee, and the detective started asking a lot of questions, such as, how long had I known Roach, where did we take the stereos from, who did we buy the marijuana from, all of which I had no idea. I answered the detective and said, "I had only known Roach since he picked me up back in Georgia." The detective would leave the room for a while then return. After making about fifteen trips in and out of the room, the detective told me. "Your friend Roach tells us that the two of you have been friends for the past two years, and that the two of you make this trip on a regular basis to come up north, and sell marijuana and stolen goods that both of you break into places and take." He says the two of you are associates together.

I had no idea at the time, but Roach was told if he would tell the detective what they wanted to hear that he would get a lighter sentence, so he became a song bird and made up the story about my being acquainted with him, and the detective believed him. I was arrested and charged for breaking and entering of a building. Roach took the rap for the dope, and for having his part to do with the stolen merchandise. I was now sitting in jail for charges I knew nothing about because there was stolen merchandise from both the state of Indiana and Michigan I had a choice when I went before the Judge to sign extradition papers for me to go from Indiana to Michigan to spend my time".

After talking with some of the prisoners in the holding cell here in Indiana, everyone said, Michigan had a better jail, and I would be better off too sign extradition papers and go there for my trial. The following morning I ask too sign these extradition papers. Then, a detective put me in an unmarked car and transferred me too a Michigan county jail. After, I had been booked, finger printed, mug shots taken, they gave me my new clothes, a bright green shirt, and pants to match, both the shirt and the pants three people my size could have fit in them, sewed on the back of the xxx large shirt in big black bold letters was the name of the county jail. Then, an old man called the jailer, or I would learn later the prisoners referred to him as the old turnkey, who look as if he needed too, have retired about twenty years earlier took me up a flight of steps. At the top of the steps was a long hallway. I would have estimated it to be about a 100 feet long and about twelve feet wide. On both sides of the hall were steel doors spaced about every ten feet from the other. Through each door was a cellblock; there were four cellblocks on both sides of the hall. My cellblock I would be living in for however much time the Judge of Michigan determined would be in cellblock C. However, the odd thing about my coming here was that as soon as the prisoners heard the rattle of the old jailer's key coming down the hall they yelled from inside the cellblocks, "Hey, is that you Lone Wolf", the prisoners had already got word I was coming, and that I was using the alias name of Lone Wolf. This, of course was something old Roach had made up and, told the police that his alias name was Hays and that I went by the name of Lone Wolf, the prisoners knew where I was arrested, why I was arrested, and more about me than I knew of myself. The old tall slim jailer looked as if he walked fast, it would put him out of breath, and after we reached the top of the stairs I stopped to look back down the flight of stairs just as we had entered the long hallway. I thought if I turned and ran back down the stairs the old man was not wearing a gun, I could reach the bottom and break out before he knew what had happen. However, the thought did not stay with me long, as I remembered there was a sergeant's desk at the foot of the stairs, and he was, wearing a gun. My body felt limp as the old turnkey put the key into cellblock C, and opened the big steel door. Just as I step through the door I noticed to my right was a shower with no curtain, next to the shower was the toilet just sitting in the open with no privacy. Then, to my left was a row of steel bunk beds. There were four beds bunk beds an eight prisoner cell block. Then, straight in front of me from the steel door I had come through was a set of bars that ran ten feet in length along another hall that had steel doors at either end of that, our eating table was sitting next to the bars. My cellblock had three other prisoners that I would be sharing the same shower and toilet without any privacy.

The first prisoner walked over to me and said, "Welcome to cellblock C. Lone Wolf, my name is Runt, this here is Vampire, and this one we call Peeps." Well, I could see why everyone called him the Runt, as he was a little guy, no bigger than a good size jack rabbit, and was about the same age as I was. Runt was in here for armed robbery his first offence. Peeps, he was an older man in his fifties, in jail for being a peeping Tom. Next was the Vampire. Vampire was in here for biting some ones finger off in a fight. Vampire and I had to have an understanding with each other before I even settled in. Vampire was a strange looking person with long stringy black hair, his eyes were as black as the midnight and looked like marbles and he had odd- pointed teeth. Vampire walked up to me and said, "Lone Wolf, I am going to come to your bunk tonight after you fall asleep, and suck all the blood from your body." I considered this as good a time as any to set things straight with Mr. Vampire, and I said, "If you come even within a foot of my bunk tonight, or any other time Vampire, I will pull your eyeballs out of your ugly head and feed them to you." "If you were vampire, why haven't you turned yourself into a bat and flew out of here?" Runt and old Peep went to laughing and said, "Vampire, I believe Lone Wolf would do just that." Then, old Vampire said, "Oh Lone Wolf, I was only having some fun." "Ok, I said, you had your fun, so long as we know where we both stand with each other because I am very serious."

After old Vampire said the things he had, I learned from that night to sleep with one eye closed and the other eye open. I learned this way of sleep so well that I could actually sleep with one eye closed, and at the same time know what was going on around me. "Welcomed to your new home Runt said, you might as well take the bottom bunk next the bars." "Yea, I agreed it looked good enough to me." Then, after making my bed with clean bed clothes I lay down on my bunk and wondered how I could have got myself into so much trouble. Runt, asks me if I would like to play, a game of cards with them, a game called spades as it took four people to play the game. I said, "Maybe later, but for now, I need to just lay here and think." I must have had more than a million thoughts running through my head on how to get out of here. Maybe, I could write a letter to the Governor of the state of Michigan, explain to him my side of the story, and plead my case before him and maybe, he would give me a pardon. Maybe, he could somehow get me back into the Marines. I would go at once. Maybe, I should address a letter to the congressional representatives. Then, I thought about just breaking out and running for the border of Canada. I wouldn't think Michigan would extradite me from Canada on a burglary charge. Lastly there was always the one thing which granny taught me as a child growing up, and that was to pray. However, I had not up until now seen one prayer that had ever work for me, unless you counted all the times, some of the strange things that happen with some of the people who had helped me, and then it turned out that these people were never there. I wanted to cry, but that was something I had learned that never at least for me helped? I was told that real men did not cry. It was true that crying before never fixed any of the problems I had.

168

If I cried from the inside no one would ever know it, and maybe, it would make me feel better.

Today was a Friday and every Friday for the evening meal, the jail was supplied by a local restaurant all the fish the prisoners could eat, with this came all the trimmings and boy did I ever enjoy fish..

The meal had.

Fried catfish,

Cole slaw,

Potato salad,

Hush, puppies,

Ice tea,

With food such as this, this might not turn out to be so bad after all it look as if at least I was going to eat very well. The following morning around seven O'clock, I could hear the turnkey coming down the hall with one of the trustee pushing the cart of food. Everyone in the cell lined up in front of the steel door and waited until the turnkey opened a small door in the big steel door called a bean hole. The bean hole was about eighteen inches in length and about eight inches wide just enough to push our food trays through it.

For breakfast here on my first day consisted of.

One scramble egg,

A piece of bacon,

A piece of toast with grape jelly,

Coffee

The jailer brought word to me that I would see the Judge on Monday for my trial, I kept thinking about what trial? Roach set me up in order to get time knocked off his sentience. However, I had no way to prove it. Another full day had come and gone and the boys here in cellblock C had talked me into playing card games with them, and I would learn from this morning to play well, or go without food. Since we had no money to play with, we made bets with our meals. Whoever, was playing partners would bet with one of their three meals for the day, sometimes we would bet our breakfast that we had the better hand, other times we might bet either the noon meal or the evening meal. After you lost all three meals for the day, you learn how to bet your hand or you opt out of the game altogether. The following Monday arrived much sooner that I had wanted it to, my court appointed attorney had brief me on what would take place in the Judges courtroom. The Judge "asks my attorney how does your client plea"? "My client wishes to plead guilty your honor" even though my attorney believed me when I told him I had been set up. He said the jurors would not buy it.

52

Sentenced to One Year

The Old Judge said, to my attorney, "I have been looking over this young man's police files from his youth, and it appears not to have been very bad." The Judge asks my attorney and me to stand. The Judge said," I have decided to drop felony charges against this client and reduce it to a circuit court misdemeanor." "I am sentencing the defendant too one year in the county jail." "Now, Mr. Lone Wolf as you prefer to be called, I trust from here on you will choose to keep better company, because this court could have found you guilty of a felony, which carries a maximum of ten years in the state penitentiary here in the state of Michigan." Then, the Judge to said, "Courts adjourn." "He told the deputy too take the prisoner into custody." At least I knew the fate of it all, and that was I was going to be here for the next twelve months. I was thinking what a fool I had been when I could have completed only thirteen -weeks of basic training with the Marines and been finished with the hardest part other than the part maybe being sent to Viet Nam. However, that was past, and I had to live for today. Someone had left a Bible on the foot of my bed in my cell and since, I had nothing to do most days but play cards, checkers, or read magazines, I knew of no harm it could hurt to occasionally pick this book up and read from time to time.

Surprisingly as it was the first book I turned to was the book of: {Isaiah 54:17 KING JAMES No weapons that is formed against thee shall prosper; and every tongue that shall rise against thee in judgment; thou shall condemn. This is the heritage of the servant of the LORD, and their righteousness is of me, says' the LORD}. My next page to read was in the book of Exodus 20:15 KING JAMES} Thou shall not steal. This was one of GODS own commandants, and I had broken that one many time before, but of course I had broken near everyone of the other nine commandants as well, except murder. How many times was GOD going to keep forgiving me, or had HE already stopped forgiving me and was just plain fed up with me and had washed his hands with me. Every time I would have a question in my mind, the place to look in the Bible would just seem to let my fingers thumb through the pages until I found the answer I was looking at the answer.

53

My Threat to Kill the Jailer

As, I was reading I had turn to the book of. Matthew: 18:21:22 {KING JAMES}. Then, came Peter to HIM, and said, LORD, how oft shall my brother sin against me, and I forgive him? Till seven times? JESUS and ask, "LORD, how many times shall I forgive my brother when he sins against me? JESUS said, Up to seventy times seven? 22. JESUS saith unto him, I say not unto thee, until seven times but, until seventy times seven.

I learned the meaning of this was that GOD had no number of times.' I could come to HIM and ask for HIS forgiveness for as many times as needed to repent, as long as I was completely remorseful. My second month behind these walls, and bars, and I could now imagine I could not spend another day locked in here? I was spending most of the nights sleepless, trying to come up with a plan that would get me out of here. I needed a drink of alcohol so badly I would have broken another commandment of the Bible and that was I thought I might even kill a man for a drink?

Then, one day from almost out of nowhere a first-rate plan come to me. It was almost the prefect plan too. The three of us could nourish our craving for an alcohol drink. I was going to manufacture our very own homemade wine here in our cell block C. With the help of a trustee too sneak me an empty gallon milk jug, five pounds of sugar, and the other three prisoners would save their apple juice, and orange juice from our breakfast. We mixed all this together and hide it out of sight under my bunk for the next three weeks. When, we pulled the jug out from under our bunk, the sugar had fermented the Juice and we had instant homemade apple and orange juice wine. As the three of us sat here in our cell we were the happiest prisoners in all the eight cell blocks here.

The wine took a quick effect and we were all four drunk, singing and having a cheerful good time

We of course forgot that just outside the bars were speakers which we could both speak to the desk sergeant as well he could hear everything which was said, inside our cell block. Of course it did not take long for the downstairs desk sergeant to hear the prisoners in our cell block were exceptionally happy about something today. Our happiness had been transmitted to the speaker on the sergeant's desk three deputies came to the cell block C, to investigate what our happiness was about, they immediately learned what had made the four of us so happy. Needless to say our homemade booze was found and the little of which was left they commandeer. Of course not one of us accepted reasonability of being the one who thought up the plan? For just a short time it wasn't so bad being a prisoner but, now the booze was gone and, I wanted and needed more. Once again, I went back trying think about how to make my escape from here. I thought about the poor old frail old turnkey, and how easy he would be to do away with. I thought he would be easy enough for me to take, I could hold him as a hostage for the keys? Yes, that was my plan to break out one final thought though would the other three prisoners going to escape with me? The three said yes, we will all go together. The following morning after breakfast trays had been taken up the old turnkey would always come back down the hall on the other side to passing out bath soap and magazines. Just as he opened the big steel door that came into the hall beside our cellblock, I reached my arm through the bars and wrapped my arm around his neck pulling him up close to the bars. I said, "Old man, listen to me, this job is surely not worth you losing your life over, now you reach down and give me the keys to this cell block." Well, in my plans I had not imagine the old man too be so stubborn and such a fool. He said, "Young Lone Wolf." I have lived a long life and all my family has all died and there is no place that I had rather be than too be with the LORD and my family, so if you feel you must take my life then you will, but I am not giving you the key." I could not believe this old man would make a decision to make such a choice that he would risk losing his live for this job? The old turnkey said, "Son, I don't believe, you are a killer, and I don't think you want to spend the rest of your life in prison, when you can be out of here in a year." He ended with saying, if you will turn me loose this will never go any further than just between us.

My plan had been unsuccessful I slowly loosen my death grip I had around the old man's throat and he walked off, and from that day forward, and everyday he treated me with the respect as if nothing had ever happened. As well, he kept true to his word by not saying anything to anyone of this incident. I felt now that I had turned into some kind of monster, what had happen to the GODLY training I had been taught in my youth by my grandparents? Where had I gone wrong?

54

Second Attempt to Escape

After my failed attempt to actually take another humans life today I could not picture how I could have turned into such an animal I had not been brought this way. Maybe, it was being locked up like an animal that I was acting as an animal. However, suddenly I would have another bright idea for my escape and still another shot at freedom. I took all my clothes and got into the shower and after getting wet; I stepped out of the shower and lay down on the floor beating myself with my fist in the ribs causing a big blue burse to appear. "I told Runt, Vampire, and old Peeper to start yelling as loud as they could for help!"

Now the noise from the prisoners reached downstairs over the intercom, the sergeant come over the intercom, and asks what is wrong in cell black C?, " Runt, answered, Lone Wolf has fallen getting out of the shower and is hurt really bad." It only took a couple of minutes and, two officers come into our cell block and seen me lying there with a horrible looking burse on my side and they called for an ambulance to carry me away to the emergency room. After a two- mile ride in an ambulance screaming with sirens to the emergency room, I thought this plan was working. After, I had an

Evaluation of my injuries the emergency room nurses moved me to the x-ray room, leaving two deputies that followed the ambulance sitting outside in the waiting room. I carefully got up, pulled off the hospital gown, and hanging on the back of the closed door was a doctors lab jacket, how much easier could this be I thought. I will just walk out and slide through a side door with this doctor's lab jacket on and no one will notice me as a patient, nor as the prisoner was.

However once again, I had not thought my plan through careful enough, I gently, open the door and there stood the two deputies from the jail one on each side of the door both deputies were armed. I gently closed the door back and removed the doctor's lab jacket and put my hospital gown back on, and waited for the doctor to come back with my x-ray report. After about an hour of waiting, a doctor walked into the treatment room with my chart. The doctor knowing I was from the county jail stuck out his hand to shake mine and to introduce himself. Then, the doctor with a whisper in his voice said, "I don't want the two officers outside the room hear us." However, he said. "I know what you were going to try to do tonight, the bruise you have is superficial, so put this thought of escaping out of your mind, because it want, work trust me he said." He continued, "I won't say anything about this phony injury you have here tonight, if you promise to go back to the county with the deputies without any trouble, is this a deal he asks?" "Yes, it's a deal doctor, I replied." The doctor said, "Ok." "I am going ahead and prescribe a mild pain reliever to make this look good." "Remember, don't try this one again' the doctor said, as he walked back out the door". After the doctor left the room, I dressed back into my county clothes and the two officers returned me too the county jail, back too cellblock C. After the big steel door open and I walked back inside my cellblock Runt, Vampire, and old Peeper said, "We never thought we would ever seen you again, Lone Wolf, we just knew you had this one pulled off?" And, you were on your way to Canada. Twice now, I had gotten away with two serious tries of escape and both times unsuccessful.

The next ten months were as if it was like in the {book of Joshua 10:13. In addition, the sun stood still, and the moon stayed, until the nations took vengeance upon their enemies. So, the sun stood in the midst the heavens and did not hasten to go down for about a whole day.}

55

I'm a Trustee

Ten months and fifteen-days, if my homemade calendar was correct
since I had come to cell block C. Today the old turnkey and a deputy
from downstairs come too our cell block and ask for Runt and me too
collect our belongings and come go with them. Now, curiosity had
filled me? Had the Judge decided to free us for good behavior after all,
no one knew or, was suppose to have known about the two episodes I
had tried pulling off in trying to break out. However, we collected our
personal things such as our toothbrush, toothpaste a comb a clean suit
of clothes. After walking down the same stairs I had walked up just
over ten months ago it felt like freedom. Next, we were taken into the
sheriffs', office and Runt and I were asks if we would like to serve as
trustees at the jail? I imagined at first that, I was going too awake and
this was only a dream. The sheriff asks us, "Did we think we could
carry out these assignments?" We both agreed that we could do this.
The old Turnkey walked Runt and I to the back of the jail, here was
a large cell with two beds, and the door would be left unlocked at all
times, we could come in and go out, as we pleased so long as we had
all of our assigned work done. Our work assignments were much the
same every day, sweep, and mop all the offices and halls, clean all the
restrooms take out and empty the trash. Go with the old Turnkey too
deliver food trays too the prisoners in the cellblocks, and when a patrol
car come into the garage dirty that we wash it.

Our first day as trustees' of the jail, and having more freedom than either of us would have ever though. Having all this freedom helped lift our self-esteem too some level. However, it was still jail, and jail, was jail.

We had even become so trusted in our position that Runt and I had talked the sheriff and he had agreed to let us wear plain white tee shirts, in place of the old green tee shirts with the counties name on the back that were issued to all trustees' too wear. We were trusted as if we were as anyone else, still we were limited to where we could go, and had a boundary of one hundred-feet of the counties property. There was no pay for our being a jail trustees' however, if one of the officers' or an office worker should bring their personal vehicle in and asks us to wash and clean it they could at their judgment pay us what they valued the worth too be. Sometime, the pay was one-dollar and up too as much as three dollars, depending on who the car belonged too.

Since, there was nothing to buy at the jail Runt other than on conversary days when we could buy tobacco personal hygiene items. Runt and I had saved a good bit of money. As a matter of fact in our first month as trustee's the both of us together had saved a total of twenty-two dollars each, all for washing personal cars of the staff here at the county jail. We had been washing one of the deputy's patrol cars when from somewhere I took that craving for an alcohol drink again. It had been much too long since I had any alcohol other than the homemade wine we brewed, and listening to my inner self-saying sneak off and go get a bottle of booze, no one will ever know. You know, I am not sure if this was something from my inner self or maybe, it was the devil telling me this thing's knowing I was going to get caught. Now, getting caught meant that for the next at minimum would be serving thirty years not in the county jail but, the state prison. Ten years for the offence I was here for, then jail break and last grand thief auto. What a mistake I was willing to take all for a drink of the devils poison alcohol. The more I kept having this conversation with myself, the more cheering the voices' in my head became. I ask Runt if he ever thought of having a drink. His answer back was he wants a drink so bad just then, that he would be willing to jeopardize the position of being a trustee for a drink. I reckon old Runt was just the same as me an full fledge alcoholic

There it was it must have been a sign for us as we were having the same gut feelings about having a drink. The liquor store was only seven blocks away from the county jail, and the proprietor there had never before seen Runt or, I so he wasn't likely to know we were prisoner from the county jail?

With our white tee shirts on we looked no different from anyone else. Then, in our third week of working as a trustee of the jail, the evening desk sergeant came to work for his three to eleven shifts, and pulled his brand new cougar into the county garage and asks Runt and I too wash and clean it up for him. He said, 'if we did a good job, there would be a bonus for you two. This was what we had both waited for. Then, after we had done what we thought was a professional job of cleaning the deputy's cruiser and it look to us sprinkling clean. Runt, and I were sitting in the officers' personal car, me behind the wheel and Runt in the passenger seat, we had the stereo up and we where make believing the car was my car. The next memory I had was after coming out of my make believe world I was in, was maybe, this was a trap to actually test our honesty, it all seemed too easy.

I started the cougar and put it in reverse and the two of us where on our way toward seven blocks to the liquor store. For just a short time, I felt as if the car actually belongs to me. I drove up in front of the liquor store next to the curb, Runt and I selected getting vodka because it had less of a smell than bourbon. Then, Runt got out of the car with his plan white tee shirt and green pants, he looked too be as any average citizen in the town. Within about five minutes Runt came out of the liquor store carrying a brown paper bag with a fifth of Smirnoff vodka. Then, before we had pulled away from the liquor store too head back to the jail before, the desk sergeant might walk out too see how we were coming alone, with cleaning his car we both took a turn of tipping the bottle of vodka up and having a large mouth full. I recall the burn as it emptied into my stomach.

Then, I made a wide u-turn in the road and was on my way back to put the car back in the exact place the sergeant had parked it. Two and a half blocks away from the liquor store and I heard more sirens than I had in my entire life, as I look into the rear view mirror, and there was so many lights flashing it look as if the state of Michigan were called to retrieve the desk sergeants, car my heart drop from my chest to my stomach. I look over at Runt and said, "Hand me the bottle, I need another drink before they take us back." I knew our next home would be in the state penitentiary for at least ten years? I pulled over against the curb and took in a deep breath of the fresh cold air, as I knew it would be a very long time before I would breathe fresh air again. Then, if there was ever such a thing as a miracle, we had one this afternoon, we sat, and watched as each of the emergency vehicles passed us by, two fire trucks, two ambulances' three police cars' not one had paid any attention that there was two prisoners from the county jail sitting here in a stolen vehicle with a fifth of vodka. I let out the air I had been holding in my lungs, and without any delay, I drove into the county jail garage, and parked the car. Before, we had left out for the liquor store, we had started washing one of the deputy sheriffs; cursers and we had completed only one side of the car. After, we had return and knew we were safe; we put our vodka in a safe place so one would find it. However, we had forgotten about washing the other half of the car. Runt and I had free liberty too go to the officers, lounge, and Runt walked right pass the desk sergeant's office, went into the lounge, and walked back with two orange soda pops.

However, as much luck as we had up until now with stealing the deputy's car our luck was about to run out. The officer who left the cruiser too be washed come back to the trustees' living quarters and found that both Runt and I were passed out drunk. The evidence was sitting there in plain sight as we had forgotten to hide the bottle of vodka. The officer said nothing about the vodka he asks, "Why is my car not finished?" Well, I stood up losing my balance, falling back onto the cot and said, "Man we did wash your car it's clean as a whistle."

"Oh, is it now Mr. Lone Wolf was his reply?" "Yea, we washed it more than, an hours ago I replied." "Ok lets the three of us walk out here and see the clean car you say you did." Well, Runt was trying as much as I was too hide being drunk, he even pushed the bottle of vodka under the bed as we walked out thinking the officer had not noticed it sitting there. The officer led the way down the hall with Runt and I trying to hold up the wall as we followed, and when he opened the door that led out into the garage there sit the curser as clean as a whistle, just as I had told him. "You see sir; I told you we washed it?! Then, he walked around to the other side of the car and told both Runt and I too come.

Well, to our shock the other side of the car had not soap or water on it? We tried to act as if we had no clue why this mysterious thing could have happen? The officer's next question was can you explain this?" "Yes, sir," I can sir, I said." I believe one of the other officers must have taken the car sir, and got it dirty, but we will take care of it right away sir. Sadly, the officer did not believe a word of my story. I assured him that we would take care of this at once I was praying that I could sidetrack him away from going back to our living quarters too where the bottle that was sitting.

As Runt and I began, washing the right side of the car the officer said, "I don't know how you pulled this all off, and I don't want to know, however it better not happen again, you know what I mean boys?" We both said, "Yes sir, we understand, it want happen again," and that was all there was to it. The, deputy said, "Now let's go back and get the vodka!" after getting what was left in our bottle and watching him step too the side of the building, and watching as the last drop of our long waited drink was poured onto the ground.

56

Early Release for Good Behavior

Nine months of being incarcerated at the Michigan county jail the day had at last come which I expected would never come at least for me? Runt and I had both somehow earned an early release from our imprisonment and to our duties as the jails trustees and for all things, our good behavior.

Somehow, we had earned the title of role model prisoner our performance were satisfying to the sheriff; and we were given a four week early release. We both stood before the Judge once more and listen to the requirements of our probation which we would be on for the next two years. If we were in any trouble within those next two years it was not just back to county jail but, to the Michigan state penitentiary. We were in no way too have in our possession, or be are associated with anyone with drugs, alcohol or weapons? We would work and pay restitution to the state of Michigan, during two year probation. If we come before the court with any charges against us within the next two years' we would serve the two years in the Michigan, state penitentiary. We both agreed that we could do everything the Judge explained to the both of us. At least I believed I could do all except the one about the alcohol. I could not go without a drink for two years. However, I was not going to let the Judge know that this was imposable. Runt and I agreed to the conditions of our liberty and the Judge confirmed us free to go. The first thing on the list, we had to do, was report to a probation officer called Hunter. Hunter was of course only a nick name given to him because of his job. He loved his job so much that it brought him great pleasure to hunt down convicts that took it upon themselves to skip out on their probation agreement. Hunter said, "I will hunt you down to the end of the earth if I have to." Well, Hunter said, "I am going to carry the two of you out too an orchard and you both have jobs waiting when you get there." Then, I said, well "I have never worked on an orchard sir." I have never before seen an orchard, what will I be doing?" Hunter replied quickly and said, "There is nothing too no, what there is to know you will learn, and you will work." After signing more papers for our conditions of release it all took about an hour.

57

Working on the Orchard

It was a little disappointing that, Runt and I would not be working on the same farm. As we turned, off a gravel road and drove up a hill on a dirt road with a beautiful white picket fence which looked to have extended as far as the eye could see? Then, as we parked in front of a huge old white two- story house. The owner of the orchard a medium sized man of about fifty years in age come out too meet us. Hunter already knew him by bring other probationers here in the past. Nevertheless, after the orchards owner walked up to the car, and presented himself too me and said, my name is, D.I. I got this name because I spent twenty- two years in the Marines as a drill instructor. Well, this was not good news to me because, I could never let old D.I, know that I had once been in the Marines for such a short time, above all what I had done too get my discharged.

However, Hunter said, "I will be leaving you now and I will see you in my office in one, month." "Remember, you better be there!" Then, old D.I said, "well come along with me, and I would show you your living quarters." Just outside the shack were I would be staying was a woodpile about twenty-foot long and about four-feet high and about two-feet wide. The place I would be staying in had one room with an old feather bed like the one my granny had when I was growing up at home. In one corner was an old potbellied stove, it too looked like the one pa and granny had, on the other wall was a sink too wash dishes, a cook stove, and a refrigerator. D.I said; "I will advance you enough money until payday so you can buy a two-week supply of food." Next, we walked out of the little cottage and up a small hill, and here was a grove of young tree's some had small fruit on them and others did not. Every few feet under the young trees was this round looking pot with a stovepipe coming out of it? D.I told me, "these pots, are called smudge pots and your job for twelve hours beginning at midnight is too walk through the grove every two hours making sure that all these pots have kerosene in them and if they run out, you will refill them, or if the strong north winds that almost always was blowing, should blow any of them out I would re- light them at once, so that the young trees did not freeze." He added this is very important, these tree are my living if they freeze I lose profit.

After we had walked through what seemed like about three hundred trees. D.I and I walked back to the cottage and he took me too buy my two week supply of grocery as he promised. It would soon be Christmas, and I wondered what a single man with little cooking experience as I had could buy and fix to celebrate the occasion of this Christmas. The first thing I picked up was a canned ham the directions said; you can eat it right from the can, So, I put this into my basket, I remembered granny always had cranberries, so one can would do for me, then I remembered granny always had nuts, a package of peanuts, so I choose some of this as well. That should do for this Christmas dinner.

As I passed the wine cooler, my mouth could almost taste the wine, I wanted so bad to put a bottle into my basket but old D.I was standing right beside me watching everything I selected.

At last, my shopping was finished. I had enough food to last until payday. Then, I would come back later by myself, even if I had to walk the three miles here. Michigan had to be the coldest place I had ever been before. My only coat I had was the old ragged coat which old hobo Joe left behind, and I had carried it around all this time. For the most part of the day when, I was not sleeping I would sit listening to the wind blowing outside the little cottage which made ghostly sounds as if someone was in great pain. When the wind was blowing making these ghostly sounds it reminded me of the time when I was a small boy at granny's', and I had come past the old building with the old wooden coffin and I had heard the same sound from the wind. My midnight shift to start arrived sooner than I wanted; it was midnight, time for my first walking, through the orchard. When I opened the door, four inches of fresh snow had covered the ground. I pulled up the collar of my old coat around my neck and wore a pair of socks for my mittens on my hands. I picked up the can with the kerosene which sit next to the wood pile and began my vigorously walk through the snow. I clumsily begin to climb up a slope to the grove, and made my first walk through the orchard. Some of the pots needed refilled with kerosene, while others needed only relit from having the wind which was gusting at twenty-mile per hour blow them out.

My walk took thirty-minutes, and I was back at the cottage huddle close to the potbellied stove as a magnet stuck to a piece of metal. Drinking hot coco and taking in all the warmth I could before my next two hours arrived and it would be time again too return out into this arctic coldness. I figured that with going out every two hours, I would have to go out into this bitter cold six times during my twelve-hour shift. I could not help but wonder if the devil and all his demons had entered into me at the time of my conception, and it would have been best for me, if mom would have just aborted her pregnancy with me, and I had not been born at all? Looking back on my life it would appear that nothing but evil things had happen to me. I could not explain, what made me do some of the things I had done. I wondered if this was true how I would get these demons out of me. I often sit here with thoughts, going back to times past trying to remember of something that was good, I could not remember anything? It was now time to wrap up again and make another thirty-minute walk through the orchard. Before leaving out, I walked out to the wood –pile and carried several sticks of wood back in and put them into the potbellied stove, so after the walk I would have a cozy and warm cottage to come to. Once again, I picked up the kerosene can and headed up the hill to the orchard grove. The wind had begun to blow with even more of a gust than before. Here in this part of Michigan the wind always seem to come down from the Canadian border.

This time nearly all the smudge pots needed to be re- light as the wind had blown nearly everyone of then out. Walking back to the cottage I thought how much easier this would be on me if I only had a bottle of something to drink as in a bottle of Morgan David wine, or a bottle of vodka. However, after returning from the second walk it was now two-thirty a.m. I still had a long night and the only thing I could look forward too was twelve-noon when someone else would take over for the next twelve hours, and I could crawl into the feather bed with the covers pulled up over my head and sleep. Then, at last, I had finished my first two weeks and it was payday, old DI had come around at eleven thirty that morning with my first paycheck minus the two weeks he had advanced me. He offered to take me to the store to buy my groceries but I explained I would rather walk the two miles into town. What I wanted was not have him looking over my shoulders so that I could buy a bottle of wine.

58

Runts 1960 Chevrolet

After I had put on several layers of clothing I was standing by the old potbellied stove.

I heard someone honk a horn outside my cottage door, wow, I told him I wanted to walk. When, I open the door to yell wait a minute, I notice it was not old DI at all, but instead my old friend Runt. There sit Runt in one of the cleanest and prettiest 1960, Chevrolet I had ever seen.

Runt rolled down his side window and said, "well get yourself in and, let's blow this place." I turned and grabbed a cup of coffee I had been drinking and a rolled up a blanket from the foot of my bed just in case we were to become stranded. It turned out Runts boss had this 60 Chevy just sitting in an old barn and he told Runt if he wanted it, he would take a little out of each of his paycheck until he paid only one hundred dollars for it. I guess the two of us thought we had died and went to a different place, because this was more like living now, a warm car, a full tank of gas, a paycheck, and our first stop oh yea the liquor. This was the first time Runt and I had seen each other since old Hunter had brought the two of out here from his office, so we had plenty to tell each other. After leaving the liquor store with a fifth of vodka, a half- gallon of wine, a fifth of Yellowstone whiskey, and a carton of cigarettes we had everything we needed to forget that we were in the coldest part of the world, at least it seem that way. Runt and I drove around the entire day, we had been up and down every country road we could find, in fact, the sun was quickly vanishing in the west and, we had no idea where we were, and furthermore we did not seem to care.

By the time the sun had completely set in the West. The old car had stopped and with either of us having any knowledge about the mechanics of an automobile other than putting it into the proper gear we were bewildered as to why the car would not move. The gas gauge showed we still had plenty of fuel in the cars tank, the car had been running like a fine tuned automobile, and then it just stopped. It was completely dark now and we had no clue as to where we were at. I was glad I had brought along the blanket I had picked up before coming out of the cottage. The weather report on the radio said, to expect temperatures to be in the minus degrees tonight, and after the last of the warm heat from the cars heater left, the forecast seemed to be correct. However, having put on the added clothing before leaving my little cottage and with a warm wool blanket I brought along, the old Chevy was warm and toasty; at least we would not freeze. I was awake the next morning by the warmth of the east sun coming through the passenger window, I strained to partly, open my eyes to see where the car had stalled during the night and we were in grave danger. After, I had fully open, my eyes, I said, "oh my stars, my words awaken Runt and he asks, "don't tell me, the law is here," No I said, "It is not as good as that." "What could be worse than having the police pick us up, Runt replied." Well I said, "We need to get out of the car and push it from where we are sitting." Then, after Runt opened his eyes and seen what I was looking at, he jumped out of the driver's side of the car as if he had been shot from a cannon. Then, we pushed the car about fifty-feet away from the railroad track that we had been sitting on through the night. We had no more than pushed the car from the train tracks that a fast moving freight train was barreling down the tracks. The engineer on the train gave a long blow of warning toward us as he passed by. I thought about what if, this train had passed by during the night while we had been passed out?

It looks as if the train was traveling at around fifty miles per hour. It would have been for sure we would not have ever known what happen? This brought back a memory of the time when, I was nine years old and my friend Jack Rabbit had been playing on an old box car and it had been hooked up to an engine that begin togging away and we were two young hobos. I was in a very bad way of needing a drink, as old Joe would have called it, the hair of the dog. The first bottle I picked up was just an empty wine bottle, we had drank every last drop of it, next I came across the vodka bottle the same thing not one drop left, surely I thought we had some of the whiskey left, but when I located the Yellowstone bottle it was the same thing, every last drop gone. I had to have a drink maybe, there was something in the glove compartment. There was something in the glove compartment, a half bottle of rubbing alcohol. I had never been so desperate, but my body was shaking out of control I turned the lid to open the bottle and after putting the bottle to my lips I turned the bottle up and swallowed about a tablespoon full, as the burn from the raw alcohol started at my lips, and it burn from my tongue down to the empty pit of my stomach was more than I could endure. The raw rubbing alcohol immediately caused me to vomit. Runt had crawl back into the car and we were both trembling from needing a drink of alcohol and from the frigid temperatures.

I had been told that being an alcoholic was a disease, somehow I can't concur with this, I believe it is a choice, I could not understand how I could have become an alcoholic at such a young age?

Without thinking, I reached over to turn the radio own and to my astonishment, it worked. The first thing I heard was a man preaching about everyone going to burn if they did repent of their sins. Well, this was not something I had any concern about this morning so I turned the channel to another station. It there was the same thing, just a different preacher, he too was telling everyone they had better get their live straighten, out and repent of their sins or they was going straight to eternal fire. So, I change the station once more. Each time I changed the station it was the same thing, another preacher telling everyone to change his or her lives, because GOD was coming back soon. Well, I decided I may was well listen, since every station I turned to was a preacher. The more the preacher began to talk about sin and how JESUS came over two thousand years and died for everyone and for every sin we were all guilty of I became a little more interested and took concern to listen to see if there might be something which I might need to hear. He talked about a scripture in Luke 23:39:43 {KING JAMES} and CHRIST, save you and us 40 But the other answering rebuked him, saying, dost thou fear GOD, seeing thou art in the same condemnation? 41. And we indeed justly; for we receive the due reward of our deeds: but this man has done nothing amiss. 42. And he said unto the LORD remember me when thou cometh into thy KINGDOM. 43. And JESUS said unto thee, Today shall thou are with me in paradise. By the time the preacher had finished I had said, a silent prayer and ask that I not be left behind should the LORD returned. I just wasn't sure if however, he had heard me since I did not say it audibly? By now, the sun was at high noon and Runt and I decided to try and, start the old car once again. Runt pushed in the clutch and turned the switch and the first try the old car fired up sounding as sweet as it did before it had stopped.

Now, if we could only find our way out. We both was certain of one thing and this was that either one of us had a job at the orchard any more. I was supposed to have been at work the night before at midnight, and so was Runt, the temperatures had dropped below freezing during the night and I might picture the rancher lost many young trees. The want inside of my body for a drink of alcohol was to the point I was eager to do just about anything to get a drink. I ask Runt to pull into the first place that was open on this now Sunday, afternoon so we could ask where we could buy a bottle of cheap wine. No, sooner than I had spoken this, I said to Runt, just ahead was a little county store out in the middle of the what seem to be no place. Runt pulled the old Chevy up to the front door and I got out and went inside. After acknowledging, the store sold beer and wine I bought a bottle of Morgan David. I ask the old woman clerk how to get back on the road that would, led us back to where we need to be. We had driven about fifteen-miles on a wrong turn off, and had to turn around and go back, there was no hurry in our returning, it was obvious either of us had a job, this much we were sure. Therefore, we would just relax and listen to the radio, and sip from the jug of wonderful wine.

59

Ordered Off the Property

I was thinking about what was going to happen as soon as Hunter got the word we had not showed up for work, and we had both failed to report to Hunter? This all look as if we had skip bail to Hunter. I remembered Hunter telling us when he was assigned to be our probation officer, if he had to come looking for, us he would look even to the ends of the earth until he found us? Hunter was another one of those types of people as the old Bull Dog the drill instructor had told me during my short stay in the United States Marine Corps, that if needed be he would bring me back in a body bag if I should decide to go AWOL. At last, we had made it to Runts place of work first and if my boss was any more upset than Runts boss was, I had just as soon leave the few clothes and personal items that belong to me and leave without bothering to go by to pick them up. The situation was not any less than what we had already anticipated, as soon as Runt pulled up in front of his cottage the owner stepped out of a four-wheel drive jeep, he pointed his finger in Runts face, and said, "Get off my property and at once." He continued with saying, you can expect the money you owe to me for your car to be deducted from you final check. "Now get your belongings out of my cottage and I want you off my property was his orders!" Runt was like me, he never had much in the way of personal things, only a few of his old clothes and that was the extent of it. After, we pulled away from Runts ex-place of work, as we did not feel the need to create an episode and have the law enforcement called out, this would mean for sure we would be going back to jail and that meant another probation violation. It also meant spending the next two years locked up in the Michigan State penitentiary now, as we drove to my place of work. I wondering if my boss old DI had already called Hunter and he would be sitting waiting for me.

As we turned off the gravel road onto the dirt road that was surrounded by the white picket fence up a winding hill I would remember this most beautiful sight I had ever looked at it was something that no artist could every have captured the real beauty I seen through my eyes. The winding road up to the farmhouse and the cottages seemed to have shortened, for some reason today, as we pulled up in front of my cottage I did not see old Hunters' car, so I felt some relived. However, the odd part, was what I could not see just as I opened the door there stood my boss old DI just then, I seen daggers shooting from his eyes, and he ask with a serious tone, "He ask were in the name of Saint Peter have you been boy?" "I have lost thirty-five, young tress because you decided not to show up for work, nor did you even have the courtesy to call me." Then, he interrupted his own question and said, "No I don't need to know just get your things and get off my property. I have already taken the liberty to put your belongings into your pillowcase." Now, "I want you and your weird buddy off my property." I imagined by what he said, and by what Runts' boss said, that maybe they was a family connection with them, as they both used the same expression, 'get of my property. Then, as DI handed me a check for five day's worth of earnings coming to me, he said there is just one more thing. I called Hunter and he advised me to tell you as soon as you received the message you were too make contact with him immediately. Well, this was not good news, however as we were driving off I noticed old DI was taking our license plate number on a notepad. As Runt and I were on our way into town to Hunters' office, we were imagining the worse things that could happen.

We were discussing since we had the car, and I did have my last paycheck that we might try to run for the border of Canada. Then, Runt said, he thought he might go out to California if we could somehow get out of this mess, and asks if I wanted to come along. I never liked the sound of all the earthquakes I had heard of there in the past. I had been in a tremor once when I was fifteen-years old and it had shaken the apartment so hard that every picture on the wall flew off.

I remember I was at home sitting with my nine-month old stepsister, dad, and step-mom was out in some honky-tonk boozing it up. I was so frighten at the time I did not know what to do with the baby I remember I took her up and pulled out the bottom drawer of a six -drawer chest and packed a blanket in the empty drawer laying the infant there closing it just enough for some fresh air to get in, this way if the entire house should crumble down and I did never made it out alive the rescue came

Looking for any survivors, they would hear the baby crying and save her. Therefore, California was not where I wanted to go. If Saint. Louis, Missouri was not to be my home then where was I to go?

This was the only place I could think quickly of and that's what I told Runt. Ok, you go on out to California and you can drop me off in St. Louis, Missouri. Another problem we had now was how we were going to get that much money for all the gas for this trip of almost six-hundred miles just for me to get to St, Louis Missouri. Well, Old Runt did some thinking for a while and then he said, "I have a way." Back at the orchard where he worked the old orchard owner had some empty fifty-five gallon barrels he kept stored in the far back corner of one of the orchards, and there was a five hundred gallon tank filled with gas for the farm equipment. Runt said, "If old Hunter would allow us to leave the state to find work this is what we will do." "We will wait until around nine-thirty p.m. This will be between the new hired men doing his rounds checking the young trees. Then, we will get one of the empty fifty-five gallon drums and tie it in the trunk of the car, and we would fill it up with the gas from the five-hundred gallon tank."

60

Hunter Office

The next thing we knew we were sitting in the waiting room of Hunter's office waiting for him to see us. Then, what seemed if time had no end; the wait was at last over.

Hunters' receptionist said, Mr. "Hunter would see you the two of you now." Runt and I drew in deep breaths and opened the heavy wooden door and there sit Hunter behind his desk.

"Come in boys' and have a seat." There in front of the huge oak desk sit two leather swivel chairs Runt sit down in the right chair and I sit down next to Runt in the left. Hunter had his head bent and seems to be reading files he had opened on his desk. Then, he closed the folders and look up at both Runt and me and said, "Well boys tell me about your weekend." What was there to tell? What you want to know, "I ask." "I want to know where the two of you where and why you were not back on the job when you were should have been." "Who wants to start first Hunter asks?" "I said, I would," "Ok Hunter said, you start Mr. Lone Wolf." "Well sir, I said, we had both been paid, and Runt's boss had sold him a car on installments, we had planned on showing up for work, just then, I went quiet for a moment. "Please, go on Mr. Lone Wolf" "Well, sir we both know that part of our probation is not too have any use of alcohol, but when we got those paychecks in our hand and we had the entire day off, we felt that we had earned some relaxation from our hard work." I can't think of anything else just now sir. Next, Runt begin to explain and he continued by saying Sir, "after we bought the liquor we drove around out on some of the old country roads and before we knew it we were lost, and the car shut down so Lone Wolf and me had to sleep in the car all night."

"So someone came along the following morning and helped you get the car started Hunter asked?" " No sir, I interrupted, that was another strange thing sir, the next morning the sun which was warming through the window woke me up, and I reached over and turned on the radio and the battery was not dead because the radio, it played just fine." "I remember every station I tuned it to there was a preacher, preaching on the exact same thing, about how everyone was going to burn if they, did not change their ways and soon." Well, I continued. 'I happen to get my eyes opened, and it was then, I noticed the car had stalled out, straddle across an active railroad track. So, I woke Runt and told him that he better get out and help me push the car away from where we was sitting, and then we had no sooner moved the car than the both of us heard the whistle of a freight train moving down the tracks at about fifty-miles per hour.'

Hunter said, "Well, this is not the everyday story I get?" He said, "I don't think in all my years of being a probation officer I have ever listened to a story as good as this one is boys'." "Well sir, I said it's the truth." I could tell Hunter could see that both Runt and I were gripping the arms of the chair so tightly that our knuckles were turning blue. Then Hunter asks? "If I let you go what will, you do different the next time?" I spoke quickly and said yes sir. "I said Sir, Runt and I would like to ask for an official pardon from the conditions of our probation and given an authorization to leave the state of Michigan. Myself, I would wish to have permission to return to, Missouri. My father lives there and I can find work there sir. And, Runt would like to go to California." Well, Hunter was rubbing his chin and looking at both of us and said, before you two come in here today I had already determined what I was going to do with you two. My heart sunk down into my stomach. I thought, this has revoked our probation and that meant the next two years in the state penitentiary.

Just then old Hunter said, "I am about to do something I have never done before. I am going to leave the room and when I return I don't want to see you or the papers lying on my desk, I don't want to see any signs either of you were here today." "You two go on to where ever you need to go to find jobs, but you better make sure the restitution the Judge ordered is paid in full as the Judge ordered you? If you stop making the payments the Judge will order an arrest warrant and, then I will need to come looking for you." The next thing we knew old Hunter had left the room leaving Runt and I sitting there looking at each other to wonder what had just happened. Was this a setup? Were we going to be arrested or shot as soon as we walked out into the streets? However, he did say that he did not want to see us when he returned to his office, so Runt went to the door opened it slowly and cautiously took a sneak look out. As he eased the door fully open there was not one sight of anyone, not even Hunters' receptionist was at her desk. The two of us still confused at what had just taken place we walked to the elevator and pushed for the door to open and then we pushed the ground floor button, the elevator doors slide open, and my heart was beating at supersonic speeds, I knew this sort-of thing could not really be happening, and if so why was it happening? Still, no sign of anyone in the building, it was as if the world had come to an end and Runt and I were the only two people left, the building seem to be abandoned. It was somewhat frightening, it was as if what I had listen to the preacher talk about of the end times, it look as if JESUS had returned and Runt and I where the only two people left behind.

The car was still sitting next to the curd in front of Hunter office building were Runt had parked it. Runt and I got in and the old car it started up as if it was brand new from the factory. Then, as we pulled away, we were both asking each other what happen back there, why did Hunter just up and let us walk out without any questions, or any punishment for our revoking the probation. I took my coat, sleeve and wiped the sweat beads that had collected above my eyebrows. I told Runt I thought we needed to find a liquor store and have a victory drink. Neither of us had even noticed this was Christmas Eve and that tonight of all nights, we were going to be stealing fifty-five gallons of gas, but then I suppose stealing is stealing. Just then, another sad thought came to my mind, as we would be on the road in the old 1960 Chevrolet on a Christmas day. I thought of how other people had families to share this special occasion with and what this day was supposed to mean. I thought about JESUS birth and his ministry and the purpose he come here in the first place. Then, after I thought about the way everyone had rejected him, some of my guilt had left me knowing that I had not been the only one who had ever been rejected even the King of Kings, the SAVIOR of the universe had been rejected, and beat with straps and in the end had to give up his own life. Well, I knew a little more about rejection than most humans alive, and I knew more about being beat with straps of leather until pieces of my skin was tore away from my body, leaving me to become a piece of raw meat. The only thing that I seemed too not have; in common with JESUS was that HE had to give HIS life for everyone, something that I, nor anyone could ever do. Our first stop after leaving Hunter's off was, the first liquor store we seen, and since old Runts' boss had taken his money toward what was due on the Chevy Runt did not have any money left, and I only had the money from a short paycheck that old DI gave me when he fired me. However, I had enough to share with Runt; since he would be going all the way to the west coast I was happy to help him out. I still had the old coat of hobo Joes' that I wore every place, mostly because it had the secret pocket sewed on the inside. When Runt and I walked into the liquor store, I sent him to the counter to ask the clerk for two packs of cigarettes behind the counter and while Runt had the clerks attention I put a fifth of Morgan David wine into the inside of the secret pocket, one more time I remembered granny again when she had read to me from the bible about stealing. Romans 7:15 {KING JAMES} 15 for which I do I allow not: for what I would, that do I not, but hate, that do I. 16. If I do that which I would not, I consent unto the law that is good.

However, I had to learn at an early age that surviving on the streets was not something you learned from book teachings, but by experience, and sometimes you had to do what you had to do, in order to keep alive, even though I knew that stealing was wrong

61

Return to the Orchard

The short winter days' sun was starting to set and by the time, we drove back to Runts old place of employment, it would soon be completely dark. Runt said he knew a short cut we could take through one of the back orchards which anyone hardly ever came in this way. After we turned off the gravel road and into the field, the fresh plowed furrows caused the old cars underneath to hit the ground in all the high places. I wondered how we would come back this way after getting fifty-five gallons of gasoline in the trunk of the car, would we ever make it back across here.

Runt knew every inch of the orchard even thought it was now pitch dark, and the only light we had was the lights from the headlights of the car and the light of a full moon tonight. We put an empty fifty-five gallon barrel into the trunk and secured it tightly with a rope next, Runt drove to the other end of the orchard and filled the barrel from the five hundred gallon tank filled with gas, the rancher used to fill his farm equipment with. It only took about ten minutes and we were bouncing back out of the field I could fell every furrow the old Chevy went over it look doubtful we were going to make it, but each time Runt would pull the gear shift down into another lower gear and let the clutch out, the Chevy crawled over one more furrow. At last, we had crossed the final furrow and there was the gravel road again. It was nine-thirty P.M. We pulled on interstate 69. We had about a twelve- hour drive, because extra caution would be most important with a fifty-five gallon barrel of gas hanging half way out of the trunk of the Chevy.

Of course, we had not thought of such things as what if someone rear-ended us, the car would explode and blow both Runt and I to kingdom come, or the law might spot us and they for sure would stop us and most likely this would be something that would get us put under the jail. Two and a half hours had passed it was now Christmas day and Runt and I were in the Christmas spirit, listening to and signing along with the Christmas songs from the radio and of course we had other spirits besides the radio we had Morgan David wine. It was now twelve-thirty AM, three hours since we had left; our average speed because of the barrel of gasoline in the trunk was around fifty-miles an hour. Just then, we heard a loud pop that sounded as if something had exploded. My first thought was someone had just taken a shot at us and missed. My stars Runts old boss spotted us and he has waited until now to take his first attempt on us, the car swerve off the road toward the right and into a ditch, Runt was fighting with the steering wheel trying to bring the car back onto the highway. Just, then the car begin to lean toward the right as if it was going to roll over, when Runt yelled out, Lone Wolf it's about to roll get ready for the explosion. Just then, it looked as if he had control of the car again and pulled, it back onto the road. After coming to a complete stop, we got out first to check to see if the fifty-five gallons of gas was still in the trunk, I guess we had done a good job when we tied the barrel in because it had not moved at all. Then, we went around examining what caused the disturbance. The right front tire had blown and now there was nothing left but a steel rim. I never, ask Runt if he had said a prayer or not but, for what it was worth I was sure doing some silent praying? Before, we had put the barrel into the trunk Runt, suggested that we tie the spire tire on top of the car just in case we were to need it, and now I was proud of his intelligent thinking because if the tire had been under the fifty-five gallons go gag we would have never been able to remove the barrel to get the tire. What we had just come through we needed to find a place to stop for the night and drink the rest of the wine while we comforted our anxiety. After pulling the old steel rim off and tossing it out into the ditch and put the spare tire, back on Runt asks if I would take over the driving until we could find a place to pull off for the night. I could see the shade of red in Runts face as if he could pass out at any moment and considered what had just gone through he deserved a break and a good swallow of wine. It had been quit sometime since I had driven out on a highway, but it was like an old saying I had heard of a long time ago, {Once, you learn, it was like riding a bicycle you never forget.} Driving the old Chevy was like driving in a new car for me it drove as smooth a silk. Forty-five minutes into my driving the weather report said, expect temperatures to be dropping into the teens tonight. I was thankful that the old Chevy had a good heater because, now it had started to mist a light freezing rain, and it seems to be sticking and freezing to the highway as soon as it touched the highway. The Chevy with all the weight in the trunk was to some advantage to us, as it gave the car more traction and we were creeping along at twelve-miles per hour. Then, through the headlights, I could read a sign that there was a rest area one mile ahead.

There were cars, pick-up trucks and eighteen-wheelers which had slid over into the ditch. By the time we had reached the rest area, it seemed as if we had drove twenty miles, but at last here it was, and when we pulled in there was just enough free space left for one more car to fit in. Well, this was it for the rest of the night. We did have somewhat an advantage to everyone else, we could sit here for the next month and let the car run and not have to be concerned about running out of gas, and I think our only concern was running out of wine before the gas did. This had been the longest Christmas, I had ever remembering spending anywhere and as I lay there listening to the freezing rain hit the top of the old Chevy I fell into a deep sleep that lasted until the morning sun awoke me.

The weather forecast, predicted the temperatures would climb to the low forties today and that was good news because all the ice on the road would melt after thirty-two degrees. Runt and I decided to wait until some of the other vehicles began to move then we would know it was safe for us as well. By eleven O'clock, everyone at the rest area had left and the traffic on the highway seems to be moving along at a normal speed. I decided to turn the driving back over to Runt and was thinking about what I would do back in Saint. Louis. I had no home there, and I did not want to go back to dads, even though I believed I was too big now for me to let him give me another blood bath beating with the leather strip, it was the principle of the idea that he had in the past.

But, what was I to do. I did not like the idea of California, and I sure did not care of the thought of Arkansas, granny as good told me that I had no home with them any longer, I knew mom never wanted me in all the years past so this was not practical. I knew how she had felt from the first time she learned of her pregnancy she hated this life that I was growing inside of her. I was hated throughout the nine months of pregnancy, while she drank alcohol, smoke cigarettes; smoke marijuana, was in a roll over car accident she had deliberately tried everything possible to terminate the term of the pregnancy. Then, after I was born into the world, she resented me, wanting nothing to do with me at all. I remember her biting me until she would bring blood out of my arms and legs; I remember her leaving me locked in a damp basement tied with a rope for an entire day.

Afterwards, she would give birth to two other children a brother and sister. She would leave me to look after the both of them, she would be gone for as long as a week at a time leaving me to feed, bathe and care for these younger siblings. So the absolutely thought of my going to Arkansas was a big no. Well, the time left to spend with Runt was fast approaching the end and it seemed like we had known each other for a lifetime. We had spent the last year by each other's side. We had spent ten months7 and fifteen days locked in a cellblock together, and then, the two of us served as trustees of the jail together we had even stolen a police officers' personal car while we were trustees."

We had come to know pretty much everything there was to know about each other.

Now in about thirty-minutes Runt and I would shake hands and tell each other good-bye for forever. For some reason this was causing a hard lump to form in my throat and a small tear was trickling down my face, which I wiped, away with my old ragged coat of Joes,' without Runt knowing that I was capable of shedding a tear. We had come within two miles my dads' house and I told Runt to stop at a liquor store that would sell me a bottle of vodka and we could have one more drink together. Then, the moment had come and Runt pulled down a long driveway at my dad's house at three- thirty in the after-noon. Then, when we both reached out our hands toward each other I could see that I was not the only one having troubles saying good-bye. I told runt no way that just a hand shake was good enough, and we embraced each other with a hug. I believe what had made Runt and I as the close friends that we had become to be to each other was that his life had been pretty much the same as mine had been. Runt was an orphan, after he was born his dad had left him with his mother, then, she took him to a neighbor's house, and left him in front of their door. Runt said, he could not ever remember seeing his parents. After a long hug and saying good-bye to each other, and saying what a joy it had known one another I opened the old car door of Runts 1960, Chevrolet and stepped out taking my old pillowcase of dirty clothes. I watched with tear filled eyes as my best friend was fading out of sight knowing I would never see him again I was wondering if maybe, I should have gone ahead and tried California, but then I knew if Runt and I had stayed together that we would have most likely ended up in some serious trouble some place. It seemed that when the two of us were together we caused more trouble than normal.

62

A Marriage and Desertion

It was now time for me to walk into the house, but just then, I remembered dad had not come home from work at this time of day and I did not want to be alone with my step-mom. Just then, I could hear loud music coming from the end of the driveway and since I had nearly a full fifth of vodka left, I thought it could not hurt if I went to see if it was a party, anyone could join, especially if they brought a bottle to share. As I walked closer to where the music was coming from I could smell something recognizable other than alcohol, it was just more than a party with alcohol, and someone was smoking that familiarly smell of marijuana. The first person I met, I ask if anyone could join, their party, sure man go on in, a hippie told me, at least this is what we called them back then. Once again, this brought some memories of when my mom was carrying me inside her womb; it remembered it was always full of cigarette and marijuana smoke. I suppose I will never know why my own mom hated the life that was growing inside of her. It seem that I was hated throughout the nine months of pregnancy, while she drank alcohol, smoke cigarettes; smoke marijuana was in a roll over car accident, she had purposely tried everything possible to terminate the term of the pregnancy in a way which would look as if it was an accident for the aborting me? Now, while I waited for dad to come home from his job, I could let off a little steam. After all I had been locked up for almost a year and then of course the short period of time I worked on the orchard, I ought to have a good time.

Then, it happened, our eyes met each other at the same time, she had long blonde curly hair that touched the top of her blue jeans that fit tightly against her hips. Her body was like that of a marble sculpture. She was making use of her body language at me too come to where she was. I was looking hard to make sure she was for real. Then, this adorable dream came walking toward me, her dark blue eyes seemed too hypnotize me as she come close and looked into my eyes. I had never been captivated so by any woman before as I was now. I wanted her to jump into my arms, but I did not want too seem to be so fast either, she looked so vulnerable, yet at the same time she looked as strong as steel if she needed to be. Our conversation started when she walked up to me and ask where had I been all her live? Her next question was would I like to dance with her, and of course, I did. One thing led to another and soon the party was over everyone had left but the three couples that lived in the apartments where the party was at. However, I had been asks too stay over as her guest and after we had gone off to our self's she ask me where I lived, as she had not seen me around her part of town before or at least in the past year.

Well, "I answered I have been in the United States Marines, and after that, I went up north and worked for a while, but Saint Louis is actually my home, I said." Well, I never really lied, I really was in the Marines I just never told her for how long, and I really had been up north working, I just forgot to say that I had been in jail for one year working as a trustee for a county jail. However, one thing led to another and I spent the night forgetting that I was supposed to go to my dads' house. Then the following day she asks me if I could stay with her, and I sure was not going to turn this opportunity down and I accepted. Before the day had finished I remembered I was supposed to be at dads' house. However, now I would not be walking up the driveway alone, I would be holding the hand of what must be one of those angles that I had read of in the Bible, this or a dream, and if it was a dream, I sure never wanted to wake up from this one. When I knocked on dad's door I was not surprised to see that he and step-mom was drunk as usual but, I had no room to talk because that was what I did most of the time now was stay drunk.

Dad welcomes me and my woman friend in and offered her and me a mixed drink which we of course accepted. Well, it would have not been polite to have said no, we were guest. Then after about the sixth mixed drink, I told dad that I would be staying with her instead. I think this pleased dad especially since we had not seen each other in the years that had passed and our past with each other had never been that great. I am sure dad knew I had forgiven him for all the blood bath beating he had given me before and I think I had forgiven him as well? My moving in with what I had believed to be an angel would turn out to be living arrangements only for the next year, when we both decided that the relationship between us was strong enough to marry. January 1973, the two of was united in holy matrimony before a justice of the peace. I did however after the first month of our relationship tell her about the jail time I had spent and that I was on probation for the next two years, which she paid all the fines that I had been ordered to pay. Two years had passed and still no child and I become worried that something either was wrong with her or me. I began to make remarks that she had put on to much weight to bear a child. The following year we become proud parents of a healthy baby girl. Three years after that in 1976, then in 1978 a baby boy was born was born with autisms alcoholic fetal syndrome. Here again is the point of the story about my mother carrying me, when she drank and smoked throughout her pregnancy with me. Mothers it doesn't pay, because you're not only hurting yourself, your now hurting an innocent life that cannot defend for his, or herself

Another baby girl was born too us again in 1980. We were thankful that this birth was normal, and still another baby girl born in 1981. However, this was another baby who would have many health problems and GOD would call away much too soon. Regardless of both my wife and I having drug and alcohol problem we were able to keep our marriage together for ten years. Ten years, of which I think for the best part, were happy ones, at least for me. Then one night in the spring of 1984, she left the house in the middle of the night without any warning signs and seemed too have vanished. She left without as much as saying good-bye to the four children she had given birth too. For the next fourteen years, she would have no contact with them.

63

The Dissappreance of My Wife

February 1983, the mother of our four small children ages two, three five and six and a woman which I had been married to for the past ten years and loved ended with a heart breaking divorce. Why was this happening? I have asked this question over a million times? I thought everything was going well, we were the owners of a profitably business, and we were actually doing very well. It appeared that we had a good marriage other than my continual drinking. Today however, as I walk into the court room on this early morning my heart would be dangerously beatings, sinking deep into my chest. I could feel a sharp stabbing feeling inside my chest which would cause the heart to feel as if it would stop. My entire body had begun to ache. It was clear to anyone, I was still very much in love with this woman which I had lived my past ten years of my life with. It was reassuring this morning to know she did not appear for the divorce proceeding, and I was awarded full custody of my four children. It was now however, that I would take the reasonability of being a father and mother to three girls and a boy whom I would later learn had autism. Later in years he was diagnosed with alcohol fetal syndrome. However, our live were about to take a 360 degree turn. We went from living on an income of several hundred dollars a week to living on food stamps and a small government check. AFDC It was mid July 1983, five months after the divorce, the children and I had adjusted from the absence of their mother not being there. It was a late Sunday afternoon a knock came at the door of our small rented trailer. When, I went to welcome who might be at the door I was greeted by a police officer who handed me a small piece of paper with a note which read please call me at this phone number. The officer told me when he took the call the caller seem as if it very important that I call the number right away. We had no phone so I got the children ready and loaded into the car to drive to the nearest pay phone I could find. Full of anxiety that this news was going to be obviously bad news? I deposited the necessary change into the phone and listen to one, two, three four rings, no answer. I was about to hang up when I listen to the most shocking voice on the other end of the phone. I could not believe who I was hearing? It was the children's mother crying and with a trembling voice she asks me did I still love her and would I talk with her about reconciliation. She told me that she had made a dreadful mistake. Fool heartedly I would be too quick to say yes. But, I was still in love with this woman and was willing to pay any price to have her back. I was indeed going to pay for this mistake which I eagerly agreed to. After two weeks of our being reconciled we were unquestionable still in love with each and this love for each other was enough that we should be reunited in marriage. I was ever so willing for this, I was as much tranquilized with her love, as the very first day that I had fallen in love with her and was married. Our second wedding was causal one with a few friends, and just two members of my family came to witness the ceremony, as no one else was ready to forgive and welcome her back into the family, but I didn't care if they ever talked to me again. Two weeks into our marriage had gone by. I was feeling happier I believe, than the first Time I had married her? I had not realized until this separation just how much I did love this woman. I believe I would have walked through fire if she had asked it of me. I would have exchanged my very soul to burn in eternal fire for her at this point and time. Then, that familiar feeling of something horrible was about to happen filled my body and sometime during the late hours of the night, my wife for the second time disappeared into the late night hours without telling the children a good bye, she slipped away, and we would net see her again for fifteen years. I had never before known anyone that could fade from off the face of the earth, as she had done.

64

A Journey of Two States

It was April 1983; the children's grandparents from their mother's side called my dad and ask him to deliver a message for me to call them? After making the call I was told by the children's grandmother that she and the grandfather would take pleasure if the children and I would move to live with them in Missouri. At least I knew something about Missouri I had lived here once when I was a teenager.

This was an important decision for me; it was a 1000-mile trip across two states, with four small children, on a greyhound bus. I would require a little time to think about this, and I would later wish I had given it even more thought than I had. However, we weren't conquering the world since the children's mother had abandoned us, so against good judgment I decided we would sell the few things we had collected, since the divorce, as the children's mother had taken everything that we had bought together. This would be the beginning of the worst nightmare anyone could expect to live through.

We were about to step into what seem to have been another world for us after our arrival here to my mother-in-law and father-in-law's house. In the beginning we believed we had been accepted as part of their family, then, the most bizarre and sudden thing happened; after our first month here we were told we would have to run along and without delay. Almost, 1000 miles from where we called home in Texas, and I have direct orders for the five of us to hit the streets.

Now, homeless and with four small children, I hardly knew in what direction I should turn. I thought perhaps if I had known the LORD, would it have made any difference to my situation. No, that nonsense was only for certain people, people such as the rich or at least this was the way I believed at the time. Only much later in my life would I have any vision for the need of a LORD. Well, I packed a light load of clothing into a couple of pillow cases. I packed what thought would be basic for a hike of some three hundred miles, the five of us started out toward the highway with a large cardboard sign that I had written the words "Arkansas" in large writing, we began the journey of being homeless for the first time with four children?.

65

Fear For Our Lives

I had chosen going to Arkansas because I had a mother who lived here and I thought she might take us in, this only turned out to be a thought. After, we had walked to interstate 70, and we had only walked a short way a big shiny black car pulled off the highway to the shoulder of the interstate highway. Getting out of the car was a large man of about 6'6" and looked to have weighed around 250 lbs. As the stranger walked toward the rear of his car, walking toward us in an authoritative way, he spoke to me with a deep tone of voice, asking me "what are you doing out here?"

Then, he told us to get into his car full of fear we did as he told us to do as he hurried off from the side of the road to get back into the congestion of traffic I observed this man seem to know his way about, as he was weaving in and out of heavy traffic in a hasty manner as if he had a wish for getting away from someone. Then, quickly, the car swerves off to the right exiting the interstate and down an exit ramp I counted as we went through seven, eight then ten traffic lights, all of which were in precise timing with each other all turning green at exactly the same time I was hoping that one of these lights would turn red so I could take the chance to grab my four small children and make a run for it?

My heart was pounding at full force, with twice the normal beats. My mind was racing I could not keep up in my mind what to do. How would I only a small-framed man weighing to my guess half what this man weighed protect the children and myself? If ever I needed this GOD, I had heard of in my youth I needed HIM now I believe it was quoted in the book of Hebrews, 13:5

{KING JAMES}. 5. Let your conversation be without covetousness; and be content with such things as ye have: for HE hath said, I will never leave you nor forsake thee.

As I tried to seize the large-scale man up through the side of my eye so that he wouldn't notice my paying him any notice and at the same time look for the precise time to set up some technique, to generate a disturbance for our getaway if only a light would turn red. As we left the city limits coming into a non-residential area, I'm sure my face had confirmed my alarm that was in me I felt limp; my throat seemed to be plugged with something blocking my breathing, then for the first time since before I could remember I said, "This man is going to take all of us out into the country and murder the Five of us? After we had driven to a remote area, the big black car came to an unexpected stop in front of a building sitting alone in the forest. Then, I notice a sign in the front yard that read. The Salvation Army, as the strange man got out of the car he in the same manner as before with a voice of authority told us to get out of the car and to follow him. I noted something different about the big man this time; it was the way in which he was walking. We walked into the building and down a long hallway, then after passing by a great number of offices we walked into a room that had a plaque on the desk that read, Commander. The stranger that brought us here told the Commander to take care o us with whatever we needed. It turned out that the stranger who had taken us from the interstate to bring us here was a Captain in the United States Army. That, afternoon we were given a hot meal to fill our famished stomachs and a clean bed to sleep in through the night. The following morning we were taken to an area in the building for a hot breakfast and a bus ticket on a greyhound bus line to Arkansas. I will never leave you, nor forsake you. HE was surely looking out after HIS children this time. After riding the big blue and white bus, for some eight hours we reached our destination of the little town of which our nightmare would be awaiting for us to arrive. The gruesome people of this town were going to torment us to the ultimate degree. From our first day we arrived here, we weren't welcomed. After six hours on the bus and upon our arrival and calling my mother she told me as soon as we were seated in the car we could not stay with her this was something I should have known before hand. Mom said, she had talked this over with her land owner and she would not allow her to let the five of us stay. Mom said I would have to take my Children and move on. However, she did say she would take us to a mission for the homeless some sixty miles away and where they would perhaps let us stay. This would soon be the beginning of our soon to meeting these uncivilized people here. This was going to e a nightmare that was actually reality. But, I accepted the responsibilities of rearing my children to protect them with my life if needed. We were at our turning point; our circumstances allowed us no further choice but to go to the mission. I had looked for this to be possibly better than having my children sleep on the streets.

Now, as we arrived at the mission we walked into the most filth I had ever before seen I thought perhaps maybe, we would have been better off to sleep on the streets this was the most unsatisfactory lodging I had ever seen. The structure was an old barn, built probably around the 1920's. It had been partition off into small rooms that would have measured around 12' x 12'; the floors were dirt the walls were of a thin layer of metal that was rusted. It was an unseasonably hot summer, the shelter's rooms had no windows, had no air conditioners or a small fan too blow away some of the sweltering heat. Massive swarms of jumbo sized mosquitoes sucked our blood through the long hot summer nights. Sleep was something uncommon. The food was considered unfit for human consumption; our breakfast consisted of part corn flakes and part weasels floating in them. The milk was 20 percent milk and 80 percent water. We did still have something to hope for though; hopes that this wasn't for eternity.

66

Threats to Hang My Children

Two months went by since we arrived here at the mission it was August 1985; we received a message from the government housing authority where my mom lived and had turned us away that we had been accepted for public housing assistance. Next what we were about to face no one should need ever live through? Even though most of time I did not live by it, as small child, my grandparents had done their very best too teach me the golden rule of the Bible, to love thy neighbor as thy self, and as well try to teach me to believe in GOD. I was trying to pass along these golden rules too my Children even though I was far away from GOD as one could possibly get. However, the people in this town would soon give another explanation for the meaning of love; they would teach us to be skeptical of everyone. These horrible people in this northeastern town of Arkansas would cause the five of us to be suspiciously of everyone. At sunset each day we would lay in our beds, terrified that someone would break into our apartment bringing considerable harm to us. It was obvious from our first day that we had come here, that these people had blueprinted too detail in doing everything in their might to plague upon us every injurious punishment possible we sat continually imprisoned inside our little apartment with constant fear for our lives.

We listen in fear of sounds coming from the outside sounds of someone cutting away our screens from our windows, sounds of grown men outside laughing and threatening how they planned to do away with us. Our clothes had been taken from the clothes line, and tossed across the lawn, many times torn to shreds; we would often come across someone wearing our clothes, we would hear them tell someone else how they came about having our clothes. As each day was frightening the children were terrified to walk to their school as their lives had been caution; that they were going to hang them from a tree between the school and their house in the nearby forest. I believed we would have been safer had we lived in some alien country. After we had lived in our apartment for three weeks, we begin to have almost a daily visitation from law enforcement, child protective services, the child welfare office and the school principal's office all which came with a lying report of allegation, which we knew nothing about. The harassment from these people became almost unbearable to the degree the only time we came out of the apartment was for the five of us to walk the children to school or cautiously walk to get our food, and then hurriedly get off the streets and back into our apartment. We lived in constant fear every day, fear for our lives, wondering when something was going to happen? Wondering how they intended on killing us? Would it be they were going to hang us? Shoot us and make it quick? No, that would be too humane for these people. Maybe, they intended on coming into our house while we were gone and they would put rat poison in our food. Yes, that would be more on their like; but whatever they had planned, I could envision I would go first just dwelling on it. I made continuous calls to make a complaint of the vandalism to our apartment and, of our personal belongings to the police. "We're not your babysitters," the police would tell me in a hateful tone. They would say, "We never saw it happen, so we can't do anything about it." Our only light at the end of the tunnel we seem to have had was to trust in GOD, that HE would surely get us out of this harassment that we were in. I knew if a miracle didn't happen these people here was going to do something didn't that they would cross that line, they had so much resentment built up inside of them and why against us I could not understand. The only way we had out was to walk out, and that would be the most dangerous thing of all the only source of income was a small check from the government, an aid for dependent children's check, and a few food stamps. We were thankful to have this and we believed it was enough. I recall reading some place about letting nature feed you, so I went out into the woods and found different varieties of berries, along with a variety of various kinds of comestible greens. With this and what foods the older children saved from their school lunch and packed home, we at least all had something to satisfy our famished stomachs with. I felt as if we were in some foreign prison camp waiting for our execution.

It hurt to listen each night as the children lay in their beds praying; asking GOD, to get us out of this frightful place praying to a GOD, who I now had come to believe had condemned us to be here. If only we could have at this present–day had the resources to have left to return to Texas; to the town we knew as our home or for that matter left for any place away from here, but we had not even began to suffer any punishment compared to what was going to come. Our weeks turned into months, it seemed as if though we were trapped in some sort of snare. With no way out of this gruesome condition, It became more and more grueling as the sweltering summer's heat continued to blaze down on this place which looked like the description from the bible given for the eternal pit . The electric company came out to shut off our electric, as we could in no way pay the bill being charged us for a three-bedroom apartment. With only a refrigerator and a small window fan, which we only ran in the hotter part of the day, our bill was three to four hundred dollars for the month.

Now, as the summer pressed on and saving back everything that we could, by late October we had put aside enough to have the electric turned back on. Maybe, the children would at least stay warm through the lengthy winter months ahead of us. It was now that I came about the well-timed change to talk with one of the elder tenants here, who suggested to me that I make a way to take my family and get out of town before something happened that he could not tell me about, but it wasn't going to be pretty if I stayed here. The endless threats, the terrorizing, the trashing of our personal belongings would have made a best seller for a horror movie.

67

A Cold, Long Walk

We had stayed alive through a long hot summer and it was now November.

It was a bitter cold night I was awakened around three A.M. by my two and a half-year-old daughter to tell me. "Daddy, I'm sick." After, I had put my hand to feel of her little forehead, I learned at once that she was burning at the touch with a fever. After taking her temperature I was in tears to learn she had a temperature of 105 degrees.

The hospital was a five mile walk and my child needed medical attention and right away. We had no vehicle at this time; and I knew it was no need for me to call my mom in the middle of the night; she would not come if it had been in the middle of the day? She would only remind me that this was my responsibility and I should have thought about this before I took on the role of being both a dad and a mom to four small children? I knew also, it would not help for me to for an ambulance. Filled with fear I ran out of the apartment and without thinking, I began pounding on any door I could

I beg with and wept to anyone I could awaken, for someone to please take us to the hospital. The answer which I got as soon as they found out who I was, was go away or they would call for the police. Go back to where ever you came from some told me, I was told I should have thought of this before I came here. The five of us had no choice but to a wrap ourselves as best we could with our ragged clothing and walk through the frigid snowy night the five stressful miles to the hospital. As the walk becomes difficult through the heavy snow of the night, I had to carry my sick child on my back as she was too sick for the walk. It took the children and me three hours to walk across the snow drifted highway. After our arriving to the emergency room, cold and wet soaked clothing we waited, and waited some more. As others come in after we arrived, everyone had seen a doctor before us and had gone on their way? As we sat shivering from the long cold walk we waited and waited to see a doctor.

After we had arrived at the hospital and waiting for three hours at last, one of the hospital's orderlies came out to the waiting area and touched my daughter's forehead with his hand then said, to me and hatefully, "Oh, she only has a fever all kids run fevers. What you have done is waste our time." He told me to take her home and give her an aspirin; he then turned and left us sitting there I had no other choice, but to do what I was told.

To protect and to serve, was perfectly clear that this did not apply to just anyone as I called the police to ask that they might send someone to the hospital to take my children home I explained that I could walk, but one of my children were very sick with a high fever we don't run a taxi service here in this town boy, and if you call back to tie up our line with such nonsense we'll have you arrested. Once again I put my sick child on my back and, the five of us took out for the five-mile walk back across the same rugged countryside that we had earlier walked.

As we walked along our way toward our apartment, I envisioned our down-and-out situation to be punishment in itself. That we had to walk in this harsh shivery weather tramping through the sludge made from the passing traffic, but now these atrocious people were intentionally veering to run through the puddles of standing water, causing us to become drenched on top of our already cold and aching bodies.

68

First Holiday

It was a Thursday twenty-six, nineteen-eight-three, Thanksgiving morning. I was up before the children this morning and as I stood with my eyes fix out our little apartment window at the new snow which lay upon the cold and frozen ground, I could also, smell mixed in the cold air the aroma from all the foods that were cooking this morning. The scent of apple pies, pumpkin pies, someone's turkey, the dressing I thought of what we would have today to eat. I could taste the hint of salt from teardrops that ran down my sad face. It was more than I could do to hold back my silent sobbing and, it become audible. I believed the children would be better off, if I was dead. I was thinking about what was the best way without them knowing I had done this to myself.

But, as I felt the sadness of this morning looking out at the dazzling snow I realize it was true we wouldn't enjoy any of the luxurious of the usual Thanksgiving meal that everyone else would be having this day, but we did however each other have, we did have some canned beans and rice that I could fix and I thought about there was someone, somewhere who did not even have this much to eat today? I believe that Thanksgiving Day went by slower than any day I could ever recall, every hour that day seems as if it were a month passing by. Thanksgiving, was at last over, Christmas was soon coming and, I was going to face-off with an even more day of another heart breaking experience with the month of Christmas than I had with Thanksgiving. I was not so sure if could make it through the Month of December, or not? It was soon going to be Christmas and the only money we had would be used for paying our rent and utilities with. We hadn't even a Christmas tree this year. However, a brain storm had come to me one which might be one I would regret if I should get caught, but I had to at least try. I was all of a sudden reminded when we were walking to the hospital crossing the rugged terrain that I had seen a couple of cedar trees beside the highway.

Now, these people would hang me from one of these trees if I got caught doing what I was about to do, but I was ready to pay the price for my children to have a Christmas tree this year. I waited until late that Christmas Eve night. I believed this would be a time everyone would be spending time with his or her family or asleep and I wouldn't be noticed. Now, I need to slip out to where I had seen the trees. It was one A.M. It was another harsh frost biting night one mistake tonight and it would be all over with I had thought it would be best tonight if I left the children at home, besides I could move more quickly by myself. There was going to be the chance I would be seen, and I might need to spend the night hiding out in the woods with the temperatures well below zero, a man could freeze to death in a little time tonight. I took with me a butcher knife and a hammer this was how I planned no cutting the tree my Children's Christmas tree. Our neighbors looked as if they were all sleeping. With a whispered voice I told them I loved each of them. I told them to lock the door and not open it for any reason I began to walk to the location where I was going to get the tree from.

The snow tonight was deep with the north wind blowing it brought with it the ghost noises that howled creepy sounds through the tall trees along the country road. It had taken me some forty minutes to reach my destination. I knew exactly what tree wanted? It wasn't going to be a very large tree but it would be a tree the children would enjoy as I slipped off the main road it was here and with the help of a full moon tonight to see by, I kneel down beside the tree then, putting my butcher knife to the small trunk I swung my hammer with all the power I had in me. Upon striking the back of the knife the sound of the metal against metal echoed a thump that the wind carried off through the cold night; luckily there was no nearby houses for a couple of miles that anyone could hear. I must have hit on the tree trunk some ten times and then I felt as a lumber jack might feel at the fall of a great tree; I had cut our Christmas tree down now, to get back without anyone noticing me, I would have to be careful for headlights from any vehicles that might be out on the highway tonight; it would not be likely as late as it was and the roads were iced over to almost impassable to be on. I had made almost my half way mark at getting home; when my feet began to feel dull numb it was becoming troublesome for me to move my legs. I had to make it; I was too close to give up now. I continued making singing chat to myself to distract the pain I was having I knew I had been out to long, but it never mattered, I was going to see that my children had a Christmas tree for the following morning even though we had no presents to place under the tree at least we would have a tree? As my step become slower and slower it was seemingly getting further away instead of getting any closer. At last I was at our front doorway at this point I believed if I raise my hand to knock on the door for the children to let me in I would pull it out of socket. But, I was here and with the only gift I had to give, but, I would be giving it with all the love I had fortunately, the snow had fallen through the night which was to my advantage as it covered all implication of any footprints. While, I was out to get the Christmas tree the children had cut bands of paper, which they had colored and pasted into chains. We popped popcorn and strung it with sewing thread, and then just outside our window were a bush that grew wild red berries on it which we also strung through thread, the tree might not have had lights, and ornaments and pretty decorations but it was pretty to us just the same.

I lay idle-awake throughout the remaining of the night. I was hoping and believing that maybe, if not for me the children would get a miracle tonight, from GOD. For a short-lived moment I believed I was going to walk into the living room the next morning and would find there was such thing as a not in a Santa Claus but, a miracle from GOD, and he had brought presents wrapped with pretty ribbons and bows, all of which would have a name tag with my children's name on them. But, then the restless night ended I walked to the living and looked for the packages that were not there it was just as bare as we had gone to bed. No Santa Clause and no GOD to answer that miracle prayer the children and I had prayed? As I stood in the dark room gazing at the void space under the tree again, I could not hold back the painful teardrops falling from my eyes down my unshaven face. There were no presents and again there would be no traditional food that one would look forward to eating on this holiday. As I was standing along in the room, I listened to the beautiful Christmas songs that were playing in my mind, and then I heard the shuffle of little feet behind me. As I slowly turned I could not hold back the tears any longer after I looked into the saddest four little faces I had ever looked into. I then broke down with heartache, tears of sadness was streaming down my face like Nigeria falls. I knew this town handed out presents to underprivileged families but, I didn't know why my children had to be excluded I noticed something however in the hands of my older daughter, and then she handed me a small piece of folded paper. As I unfolded the paper I started to read the note: "Dear Daddy, Merry Christmas, and Dad. We just wanted you to know that even though we don't have any presents, that we love you anyway and even though you sometimes get mad at us we know that you love us, so we wanted to tell you today, that we're sorry for getting you upset and one more thing it don't matter about the gifts, because we have each other and that's the best gift anyone could have, Merry Christmas Daddy, from all your kids." I remembered reading once in the book of the Holy Bible, where Satan was permitted by GOD to experiment with a GODLY man, by afflicting plagues and tragedy upon him, seizing all his belongings was consented in allowing him to even kill this man's seven children.

I remember how appalling I recalled conceiving this was, a GOD that was supposed to love us, would tolerate such a thing to happen and to a man that had done virtually nothing to deserve this. I wondered now, if this same GOD that the Bible tells us about was using us in the Same like manner as this man named Job.

69

No Food Left for You

It was now, New Years day 1984, still no changes. On the third of the month it would be the time of month to receive our monthly food stamp allotment it was time to go shopping. Having no one to ask to take us to a local market to buy our monthly food supply, not even my mom could find the time to be concerned with us? We would be pushing a grocery basket with our month supply of food over snow and ice for five miles each way. This would make our total walking for the day come to a total of twenty miles. It would take us the entire day to complete this shopping day. The grocery basket had to be taken back to the store the same day, or the store manager said, he would call the police and tell them I had stolen the cart. The last trip today, I would take a chance and leave the children at home while I returned the grocery cart back to the store and returned by myself?

Every step seem further away, as the children's painful walk through the frost biting cold would stop them in their steps to explain how much they were hurting, with teardrops almost frozen to their little cold and swollen faces they would ask, "Daddy, why? Please let's get out of this horrible place. I made an effort to stop my mind to close out the cold and to think this GOD, I had heard so much about all my life HE would surely send someone and offer help to our desperate need. But every car and truck only rapidity passed us by with not one having enough passion of human kindness to stop and offer us help.

But, as the first trip of the five mile walk there and to the apartment was over I now had to go back again, and make sure the manager knew I had returned the basked and then to walk back to the apartment this was a twenty- mile walk today. The day was not finished, now the children had to have food fixed? The picture here is if I would have had anyone to have helped just a little would have meant so much to me and my children?

But, no friends no family, oh there was a brother and my mother but everyone had every excuse there was?

The long winter made its slow progress, with many days a copy of the one passed, and as spring of year had come and gone, we were headed into a long hot summer to bring us what, we would not have wished to have known. If only there could had been a way to see our future at this point? It was now July, nineteen-eight-four. This place looked every day as if it was a place which GOD had forsaken. What we were about to experience next was the worst was to come yet a local radio station announced that the government was giving away commodities, of cheese, butter, powdered milk and even some powdered eggs, along with some other government foods. I remember this day all too well it was an extremely hot day the five of us walked about three miles to the place that had been announced and when, we arrival here, we had to go through a big double iron gate we were the only ones who had walked, everyone else come by vehicle. It looked a little odd however, that all the vehicles here were mostly late model vehicles many were band new ones.

I could not help but question myself how could these people be qualified for this kind of assistance? None the less as we stood suffering in the open sun with temperatures of around 105 degrees and, as others had come in after we had took our place in line with their car, we were moved back one car at a time further behind in the line by each car, if we had not moved out of the way we would have been trapped between two vehicles. We had stood through the heated day, when at last it was our turn to go through the line that was giving out the food when they said, "You should have got here earlier; we're all out of food as we walked our way back to the apartment, filled with bitterness toward these people and I suspect toward GOD as well, I could not for my life imagine what we had done to be worthy of all the turmoil that we had already lived through, and it had only began. We continued to remain closed inside our apartment barricading ourselves from the outside world. The hot summer Months hung around and we were without as much as a fan to cool by. It was now time for the children's school to start, but we had other plans unfortunately so did the authorities here. It was 4:00 P.M. We had been all this day, busy packing what few possessions we could I was hoping to move as far away from as from this place as possible I had taken all I could and I had this sixth sense that something was about to take place that if I did not leave now, I would forever regret it.

Now, as I have not talked about it before, we had gone out of town and bought a used vehicle on a payment plan however, the car broke down a month after we had taken it home, it had been in the shop all this time while we had to continue to pay for the car as well as the repair bill to have the car fixed. Today however, we had paid our lat payment on the car and the repair bill.

Between our trips from the car to the apartment there came a shattering noise as if someone was trying to break down our door, at my running to see who was causing the disturbance, I was alarmed to discover that standing at my front door was the sheriff, the school superintendent, a lady from the child protective services and a probation officer. I wasn't on any probation, but all these people without even asking forced me to the side and pushed their way inside our apartment. The sheriff began first to talk; telling me that they had legal papers to remove my four children and that there was nothing I could do about it. This was the sixth scene that I had felt earlier upon listening to this I felt complete hopelessness, my feeling nauseated and being tossed as if I were like that of a small boat being tossed on a dark, violent and restless sea. If only I had known why all these horrible things had happened, I might have accepted it. I had to question the LORD again, why He would be punishing four innocent children?

I believed they had gone through enough by their mother deserting them at their young age. Although I knew beforehand that it was no purpose in it, I began to try to rationalize on our behalf with my unstable speech that sounded as if I was drunk. I told them that as they could see we were packing and that we would be leaving their little town, as it was perfectly clear that no one wanted us here from the first day we had come to town. It came to my mind now, if anyone had ever told these people about JESUS, and what HIS words say in John 3:16, (That GOD so loved the world that HE gave His only begotten SON that whosoever believes? In HIM should not perish, but have everlasting life.) After what seemed a long time of their conversing with each, the sheriff said, "Well, this is good that you're leaving our town, be sure that by this same time tomorrow you are nowhere to be found and if you are still here, you don't want me to tell you what will happen."

70

Beaten Unconsciousness

A few hours after the group had left from visiting me and while we were yet busy with making everything ready, we had yet another visitor to come knocking to our door. This man was a large-scale man, who probably was around 6'0" tall and looked too weighed around 200 lbs. He asked that I step outside? As I stepped through the door it would be the last thing I would remember for a period of some ten minutes when I awoke from being beat unconscious my eyes had been beaten so that they were swollen shut I was bleeding profusely from my nose and mouth; I felt as if I had been run over by a large truck. After recuperating my full awareness I suggested to the children we go to bed, as we would have an earlier morning that would begin our day of about twelve hours of driving. I wish I had known the LORD as, I did later in life. I also, wish these people had known HIM, and then they would have known that GOD declares to us in the book of Leviticus, 19:18, "But you shall love your neighbor as yourself."

Sleep was not easy tonight and with the enthusiasm of the coming morning, I was in pain from the beating that was very intense and my sleep was difficult. Then, sometime during the night my pain lessened, when I was awakening by the most hair-raising scream I had ever heard before. After calming the youngest daughter's who was in shock and having turned on a light too look into her pale face; I wasn't certain who would pass out first? The skin on my body seemed to be crawling

I expected my heart stopping before I could calm her over beating heart from this horrified stage

"I saw that man daddy, the man who came today and beat you up. I went to get a drink of water and he was climbing through my window and he had on black gloves and a big knife in his hand." I will always believe this was one finial attempt on our lives and had the daughter not went to get the drink we would have all been murdered that night; but GOD had a reason to save our lives that night and I will always be thankful to HIM for this. After this, I remained to sit the rest of the night on lookout, watching, listening to everything that moved. Then, at last the sun crown through the gray, cloudy skies and now in just a short while the five of us would be westward bound. What a glad day this would be!

71

Going Back to Texas

It was first dawn and we ourselves got into our overloaded car, as if we were sardines. I now begin to have terrible thoughts creating inside my mind, all the negative things that might happen we never had a spare tire, or a jack. As I drove, I prayed I never knew if GOD was listening to me or if HE even wanted to be concerned with me or not? But, I was still praying and I was doing some dreaming about when we relocated back in Texas, with a bit of luck, things we're going to get better for us. I knew I should have been praying for these people here, who had brought such grief to our lives that they might find JESUS CHRIST and they find in the word of 1st John, 1:5{KING JAMES} And the light shineth in darkness; and the darkness comprehended it not.

And in 1st John 4:8 {KING JAMES} it says He that loveth not knoweth not GOD; for GOD is love. Sometimes, we can be stubborn in our praying for someone when we're considering only ourselves and this is when we should be praying for the other person, our neighbor; in this case, our enemy. Again, I wish that I had known the closeness of the LORD. As I later proceeded to experience HIM; I would have been quoting the twenty-third Psalms to these people. Psalm TWENTY-THREE {KING JAMES} 1. The LORD is my Shepherd; I shall not want. 2. HE makes me to lie down in green pastures; HE leads me beside the still waters. 3. HE restores my soul; HE leads me in the Paths of righteousness for HIS namesake. 4. Yea though I walk through the valley of death, I will hear no evil; your rod and your staff, they comfort me. 5. You prepare a table before me in the presence of my enemies, you anoint my head with oil; my cup runs over. 6. Surely goodness and mercy shall follow me all the days of my life; and I will dwell in the house of the Lord forever.

The first hundred miles had gone without any problem; I believed it actuality had all gone to well But, the trip had just begun too. Now, as we had not eaten since the day before, I believed it was time for us to stop at one of the convenience stores for some snacks. Still in the same state, I was somewhat uncomfortable, fearing these people were of the same breeding as where we had formerly left. I was comforted after we had stopped and was all safe and back in the car and driving toward Texas. The soreness from the beating the day before had begin to increase again my eyes were starting to grow shut and I seem to be seeing in multiples. It was a fight to keep my eyes open, at every breath my ribs felt as if someone was cutting my insides out, the children had now fallen asleep and I had rolled down the driver's side of the window to let the cool night's air blow through onto my sleepy face, my pain had gone to Unbearable I imagine I had many ribs broken and did not know why? I had never before seen this man that came to our door that day and beat me this way?

Six hours after we left a town which Satan himself had power over, a town that should have been named after him? After now six hours of driving we crossed over into the great state of Texas. It was a feeling that an ox might enjoy from having the yoke removed from around its neck after a hard day's work. At last we were back on Texas soil, I now had to have something for my pain.

I had purchase a bottle of whiskey at our stop back in Arkansas and I swallowed down a large Mouth full I could feel the burn from the raw straight bourbon as it went down into the empty space of my stomach, I knew that this wasn't going to repair the damage but, but I look forward that it would minimize some of my pain. We now had a long open breadth of Texas highway which would seem to be endless and then, after some ten hours of driving I witness something which

I reckon I was never going to see; it was the rising of the great Texas sun. What a beautify picture! We had now been ten hours on the road and at last the town, we had for so long prayed that we would live to see, again was in sight. We must have all shouted at the same time; it Might have sounded as if we were a party of raiders charging straight through the middle of town.

I look forward now that the constant, horrible acts of being knocked around; and of feeling our lives were in a daily jeopardy would now be something of the past. At least for now the feeling of freedom was once again within us. Now, that we were back, the children would need to be enrolled in their schools, I would need to locate a place for us to live, and getting food for my children to eat would be our first needs, and I prayed that we would not have the same outcome as we had in Arkansas. Our first two weeks did not go as well as I expected, but still we were much better than what we had left back in Arkansas for now anyway. I did find a place to live and, even though it was an old shack of a house, it was place we could call our own and it did have a stove and a refrigerator. For the rest of our furniture I took cardboard boxes and cement cinder blocks to make our tables and chairs with. I knew how to do this from experience in Arkansas we used empty vegetable cans for our drinking glasses. We also made our plates from cardboard boxes; with this and some pots and pans that were given to us we felt fortunate to have all of this although we did not have much, we still at had each other, at least for now we did. Now, that we had put down roots in our own place, the children's check would be transferred and maybe, my step mother would watch the children for me while I went to work; but, this turned out to be wishful hope. Before, we would receive any food stamps or money I had to do some pan handling begging on the streets for money to buy my children food until something came in. As I was out looking for work I had a chance to meet a woman who told me that there was a place in town that I could go to once every three months and they would give me food items such as flour, sugar, corn meal and some canned goods. Oh, did this ever bring back memories to the time we had walk three miles in Arkansas and then after standing out in the extreme hot summer all day to be pushed back to the back of a long line and then be told, we're so sorry we just ran out of food. So, even though I was somewhat a doubting Thomas, I went and surprisingly did get the things I was told I could get. It was now another November; only this November would be in the town we called our hometown and hopefully this one wouldn't be as sad as the former one. I always believed that there were yet some helpful people left in the world and, this Thanksgiving it would prove to be true and one which would be a most memorable one we had in the past. People from local churches brought in foods of every kind, turkey that had already been cooked, dressing and baked pies. There were even fruit baskets for the children to enjoy. This was almost too much for me to accept it was as if maybe, I had gone to sleep and was imagining this Thanksgiving dinner. November seem to pass hurriedly by this year, unlike the ones we had past lived through. Christmas, was now on its way and like thanksgiving it too, was coming on considerably to speedy for me. Although, we would still be on a fixed income to spend money this year on Christmas presents would not be much I would not have to take a chance on some deranged person dangling me from a tall tree. My oldest daughter's teacher told her she had bought a new Christmas tree this year, and ask if we would like to have her old tree. I had no problem with second hand and we accepted it with pleasure. This year we had a Christmas tree that I would not need to go into the forest and risk my life for; we would still not have any of the fancy ornaments to garnish it with. But, it would give us the experience of making the old fashioned kind as before. This Christmas Eve we went out into the woods and found wild berries the children again; popped popcorn and we cut strands of paper and glued them into paper chains. We hung pictures of animals and other things on our tree we believed we had a pretty Christmas tree. It was on Christmas Eve night that local organizations, church fellowships, and people from surrounding towns came to bring presents and more food than we would eat. This was the best Christmas that we had known since the children's mother had seemed to have vanished. The New Year had now come and we were looking for a more fitting place to live, as our neighbors consent to parties and fights into the late hours of night. Rentals appeared to be plentiful as we located a very pretty and spacious two- bedroom home and, it looked to be located in a decent neighborhood. Our rent however was much more than we had been use to paying out based on the fixed income from the welfare checks the children drew the landowner decided to reducing fifty dollars a month from our rent in exchange for my keeping a trailer park mowed, which he also owned. Only if this would work out for us, but somehow I already knew that it wasn't going to. I did not know why I continued having over and over visions of things that we're going to happen before they happened, but each time just before something bad was coming into our lives I would somehow know. It had now been a while since one of the children had been sick, In fact I suppose we were well over due for any sickness in the family but, now it had found its way back into our lives. After having one of the daughters examine by the family doctor for an earache it was learned that it was more serious than I had thought. She had lost forty percent of her hearing and surgical tubes would be needed in order to help correct this problem. Shortly after we had returned back to Texas our car had broken down again, and once again we were without transportation and no money or a way for my daughter to see this specialist to do the operation, which was some sixty miles out of town? I was going to get my child to this town some sixty miles away even if I had to walk there with all four children. Although I still did not place much confidence in the Lord at this instance in my life and it wasn't because I did not believe in His existence; but I had not realized anything that He had one for us. Again I felt that we were being used as old Job was used.

72

My Daughter's Surgery

By chance It happen I had come across an old friend I had been familiar with for many years, he begin to tell he was having some financial problems, but if I could get fifteen dollars for the gas to travel the sixty miles he could take me. I imagined getting fifteen dollars wouldn't be such a difficult thing to accomplish, but this was as if I were asking for a million dollars. Medicaid would be paying for the expense of the surgery and the Department of Human Services were going to give the money I needed for the trip back anyone who showed a receipt for this small loan of fifteen dollars.

My own father owned a full service gas station here in town, but even after my explaining to him he would get his fifteen dollars back, he denied me and his granddaughter the help. I could not believe he was denying his own granddaughter the fifteen dollars in gas to have this needed surgery I could not understand in my mind what my child could have done to him that he would say no I as well could not understand what I could have done to any of my family that they had all my life showed me no love? And, wasn't only me this was for a child who could not have possibly done anything to anyone I wondered if it was possible that I was an illegitimate birth, and my parents where to ashamed to admit this to me? Something wasn't right I relay never thought I looked peculiarly like the rest of my family, I never acted like any of the family, for some reason I was just different?

But, would I ever learn the truth?

I beg with my dad, promising him if the human services fail to pay back this money I would come and work to pay back double the amount the fifteen dollars we needed. Then, after dad called for himself, he agreed to make the loan of fifteen dollars for the gas. It was January, the twenty-sixth, nineteen eighty-eight. The surgery was scheduled for six A.M. As my friend and I, along with the four children, headed out for the sixty miles to the hospital I felt that restless feeling that in just a short time one of my children would be put to sleep. My clothes become wet from my sweat I thought only if her mother were here during this time to help? I was here though and nothing could have stopped me upon our arrival to the hospital this morning the staff was set up and waiting to take her straight into the operating room. I had never before had one of my children put to sleep this was presume to be a safe and simple operation however, I learned from past experience of course to always expect the worst to happen. An hour and a half had went by slowly then, I watched full of fear as the doctor looked, as if he was in slow motion walking toward me with the bad news of something had not gone as they had expected. "Mr. Long wolf?" How about you and I go to get a cup of coffee? I feel as if my heart had leaped into my throat, I could feel as if I were going to faint I believe the doctor seen my face turn pale and he announced your daughter is doing just fine, She will be in recovery until her vitals are back to normal and then you can go in and see her" I took a deep breath and a heave a sigh of relief charged through my body.

I think I should have said, thank you LORD, However I somehow could not get those words out of my mouth. After returning home I had to fulfill the responsibility which I promised the landowner in looking after the trailer park, for our deduction of our rent everything was seemingly going too well at least until the strike of more suffering. My hunger for the affection and the companionship of someone that I could share my life with, and someone who the children might eventually love enough to look on as a mother figure, I happen to meet a young lady who I had in the past known the acquaintance of and she too had been the mark of desertion, left with raising three small girls to along. Our coming together proposed her to ask that we might see each other steady to anxious on my behalf, this was now about to bring more tragedy to my family. Our fourth day with each other, we decided to take the children to a nearby lake for a day of entertainment when the day ended, my now new girlfriend dropped myself and the children off at our house and then, she told me she would not be coming back, as she had decided to move out of state to live. This left me with that old well-known feeling I had all too well been known with me I was sure there would be no use to question her decision and just leave it as it was. Well it was not until the following day did everything become visible as to why she left. I noticed my wallet containing the children's check of over three hundred dollars, and sixty dollars in cash was missing. About two weeks went by when I received my wallet in the mail with identification still intact; no money, of course. This happened at an inconvenient time, as it was time to pay the rent and this was all the money we had I was asked to move and without delay. For us to ever live in another mission again, after the one we had stayed at in Arkansas, was something I promised I would never do but it looked as if this vow would be broken, as this was the only choice we had other than we sleep in the streets. Even though I had a father and stepmother who had more than enough room it was out of the question. At least the mission was clean and had floors and walls and did not have any bugs in our food. As we left the mission the following morning with no place to go and no one to turn to, this wasn't exactly what I had expected when we had chosen to come back to Texas. But, as I walked the streets today with four children I had to beg enough money from people to feed the children. Then, as opportunity would have it, we happened to walk up on a family that their job had called them to move to another city and they needed to move at once, this house they were moving from they just happen to own

I believed at first maybe, these people were angels, if there was such a thing? I was summon to come to where they were and ask if I needed to make a few extra dollars; of course I did. After they listen to my story of our need they said, that they needed to leave some things behind and if I wanted to move in today and watch over the place I could have the first month's rent free. This was almost too good to be true and for a while it was; at least until more serious sickness would fall on us again.

I had taken my youngest daughter to see a doctor for some growths that was growing on her arm and buttocks. It was recommended these growths be removed by a plastic surgeon, and as soon as possible I was told they would turn into cancer if they weren't taken off at once. Once again the surgery would need to be done in the city some sixty miles away and we still had no transportation to get there. I don't know how our local radio station learned of our need of a ride to the doctor, but it was broadcast over the local radio station. Before, the day had ended I received more reaction from the local town than I could have ever expected I accepted the first Good Samaritan that offered. The following morning at five thirty the children and I were picked up to drive one hour to the city where the surgery was scheduled when, was it all going to stop? This time the surgery had to be done because the doctor said; if it wasn't there was a good chance that these moles would turn into cancer. What next? Three hours had crawl by of waiting and no one had come to inform me of anything and I was starting to get nervous. At last I looked up and saw the surgeon who had performed the surgery coming down a long hallway. Once again all had gone well, but I imagined this was about all the good luck we were going to have. This was two in a row; I could hardly believe it. I was told upon leaving the hospital I would need to keep a close watch on the child for the next couple of weeks, or until the sutures healed completely. Several days had passed of our being home and, it was a hot summer day when the child who had just previously had surgery asked that she might get into a wading pool with the other children I had forgotten that the wounds might not have healed yet. I was told to keep the wounds clean and dry, but my negligence of giving permission to get into a contaminated wading pool nearly cost my daughter's life. Before nightfall, the wound area had become infected and she had been hospitalized with a temperature of a 106 degrees. Fortunately for us, neighbors here weren't as they were back in Arkansas, when I had pleaded with and cried out to those hateful people on that cold winter night that one of my children was deathly sick and needed someone with a heart and take her to the hospital. Not one helped us; they offered to send me to jail if I didn't leave.

However, tonight I had another serious problem, I have a very sick child in the hospital and the hospital staff required a member of the family stay with the child. I explained there is no other family member? But they insisted I would need to stay. This now left me with in a burdensome position I was going to be leaving the three children at home by themselves, because I knew beforehand my going to my parents and asking them to watch the other three children while I was at the hospital were out of the question? I began to think over what it would be like to have a family who looked out after each other, and was there for each other when needed? As the three Children and I walked across town, thinking over our circumstances, we arrived at our house as we walked into the front yard a friend pulled into the drive after a short conversation, then rationalizing my need, my friend volunteered to take care of the three children as long as it took for me to be at the hospital. It was three days before the doctor gave us the comforting news that she could return home.

Upon our rejoining with the other family this day it was going to bring more bad news, something we were accustomed to anyway. While we had been at the hospital, someone had broken into a building on the property and stolen many valuable items that the land owner had left behind for me to watch and, the landowner by some odd chance had showed up today. As the items that had been stolen weren't already enough to have made the owner crazy, he had come for the next month's rent which I also never had due to the sickness we had just gone through. His response to all this was it was it's not his problem and I need to move out and don't drag your feet. I question if we would ever get settled long enough to at least get everything unpacked. I did not understand why once in a while at least something could go right; were we cursed for life?

73

Dropped from the Welfare Program

It was time to move again, our next place was much too small for the five of us and it had a many of problems. Rats, bugs, leaking water pipes but, it were a roof over our heads and we would get used to it. The nights were long and depressing, memories often would trouble me images of the past haunted me; all the unhappiness, of the past mistakes the dishonest things I had done to everyone.

I accepted I had been a dishonorable husband to my wife and likely her leaving the first time was mostly my fault. All these things from my past continued to weigh down on me, but there was nothing I could change about it now. After each day's sun set in the evenings the children and I would share time with each other. Reading Bible stories or listening to a radio, as we could not afford television. This, would remind me somewhat of the years before electricity had been invented soon we found the sun had disappeared behind the horizon and the moon had filled the night along with all the bright celestial stars I would sit looking at the children sleeping on cots made on the floor, as the moon radiated through our window with no curtains. By now we had come about a new name throughout the community, we were now being called the Scavenger family and it did look as so, as we walked the streets for miles looking within every trash can we come upon; taking anything that resembled aluminum can which we could sell for money to buy the things which we could not purchase with food stamps, and of course some whiskey for me. The welfare office had now send for me to come into their office for an interview to see if we were still qualified of any further assistance on the food stamp program. I t was not easy for me to accept, how much time had gone by since the children's mother had abandoned us however, after meeting with the case worker she reminded me the younger daughter would soon be six years old and, we would be dropped from part of the program on her birthday. However, as I attempted to find some type of employment which I might be qualified to do.

My not having worked since the disappearing of my wife and I had lost the business, I did now know what I could do? But, I would have to do what I was told or they would stop everything we were getting. Shockingly enough, I was hired upon my first application as a short order cook I expected I could do this, as I had been cooking for four children over the past years now. Anxiety kept me from sleep through most of the night; from visualizing of what could now be a promising and hopefully brighter life for us? But, tormented again with my dreadful luck I wasn't going to get to go to my first job. Before the sun had chanced to rise, I was awakened by one of the children having difficulty with her breathing upon having her examined it was not an option, but she should be hospitalized at once for an upper respiratory infection the doctor concluded this could not wait.

Needless to say, they could not hold my position for me over the next few days that my daughter would spend inside an oxygen tent. Not getting the job wasn't exactly the worst thing again I was in need of someone looking after the other three children? However, it worked out that the hospital staff would allow the children to sleep the waiting room and the nurses would take turns watching after them. After all the things we virtually took on would not have been an easy task for two parents to do and, some might have cast in a white flag by now; but I kept trying to believe it would someday improve it looked as if though things had no other way, but to get better, or so that's what I thought. Little did I know that up till now it was only a small taste of what was yet to come? After, we had returned home from the hospital

I was going to still need to care for my child. I would have to leave the four of them at home by themselves for a short while until I could walk to the drug store for the medication, which would be needed for the next two weeks. While I was at the pharmacy today, I was told by one of the checkers she had a son who needed someone in his custodian department to help He cleans a department store at nights. That, afternoon as she promised me I had an interview with her son and on the next morning I was picked up and taken to the department store for a three hours test. When the test finished I was told I would be informed of the test results that afternoon of whether or not I had the job. At last the results were back; I had passed the test and was told that I could start to work the following night. Getting up the next morning, I had walked the three smaller children to their school the usual three miles, and then when I had so cheerfully told one of the other mothers about my new job and that I was in desperate need of a babysitter, without hesitation she proposed to take the job of caring for my children. My first night on the job, I had not been told I would be locked inside this store for the next ten hours and this caused an uncomfortable feeling to come over me. As the night inched into the earlier morning hours my far-sightedness was turned toward my children. Until now, I had not yet been away from them all night.

74

My Job

Morning at last came, the sun had come up and the store manager came in to unlock the doors

At last I could go home to my children. On our way home this morning, I began having that old well-known feeling, the one where something always was going to happen but, when I arrived at the house all the children were well and all safe. Later this morning after I walked the two children to their school again and had returned home to lay down for some sleep when I heard a knock at the door.

That forceful reaction inside came over me as I was going to the door; I knew whatever it was it wasn't going to be good. After opening the door, I stood face to face with the children's babysitter and with tears in her eyes, she said, she was sorry but her husband told her he would not allow her watch my children any longer. Well, I knew it wasn't good and this set back wasn't as if it were something I wasn't used to and I did have a few hours left to try and look for someone I knew better but, for the benefit of doubt, I went to my dad and stepmother and got of course, the answer I expected to get was no, the day passed and it was time for me, to go to work and no babysitter.

This job meant so much to us, having no choice and against my better judgment, I sat the children down and explained to them how important the job was to us and I was going to have to leave the eleven-year-old sister to look after them. Leaving for work, I explained once

247

more that it was most important to not open the door regardless who they said they were. This was a painful thing to do this night as I left for work. This night my work must have been poorly carried out as ever second of the night I thought of my children at home alone every siren I would hear caused cold chills to run the length of my spine I could imagine all the likely things that could be happening such as the house catching fire, someone breaking in and taking my children's lives while they were asleep I was a total wreck.

75

My Surgery

Then, that all unfortunate luck happens again, after only a few days of working bad luck would cash in on us once again I had expected this day, but I had tried to put it somewhere in the back of my mind hoping that just maybe, this time I was wrong. I had this large boil that appeared on my buttocks, which had become most painful for some time? I had put off being looked at by a doctor much too long then, after an examination I was told it would need to be removed as soon as possible.

Hospital again and, this time it was me down and again I had more problems as there were no one to stay with the children. The hospital had been more than generous with all they had done the past to help me. And, this time it was I that was here; and they would go beyond the call of duty to help.

As before I had no one to look after the children as I was being put to sleep and undergoing only a minor operation? But, one again they were allowed to stay in the waiting room while the staff took turns watching after them. I awoke a few hours after the anesthetic to find sitting beside my bed one of the hospital nurses waiting for me to awake. My first question was where my children are? I learned that the staff had decided to give the four of them a private room to stay in as I was going to be here at least through the night. The following morning after breakfast the chief surgeon made his visit to my room, and after some professional lying to the doctor I was permitted to go home, providing I promised to stay in bed for the next seven days. Even though I had still not reached the place in my life was I thought I needed a higher power to turn to, {GOD}? I still believed that there was a GOD. It was only that I had not seen anything GOD had done in our lives, at least for the better. I recall reading in the book of 1st John, 4:4 {KING JAMES} 4.Ye are of GOD, little children, and have overcome them: because greater is HE that is in you, than he that is in the world.

Not having a family to turn to during a time of need makes the world a sort of imprisoned place and more so if you don't have GOD to turn to. I now needed to build up strength, but to keep my promise to the doctor to stay in bed was broken as soon as I returned home there was just too much to do with taking care of four small children along. Coming back to the house, to find that the landowner was not only there for the rent money, but he had come to say that he was raising the rent which we could not afford, not to mention that we was over paying for this dump as it was. Sick and in need to recover we had to move again. Our next place was outside the city limits and it was frightening me having to leave the children alone in the country while I went back to work. It was now that I would have no choice but to quit my job and go back on welfare which the children were still eligible to receive. I am now reminded of the book of Ecclesiastes, the third chapter verse two. {KING JAMES} A time to be born, and a time to die; a time to plant, and a time to pluck up that which is planted; everyone will lose someone if there live My learning of the death of my stepmother was of no surprise as she had suffered with cancer for a considerable amount of time. Her strange way of parenting which had in my youth to cause dad to cause to use excessive punishment upon me, to the measure of beatings with leather that would cause cutting into the skin for blood to pour out of me. It had now been two weeks passed since the death of my stepmother and my father had sent us a message that he needed to talk to me. The children and I walked to the place of business that he owned. I near fainted to learn the news he had for us. My stepmother had will before she had died that the children and I have a nineteen seventy-eight Cadillac that belonged to her. I Could not believe my dad was going to honor my step-moms request after all the times I felt that he had turned his back on us in the past and he was going to actually give us this, no payment, just drive away with it. For the first time in a long time we now had our own car, at least for a short time. I suppose that the countless nights of sitting up with sick children, mishaps that sent me to take the children to the hospitals were all just part of rising up the children, it would be defined that we had been through our part of troubles. My memory is now taken back to a nightmare, when a team of doctors diagnosed one of the children to have a concussion, which might leave the child with permanent loss of memory.

76

A Terrible Fall

The children and I had went to a local department store on this late August afternoon for some supplies I would not have imagined such shocking thing could have happen, even with all our bad luck we already go through? However, what should have been a safe trip would turn out to be another heart stopping experience we had only been in the store for a few minutes when I heard this ear piercing scream that call out, "Daddy help!" Regretful to say I was the daddy that was being called for.

As I ran toward the cry as hurriedly as I could and only in the next aisle my legs felt as if all the feeling had left both of my legs as I weaken at what I was looking at. There, lying on the floor was one of my daughters, semi-conscious at this point I was doing some screaming now for myself screaming for anyone to call 911. Someone had heard my cry and called for emergency help the first responders, where there within minutes of the call and they worked hurriedly to brace the neck of my little girl, as they rolled her onto a flat board then, raised her onto a stretcher and the ambulance was at once speeding off from the parking lot, with screaming siren sounds that sent chills throughout my body. My heart pounded with the sound of war drums, as I followed close behind the ambulance rushing through the city's traffic lights, I thought to myself what this curse on us was?

It was time again for me to question GOD, What were we guilty of? How could anyone warrant all that we had been already been through? I asked God what was this plague HE has sentenced to us? I could not even imagine what Job must have felt like after GOD allowed Satin to do all the things he suffered Job through. Maybe, it was the wrong time to ask GOD this; maybe there was a right time and a wrong time to ask GOD questions. Maybe, HE didn't want me to ask HIM anything; maybe HE didn't even hear me at all? But, I wanted to know why had we been through all that we had been through? It did not seem fair at least once in a while we should have something for the better to happen, this was outrageous. I now have a daughter who is an honor role student and now she was unable to remember her own name. The doctor at the hospital advised me that since they were not equipped to make the tests needed at their hospital that she would be transported to a larger facility some sixty miles away again. I hadn't thought of where I was going to leave the other children as we followed close behind the ambulance to a strange city. But, after getting the child admitted and she had been given a room, tests were to begin on the following morning. Trying to sleep tonight night was uncomfortable as the three children and I were packed in the car like sardines. Then, the restless night ended. After, I had taken the children to the waiting room and I rushed off to the nearest elevator and up to the sixth floor, I could only hope that I would find them as I had left them. Stepping off the elevator I walked into my daughter's room to find that they had already begun the test and the specialist had already found the bad news that was waiting to be told to me. The doctor informed me that she was hurt quite seriously in her fall. As for the memory loss it would return on its own. The spine however, will require long term rehabilitation. All this happen from a spill of lamp oil in the floor of a Wall-Mart store, they alleged no responsibility that this was their negligence. Wal-Mart never paid as much as the hospital bill.

77

A Horrible Car Wreck

September nineteen eighty-eight, I had been drinking beer and whiskey all day of course this was a common practice for me, to be drunk ever day. It was toward the late evening. I was about to have the most bizarre change in my life that I had ever had I would have the most out of the ordinary acquaintance which I had ever made and it would in the end be the worst downfalls in my life, even from all the previous chaos I had lived through.

It was near dusk on this day, someone knocked at our front door the oldest girl went to see who our visitor was when a young woman stepped inside the doorway, and she asked in a French accent that she might speak with me? As my daughter brought this young woman to where I was sitting drinking beer and whiskey; I looked up at what had to been the most captivating woman on earth.

I had never before seen such a beautiful woman; at least not since I first looked at my step sister. She was even more beautiful than my wife when I first meet her. She told me that someone I knew had sent her to ask if they might borrow my car. I asked that she sit down for a moment while I thought this over as I now sat looking at this ravishing woman her beauty seemed to be dripping off of her angel looking face.

As I was looking upon her beauty, I notice as well someone had beaten her severely my asking her what happened to her charming face, she then began to sob and to tell me that her boyfriend did this to her all the time. As I took her be the hand and then looking into her big brown gorgeous eyes, I told her that she was not intended to be anybody's punching bag I told her that she did not have to go back to this either, that we had an extra bedroom that she could stay in.

After we had talked for some time it had become late and she decided to take my offer, at least for the night. The following morning I was the first up and happier than I had been since the children's mother had left then after her and the children had awakened she asked that she

Might use the car and that she and the oldest daughter could go and get her belongings from where she had been living? She said, she was tired of being beat on, and that if my proposal was still available that she would like to move into the spare bedroom I was believing for the

First time that GOD had sent this woman to me and if He wasn't sending her I was thankful to whomever or whatever was responsible for filling this long time emptiness that had been in my life, and replacing it today with more happiness than I had known in so many years she

Was an angel and as beautiful as any that, one would ever look at.

How could anything about this be wrong? With her moving in on this day I was ecstatic I would not have been convinced that I was ever going to experience the emotional feelings I was having Three months of her being there every morning, would soon end and with not only a shattered dream of our relationship ending, but three most important people in my life to come near an end before their time I thank GOD for sparing them with what they got out with.

It was an early summer afternoon I had left to spend a day with a friend at a neighboring lake taking with me my youngest child leaving the other three with, now the love of my life as my friend and I was visiting listening to a police radio, when I listen to some unbelievable news coming across the police scanner as I listen to what was near unbelievable, when the dispatcher call to the portal car.

That, a registry came back to a car registered to me then, with the next voice came from the portal car for two ambulances to be dispatched to the scene, my heart almost stopped "Please, my friends get me to town at once!" "That's my car in that wreck."

As we now at least had ever right at least seemingly to break the speed limit, my friend made no hesitation to make our way back into the city limits as we rounded a curve in the road I witnessed the most upsetting scene that I had ever witnessed, in my life. As we came near the crumple and tangled vehicles, the sight was ghastly, glass was scattered across the pavement, and pieces from the two vehicles were thrown along the sides of the road. Then, as we were being signal to stop at the police barricade; that we could not continue any further, I leap from my friend's vehicle much before my friend had found a place to pull over and stop. I ran with what felt as if my feet were never meeting with the ground, paying no observation from all the screaming on lookers which had stopped to look.

My attention was on one thing: getting to the car where my children were they, were three of my children in that now mangled thing which used to be our car after getting to the car and looking inside, I could feel a fainting feeling coming over me when I looked in and noticed all the blood that was saturated over the seats and the tiny pieces of smashed glass that lay throughout the inside of the car. Can someone please tell me where my babies are? I had been so addle that I had not seen the two ambulances leaving with the screeching blast of the sirens. I recall little more of this sight later when I came to my sanity; I was at the emergency room with my three children and a woman that I was insanely in love with. All were being treated with multiple lacerations and broken bones, and I could only imagine what else. As I ran from one treatment room to the next, checking on this child, then the other, then to check on the woman of my life, I was actually in need of some treatment for myself, for a nervous breakdown. Looking at each one with blood-drenched clothing, their bruises and severed faces it was nearly more that I could suffer. After several hours in the emergency room, the crisis was at last over. The three girls had sustained multiple cuts to the face, which required numerous sutures to the face and legs I was told they would not be a permanently disfigurement.

One of the girls had also sustained a broken leg. The three girls were released but the woman of my life was another story, as she had blacked out numerous times since the accident, and was being held for observation for a possibly of some swelling on the brain. As the three girls and I left the hospital we now were without a car again, since the one my deceased stepmother had left to us had been towed away after being affirmed totaled. However, after getting home with the children, and finding out from the oldest girl what had happened to cause the wreck, or at least as much as she could remember. She said, could only remember going around a curve in the road at a very high rate of speed, probably some 70 MPH when a jeep pulled out in front of them and they could not stop in time in time. The following morning my girlfriend was released and I was able to bring her home, after a few days of her recuperating she told me that she had decided that she would return to her former boyfriend. I thought this break up would be the nervous breakdown in my life, I had even thought of taking my own life. I really didn't know what good I was to anyone with all the things that had befallen on me. It was as if it was a sign for me, maybe, from satin but I wasn't sure of this, so I began drinking more heavily than I had ever before. I was drinking a fifth of whiskey a day, plus sometimes a case of beer and most of the time some drugs as well. I was spending the children's welfare check and trading food stamps for fifty cents on the dollar I had to lie to our landowner about where the rent money was. I would give a hundred dollars in food stamps and gets in return fifty dollars in cash for a 100.00. I stopped caring about me, about the children, about anything. I quit bathing, or cleaning the house. I had quit cooking for the children I had become a full-fledged alcoholic and drug addict I awoke each morning with my first needs being a drink of whiskey to steady the uncontrollable shaking and the last thing at night was to pass out drinking my alcoholism had amplified so rapidly and to the point I did not know if it was Monday or Friday. I was having days I could not remember my own name my children even become strangers to me I was sick and needed help but did not know where, or who, I should turn to get this help. My negligence to the children had become grievous and to the point something more severe was about to happen. Even from all the past. I couldn't comprehend anything being more woeful than what we had been through already but, lurking around the corner was the same tempter that had lied to Eve in the beautiful Garden of Eden and I had become so blinded by the drugs and alcohol I can admit with my not knowing the LORD, as I should have, I was open prey for satin.

78

The Daughters Dissappearance

April, nineteen eighty-nine, the children had walked to their nearby bus stop about one hundred feet from the house everyone had told me good-bye this morning and was off to school as usual as any other typical day. I was drunk this morning as usual and would end the day in the same way.

However, today as it came to a close and as I stood in the window watching for the children's school bus to come to its usual stop, I watched one; two, three children get off the big yellow bus something was wrong today and as many times as it had happened before, I had the gut feeling again of something not being right. Todays, insight of something about to happen would not be good after, the three children come into the house I asked, where is your sister? The oldest girl had not come home this had never happened before after questioning each of them, their only reply was "Daddy we don't know, she didn't get on the bus at school." At first I thought I should wait to see if maybe, she had gone home with someone then, after an hour had passed and still no daughter I decided I should call the school before everyone had left as I spoke with the school's principal he advised me that she had not been in school all day.

I then began calling close friends whom I knew she was acquainted with some told me they too had not seen her the entire day, others told me they seen her talking to a strange man and after that she had disappeared. At this I dialed the police to file a missing person report then, after doing what seemed to have been the most uncomfortable thing I had ever done in my life, I gave the police a picture and a description of my daughter and what she was last seen wearing. The police however, told me it would take twenty-four hours before they could file the report the following day the word was out "missing, thirteen-year-old, long blonde hair, blue eyes, weight sixty-five pounds, last seen wearing blue jeans, a gray western shirt and tennis shoes. By now students were coming to the house with false reports of this stranger she had been talking too and had taken her by force.

I was hysterical at this point this has to be the most terrifying thing a parent will have to live through, all the negative thoughts that filled my mind the third day had come and gone and there was still no evidence the police were even close to finding my daughter. I placed posters throughout the city hoping this would lead someone to knowing something? One week had gone by and no information of her whereabouts. I was sensing this extreme uncomfortable sensation about this, as nothing before had ever turned out right. Too much time had gone by if she had been taken with force I knew the real truth was, she would not be found alive. Oh, I know a person should look at things with a positive view; it says in the book of Romans, 4:17 {KING JAMES} before him whom he believed, even GOD who qucikeneth the dead, calleth those things which be not as though they were. But that was for people who believed in positive thinking?

It was for people who at least some of the time had positive things to happen in their lives and nothing positive had happened in our lives, at least that I could acknowledge it was now the closing of the second week of her mysterious disappearance when the police arrived at the house. I knew at sight of the officer as he walked slowly into our yard this was it, it was either bad news or the good news I took a deep breath and was ready for the Worst. Mr. Long wolf He asks me? "I was sent to bring you some news your daughter was found this morning. We don't know all the circumstances yet but sir, your daughter is being held at the Police department for an investigation as to why she ran away from home?" he added, "She seems to be O.K." Now, as the police were leaving, a lady from the child protective services were driving into my driveway she also addressed me, "Mr. Long wolf? I have official authorized papers to remove these children from you custody" well, I had something to say about this and it just happened I was also drunk and high which gave me the self-confidence I needed and told her the best thing she could do was to find the u turn that she had came from and as quickly as possible, and if she came back she might best bring with, the United States Marines. Unfortunate for me we did not have a vehicle or, I would have not been found when she returned however, I did not have a vehicle and there was no place for me to run to I had no choice but to wait to see if she would come back. It had been around three hours gone by when this lady came back and she had not brought with her the Marines as I had suggested for her to do so. However, she did bring with her what looked as if though it were the entire police department with

Police now swarming all the way through my house, the children was running in every direction as little mice being chased by large cats, they were protecting themselves under beds, in clothes closets, concealing themselves where ever they could to best keep the police from finding them. It looked as though with the large number of official vehicles at our residence that not only I was wanted, but the children as well were wanted by the F.B.I. The police had broken down two of the doors and had torn off four screens from the windows rushing in wrestling me to the floor. They had even broken up our end tables during our struggle. This commotion went on for about five minutes and the police now had my three children. Then watching, in total self-defense, with tears flowing down my face I will never live long enough that I should stop thinking about this day. Their small voices will forever haunt me in my dreams should I live to be five hundred years old. Their cries of please don't take us away from our daddy, please daddy make them bring us back. But, as I could do nothing while I was being held by force with three police officers holding me down, plus the fact that I Was also hand cuffed, they disappeared from my eyesight.

79

Loosing the Children

Today my life and the children's' life which I lived for stopped; everything which could be taken from me had just been taken what else could GOD take from me? What did God want from me? Somewhere deep inside me, I knew it wasn't GOD'S fault but, I had only HIM to blame.

The written word as I understand it says's this GOD, is above all, HE can do all things, nothing is impossible for HIM. So, why has HE allowed my children to be taken away from me, why didn't HE stop this? Yes I felt it was most assuredly GOD'S fault. I cursed the GOD for having allowed this to happen to me, who was this GOD anyway, what right did HE have to do such a mean and spitefully thing to anyone? I believed HIM to be a GOD of love, why, would HE do such a terrible thing to anyone? There could not be such a GOD of love that would do such a thing. I now believed HE was an imaginary figure. I believed that somehow HE had lost HIS power to do anything?

I had never before go through such hurt as I had to this point and I had lived through some troublesome pain in the past, but this one was the most hurtful of all. I was traumatized inside; GOD actually made me ashamed of HIM. It hurt to think, it hurt to breathe at this point I was convinced the suicidal thoughts I was having were the right thing to do. This was something too burdensome to live with, but as a substitute and a much easier way out of this, I would choose to drink myself to death, maybe, this too was what GOD wanted me to do?

Some seven days had passed after the children were taken from my guardianship as if a thief's had come in and taken away my children I had not had a sober day in the past seven days. I could not remember when the last time I had been asleep, or even a bath had, or ate. I don't remember how I showed up at, or how long I had been at the bar from which I had made a phone call from to some members of a church which I had been acquainted with through the children going to church. Then, after making a call which I later did not remember making, I continued with my drinking myself to a coma condition which was what I regularly did some time shortly before closing time for the tavern, I caught sight something in the bar that didn't look appropriate to me. I could not believe what my eyes were looking at my first thought was I had sure enough drunk myself blinding crazy my second thought was I knew it all along; he was as much a hypocrite as I had always known he was.

For some reason beyond my knowledge, the LORD which I had not come to understand in this era of my life was not yet ready to give up on me. Well, the person standing in the doorway was the person I had earlier called and he had come to my appeal for help? One could not have paid this man enough money to take a drink of alcohol, but he was there to rescue me because he believed this was what his JESUS would have him do? {WWJD} The following morning, I awoke in my same manner I had been waking up for some time. I awoke in the quivering condition, of uncontrolled shaking hands to the measure that I could barely stand it. I did the only thing I knew how to do to control it; I started the day off by using my own medication, a strong drink of whiskey. This was the customary medication prescribed by an alcoholic to steady the tremors, known as the DT's. I knew I was becoming poorly in health and I was past a point of needing help. Once again I called on these church friends to ask if they might know a way for me to get into a hospital for help and hopefully I could get sobered up. I was now at the bottom of the pit and pulling my own grave in on top of me. Although I had made this call I think was one of the most important calls I could have made.

I needed psychological help as well, as physical help and, then of the most important help of all that I did not realize, I was in need of help from a GOD that I was not ready to surrender and of course HE was at the time somewhat of imaginary for me. However, today was not the day for me to stop drinking or, to surrender to GOD?

My body was calling for its necessary drank which I on a regular basis was use to having. But, after my phone call a chain began to connect together, as the first person I had called and pleaded for help understood the gravity of the desperate need I was in for help. To get someone admitted into the state hospital, which was the only, free drug and alcohol treatment center within two hundred miles had a six months waiting list. I expected by this time I would have drank myself to death? But, after calling judges, attorneys, doctors and drug and alcohol counselors another prayer was answered, as I was to be admitted on the following morning. I recall this sixty-mile drive two the hospital on this morning very well, Satin, was working some overtime today as he was filling me with the thoughts that I was making a big mistake. He had now caused me to believe all his lies, that I was not an alcoholic, and that everything would be ok. I could almost hear his audible voice saying, why are you putting yourself through this? I recall we pass one of the liquor stores which I had paid many visits to however, I was seated between two men in the back seat and they were not going to buy into a made up story of my need to stop to use the restroom?

Much sooner than I wanted we had at last arrived to the State hospital, a hospital for anyone having mental problem and a hospital for drug addictions and alcohol addiction. I was hoping that my church friends were going to let me out at the front door of the admissions and leave? This however, did not go as plan. I believe if they had have just dropped me in the front door and pulled away, as soon as I had seen they were out of sight I would have run; I needed a drink and in the worse way. After, being admitted, I was taken to a second floor, then through countless other doors. At the admissions today day and after, I had said good bye to my friends who had made this speedy for me. I wonder if this was an institution for drug addicts and alcoholics or had they brought me to prison?

As we entered through one last door, which was also made of heavy steel and was locked behind us. Here, I would come together with others with the same sickness as me. For the next five days I would be here for detoxification, or to dry out. I could not help believe I had made the wrong evaluation about myself. I watched grown men playing with excrement matter which was in their diapers they were wearing I knew now more than ever I wanted to run, but there was nowhere to run to. We had come through at least four heavy doors made of steel and all had been locked behind us as we came through them.

I was not sure that coming here was going cure my addictions my coming here was more for my children than for myself as I had some hope that if I would do what the program was purposed and I got sobered up, my children would be returned to me. But, now I was here I could not imagine going to bed tonight, to sleep sober without my love that was the whiskey. My admission here was for thirty days and providing I worked hard on completing the program. I felt my coming here to do this treatment would be something my children would find disgraceful in me and I did not need any more shame than, I already had. When, the police found my daughter she had told them that not only was I an alcoholic and a drug addict, but that I had tried to sexually abuse her. This will be something that I will go to my grave denying. I had not done this horrible thing she was claiming; I could have never done such a disgraceful act to any of my children, I loved all my children to such I would have walked through fire for them. I knew this was a lie another lie straight from the devil;

I knew someone had influenced my daughter to tell this lie just my being an alcoholic and drug addict was not is enough to remove my children they needed something more to remove the children and this was it I had taken these children in under my wings for the past five years.

I would later learn that the reason with telling such a lie was she had seen this addiction was killing me, and I had neglected them, and it was true I had unloaded the responsibilities of parenting on her, but this was under no circumstance true I would have laid down my own life for any of them I could almost hear an audible voice telling me that I was never going to have my children back and, this treatment here was all a useless cause. I was trying with all I had in me to make this program work I went to all my assigned classes, I had my homework done on time and I tried to get along with everyone. Each day here looked as if it was a week, getting over. Listening to everyone tell their story of their past drinking experience only caused the urge for me to want another drink?

Then at last, the thirty days ended and it was time for my discharge and I wasn't sure if I was cleaned up or not, but I was ready to try my new life back out in the world without the use of my alcohol, I was going back to the same streets I had left some thirty days past. The same people I had ran with and they had not changed. The same drug dealers were here, the same users were here and also I was going to be living with my sister who was an alcoholic as well. I was going to need more courage than I had ever had before. On the day of my admittance into the treatment center I had been given a physic al examination to find the condition of my health, everyone got one; mine was on the poor side. The doctor told me that in all his practice he had not seen a person of my age with their liver in the condition, which mine was in. He said it was caused by nothing other than all the drugs, and alcohol I had used. My body was shutting down, I had turned yellow and my brain could not remember to do what it was intended, I would often forget to go to the restroom.

However, I was told, if I could stay clean and sober for next six months, get a job, and go to the entire alcoholic anonymous meetings and to visit with an assigned psychologist once a month I had a chance of having my children back. Today, I believe my greatest weapon against this addiction I had would have been GOD all alone, I had Godly people talking to me to try and help but, understand I was a heathen. I had been a heathen all my life, so I couldn't see making any changes in my life at this point; anyway it was GOD'S fault that my children had been taken away! Why would I want to serve this GOD, who had done this horrible thing to me? I thought GOD"S love had done all this to me anyway. I wondered where GOD, was all this time? Was HE too busy helping with answering more important people other than me? Was their prayer more urgent than mine?

I understood that HE was to be an omnipresent GOD, able to be every place at the same time. I thought GOD"S word said, in the book of Hebrews, 13:5, {KING JAMES}. Let your conversation be without covetousness, and be content with such things as ye have: for HE hath said, I will never leave thee, nor forsake thee. Well, I actually had the feeling of being forsaken now, and furthermore, I couldn't see anything this so called GOD had done for me, except cause a mountain of misery to fall on me. However, their six-month plan for me seems to be fool proof enough and I judged I could beat this. Everything looked to have started out well enough; I found a job working as a certified nurse's aide I had my own apartment the church brothers and sisters who had made it possible for me to get into the hospital had financed me a car. I had made the half-way mark into the six months; I had done everything that had been asked of me to do then, the desire that I had for wanting my children back was challenge by a craving for drink of alcohol. On one of my day's rest from work and as I was enjoying driving around in my car I heard an old familiar voice in my head as I passed a liquor store the voice said to me you do know you have been healed of your alcoholism, and that a drink will not hurt you. Go ahead and get you something to drink, after all you have been working very hard you deserve some refreshments.

It was today, that I would lose my sobriety by listening to the devil telling me remember, you've been healed of your alcoholism? You are no longer an alcoholic it was without delay the depression came back as soon as I had the first drink that led to the second and to the third and so on. A week passed I forgot to go to work, I lost my job, I was evicted from my apartment and when I woke up in jail, I could not remember where I had left my car. I sat on the side of my cell bunk with my head in my hands hoping I had not killed anyone, I felt ashamed of what I had done, because now there was no chance of my having the children returned.

I had thrown away all my chances to have my babies back again all because I listen to Satin once again, why could I not ever take time and listen on something that GOD might be trying to say to me? How could I have been so slow-witted for allowing such a thing as this to have happen? It was all for the taste of just one or two drinks of whiskey. I had just thrown what life I had left out the window. Much too late for me now but today, I believe it's so important to teach young children the love of "JESUS," Proverbs, 22:6 {KING JAMES} 6. Train ups a child in the way he should go, and when he is old he will not depart from it." I was taught by dear GOD loving grandparents in my young to worship GOD. But, I allowed the devil to lead me away from this teaching. The word says, in John, 10:10 {KING JAMES} the thief cometh not, but for to steal, and to

Kill, and to destroy: I am come that they might have life, and that they might have it more abundantly. So if I had applied some of the things I had been taught as a child, I believe our lives would have been a better, one than we had. I should have remembered that in Philippians, 4:13, {KING JAMES}. I can do all things through CHRIST who strengthens me."

Well, I went before the Judge and was sentenced to ninety days in jail for driving under the influence of alcohol and a fine of fifteen hundred dollars, which I would be serving additional time in jail for to pay as I did not have fifteen-hundred dollars. The Judge had shown me some leniency and I received a total of ninety-days in jail. I was offered to a work program where you can get your sentence reduced. However, this only lasted for a few hours after I was taken from the jail cell and was working on the city's streets I confronted the guard and told him I could not do this my reason, I was known by almost everyone here in town and, I did not want them to see that I was a prisoner?

No problem it was back to being locked up and serves out my full sentence. Sometimes knowing the right person can make a difference in one's life and it happen my father was a very close friend with sheriff, and when he learned who was in his jail he sent for me personally to come into his office. The jailer came to my cell and told me I had a request to come to the sheriff's office. After, we entered the sheriff ask the jailer leave I was told please sit down, I was ask if I wanted a cup of coffee or a soft drink? No thank you I said, why am I here I ask? The sheriff said, lone wolf; I have known your father and you for a very long time. I understand you made a mistake by driving your vehicle while drinking me also; understand why you don't want to participate in the work program.

Because, I am friends of your family I am going to offer something that I as usual would not offer to anyone else? Once anyone refuses to work you just stay locked up until your sentence us served, however, under the circumstance I don't like the ideal of you being in the cell with the people I have in there. These are some really bad men and very dangerous. I'm going to offer you a job cooking in the jail's kitchen, please say you will accept my offer, so you can do your time and get out of here. Ok, I can do this. The sentence was reduced from ninety-days to forty-fives days. After I had served out my time, I had been given consent of visitation privilege with my children, under the supervision of child protective services; I had no problem with their rule, I felt that it was an honor to be able to see my children. This visit was to be some sixty miles away, I would need to provide my own transportation, and I was going if I had to walk. Once again I need to hire someone to drive me the sixty miles I was more excited today from this visit than a child would have been waiting to open their Christmas gifts. My heart was overwhelmed with unspeakable Joy the visit, however, was somewhat saddened when only three children showed for the visit as the oldest daughter had chosen not to come with the others to see me but, this was all right. This was my first visit since they had been taken away and placed in foster parent care, and if this visit went ok with their regulation of the child protective services I would be authorized to see them once a month but with continued supervision. At each visit the children had looked as if they had grown up from one visit to the next. Each visit caused a gnawing sensation on the inside of me and the only way this would leave was to take a drink of whiskey. I was missing out on watching my children grow up I felt at times that I would seize the children and run, run as far as I could I supposed by now that my stay at the treatment Center had not proved to help me much; at least I wasn't showing that it had I reckon I went to the treatment more for the children than what I should have, that was for me; however, I had been confirmed an alcoholic, but this could not stop me from loving my children.

80

The Children Were Separated

It had been six months since my children had been taken from my custody and I was now going before a board of the department of Human Services to hear if I was creditable to have my children given back to me. The board had already decided before hand, that I would not have the children reconciled back to my custody I knew their answer before I went in, but I went anyway. I was back to my old drinking habits which I thought I was hiding, but somehow I did not have it hid as well I as I had believed. I was now at the phase in my drinking that I was undergoing blackout spells again, but I do not believe I had ever had a spell that I would not have remembered bringing any harm to my children, even with what my oldest daughter had accused me of doing. It was the first week of December and I was sitting in council room with twelve members for the child protective services, all of which would tell me in their own way just how sorry I was. They made me feel lower than dirt itself, and no, I wasn't going to get my children back, not in this lifetime.

It was just a few days before Christmas and I would get one more visit before Christmas. It would be my first Christmas without my children. I thought I had in the past spent some lonely Christmas but this was the most depressing one ever I felt as if had no one, and GOD was the furthest thought in my mind. My privileges were taken away to visit the children then, as the years went by and the children were all growing up, I would soon lose the relationship as father and my connection with all four children. I later learned they had been divided into different foster homes and the boy had to be institutionalized in a home for the mentally retarded I must have cried an ocean of tears.

Once again I am blaming GOD for this. I did not understand why this GOD that was supposedly a GOD of love had consented to all that had happened to us. Then, I learned the traumatizing news that the baby daughter of the four had a tumor on the brain. The tumor lay on the optical nerve, which made her an inoperable surgery candidate. The good news they told me was they didn't think at the time the tumor was malignant and that they believed that maybe, she was a candidate for chemotherapy and radiation. I wondered what GODS' plan was this time? Was HE actually going to take my daughters' life at this time I in her life, after all she is an old woman of four years old?

I could not read GOD'S mind I could not pray and ask HIM to heal my daughter after all HE had never in the past answered not one prayer that I had ask of HIM or at least that I had recognized?

I would never acknowledge it at the time that it was GOD but, something did happen that the many radiation and chemotherapy treatments she had taken begin to reduce the tumor and after one year she was in remission.

81

Living on the Streets

Just now my life went to the gutter once again. I was homeless living on the streets, sleeping wherever I could find to curl up at night, sometimes under a bridge, a cardboard box in an old abandoned building. My foods come mostly from what I could recover from garbage cans, begging, and shoplifting. I did whatever it took to stay alive living here on the streets is about knowing how to survive. Doing what a con-artist does best, I begged enough money to buy a cheap bottle of rut gut wine? I had lost track of just how long I had been living on the streets on this day after I had my fill of some old cheap wine, I had a few small coins left offer. I made a call which I promise to myself I would never do.

With my shaking hands I called my mom. Again, as in the past I felt the sixth sense not to do this because I knew of the outcome beforehand. After all she had just a few years past turned the children and me away sending us to live in that sickening mission where we ate the weasels in our cereal. I will never live long enough to forget this nasty place for as long as I live? I will always have memory of mom telling me her lord said, that me and the children cannot stay here with her. It was after this she put us in the mission. It was after the children and me left the mission and returned and, we had taken an apartment that I had spoken with my mom's landlord and her land lord told me

Mr. Lone Wolf this was a lie from the lower pits of the earth." She said, "I told your mom you and your children was welcome for as long as it took to get an apartment." None the less regardless of the past I was desperate to leave the streets. Hopefully, I can clean up again?

To my astonishment she agreed for me to come. Now, I needed money for my bus ticket once again, I had learned the business of being a con-artist and I would pan handle enough money to buy a one way ticket to Arkansas a place I had made a solemn vow I would never return here. After all, this was the same city the children and I lived just a few years past, where we had been tormented, and threatened with our lives. I can't imagine why I thought they had changed in just a few years? But, sometimes desperate people do desperate thing to survive and I was desperate. Now, for the next twenty-four hours I would be without food or drink until I arrived in Arkansas. As I only had money enough for the ticket on the bus, not even enough for a small cup of coffee.

As the long journey finished, exhausted and famished me was meeting by my younger brother as I stepped off the bus my sixth sense filled me instantly I knew once again I had made the wrong decision by coming here. I was asking myself why I didn't just stay and live on the streets. However, I was here I was tired I need something to fill the pain in my hungry stomach I could also use a strong drink of whiskey? I knew my brother was as well an alcoholic It seemed as if this was tradition of our family going back to our father. I did not understand where our father acquired his alcoholism from, as his parents were strictly against the use of this drink. Our mother also, came fond of this cocktail as well. Her father was a half Cherokee Indian and enjoyed the fire water very much so it may have begun there? However, I was not embarrassed to stoop to ask my brother if I could have a drink it's under the seat he told me. So with trembling hands I took a large swallow of the straight whiskey. Mom did have food cooked when I arrived, and I did eat until I was full arriving on a Saturday gave me the weekend to rest. Monday morning I went to apply for food stamps assistance. To my surprise I was given $75.00 per month. I believed that $75.00 of this would be enough for my share to stay here? With any luck, I would find work soon. But, I knew it wasn't likely anyone would hire me. I knew if I wasn't at least pretending to be looking for work that it was about to break loose with my mom. My guts told me she really never wanted me here, but some people need to put on a show for a look good to others at the end of each day as soon as mom comes from work I would give my report of every place I had search for work one of the employers was a retirement home. Shortly after I had lost custody of my Children I worked as a nurse's assistant I even was a certified nursing assistant I had always enjoyed working with the elderly. Mom was never educated with the use of electronic equipment, and I had secretly hooked up a recording devise that recorder all incoming and outgoing calls. However, I secretly learned mom never thought that a man should work as a nursing assistant only a man who was gay would do such work; she had made many comments to her brother on the recorder about me. I think he must be gay, she told her brother. What man would want to work doing a woman's job why, I've never heard of anything such as this in all my life she said. Then, another conversation was. I don't know what I am going to get rid of him? I'm sick of him being here I can't stand it. When she came in from work I would have the house clean and her dinner ready and on the table. Nothing ever pleased her. Mom would make a complaint if the sun came up and if it went down, if was raining or if wasn't. I enrolled in a class to receive my GED and I was call terrible names for this again, she told her brother and two friends of hers. Why, I have never heard of such a thing as a grown man going back school sitting there with all those young people. He must look so retarded sitting there?

Now, I had just about taken all I could something had to change fortunately my brother had an old military canvas tent which I took loan of and set up in the back of my mom's house. Along with a kerosene heater and an air mattress, I had my own little piece of the world.

Now, I needed whiskey. In the days when they gave you paper foods stamps you could most of the time get cash back, or you could sell them for fifty cents on the dollar. I used this method to get my smoking and whiskey money. Living in the tent was little a better than under a bride, the stove keep the inside around 40 degrees and of course the alcohol helps my kerosene heater also served as a means to cook on. The top was warm enough to heat a pan of soup on and to keep coffee warm to drink. It was cold enough outside that I could keep perishable foods outside the tent at night I had a kerosene lamp to write my log of what happen through the day as well as read. I took even a slight interest in reading the Bible I can't imagine. However, I often would read until late hours falling asleep.

82

My Dad Dies

An unexpected phone call came to my brother that our father was dying of cancer going to pay last regards I had to make a difficult decision, as my second step mother now, was in a desperate need of someone to move in to help with caring for dad. It was a difficult choice because the past came to my memory of the many times, the children and I had needed help and we had been turn away. However, I search myself and decided after all, he was my father and at most I owed this to him?

Dad suffered and fought with his cancer for a year after I had come home I watch as a miracle took place in my dad's life, as he turned his life around from the hard core person I had always known him to be, to a man who had asked "his living GOD into his heart, asking GOD to forgive him of his sinful life that he had lived? I am positive GOD did grant this prayer to my father and today he suffers no more, as GOD called him to that everlasting home in heaven. I plan always to believe there is indeed a GOD, who started this earth, created man and every living thing on the earth I accept this same living GOD, fulfills prayers; I had not on the other hand understood why GOD, had never answered one of my prayers my presence in a church had never been continual however, this had nothing to do my believing in GOD?

I've tried many places of worship, in the past and I would always find the same thing in all f them; they all had at least one person in their congregation that looked down their nose at who I was.

I knew exactly what they were thinking of me, not that I'm a wizard, but I've come to recognize these people. At my first becoming knowledgeable with these types of people, I had hoped they would be rare, but I learned quickly they were in every place of worship I had been to. They were all easy to spot; they were like the Pharisees and the hypocrite, making long and exquisite prayers in public places, wearing their priceless jewelry with their expensive clothing and to have a marked place of someone in a lower place in society to sit.

Until now from what I had seen in all the churches, I was picturing GOD was for the rich people and, the poor man did not have a chance, because from what they had portrayed to me, GOD did not have time for anyone who was in the lower class. I knew however, there was something missing in my life. It was as though I had this emptiness no matter what I tried I could not fulfill the loneliness that followed me. I didn't know at the time that what I needed was the LORD as my personal Savior. I knew that I was hunger for a companion to share my life with, but the chances of this happening were less than someone walking up and handing me a million dollars.

83

The Witch

Before my dads' death, I had taken a job as a nursing assistant; I had done well with leaving the drugs and alcohol alone for close to three months now. I had impressed myself and had overlooked the tactless people who believed they were better than me and I started to church. Still, I did not trust in what anyone had to say about faith, and about the need for going to church, for now church for me was probationary. I still had not recognized anything GOD had done for me? I understood the statement that GOD works in mysterious ways this much of my religious teaching of my youth was rooted inside me. I predicted when, I was born GOD had cursed me, and GOD did not bless anything which was cursed, and I had lived forty-one years without a GOD in my life, why should I change my life now? HE hadn't cared about me in the past to stop all the terrible things that happen to me, and if that wasn't enough, HE gave the devil permission to all the revolting things that came upon these innocent children oh, I did fear HIM alright; I feared HE was going to allow the devil to bring more evil to my live. However, as I was the only male nurse at the rest home, I was assign to work rotating shifts and work where ever they were short a nurse I suppose the old wise saying has some truth to it, about romance can happen in strange places, and, I further expect GOD has HIS will for all of us as well? I had the ideal that going to work might reduce some of my anxiety which was increasing inside of me; I felt at times I would explode from the mountain of problems that had been stored inside me over the past years. If only I had someone to trust, someone I could tell all my troubles to, someone who would listen? This night at work would bring forth just that person I had worked a day shift on the two to ten shifts then; as my shift had ended I was ready to go home I was asked that I stay over and work the ten to six shifts. I remember my detesting working with the second shifts charge nurse I had no desire to work with her even though I had never actually meet the woman I would notice her coming on duty as I was leaving, she came into the building as if she owned the place, she went through ever single residents room making an inspection of everything If one thing was found unsatisfactory you would be written up, no I wanted nothing to do with her she had a nature that no one cared for. Oh, she did however, reminded me of a princess in a storybook I once remember reading at the same time she reminded me of those sitting in the church, those that thought, they were better than thou kind of people. She was in my opinion a first class witch, respectfully putting it I had no plan of working with her in spite of the attractiveness she looked to have. Up until now, I had been with many Delilah's since the children's mother abandoned us, and I thought I was a very good judge of people at first sight. However, as the night went on I had finished my work which I had been assigned. Then the witch, the charge nurse called me to her desk to report my assignment. After giving my report of the work I had been assigned, we had time for some small conversation I learned afterwards that I owed her an apology she was remarkably attractive she had fiery long red hair which she often let down to fall loose on her white nursing uniform. Now I had also, had learned that night she might have some money put away and I may as well be the one to help her spend some of it, only I didn't know that GOD was setting me up on this one and things were about to backfire on me. My six censes was not working as it had in the past I did not foresee what was about to happen this time? I was thought of myself in the past to be a professional con artist. Apart from, my attitude I had carried around inside me, that GOD had never before answered any of my prayers, I continued to pray just the same. Well, I continued to pray just in case HE decided to answer a prayer for me? One of my prayer's was that I HE, send me a woman to share my life with I was about to get a example in being careful what you ask GOD for, because HIS mercy might give you what you desire, as now this person I declared I would not as much as work with was soon going to be my wife. As I talked about before, this had to have been the work of GOD, as at the end of the shift we had made plans for our first date.

84

My Dreadful Double Returned

I believe I was ready to be truthful with myself as well to everyone else, but my old arts of the trade of being a con artist was beginning to work overtime and my now fiancée had not seen the other side of who I really was. I had been impersonating someone who had changed his life from being a miserable drunk to someone who had turned their live around and was now living their life for the LORD. I was giving my best recital of all time of a man who wanted to serve GOD and wanted someone who wanted the same thing. We went on our first date, with her suggestion we attend a church, which she was a member of I play acted to have been in favor of this after all, I am professional con artist. That date would to lead us to many more and things would move well for the next year at which time we decided we wanted to share our lives with each other and had set our wedding date. Then, that unpleasant double of mine, the evil spirit inside of me, once again took control of my life. I was back to using and abusing the drugs and alcohol. Needless to say, the marriage was called off without forewarning after awaking from a drunken trance, I awakened to find all my personal belongings had been moved, at which time I was ordered I would also move on, or the police would be called to escort me away. This move on part, I was all too familiar to me, I had heard it many times in the past I recall, this from the children's mother's parents telling us this Then, there was my mother who had told us this and last there was my dad had told us that we would need to move on. Fortunately, for me I had a friend who would be taking me in to keep me from having to return to the streets in exchange for helping take care of him, as he was an elderly gentleman.

I was now going toward the bottom of that old familiar pit again this time; I was at my lower most and pulling it in on top of me. I was somewhat much worse this time, than I had been before when I had gone to the treatment center I would watch for the first time, actual death knocking at my door. I in fact acknowledged an out of body experience, meeting with what it will be like on the other side, that is waiting for the unsaved of this world. I have heard the African American complain all my life, they were once slaves to the white race, and we now owed them something for this. How true this statement is that not them, but their forefathers was once used for slavery, but this was also over a hundred and eighty years ago. My white bloodline were also used as tools of slavery, that proof is in the Holy Bible, beginning in the book of Exodus when Pharaoh, the Egyptian ruler held my family hostage and as the word reads he knew far more about punishment than the white man ever knew. I point this out now because; I have been a slave to an even much worse ruler than Pharaoh. I have been a slave to Satan all my life. I have been a slave to Satan, the strongest defeater of all

I have for so many years had been a slave to Satin and could not see he was taking the life out of me, his tempting me with the drugs and alcohol which he knew I was not strong enough to refuse I lay this night at the doorstep of my death. I had stepped over the edge to take from Satan's hands a bottle of his toxic poison, knowing full well I was trading my very soul for this cheap bottle of whiskey, and just as I was about to authenticate the deal with satin something happened.

85

A Place for the Unforgiven

Several weeks after coming here to my friends home, and to add he as well was another full fledge alcoholic. I had not taken in a sober breath in those several weeks time. I was resting on a davenport in a dark room with cramps in my stomach so severe I was wishing either, I could get better or die. I had even told GOD to either kill me or heal me, when some time into the late hours of the night my pain was interrupted with a strange being in the room. I recognized at once that whatever this being was, it was not a worldly being in the dark room with me. My pain which I had was taken away immediately I enjoyed a total relief from pain and everything of this earth. Then, in the blink of the eye I was looking at myself at rest on the couch as I now was a spirit drifting over what I was assuming my lifeless shell of a body. Instantaneously, I was standing face to face in the center of a lake of fire, which I would learn had been made ready by GOD for the lost in CHIST and had given this place the name of Hades. It was as if I was standing in the midst of an ocean and looking to my right, to my left, to my rear, forward upward and downward was nothing but fire. Fire was everywhere I looked. Nothing could withstand this fervent heat, but, yet the spirit of GOD was safeguarding me in the midst of all this experience, this fire was not touching me. Matthew, 8:12 {KING JAMES} says but the children of the kingdom shall be cast out into outer darkness: there shall be weeping and gnashing of teeth.

"I could not look at anyone's image there. I knew however, there were as many souls that had died and were sent here, as there were people on earth. I would have believed also, with all the fire which was walled around this endless place of damnation, that there would be light, but it was complete darkness, a dark which I had never before seen on earth. I stood in a frozen position listening to the frightening screams that were penetrating into my spirit; this was continuous as souls entered this place.

The stench of death surrounded the darkness of this gruesome place their agony was never going to end; it was indeed a world with-no-end, this was the eternity, for unrighteous. I could hear what I believe was old Satan's demons in a far place some-where, rippling with his laughter at what seemed as if every second a soul had come in. It was apparent as every time a new soul entered here the blaze would burst forth with even more flame. I'm not sure how long this visit had lasted, but one second was enough to last me a lifetime as instant as I was getting here, in the same nature I came back. No man could have built such a machine that could travel as fast without burning up in the earth's atmosphere. It was like you were in one place and then you were some other place without feeling the maneuvering; I was moving as in the twinkling of the eye.

As I re-entered my room, in which I had been at rest on the davenport, I likewise looked once again at the lifeless shell of my body without a soul; the same one I had observed when I left with this strange light. It was peculiar to look at myself and knowing I am not there, I knew when my spirit returned back into my body I was going to have the mortal responsibilities again, and I was going to be unhappy to leave this angelic spirit that I now was. However, I did not feel the transfiguration, it also was as the twinkling of the eye and I was once more my human self again, with exemption of the excruciating pain I had before this took place. This pain did not return all of a sudden I was on my hands and knees beside the sofa weeping, as I prayed about the horrible place of torment I had just paid a visit to as I prayed, please forgive me of my immoral life that I have lived.

I know I have rejected YOU all these years and have turned my back on YOU I know I curse you and blamed YOU for all the things that happened through my years here on this earth and I'm remorseful for this. GOD, as a child I was raised and taught to believe in YOU.

GOD, YOU accepted and old disgusting sinful sinner that I was that YOU came and paid a price which YOU did now owe, and one that I certainly owed, but could have never paid. Delivered me LORD from these drugs and alcohol I am addicted to use me, Oh LORD, where you will, Amen.

GOD began immediately to speak in the stillness of the night, as I listened in my now horizontal position to what GOD had to say to me. HE said this was indeed a place for the unrighteous. HE said however there was no excuse that anyone should have to spend their eternity there and HE made no apologies for those who were sending themselves there. GOD said, HE did not send people to this eternal place of fire, but people sent themselves to there by rejecting HIM.

Then, GOD addressed me, saying, "lone wolf, I'm not going to make you change your life to live for ME. You know the difference between right and wrong and I have given you, your own choice, but if you so choice to follow ME I will give you the promise of everlasting life in My Kingdom and I will never leave you nor forsake you, my son." "On the other hand, son, the things which you witnessed will be for those who choose to serve my adversary, Satan his kingdom will also be eternity and I have given you a firsthand look at what his world has to offer." As my LORD continued to speak, HE said, "Your sins are forgiven, your deliverance from the drugs and alcohol are granted, your healings, your addictions have already been paid for, my son." Then, HE said "I have something to request of you, my son?" Me, LORD! What could I possible do for YOU, LORD? I had tried it all, the dance halls, alcohol, drugs, lust, gambling. I had listened to and tried everything that the devil had offered me. There wasn't any

At lasts that worthlessness which had been inside me for this entire thing that I would not have tried. Tonight, however, Satan had been defeated. As GOD continued to explain to me HE wanted me to go out into the world and preach HIS word I could have fainted at this, LORD I said, "I don't mean to question YOU, but are YOU sure? This is lone wolf you're talking to." "Son, "I know who I'm talking to." Then, the LORD began to show me visions of place I was to go, He began to give ms scriptures from the Bible, and the LORD said something I wasn't expecting. HE said, "My son listen and be careful of Satan he will not take this without a fight. He will be on every corner you come to, he'll have a trap set in every highway you take, and he'll use people that you would never expect. Resist him in MY NAME and he will have to flee." After spending an entire night speaking with the LORD without sleep, I could not remember when I had felt so good. It was like what a million dollars Might make a person feel like. I felt as fresh as if I had slept a week. I had just been given a second chance in the life to prove that I could be that GOD wanted me to be?

86

The Marriage

As the dawn of day came, I wasn't sure what my ex-fiancée would have to say upon my sharing with her this experience, or if she was willing to talk, but I had to tell someone of this extraordinary thing which happen to me. I imagined I would start by sharing what the word says in the book of Matthew, 19:6{KING JAMES} 6. Wherefore they are no more twain, but one flesh. What therefore GOD hath joined together, let no man put asunder.

"Satan, had been dancing in his paradise since our separation, he believed that he had achieved his will instead of GOD'S will, but Satan is a liar and loser and has been since GOD hurl him and a third of his angels out of heaven. Now, it was time to take back what he had stolen from us I remembered what GOD said, to me earlier about confronting this snake in the grass in HIS NAME and he couldn't withstand the name of the LORD and that's what I did I simply said, "Listen you devil in the Name of my LORD you turn loose of my life I stand before you in the name of JESUS satin That's was all it took, when he heard the name o JESUS he fled like a scalded dog Well, I had to make the call and see if my fiancée would at least listen to me.

Before the day had ended we had made plans to talk over reconciliation I'm not sure who was the happier to see me, my fiancée or the baby of the family. My wife-to-be had a twelve-year old boy she had named Toughie, Toughie had been a baby all his life, you See

Toughie was a part poodle and part something else no one knew what. I said, the other part was grizzly bear, as he would attach anything that moved so long as it was bigger than he was. However, he was worth his weight in gold I remember during some of my days of being hung over Toughie was the closest thing to a human's love that I could get to feel sorry for me. When I would snuggle up to him to tell him how much I was hurting and how sick I was he would whimper as if he was crying for me.

Sometime after our marriage old Toughie's heart failed him, as he was quite old, but he will always be remembered. I've learned that you cannot always know what GOD'S will is for you, but I know that HIS will is what's best for you. I've also learned that you cannot out give GOD, for the more you give to HIM the more HE will give in return and all HE asks of us is to give HIM is our love. On December the 8th, nineteen ninety-four I was married to the woman I had vowed that I would not as much as work beside. A woman I came to love from our first date, after we had went to her little Church and mostly because I had learned she might have a little money salt away.

I had intended all along to take the money and run but, GOD had other plans, and I suppose it just proved that GOD still works in mysterious ways. Coming into my family was also a young step daughter of eighteen years old who also, had a new born baby of five months old.

The step daughter having lost her dad at seventeen-years old and the new born of course who would never knew her real grandpa? However, the step daughter would go on to give birth to four other babies, all of which would always address me as there grandpa, and the step daughter has continued to call me as her dad even though her mom and I have been divorced for many years now.

87

Second Divorce

Well, all that starts well does not always ends well. After 13, years of marriage to this woman it had now come to an unexpected end. I suppose this should have not come to a surprise considering her life had been control by siblings in every part of her live, this included our marriage. And, then there was something I had always felt during our thirteen years of marriage and this was I don't think she ever got over losing her deceased husband? It was as if I was living with a ghost in our home? Actually this came rather sudden when one day out of the blue she said, she needs to move on an ask for a divorce? Why this did not hurt me I am not sure but, I totally agreed with her and told sure only she would pay for everything. She took only her personal belongings and asks for a hundred dollars to live on until she took her pay on the first of the month. We said good bye and we each went our separate ways.

Having only a seventh grade education of which I partly blame myself and partly blame my parents for moving me around across the country and the alcoholism in my parents I was not getting the proper learning I could have otherwise. The, education I obtained after dropping out at the age of 16 would be self taught. My dad said, I had an alternative to go to school or go to work and lastly I was old enough to drop from school and I was old enough to leave home and live on my own. Trying to work at 16 was not easy. I began my first job at picking cotton which I learn the first day was not my consideration of an occupation that I wanted a career in. Later you will understand this statement. Even though I had never been more than five hundred miles in any direction I had seen movies of the big cities and movies of foreign countries on the other side of the world.

Now, I was raised a country boy in a very small township in North central Arkansas, with a population of around 400. I had until dropping out of school been no place further away than about 500 miles. In the small township where I grew up in, everyone knew everyone else. They knew all your siblings, your mom, and dad, your grandparents, your cousins, uncles, aunts, how many dogs, and cats you had when and what you ate and when you went to bed and got up the next morning. I had always felt that for some reason I had no distinctive resemblance with the rest of my family, I looked different, I acted different, and I talked different. Here everyone was slow, they walked slowly, they talked slow drove slow. I wanted a faster paced world than this; here it looks as if everything is at least a hundred years behind time. I always wanted to go places, see things meet new people. I did not belong here my being different would always be a mystery to me however, being here seemed hopeless that I would ever get out. Growing up in this era there was no video games or any computers. The closest thing to a social media would have been through the mail. So, even at the time of my second divorce I had no experience of the new technology of the World Wide Web. My dad said, I had an alternative to go to school or go to work and lastly I was old enough to drop from school I was old enough to leave home and live on my own.

88

Polish Woman

So, how is a boy from such a poor rearing from a small town, of northeast Arkansas with no education end up moving to and living on the other side of the world? You would think impossible. However, after the divorce I had heard of a lot of people using this social media on the internet to meet people for different reasons. Just for a friendship and others for a lasting relationships, which was the one I was most interested in I did not believe at the age of 56, I wanted to be alone for the rest of my life. Still my not being educated in the new technology world I purchase an inexpensive laptop computer, if it crashed it was not so much loss.

Living in an elderly friend's car garage after my divorce was just a slight step up from being better than living on the streets. But, having been declared disable from work after three back surgeries I was not in the position to afford rent any other place. This however would be a red flag to finding a fitting mate for me as a companion on the social media it was not likely that anyone would be looking for a man living on disability and in a car garage.

However, as my learning the social media begin and the hunt to find the hopeful woman for me who I was looking for and hopeful the same thing she would be looking for? This was much easier than I had imagine, almost instantly I had more women that were in love with me than, I could keep up with. There must have been at least a dozen attractive young women who sent me their picture and, they were all looking for exactly as I had described myself as on the profile of myself. We were an instant match for each other in every way. After some four months of chatting with all these beautiful women who had falling instantly in love with me. My irresponsibility with this new social networking and wanting to have the companionship and affection of a female I was easy to fool. I actually believed all them when each told me they were in love with me this was working until they ask for large sums of money that I send them to travel to the USA from their foreign country they were from.

That instant love they had for me vanished just as quickly as it began, when I explained that I was a poor boy living on disability and living in a friend's car garage and explained I had no way to send the money. As this now becomes a daily habit of playing mind games I was not expecting anything to ever become serious with this. However, more phenomenal things have happen so the games went on. Every day a new pretty face, a new name the same line of I am in love with you boy, I had taken all this in at the start, and now I had learned how to play the mind game right back it had taken me some time to learn that these were all the same person with different pictures different names.

I had women who were allegedly living in Africa doing missionary work, women from Scotland, Russia, and Ireland even a women from England that was going to dental school. Why would a student that is about to graduate from dental school need me to send her money for her to travel to America to meet me if she was really serious about meeting me. But, I was blinded by the fact that these young beautiful women were interested in me had I have known I was such an admired man I would have never married the first time. Then, as fate would have it I open my email one morning and here was another woman. A woman who had simply written me a letter from a website called plenty of fish. After, looking at her profile on the plenty of fish website, everything looked to be in order and for the first time it looked genuine. She was from Sweden and was genuinely a most attractive woman our age difference was only seven years apart. In order to keep a happy wife and for me a happy life I will not say who was the older was. We did however, have somewhat a slight commutation problem. You see I spoke no Swedish and she was beginning to learn how to speak the English language.

And, again this was a woman from the other side of the world, the other dozen are so had been as well, and all wanted me to send them money sent to them. I was not going to fall for this again. Our meeting on the dating site in April set in motion a daily meeting and chatting with each other. We exchanged phone number and email address. Having a seven hour difference in time was somewhat of an encumbrance at the beginning trying to remember when she was getting up or going to bed. We had chatted now from April until September 2008, when we believed from our written words to each other that we were in love. At the time either one of us had a web cam and the only pictures we had of each other was from those we had taken and downloaded and sent to each other, but we where captivated by each other, and was anxious to meet as soon as possible.

The stumbling block with our relationship was this beautiful little woman lived on one side of the Atlantic Ocean and I lived on the other side. But, without any hesitation I felt this to be without a shred of doubt the love of my life. How would we ever get to meet in person? I surely was not financially able to travel to Sweden. Furthermore, I would need a passport; I had never seen a passport. After all I was still the boy from the country that had never been out of America? Then, one day she sent me an email and asks where the closest airport to me was, and if she flew to America would I meet here at the airport? Ok, now I am waiting for the next punch line to come?

Can you send me some money so I can come to America to meet you? I must plead guilty here

I was a doubtful, that this attractive woman was actually coming to the United States, from Sweden to meet me? So, still with the doubting Thomas, I thought what it was going to hurt if I drove to the DFW airport in Dallas, Texas and she did not show up.

No one would ever know I had made a dupe of myself, by going to meet a woman from the internet that promised to meet me there. After all, it was only going cost me a tank of fuel so who was going to know the difference? Well, the day came she had actually e-mailed me her flight itinerary, and after doing some checking it looked valid. Mind you, I understood that not only is this a woman I know nothing about other than our emails and chatting on the internet, and someone who is also five thousand miles across the Atlantic ocean, It was likely more frightening for her to fly to America from Sweden to me strange man that she as well knew anything more me than what I had told her about me. For all she knew I could have been a rapist, a murderer and yet she had trusted that I was everything I had told her I was. These relationships are not always advisable as it could be very dangerous.

However, In order to make her more feel more relieved upon meeting me for the first time, I took my youngest daughter and husband and granddaughter to the airport to meet the beautiful woman from Sweden. As I nervously sat in the terminal waiting a while, then up to pace across the floor for a while waiting as if I was an expectant father for his first time. Every few minutes I was up to check the arrival of her flight number. Then, at last the announcement came over the public address system that her flight had just landed. I watched nervously as everyone on the flight had exit off the plane from Sweden, I did not see anyone who looks as the picture I had of her? Well, just as I imagined guess what? There was no woman on that flight from Sweden I had been stood up; I was the laughing joke of the day. I was betting she was sitting back in Sweden having the best laugh she has ever had in her life was guessing she was saying, to all her friends and family, I wonder if that cowboy in Texas really thought I was coming to America to meet him. I bet he is sitting there at the airport looking like a big fool waiting for me. I wanted to cry; I wanted to laugh at the same time how could I have let this happen to me again would I ever live long enough to learn my lesson? I told my daughter to take me back home she's not on the plane it was nothing but a joke. But, then, my daughter asks, dad is this woman short, yes I said, does she have short blonde hair, and wears glasses? Sure I said. If you're trying to make it worse you may as well have a laugh too daughter. No dad I'm serious I think I see her coming. Then, I looked up and though the security doors my heart come close to jumping out of my chest. There she was, just as the picture I had of her from the internet. Wow, she was as beautiful in person as the picture I had of her. Then, when are eyes caught each other she came running toward me and said, are you my lone wolf? You are really here, wow, I can't believe me she said. I knew just from her writing, and from some phone calls she had an accent, I answered her and said, yes I am your lone wolf and you are my princess from Sweden? Yes, yes she said. I was not sure at first if it was a good ideal for me to bring my family along on this first time to meet her, but I was happy afterward that I had my van had three rows of seats and we were able to sit in the back row while my son-in-law drove the sixty miles back. I was so happy this night as we drove back to my daughter and son-in-laws home. We could hold each other close taste each other lips, for the next sixty miles. When GOD gives HE truly does not give junk. GOD has at last given me the best there was it's like HE took one of HIS own angels and dropped her to earth just for me. I can never remember in my life time being loved the way I am loved by my princess from Sweden my princess from Sweden's was here to visit for two weeks and in those two weeks together we had so much to talk about. It was if we had known each other our entire live although, I could speak no Swedish at all and she was learning to speak English we often had to draw pictures to speak to each other these two weeks of her stay I would stay with my youngest daughter and granddaughter. I had told her that I lived in a car garage, but it was a little embarrassing to take her there just yet those two weeks seen to have gone by as if it was only two days. Then, having to take her back to the airport was one of the toughest things I could remember having to do I was full of fear that I had not been everything which she had expected in me, and this would be the last I will ever hear from her again? The feeling of something might go wrong in the flight across the Ocean to her home in Sweden. I stayed awake for the next twelve hours when I was relieved to receive her text message upon her arrival back that all went safe and she had returned home. I was also, relieved when she told me how happy she was that she came to America to meet me and that she was returning again the following month. It was now October; my Swedish fiancé was back in America again for another two weeks. Our first two weeks visit was as if it was only a couple of days' again, and I was once again we were back at the airport, only this time with tears in my eyes and a lump in my throat that blocked my air way making it difficult to breath and to swallow although there is a vast Ocean separating us and many thousands of miles between love, has no distance that will keep us apart. It seemed as if we had a love which began in heaven, our heartache of missing each other was so deep that in less than a month my Swedish angel was on her way back to America to see me once again. And, once again we met at the airport for another two weeks together our love seems to grow stronger each day and the miles between us and the Oceans would not keep us apart. Once again I was on cloud nine to be with her but as before the two weeks went hurriedly by and back to the airport to say goodbye again as before I waited nervously for her to contact me telling me all was well. Then, she bomb shell me with another wonderful surprise when she said she was again coming back in November for another two weeks

89

My Wifes' Mothers Death

It was now November, once again as she returned back to America. However, this time after picking up my fiancé up at the airport I took her to my studio apartment, that was my garage where I had set up my little make shift apartment. I know she was trying to make me feel comfortable by telling me that the place look nice I knew that this was not something that she was us to living in. We begin making applications for to stay in America from the first time she had come to America. Now, this being her third time here we had almost completed everything required we were advised by our local Congressman's office that if we wanted to be married all we need was a piece of identification and go to the local Justice of Peace office. After getting settled and just a short while we were working on paper work to arrange for her to stay in America. My lifestyle of living was something I was accustomed to, I was able to cook full course meals on a two burner Colman stove, cook outside on a grill, sleeping in arctic sleeping bag through zero degree temperatures taking baths by a water hose, when the temperatures would allow it but then on the other hand I was not sure my new Swedish bride was capable of the same life style as mine?

Shortly after my fiancée's return this time she received a call from a family member that she needed to return to Sweden and without delay. My fiancé's mother had taken gravely ill and the family was asking everyone to get together at the hospital to pay their last respects. This was at the most inconvenient, time as I had never before been out of the United States and therefore I had no passport. The usual time to process a passport is three weeks, I needed one at now, once again, our we went to our local Congressman Office and was instructed the two of us to have the Doctor of my fiancé's mother fax a letter explaining the urgency that she was not emotionally stable to travel the five thousand miles under the stress of her sick mother and that we go to the nearest passport customer service centre with the doctors letter and request an emergency passport. Within hours we had the fax from the administering doctor in Sweden and the emergency passport for my first foreign travel was ready. I believe death has a time for each one of us and when GOD calls it waits for no one. GOD's word says in the book of. ECCLESIASTES: 3:1 EVERYTHING HAS ITS TIME. Now, as we was flying at 38,000 feet and this is my first time to be back in an airplane since I went from Missouri to Paris Island to the Marines when I was eighteen and, this flight was not just a few hundred miles, this was a five thousand mile flight across the Atlantic Ocean, I can admit it was making me a little nervous. This was not how I had imagined my first trip to my fiancé's country, although her mother could only speak in Polish I was still anxious to meet her for the first time however, as I mention before death waits for no one when it's time. As are long journey to Europe ended and our arrival to my fiancé's apartment where her youngest son and his fiancé were living we were met at the by only opening the door as much as necessary with the security chain on and was told by the step son fiancé to leave the property at once she said, you are not welcome here.

We were told that we were too late that my fiancé mother had passed the day before. Next we were as well threatened if we did not leave at once the police would be called. Tired, sleepy, hungry, needing a bath from the long trip and with the November cold here in Sweden was the coldest place I have ever been to in my life except maybe, when I was a young man and had went to work on the fruit farm up in the state of Michigan?. My being a foreigner here in another country I did not need any heated argument. I requested to my fiancé we leave and return to the airport and change our flight scheduled at once to return to America. With no clue even as to where they had placed her mother, so that she could at the least go to say goodbye and have a change for my fiancée to grief...

90

Back to America

So another long journey back across the Atlantic to the USA. I was in shock that anyone could be so cold hearted in a time such as this to turn their own relation out into the cold after a five thousand mile trip without as much as saying please come in and have some warm tea and rest. I think It reminded me of my past when the children and I had been turned out into the cold winter streets

I could not see how it was my fiancé wrong that we did to get to her mother in time before, GOD had called her home? I realize GOD says, we all have to forgive one another, but it is very difficult to forgive people such as this. I think I can forgive but to forget never, in a million years will I not remember this day. But, home and at least I feel safe being back in my own country.

We had now determined this time we were somehow going to accomplish her staying in America permanently. We had a social security number for her as well as a resident's card, so we had the necessary things we needed to get married. It was now December the 1th, little did the two of us know after we awoke this morning and without a clue that before this day was over we would be married, Mr. and Mrs. Lone Wolf. Upon our appointment today we had arrived at our local congressman's office for help with finishing the lat of the legal documents for my fiancé to stay in America. It was today that we had been told to take our Identification, drivers' license to the Justice of the peace and he would marry us, and that was how we became Mr. and Mrs. Lone Wolf.

I would always take a pleasure in remembering our first disagreement not long after we had been married I remember during the quarrel I walked out to sit in the car to avoid any additional argument. After locking the door and sitting listening to the radio she came to where I was and told me to open the door. I pretended I did not take notice of her at the window. However, I had not remembered that she had a spare key to the car and when the door open and she began to flog me on my leg with her shoe I was pleasured to understand very well that she had other ways to have a conversation with me. Then, there was talking with her hands when one day she throw her hands up over her head and moving them as if they were a pair of long ears telling me that I was acting like one of these she was trying to match up to me to a donkey.

Thoughts now continued to trouble my mind why would my new bride permit herself to come from Sweden living on the tenth floor of a high rise three bedroom apartment, working making a good income to now move to America to live in a car garage. No heat, no bathroom, no place to keep our food other than an ice cooler and our only income would be my disability check? Could there actually be such a powerful love as ours, if so I had certainly never seen this before. I wondered how long this could last before she would become conscious she had made a dreadful mistake, and she was going to tell me that it was over and was going back to her live in Sweden. For me this way of live was not all that unreal, I had lived out on the streets homeless under bridges, living in tents,

In fact this for me was a step up toward luxury. However, the love seemed genuine, as each day passed we both acted as if we had a million dollars there is an old saying is only in America a happy wife a happy life, and I was hoping that as long as she was happy, I was going to have a happy life. One day we were out only to look at new vehicles, knowing this was hopeless without question with the amount of income we had. I had my small amount of disability and she had a very small amount of income from her retirement in Sweden this surely would never be enough to qualify us to drive away with a need vehicle? Need more to be said, about this, we were accepted for a loan to purchase a new car next we applied for a government assistant apartment and were as well approved for a two bedroom apartment, now, at least this would get my new bride out of this horrible living condition of living in a car garage at lasts a civilized way of living we had a place to bath, a place to keep our food, a real stove to cook on, heat to stay warm in the winter with without having to use an arctic sleeping bag and air conditioner to stay cool in the summer, not to mention that we were driving new 2010 Cobalt only in America I say.

I had to question, how long this could last this was much more than I could expect coming from living in a car garage this was about one step up from living in a barn and now into a nice two bedroom apartment, from driving an old van with over two hundred thousand miles on it, and now driving a new vehicle that had seven miles on it, these were miles from moving it around on the parking lot. This was almost as good as going from rags to riches over night in all my experience in life before though, anytime something for the good happen there for sure was something bad going to tag along. We had stayed alive living in the old car garage for two years before at last finding this place with customary conveniences. And, now time seemed to have fast forward for us and it was if it over night when we become aware we had been here at the apartments for five years now. The wife was getting homesick for her country and to see her children and grand children we had been going back all along spending six months there in Sweden through the summer and back to Texas for six Months during the winter as the winters there are harsh.

91

The Death of My Baby

So, now I will need to make a complete transformation of my life I have always before been able to adjust to anything I choose. I had self educated myself after dropping out of school at the age of sixteen, I had accepted my birth mother wanted nothing to do with me from the time of my conception? I had learn to take care for myself at an early age but, now making a devotion to move to an foreign country to live permanently maybe, this was the biggest decision I had ever had to make a decision on before? It was not a question of if I loved my wife, because I truly loved her enough to live at the end of the earth with her if this is what she was asking of me. I was having difficulty because I could not speak the Swedish language, and my wife could speak five languages,

Polish Swedish Russian and Yugoslavia. I felt like I was illiterate because. I could not read their language or speak their language? Another thing was their type of weather; it was much different than from what I had been use to here in Texas? The winters in Sweden were six months long, and through most of the winter it was dark about eighteen hours a day. Nevertheless, I had to appreciate she had come to first America to confirm to me she truly loved me enough to leave her country and family leaving everything behind to be with me and to live in a car garage. I believe this was some powerful love? I expected the least I could do was to give back in the same matter of love and prove to her I loved her as much. Up until now it would appear with me as if all I had experienced through these years was, GOD HIM SELF had been testing me, or it was HE HIM SELF allowing Satin to do this dirty work on me I was not sure which? I recall from past times reading the bible of the story of Job where GOD allowed Satan to test him however, even with Job this only lasted for at total of seven days my test has been going on now for years?

I have hoped that after all the years I would have been through enough? In the very beginning of all this just before my children's mother abandoned the five of us things were apparently going ok?

Everything seem to come about on us afterwards? Yes, they were my children and I rightly should have taken them, I was the father however, I must also, say that I did not have to do this I was still young in my thirties I could have said, no I have a life to live I could have taken the four of them to the child protective center and dumped the all out and disappeared, driving off into the sunset just the way their mother did. No, parent should ever need to have the responsibility of being left alone to raise their children. I two people are responsible enough to make a baby then, they should as well be responsible enough to love this creation that they choice to bring into the world?

It takes both to conceive the child and it should take both to stay the course and raise the child as a family, and further it should be in a Christian family. Alcohol and drugs can come to anyone at anytime. They come to all colors, to the rich, and to the poor it has no favorites to whom it will attach it's self to. Once you have conceded to this and became a victim to the addiction it will become your new love affair. I loved my children and still do as much today my children more than anything I could have been given on this earth there was and still is nothing that I would not do for any of my children, but the power of the drugs and alcohol overpowered me the temptation of these addiction were more powerful than I was able to resist by myself? It took away so many years of my life that, before I was capable of finding and accepting a higher power greater than anything on the earth, that power being the almighty GOD to deliver and set me free from the poison of Satan's drugs and alcohol. James 4:7 {KING JAMES} tells us. Submit yourselves therefore to GOD. Resist the devil, and he will flee from you GOD.

Strangely enough to me I felt I had submitted myself to GOD many time and I could not see that the devil had left me? However, as you have read from my book of all the horrible times the five of us encountered GOD, surely HE must have been there with us otherwise no one could have possibly come through all of the horrible thing s we had went through? So, I would still advise anyone reading this book if you are going through a related situation, pray, pray, pray and pray some more. Please let GOD lead, let GOD be the head and not the tail. Please understand I had drank many bottles of alcohol looking for the answer at the bottom of each and every bottle I drank, and I never found an answer at the bottom of any of the bottles? Every bottle I started drinking Old Satin would tell me this is the one, as soon as you have finished this bottle the answer you are looking for is waiting at the bottom of this bottle. Remember Satin is the father of lies?

After having my children removed from me and they had all been placed in different foster homes across the State of Texas, and my autistic son who was placed in an institution for the remainder of his life. I had up until now believed GOD, had put me through all of the past happenings for a test?

And, I had likely been through all the test there was on GODS list. Not, so. GOD was not finished testing me still? I have been asking questions which had no answers? Is this really GOD doing this to me, or is it Satan. Even if it is Satan why if GOD has all the power that HE, holds why is HE continually allowing Satan to test, and torment my life? GOD, or Satan, I don't rightly know who it is doing this to me, but now it looks as if someone is going to take at least one more attempt at me to try and break me.

I had to wonder at this point if maybe, I should have in my earlier life sold my soul to the devil Everything, in my live that I can look back on looks as if it was against me. However, I continually recognize the world had a creator, that being GOD. I also believe it is possible there is two gods. GOD the CREATOR, GOD the FATHER GOD the HOLY SPIRIT. This is the first GOD.

Then, there is god the devil, not comparing the devil to GOD our CREATOR, but many people worship him as their god. Many have not waited until the great tribulation, to mark their lives as Satan's followers and have already sold their souls, as payment in exchange for a more prosperous life now.

May 2015, my wife and I had been spending some time with my youngest daughter and granddaughter before we left for our overseas trip to move to Sweden. It had been a nice spring day and the daughter and her husband had been working in the yard planting flowers, my daughter loved plants and flowers. That evening she begin complaining of pain in her hip, as the evening passed the pain became more intense. By morning we had to rush her to the local emergency room after a short examination it was decided that she should be transferred to a larger medical center with a trauma center and, more advanced equipment? After, the transfer and as hours passed with what looked as if nothing was being done for my child, and my listening to my child cry out in such suffering from the pain I was becoming very upset. It had been at three hours and still we have not seen a doctor, some pictures had been taken, but no one had given us any diagnoses, they had started her on an IV drip of morphine, which was not elevating any of the pain. The staff had threatened to have the hospital security come and accompany from the hospital faculty if I never settled down. Then, after eight hours of waiting we at last spoke with a doctor offering his apologies for the long wait for an answer which he did not have?

The following morning my daughter had made a turn for the worst, now she had been moved to the critical care ward and was hooked up to a life support system and still no one has an answer as to what is going on? To look at your young daughter lying hooked up to a life support system to keep them alive was just about more than I could do to survive. Again, I knew that GODS word says in 2 Corinthians 12:9 {KING JAMES} And, HE said unto me, MY grace is sufficient for thee: for my strength is made prefect in weakness. Mostly gladly therefore will I rather glory in MY infirmities, that the power of CHRIST may rest upon ME. My grace is sufficient for thee: But, I can honestly say I was having doubts about this.

I have always been a person of question? Why does the bible tells us that we serve a GOD that loves us unconditionally, and this same loving God allows all the horrible things to happen in the world to innocent people, little babies born with missing limbs, blind, deaf, mute born with terminally disease why does this loving GOD allow all of this to happen? Why, does my daughter who is a GOD fearing woman, GOD loving young woman lying here on life support? She has a loving family a nine year old daughter who was also, one of those innocent children born with a terminal disease. She was born with a brain tumor has undergone chemotherapy and radiation for nine years of her life; she is now blind in her left eye because of all the treatments. So, why does GOD do all of this? Why can't he say enough is enough? It looks as if HE will never stop attacking us? I feel my life is being punished for something that should be over with. Surely, HE would sympathize at some point and forgive me? Maybe, what belief I have had, has been all hopeless? Should I just stop praying altogether? This praying does not seem to be working at least for me anyway. We all think at times, that this should not be your child, here but you? However, it's now been five days and there had been some improvement. The life support had been removed. Miraculously after one week she was being released to return home.

This was indeed a mystery to me because still no one had given us a reason as to what had happen in the first place? Was this going to be a miracle, or was GOD, going to be sitting up there just laughing at me again time would tell? Our visit here with my daughter turned into a much longer stay than we had planned for and we had been away from our home some one hundred and fifty miles away. We needed to return there and then make a trip to the State of Arkansas for some legal business. Following this trip we were making our plans to move to my wife's Country of Sweden.

Now that the daughter was released to return home we felt safe to leave. Now, to say good bye and assure her that we would come back before we left for overseas. So, we were on the road for a six hundred mile drive to Arkansas. This, would be an overnight stay in a Hotel, take care of the legal matter the following morning and quick visit with my mom and back on the road to Texas, to pack our personal thing and make the arrangements for our movie to Sweden.

It seems that this visit was different with my mom than any other visits before. I actually heard her say, I live you to me. It seems as if we somehow put all the past difference behind us this day

Maybe, it was GODS way of trying to tell me something? However, after this last visit I would have a reasonable commutation with this woman that gave birth to me my mom.

How, was a Country feed boy like me to end up in a position where I am? Well, it's time once again I bring back that; I have a feeling about something that is just not right again? Why, did the doctor, never tell any of us what they diagnosed my daughter to have had? Why, did they have her on a life support system? There were too many unanswered questions oh, well, maybe, it's ok? Our trip to Arkansas went well, the legal matter was resolved, and our visit with my mom went reasonably well. Now, our trip back to Texas, I could only hope it went well?

We had been back on the road toward Texas just over thirty minutes. My cell phone rang, I could see from the caller id it was from my son-in law in Texas. When, I answered hello, my son-in laws voice was crying, He said, dad she's gone. What are you talking about, I ask? My heart almost stopped for a moment. My wife was listening over the speaker phone and began to cry I had to find a place fast to exit the highway to get myself in order. I had a six hundred mile trip I had to make Then, someone took the phone from my son-in-law and begun to try explain what happen?

I was told on this morning for unknown reason my daughter had stopped breathing and after calling 911 the first responders were not able to revive her? After, my daughter's death I believed that it was GOD'S finally completing HIS mission with totally destroying me.

The death of my daughter removed and left a sink hole in me the size of the moon. Why, did HE do this? Is there an answer? I have no choice but to accept it, I can do nothing, GOD is GOD. HE has absolute control and power over everything. I cannot change HIS mind, HE has already made up HIS mind and this is HIS will. So, I have to carry on believing and, yes now more than before. Why? Because I know my Daughter believed in HIM, so I know she went to be with HIM. If I ever wanted to see her again, I have to accept everything HE puts on me regardless of how violent the stormy sea may get.

92

The Funeral

Having to go to a funeral is something which most ever family experiences having to go through

It's just part of life's cycle; I have to understand it's another one of those plans of GOD'S that we don't understand fully it just doesn't seem right? This is more than ever true when a parent is burying their very own child. There is no deeper hurt, no deeper pain I fully understand that GOD gave HIS only son to be a sacrifice for our sins. I know that it was us that owed for a sin that we could not pay. However, GOD got HIS son back He, has taken my daughter and I don't get to have her back.

However, today was the blackest day I could ever remember. Looking down in the casket at my baby daughter I felt numb, I felt anger toward GOD. This was a young woman who loved life, loved her daughter and husband; there was no reason for this at all. As everyone was called to be seated I was expecting to sit on the front roll with the rest of the family however, as the funeral directors were placing everyone in their seats they directed ne and my family to a second roll seat. My daughter's husband's family and friends were seated in the front roll. Had it not been for creating scene I would have refused to be placed in the second roll, this was my daughter lying there and I had every right to be on the front roll. However, I managed somehow to keep myself contained I did however, just as everyone was called to pass by the casket and say their last goodbye, and they always start with the back roll and work forward letting everyone look one last time and then shake hands and hug the family of course the family on the front roll which I was not.

I was thought of as a non family member. However, I rose up and pushed myself in with the other viewers and went to my daughters casket to tell her good bye and that I loved her. Then, I quietly told my wife and son and a step daughter, who were sitting on the second roll with me, lets' go and we left the Church. I would like to mention that my being placed on the second roll was the work of my son-in-laws evil sister. Another interesting thing today was that the mother of my child did not have the moral sympathy to attend her own child's funeral. There was not as much as a flower sent from her. One last stop and that was the grave site where they were putting my daughter to her final resting place. So for now, good bye my daughter rest in peace dad hopes someday to see you on the other side my child.

I Love You.
Dad,

You know GOD does not get upset when we get upset with HIM. HE knows our ways are human ways we are all like the parable of the lost son.

Luke 15:11-32 {KING JAMES} there was a man who had two sons. The younger one said to his father, father give me my share of the estate. So he divided his property between them. Not long after that the younger got together all he had, set off for a distant country and there squandered his wealth in wild living.

After he had spent everything, there was a famine in that whole country and he begin to be in need. So he went and hired himself to feed the pigs. He longed to fill his stomach with the pods that the pigs were eating, but no one gave him anything. When he came to his senses, he said how many of my father's hired servants have food to spare, and here I am starving to death! I will set out and go back to my father, and say to him. Father I have sinned against you. I am no longer worthy to be called your son, make me like one of your hired servants. So he got up and went his way to his father.

But while he was still a long way off, his father saw him and was filled with compassion for him, he ran to his son and threw his arms around him and kissed him. The son said, father I have sinned against heaven and against you. I am no longer worthy to be called your son. But the father said to his servants, quick! Bring the best robe and put it on him. Put a ring on his finger and sandals on his feet. Bring the fattened calf and kill it. Let's have a feast and celebrate. For this son of mine was dead and is alive again, he was lost and is found. So they begin to celebrate. Meanwhile, the older son was in the field. When he came near the house, he heard music and dancing. So he called one of the servants and asks what was going on. Your brother has come he replied, and your father has killed the fatted calf because he has him back safe and sound. The older brother became angry and refused to go in. So his father went out and pleaded with him. But he answered his father, look all these years I've been slaving for you and never disobeyed your orders. Yet you never gave me even a young goat so I could celebrate with my friends. But when this son of yours who has squandered your property with prostitutes comes home, you kill the fatted calf for him. My son, the father said, you are always with me, and everything I have is yours. But we had to celebrate and be glad, because this brother of yours was dead and he is alive again, he was lost and is found.

No matter how far away we may drift away from our Heavily FATHER HE will always be waiting to welcome us back in HIS loving and forgiving arms.

If you are someone going through troubled times remember, Proverbs 3:5 {KING JAMES} Trust in the LORD with all your heart; and lean not unto thine own understanding.

THE END

About the Author

Contact: <u>longwolf49@yahoo.com</u> Born 1952, in a rural town of Arkansas. Had it not been for the love of GOD fearing GOD loving parental grandparents? I would most likely have been placed in an orphanage home? My wandering away from the GODLY guidance I was taught in my grandparent's home and turning to drug and alcohol, I had become by eighteen years old an alcoholic and drug addict, these addictions would be the cause to many problems in my young life including spending a year in jail. This, life style would continue for the next thirty-eight years when GOD gave me an out of body experience showing me what the eternal place of fire would look like for the un- repented sinner. The old saying you can't judge a book by its cover has never been more meaningful than, it has had for me. I left school at the early age of sixteen years old with only an eighth grade education, other than a GED I later would acquire in the military, I would school myself.

Having lived the life of this character in my story, I feel experienced to have written this exciting novel of the unwanted baby and the sequel of a father with custody. My prayer is by sharing my story is for the purpose of touching someone's life that may be experiencing some of the difficulties which I had suffered through? I believe there is always hope? However, I needed more than just hope, I needed a much higher power than, myself and that higher power was GOD. It would take many years for me to understand that HE was the answer. Having been rejected by my own family and turned into the cold winter streets with my four children in the sequel, after the children's mother deserted the four of them, our being homeless, cold and often hunger would seem as if GOD had a vindictive against us. I imagined from after the entire tempest I had suffered GOD had at last finished with HIS punishment on me, or HE had forbidden Satan to stop his torturing me. But, there was still more to come much more.

Face book: Lone wolf

Twitter:

Instgram:

Printed in the United States
By Bookmasters